Through the Folded Stars

By Jenna Avery

Contents

Also Written By Jenna

My Ashes: Memoirs of a Misbehaving Woman
Come Back To Me: A Dark Romance Thriller
The Singularity
Through The Folded Stars
Skies of Avalon
Glittering Skies

For Susan. I hope you've found joy in the stars. You aren't here to read it, but it wouldn't be here without your encouragement.

Prologue

The announcement of the asteroid was a PR nightmare. Whoever leaked the information to a gossip magazine before the president could address the nation has a special place in hell reserved just for them.

No one believed it at first. Even Dad scoffed at the gossip rag, claiming the world was going to end. It was the same source claiming body snatchers were in Congress a couple of years ago. The claim went viral, and suddenly, there were meme videos proving all the ways the old congressmen were aliens in disguise.

It was actually convincing for some of them.

So, when the end of the world was announced right beside a claim that the late Dolly Parton gave birth to triplets, who would have believed it?

The government was plenty happy to let it get dismissed as tabloid fodder. They still hoped that creating bunkers and preventing panic was the solution.

Of course, there was never a solution. None they would ever know about.

By the time people realized the truth, the government had come to the inevitable conclusion: We were doomed.

The apocalypse is a great equalizer. The rich became as terrified as the poor. All tried to bargain with invisible gods, swearing new and old fealty.

For me, science is my god. I inherited the religion from my parents. For the last two decades, we've worked tirelessly toward a singular goal: to travel through time.

It was sheer luck we figured it out right before they announced the end of the world. We had a way to save our family, to save ourselves.

Except no one told me what a lonely experience it'll be. The guaranteed heartbreak. And the kind of love so incredible, it's worth traversing universes for.

Chapter One

Rocky Road Ice Cream

All I can think, as I look at the asteroid above me, is how much it looks like Swiss cheese. Moldy, dirty-looking Swiss cheese. The debris ripping off its jagged edges burns in the atmosphere, sprinkling into the sky like ominous shooting stars. There are only thirty minutes left until it destroys the entire world. My skin itches with the fearful urge to escape.

The flannel blanket presses into my ear as I peek at my cousin, Piper. Her hands cradle her head as she gazes up at the orange sky. Some stars are defiant against the glow of the asteroid, still twinkling despite the hurtling rock of doom trying to dim their vibe. Even as her galactic executioner draws closer, her face is full of wonder.

Unaware of my stare, Piper asks, "Do you think the stars will be the same in the different universes?"

"I don't know," I admit. "I'll let you know when I come back."

My eyes skate across her features, soaking in the freckles along the bridge of her nose. The way her long, black hair spreads around her head resembles a halo. Even the way her lips part as she huffs out a breath of frustration. I'm desperate to remember it all. Soon, memories will be the only thing left.

Piper turns to face me, resting her head on a hand. "Seriously, Saira, you need to tell me *everything* when you get back."

She acts as if we've ever had secrets. As my best friend for twenty-six years, there's nothing we don't know about one another. "I'm going to collect data and samples, come back, and take the family to whatever place I think will be safest. Or whatever Dad thinks is safest. It's just a big science experiment, nothing else."

With a scoff, she pokes my cheek. "Sai! Don't tell me you're going to travel through time and *not* have some fun."

I bring up a hand and pinch my fingers together. In the sagest tone possible, I declare, "One does not simply travel through time and 'have fun,' Pipes."

The joke lands, and she grins. "You aren't going to Mordor, you soggy taco. I mean, you're going where no one else has." She bites her lip, then adds, "At least from this Earth."

Somewhere behind us, there's a crash and raucous laughter. Our attention flicks to the patio where our family is getting wasted, ignoring what's about to happen. Like most people on this planet. It's amazing how much people will ignore, even when certain doom flies toward them. As a scientist, it's been fascinating to observe the collapse of society. As a person unable to stop the inevitable? It's been heart-wrenching.

Piper sits up, and I do the same. Piper's carob-colored eyes, shocking against her tawny skin, refocus on my face. Her fingers play with the locket around her neck, rolling the chain absentmindedly. "So you're telling me you're going to travel to new worlds and not actually step out of the scientist role? Lamest pseudo-vacation ever."

I tilt my head from side to side. "Maybe. Maybe not. There's no real way of knowing where the hell we'll go, anyway."

She holds up a hooked pinkie. "Pinkie swear you'll bang someone. *Anyone.* And maybe even relax for a time or two."

"Isn't banging someone supposed to be relaxing?"

She snorts. "Depends on the person." Falling over like a sack of flour, she flops onto her back. "I can't believe I'm going to be dead in less than an hour."

An abrupt yet suitable topic change. Piper's never been the type to mince words.

Fiddling with a metal buckle on my boots, I say, "Yeah. Crazy."

What the hell else should I say? *Sorry to leave you, but I'm abandoning the whole family in the hopes we can save you one day.*

It sounds pathetic, even if it's true. But we've had talks. The cry sessions. Copious amounts of denial and anger. Now we're just accepting she's staying here to be killed by an asteroid while I travel to new worlds. Or get sucked into a black hole and crushed to death.

It's a real toss-up.

And really, really, *really* unfair.

She sits up again. Her hands fumble at the back of her neck, and the locket falls an inch before she pulls it away and holds it out toward me. "I didn't know when to give you this. Guess this is as good a time as any. Open it when things get too hard."

The tears I'd assumed were long exhausted reappeared, blurring her beautiful face. "Are you sure?"

She looks at me like I'm stupid. "What the hell am I going to do with it?"

Sitting up to face her, she drops it into my palm. I'm about to pry it open, but her hand covers mine.

"Don't. Only open it when you really need a reminder of why you're there."

"Yes, ma'am." After giving a little salute, I wrap it around my neck, clasp it together, and tuck it into my black T-shirt. "Any other last requests?"

She pretends to think, tapping her chin. Her face lights up, and she points her finger. "Oh. I know. Get laid!"

I groan and rub my hands over my face. Sometimes, she's maddening. We're both different in so many ways, and focusing on romantic entanglements is one of them.

"For the love of Betty White, Pipes, it isn't that big of a deal."

Piper's always been the outgoing one. Me, not so much. My entire life has centered on becoming one of the best particle physicists in existence. She's always been the one rattling against the self-imposed bars of my introverted prison cell, begging me to live a little. Every margarita I've ever consumed had her fingers around the glass stem first. Without her encouragement, I'm not sure I'll have the courage to live life the way she begs me to.

Piper's eyes narrow. She's attempting to look intimidating, but it's impossible when we've known one another since diapers.

She tries anyway, waggling a finger at me. "If you show up a year from now." She pauses. "Wait, a year ago. Or last year. Whenever you're reappearing, you better have done the horizontal tango with at least one person. Or I'm going to ..."

I raise an eyebrow. "Going to what?"

She juts out her lower lip and gives me a stink face. "Or I'm going to tease you in whatever world you drag me to for as long as I live. I'll tell people you're a celibate twenty-six-year-old. I promise."

"Got it," I say dryly. "I'm quaking in my space boots." I push off the ground and brush grass off my legs. "While taking samples and gathering data and trying not to die between wormholes, I'll try really hard to get laid, so my best friend doesn't tease me forever."

"Good. Glad you understand." She gathers the blanket and stands, staring at it with bewilderment. "Why the hell am I cleaning this up?"

She tosses the blanket back down on the ground, pauses, then kicks it for good measure.

I laugh, my heart light, just for a second. "I was wondering the same thing. Come on, I gotta go find my dad."

We turn back to the house and head toward the party. I know it's time to say the pretend goodbyes — no one else knows what Dad and I are about to do — but honestly, I just want to find Dad and leave. Goodbyes are hard enough, and, to be honest, some of them I'm not sure I'll miss.

Case in point: Uncle Nik.

He's an alcoholic on a good day, but as we get closer, I see he's absolutely *wasted*. Judging from his tone, he is well past his argumentative phase. He's swaying in the same tattered sneakers he's worn since he was seventeen, jabbing a finger at Aunt Trish. She's not much better off either, wildly gesticulating and screaming about the credit card debt he racked up over the years.

Those two are Piper's parents, and let's just say she isn't the biggest fan of them. Aunt Trish is Dad's sister, and more than once, she's complained at family dinners about how Nana favors Dad. On top of that, since Piper turned eighteen, they've been trying to marry her off in an arranged marriage. Aunt Trist claims she's afraid Piper will die alone, but I secretly think she just wants something Dad doesn't: a married daughter.

Piper has avoided marriage by rejecting every suitor. I guess today marks complete success in that department.

Instead of trying to make things right with their daughter, they're arguing about the dumbest shit. I'd like to say it's surprising to hear people yelling about something that won't matter ever again ... but I'm not.

They call it PocDis. A cutesy-sounding nickname for the official diagnosis: Apocalypse Dissociation. Some people can't handle seeing death hurtling toward them, a guaranteed time and place when the world ends.

So, on the eve of their death, people argue about finances. Sex. More finances. More sex. Truly banal behavior.

"Piper! Get your ass over here and show Robbie how a keg stand is done," one of our cousins, Marco, screams from inside the house. Piper grins and bounds off to have her last swigs of beer ever.

This is getting too depressing. While every second with Piper's a fleeting gift, there's nothing appealing about comforting her while she vomits up said beer.

I spin in a circle, looking for Dad. Finally, I spot him by the pool, talking to Nana.

Well, never mind. Not going over there now. Nana is the definition of an overbearing matriarch. She gets away with it by stuffing us with delicious food, which is nice. Right now, however, it looks like they're arguing. No thanks.

Turning in the opposite direction, I weave through groups of seated family members, hoping to find Piper again. I'm stopped along the way by various aunts and uncles, giving as brief a goodbye as possible. It's been said enough. Plus, if I sit here and mourn their loss too much, it might make things feel impossible soon. They need to stay alive in my mind.

Finally, I see Piper at the keg, being held upside down by Robbie and Marco, while she chugs beer. It dribbles past her lips, running down her cheeks, and plopping on the already-wet cement.

"Go, go, go!" My cousins cheer her on, their foreheads slick with sweat and eyes glazed from the booze.

Finally, she taps the keg, and they help her down. She stumbles with a goofy grin on her beautiful face. "I did it!"

Everyone roars their praise, arms up in the air, enjoying her victory. I even clap for her, because why the hell not?

Spotting me, she bobs and weaves through the crowd. "Not a bad way to close out my life, don't you think?"

Unable to say anything negative to her, I plaster a proud smile on my face and link one of my arms with hers. "Few could ask for something better."

Words slurring, she crows, "I'm the Booze Queen now."

I nod in agreement. "The one and only."

She stumbles into me, and I help plant her in a chair. She grins from ear to ear, peering up at me. "I thought you were going to find your dad?"

I grimace. "He was with Nana."

"*Ugh.*" She looks like she tasted something disgusting. "Did you know that yesterday she told me it was a shame I never got into better shape? And it's why I never got married?"

Extremely unsurprising. "Yeah, well, she's been telling me to lose weight since I was nine."

Piper looks me up and down. "You're hot stuff, bitch. A Badass Bitch Scientist. Who cares if you're a little floofy?"

Glancing down at the extra fat on my tummy and the thick thighs I inherited from my mother, I shrug. "Apparently, Nana."

Sighing heavily, her face turns dreamy. She yawns. "I need a nap. Do you think I can just sleep through the apocalypse?"

"Probably, yeah." There is — was — an entire pharmaceutical movement, selling the ultimate amount of drugs to maximize the dissociation this past year. "There are pills on the table. Want me to get you some?"

Hell, I'm tempted to down a few. Except Dad would murder me. It could very well skew the vitals and recordings. The Mission comes first, even if anxiety is carving a hole in my chest.

She shakes her head vigorously. "Nah. I want to watch it with my eyes open." She peers up at me with one eye bigger than the other, like it'll improve her focus. "You need to get out of here. Go. Scoot. I'll be fine."

I squat next to her, grabbing one of her hands. She intertwines her fingers with mine, squeezing tightly.

Swallowing the lump of emotion lodged in my throat, I choke out, "I love you, Pipes. More than anything in this world. Or any world." I reach up and brush a sweaty hair off her face. The lucidity in her eyes is fading fast. It's okay. No one wants to face death with eyes open.

Her smile is one of kindness and pure love. "Hey, you remember when we ate an entire tub of ice cream in high school and then got sick all night? And then had ice cream for breakfast because you were so sure it was like the hair of the dog?"

I laugh, a tear dropping down my cheek. "Yeah. Not one of my smarter moments."

She giggles. "Well, when you come find me again, promise me we'll do that. Get sick on ice cream while you tell me about *all* the steamy sex you had."

I blow out a deep breath with as much patience as possible. "Deal. You can even choose the flavor."

"Rocky road?"

"I love rocky road."

Gnawing on the inside of my cheek, willing the sobs to wait a little longer, I release her fingers and stand. Leaning down, I plant a final kiss on her forehead. "I love you."

"I love you, too, Sai."

JENNA AVERY

I walk toward Dad, leaving my best friend to die.

Chapter Two

Don't Forget: Mission First

Bracing myself, I make my way to Dad, who is, unfortunately, still talking to Nana. They seem to be in a heated discussion, but a quick glance at my Scout tells me we're running out of time. The Scout only does four things: leave a universe, create a glamour so it blends in with any outfit, and show the current closed timelike curve coordinates.

It's my lifeline on this entire journey, and I'll be taking it off as little as possible.

With anxiety lodged in my throat, I walk up to them and assess the situation before interrupting. Dad's frowning at Nana, pumping his hands up and down in an effort to calm her down.

Thick salt-and-pepper hair pulls back neatly at the nape of his neck with a piece of brown leather. Laugh lines crease the corners of his eyes. I look down at the gold wedding band still on his ring finger. Mom died of an incurable cancer when I was twelve. It broke both of our hearts.

Fourteen years later, he's never stopped loving her. There's something romantic about not letting death or time separate their love. Dad sees me first and smiles warmly. Nana, however, looks distraught. Something tells me he could use a hero right about now.

Stopping next to Nana, I point to the Scout. "Uh, we, uh, need to go on that walk."

Nana sighs, wringing her wrinkled, tawny hands. She narrows her wrinkled eyes at me. She's aged beautifully for a seventy-eight-year-old woman. Even her black hair has only faint streaks of gray. "I can't believe you both are willing to do this. It sounds so dangerous, and for what? Possibly find yourself in a universe that might have ants the size of horses?"

Anger flares as her words sink in. Somehow, Dad has made this situation harder than it needs to be. I glare at him. "You swore you wouldn't tell her."

"What?" Nana whips her head at him, tears glistening.

He winces. Placing hands on her shoulders, Dad says, "We'll be back, Mama, before you even know we're gone."

"But I *do* know you're gone. And what if this skort breaks? What if you don't succeed?"

In this family, she's the centrifugal force. Nana has the best intentions, but she's a worrywart and a bit of a pessimist. She acts like this only because she loves us. Doesn't make the boundary-crossing behavior any better, though.

"It's called a Scout," I say patiently. "And whether or not it works, the worst outcome is we die somewhere else instead of here with everyone else."

"Saira," she gasps, an elegant hand fluttering to her chest. "No need to be crude."

Jeez, we're never getting out of here.

"Mama," Dad interjects. "Saira is right. Time is of the essence, and we need to prepare to leave."

Her face crumples. "Abraham Ismael Andromeda, you're going to leave me to die here?"

I lift my Scout again, tapping it with a nail. "Dad. We have ten minutes."

Now, her distraught expression spears toward me. "What have you done to prepare? Can I give you food to take? I know you love my chocolate chip cookies. I think there is still some left. Are you sure I can't join? How have you readied for this adventure?"

Her questions take away some of my frustration. She's trying to show her love in the best way she knows how. "Nana, you need a walker most days. I don't think you'd be able to escape an angry chihuahua, let alone an alien with six legs and a penchant for the flesh of old ladies."

Dad swears under his breath while Nana's face pales. Clearly a joke funnier in my head. I try to look contrite. "But I've been to some wilderness classes when Dad and I haven't been working on the tech."

She doesn't look comforted, tears beginning to glimmer in her soft eyes. I reach for the hand not pressed against her chest. "Nana, we'll be back. I promise. Everything will be okay. I love you."

Before I cry with her, I press a kiss against her soft cheek, smelling her scent of jasmine blossoms. I step away, waiting for Dad to convince her to leave. It was hard enough to walk away from Piper.

Walking over to our packs, I do a triple check on the supplies. Everything is still good to go, including the analyzer, freeze-dried meals, and camping gear. Putting on the sleek jacket he made me, I admire the softness of the indestructible, yet breathable, material. Dad calls it Chronoweave. At any other point in time, he'd make a killing selling it on the market. I make sure my boots are tightly strapped and then re-braid my dark, curly hair.

Finally, Dad sidles up to me, somehow looking twenty years older. "I shouldn't have told her. There's no guilt quite like a mother's guilt."

I cock a brow. "I wouldn't know," I say dryly, motioning to his pack. "Everything looks ready."

Dad gives me a chastising look at my dead mom joke, then looks up at the asteroid. The land grows brighter as the asteroid grows closer, reflecting the sun even in the dusky light. The burnt-orange hue makes everything appear even more apocalyptic. Dad leans down and grabs my pack first, handing it over.

I sling it over my shoulders with a grunt and tighten the straps. Dad does the same, then holds out his Scout for me to see. It shows our current location on the closed time-like curve coordinates. He taps at the glass facing.

"Pull up the first set of coordinates."

I do as he says, holding down the button. I'll never not be grateful for him figuring out a way to take something complex like particle collisions and boil it down to a watch-like invention. Creating a singularity by allowing atoms to collide is no easy feat.

He's programmed the final destination required for the time travel course. It isn't clear yet exactly how many stops there will be. The dimension of time is far too unpredictable, even for us. Dad estimates at least six, but I'm not holding him to it.

When we get to our respective destinations, we'll be scouting out the flora and fauna, any cultures and peoples, as well as the landscape. We want to bring our family somewhere safe or as safe as anywhere else can be. Statistically speaking, one of us is bound to find a suitable option. We can't save the world, but we can save our family.

My heart hitches with anxiety. I wipe my clammy palms on my black pants, but the material is waterproof, so the moisture smears on it. Gross.

"Saira, are you with me?" Dad says gently, interrupting my reverie. He's peering down at me with curiosity.

My body trembles with fear and adrenaline. "After this, we won't see one another for who knows how long." Voice cracking, I say, "I don't know how to do this without you."

Dad gathers me in his muscular arms. The warm embrace is a battering ram against the surge of emotion I've tried to hide behind a wall of steel determination. His scent reminds me of warm earth. As our last moment together for the foreseeable future, it's excruciating.

It's been he and I this whole time. We've rarely gone a day without seeing one another. After Mom died, he buried himself in time travel research while I completed my degrees to catch up as fast as possible. All I wanted to do was to be his equal. Help him achieve his lifelong goal, like Mom had tried. Ever since achieving my postdoctoral, we've worked together every day.

The terror inside me is a yawn abyss, threatening to swallow me up, one chunk of sanity at a time. My lower lip quivers, and I chomp on it, tasting blood when my teeth cut into the skin. Dad tries his best, but he's never handled my tears well.

He says into my hair, "Do you remember what to do?"

The sky is brightening as the asteroid hurtles toward us. It's almost like daytime now, even though it's near midnight. Soon, the whole Earth will be on fire. We'll be an extinct species on a dying planet.

"Saira."

Dad's voice is more insistent as he gently pushes me away, still holding my arms. The air between us is chilly, like he took all the warmth with him. I gulp air like a fish on land. There's not enough oxygen. Why isn't there enough oxygen?

An edge of frustration curbs the edge in his voice. "Saira. Are you with me? We're running out of time."

Thoughts race through my mind, flitting past before I can get a grip on them. I need to get my shit together. *Focus.*

This is only the beginning, not the end.

We're doing this for the people here.

They deserve a redo of this moment.

They don't deserve this moment at all.

Piper deserves her ice cream.

This final thought brings me back to the present. Inhaling deeply, all of my fear leaves my body as I exhale. I can do this. It's only for a little while.

"Yeah, I'm with you."

He watches me closely for a second before nodding. "Alright. Tell me again what you're going to do first."

My words come out on autopilot. "Arrive at the destination. Take air and soil samples. Write observations in the journal. Find the locals. Ask questions. Leave when I think there's enough data gathered."

"Good. Mission first, everything else second. Only skip a destination if absolutely necessary."

He tightens the straps on his backpack. Flipping my black braid over my shoulder, I take a deep breath.

"Wait!" We look over, cringing when we spot Nana hobbling over, holding two plastic bags filled with her infamous cookies.

"Goddamnit," Dad says under his breath. He rushes over to her. "Mama, we need to go."

Her disapproving glare would make most people wilt. "My son and granddaughter will not go off without some of my cookies to fill their bellies."

The fight goes out of him. His throat bobs as he takes the bags out of her shaking hands. The burning in my eyes makes it hard to see. I wipe away a tumbling tear as he gives her one final kiss on the cheek.

He approaches me, twirling a finger. I turn, allowing him to unzip my pack and stuff the bag into it. I do the same for him. It's bizarre stuffing cookies into the backpack, like we're simply heading out on a hike and picnic.

"At least we'll have a snack when we land?" My voice quavers, the joke falling flat.

He sighs, giving Nana one last look. She's standing there, lower lip wobbling. Behind her, our family points at the asteroid. No one is looking at us. Scanning faces, I'm disappointed the only face I want to see is nowhere to be found. My last goodbye to Piper will have to be good enough.

We place the badass-looking black oxygen masks on. From the outside, it looks like one solid piece of black glass, but inside, it's a two-way mirror. The world flickers to life on the screen with constantly adjusting analyses in every corner. It shows the stats of the world around me, which will be helpful once I reach the next location.

My lungs fill easily with air even without an attached oxygen source. It's because of Dad being nothing short of a genius. Two summers ago, he discovered a particle conversion formula that converts carbon dioxide into oxygen by essentially convincing particles and molecules to shapeshift. A literal lifesaver.

Somewhere in the distance, a louder *boom* sounds, and the ground vibrates beneath us. Chunks of large space rocks blazing through the clouds. Nana slumps against the ground. I cry out in alarm. Instinctively, I take a step toward her.

"Saira! Pay attention," Dad barks, holding up his Scout. He glances at Nana. His eyes fill with regret. But Dad is a scientist first and foremost. So while Nana curls into the fetal position, resembling a frightened child, I hold up my wrist. The Scout's face lights up, showing the co-ordinates to the first destination.

If we're lucky, we'll meet here approximately sixteen months from now. Piper won't be dead. Nana will be able to make more cookies for us. This pain in my heart, this wretched decision, will be nothing but an ugly memory. More booms crash into the land, trembling the foundation beneath us.

"Dad," I whisper, my voice barely above a whisper. "I'm scared."

His expression softens. Placing a hand on my shoulder, he gives it a gentle squeeze. "We'll see each other soon. When in doubt, leave. Before you know it, we'll be together again."

"Promise?"

The only clue to his smiling is the squinting of his dark brown eyes. "I promise. Now, let's go travel the universes."

As another explosion rocks the world nearby, we press a button on our Scouts, and existence folds in on itself. Taking every molecule of my soul with it.

Chapter Three

What Kind Of Revolution Is This?

The media constantly portrays time travel in a limited way. It's usually either traveling into the past or future. Linear and non-dynamic. For most people — i.e., anyone not Dad or I — time travel is a dream or hoax. Books, TV shows, and movies can make it up as they go.

I've spent nights considering what it might be like. Would it be like falling a short distance? Maybe a gaping hole into the next world? It could even be something silly, like disco ball lights.

Sadly, there are no disco balls. Instead, it's like a mountain pressing onto every molecule, making it impossible to suck in air. Total darkness pairs with the roaring sound of static, leaving my ears ringing. A bright flash of light forces me to cover my eyes, my pupils overwhelmed with the changing light.

White light swallows me whole, and the pressure evaporates. I slam against something hard, and the oxygen mask almost slides off. The screen fogs temporarily as I hyperventilate, trying to orient myself.

The first thing I notice is the smell. It makes its way through my mask, causing an immediate gag. What the hell smells so bad that it gets through my mask? It smells like Uncle Harod did after eating three salami sandwiches with extra cheese.

Glancing down at the ground, I cringe as my fingers scrape against filthy, wet cobblestones. There are scraps of something unidentifiable.

Jerking my hands back, I wipe them against my pants and groan. Time traveling has already proven to be less than glamorous.

And we definitely didn't consider the need for hand sanitizer.

A quick scan of my body shows that everything seems in order. Piper's locket moves against my chest, answering my next question. Mom's ring glints in the sunshine as I move my fingers. Everything appears to be as it should.

Looking around, it's clear I'm in an alleyway of some sort, with brick buildings on both sides. It's currently vacant, but the sound of angry voices comes from nearby.

A wave of nausea rolls makes me grip my stomach. The smell is horrific. Terrified of throwing up in the mask, I scan the stats. A small blurb on the screen flickers green, signaling the air is safe to breathe. I yank the mask off in hopes that the fresh air will help the queasiness.

This is a very incorrect assumption.

Instead, all I smell is excrement. Smoke. Something rotting.

It fucking *reeks*. I'd rather smell Uncle Harod's sweaty armpits for a year than deal with this stench.

Shoving aside my mental tantrum, I get to work. Slinging off my pack, I pull the analyzer out of its pocket and press a large orange button. It's muscle memory to type in the password BettyWhite628. A small, clear spoon pops out. Pressing the edge of the spoon against the cobblestone, I scrape a small bit of the stone into the shallow indentation and slide it back into the analyzer.

Immediately, the information aggregates. Most isn't necessary data, but some particular stats catch my attention.

Location: Paris

Year: 1793

Dissolved oxygen (DO): 5 mg/L

pH Level: 7.5.0

I wrack my brain for facts. The stats only offer years if they're on a similar enough timeline. Some parallel universes may be so different from mine, the tracking of time isn't detectable in a way the analyzer can process.

The appearance of a definitive year is both promising and daunting. If this is the same historical timeline, then this is the French Revolution. I hope I'm wrong, because this was *not* a pleasant time to be alive.

Trying to stay on task, I place the oxygen mask into its designated pocket of the backpack and stand on wobbling legs. Another wave of nausea makes me gag. This is a rough start to the entire journey.

I lean against a brick wall and carefully examine the alleyway. It's filthy, with murky puddles sinking into worn cobblestones. Beyond the buildings, a crowd roars.

The entrance to the alley is about twenty feet away, and from here, there's a throng of people pushing and shoving, all trying to walk in the same direction.

Everyone is wearing a clothing style I've only ever seen in movies. The women wear coarse-looking fabrics in muted shades. Most of their skirts have tattered bottoms, with random patchwork sewn in. The men look little better, with worn-out trousers. Those lucky enough to have shoes on their feet have the occasional toe poking out. Almost everyone looks a certain level of filthy. Explains the smell.

The one thing they all have in common is the rage and excitement on their faces. Especially the ones with weapons. Clubs, pikes, muskets ... these people are ready for violence.

Yep, this is the revolution.

My immediate impulse is to leave, but Dad will be furious if I leave without taking observations and samples. I attach the analyzer to my utility belt and heft the pack over my shoulders. Time to get to work.

There's a faint thud, followed by a roar of appreciation. I glance down the alley again and watch the crowd surge. So far, no one has noticed me, but I know in my bones that won't last.

I walk in the opposite direction from the crowd. The other side of the alley is farther away but seems clear.

It's hard to breathe with the overwhelming stench of everything. The buzz of flies is relentless. Piles of fecal matter litter the cobblestones alongside rotting garbage. I swear it's already seeping into my pores. It's only been five minutes, and a bath has never sounded so good. Why the hell did we not pack sanitizer?

The other side of the alley opens onto a wider road. Horses hitched to empty wagons wait patiently for their drivers. Shop stalls stand empty, boarded up against theft. A kid runs across the street, disappearing around a corner. A wagon with a too-thin nag plods past me, the man holding the reins, sucking on a pipe, not even sparing me a second glance.

The hairs on my arms rise when I notice a flickering light coming from the front of a building a block away. A group of people crowd together like moths to a flame, their faces pale from whatever they're looking at. Glancing over my shoulder to see if anyone is watching, I slowly make my way to the cluster of people.

It isn't the warm glow of fire, but the fluorescent glow of a screen. Like there's electricity here. Which is impossible. They still used oil lamps and candles in this time period. For fuck's sake, they're shitting in the streets. There's no way they have—

Oh.

The source of the light appears from behind a tall window of a brick building. It's about seven feet off the ground in a small alcove built like a storefront, but multiple screens tilt from different shelves down, all streaming the same broadcast. If I weren't so shocked at this twist, I'd laugh at the dystopian hodge-podge collection of screens.

No one notices when I edge closer, straining to see what's so fascinating. The images are vibrant, bringing out the color of fresh blood even more. When a pale-skinned woman wearing a dirty chemise stumbles onto a wooden platform, the crowd surrounding me murmurs their blessings as the mob in the broadcast roars in approval.

The woman's pale face is blotchy, her wide eyes puffy from cry-ing. She struggles as two plainly dressed men shove her toward a rust-stained guillotine. An executioner, face covered in a shabby black mask, steps up to the guillotine's release handle.

23

New little squares of light appear in front of me as someone forces the woman to her knees. People in this crowd hold rectangular pieces of metal with tiny screens on them. Red recording timers begin.

They're holding mobile phones, like the ones popularized in the early twenty-first century. I bite back a gasp of shock, not because the woman's neck stump pours out her lifeblood in sharp spurts, but because these people are filming it.

This might be 1793, but it's not *my* world's 1793. Everything is suddenly more unpredictable.

Backing up slowly, I look around for a place to hide. The buildings are compact and dilapidated, with doors and windows boarded up. Stragglers approach the group, eyes focused on the screens.

A man at the back of the group turns around and peers at me with curiosity. His wide eyes focus on my outfit. Then my backpack. His expression turns suspicious. Shit.

Unwilling to chance a conversation, I speed walk away from the group of onlookers. Dad said to leave when in doubt, but ten minutes isn't enough. I need to try and last at least a day.

Shadows grow longer, so the sunset won't be too long from now. There has to be a place to hunker down in for the evening. Hopefully, it's a safe place; as safe as this place can be.

The more I make my way through the clusters of homes and storefronts, the more I notice the peculiarities. Where I expect gas lamps, there are electrical lights. Behind patchwork curtains, I see more flickering TV light. I swear at one point, I hear the roar of a car engine.

It's an odd juxtaposition, seeing electricity in dilapidated homes that look like they belong in a fairy tale. Down the cobblestone road, thin horses pull rickety carts. The few people I encounter are also emaciate, their gaunt eyes darting from my face to my clothing, then away to the distance. I can't tell if their sneers imply I'm out of place or if this is how people are here.

I walk until my hips ache; despite that, no answer of where to stay appears. The sky darkens. It's becoming clear I need to find a dark corner to curl up in. The idea fills me with dread, and not because the streets are filthy. I've never even left the country—now I'm in the nexus of the French Revolution, looking for a shadow to sleep in? This doesn't even feel real.

In the relative safety of Dad's lab, time travel sounded glamorous. Maybe even fun. Go observe new worlds, collect samples, and find a safe haven. Preparation? Easy. Do some wilderness classes and walk on a treadmill while annotating research notes. My pack contains top-of-the-line survival tools, including a tent; however, we never considered landing somewhere a tent would be impractical, which was phenomenally short-sighted. We're scientists, not Rambo. Even so, I need to give this place more than a few minutes. It's what he would want.

Since I don't really know how to exist in a world where he's disappointed in me, I need to give this place at least twenty-four hours to say I tried.

The doubt is creeping in, though.

When twilight gives way to the darkest sky I've ever seen, I know it's time to find the dreaded spooky slice of shadows.

I find a small alcove between a set of ramshackle, wood-paneled homes. There are no nearby street lamps, which should be alarming, but hopefully, it'll offer a sort of safety blanket.

Sniffing the air, I'm relieved there's no immediate scent of feces. Seriously, did they defecate literally in the streets here? My skin itches, imagining invisible bugs crawling over my skin.

I sling off the backpack and gently place it on the ground. It'll make a good pillow, at least. Leaning against the wall, I slide to a squatting position. I groan in relief, rubbing my aching knees absentmindedly.

Despite the insulating material in my pants, the cold ground still seeps into my skin. My body shivers, either from shock or chill. Tucking my legs to my chest, I force myself to take deep breaths. I'll try to find some food to take samples of, and if I'm lucky, I'll find some samples to take off a couple of people. Then I'm out of here.

Despite the chill, exhaustion weighs me down. It's stupid to fall asleep, but my body doesn't care. As hard as I fight it, sleep overtakes my senses, burying me from this reality.

Chapter Four

Tea and Dry Biscuits

"**E**xcuse me, *mademoiselle*, but what are you doing by my door?"

A heavily accented voice jerks me awake. I sit up and frantically look around for the source of the voice. It's still nighttime and even darker than when I fell asleep.

I squint toward the voice. "*Bonjour?*"

The word feels so odd to say. At home, everyone has an optional translator implanted, letting them speak and understand thousands of languages, including various versions of French. It's not going to be perfect, but it's certainly helpful here.

"*Bonjour?*" The voice sounds even more impatient. "What are you doing here by my door?"

Finally, a shadow separates from the wall, and the slim figure of a woman appears.

I stand. "My apologies. I needed a place to rest for a bit. I'll go."

There's a beat of silence before she speaks again. "Are you all alone? Do you have no place to stay this evening?"

My hands grope for the strap of my backpack. I heft it onto my back. "No, but I'll leave right now." I clip the strap across my chest, securing the pack. "Again, I'm sorry."

I try to scoot past the woman, but she gently grabs my arm. "Wait one moment. I could never live with myself if I did not offer you a place to rest."

The hand holds firm when I try to pull away. "That's alright; you don't have to. I'll—"

"Don't bother arguing," the woman says in a practical tone. "You need a place to rest, and by the temperature of your arm, a place to warm up as well. Come inside."

She guides me toward a nearby wall I had assumed led nowhere. Even now, I don't see a door. The shadow of what I assume is her other hand waves, and a touch pad appears. The keys glow light blue, casting an eerie hue on my savior's face. Her fingers expertly input a code. To my surprise, the wall retracts and slides into itself, revealing a dimly lit living space.

The woman steps aside to let me into the cozy space. A fire is lit on one side of the room. On the other side is a small bed covered in pillows and quilts. In the center of the room is a worn-looking table with two matching wooden chairs. In another corner sit a small modern-looking stove, a metal basin, and a butcher-block counter. Cooking utensils and half-cut vegetables spread across all the surfaces.

There are other signs of modern technology, including a small TV attached to the wall opposite the bed. The door behind us closes quietly, but its near-silent automated locking still makes me anxious. Less than twelve hours in Paris, and my nerves are already fried. It's impossible not to feel on edge.

"Come sit by the fire," the woman orders, but not unkindly. She makes her way to the fire, throwing in a log. The fire crackles and snaps greedily at the fresh wood.

Noticing my hesitation, she motions impatiently at a rocking chair sitting adjacent to the fireplace. "I will not hurt you. You're going to catch a chill if you don't warm up. I imagine the stones aren't the most comfortable."

Her honey-blonde hair is loosely tied at the nape of her neck. A décolletage shows off her sharp collarbones. A dark yellow corset complements the white puffs of cotton covering her shoulders, the yellow fading to a dark orange skirt. It's multi-layered and looks far warmer than my current ensemble.

Peering around the room, nothing screams danger. The woman's insistence on helping is endearing, but it also increases my sense of unease. I'm in eighteenth-century France during a revolution, except they have technology. This isn't a world I can even pretend to understand.

A chill races down my spine, causing a violent shiver. She sucks her teeth and bustles over to her stove, ignoring my refusal to move. Metal clatters against metal as she pulls out a black kettle from a cupboard and places it on the cast-iron stovetop.

As she prepares what I assume is tea, I edge my way closer to the fire, the scent of ash increasing with each step. When I reach the rocking chair, I place my backpack on the ground. My shoulders ache with relief, and my resistance to the strange situation cracks. There's no way I can function on this entire adventure-journey-experiment-thing constantly conjuring possible problems. It's a terrible idea to approach this journey with suspicion at every turn. It might break my soul if I do.

Trusting the woman's intention, I sink into the rocking chair, allowing my tight muscles to relax. A sigh of relief escapes my lips, and I catch the woman glancing over her shoulder with a knowing smile.

She fills the kettle with water from the faucet as she asks, "So what were you doing, sleeping there on the street?"

Leaning forward, I hold my hands to the warmth of the fire. "I didn't know where to sleep for the night. It seemed as good as any spot to relax."

The woman scoffs and turns on the stove. It clicks, then flares to life. They have piped gas here? What the hell is going on?

"What if I had been a man? Do you think it would have been safe then?"

My eyebrows raise. "Are the men here dangerous?"

She pauses in her ministrations to turn and face me. "Is this a serious question?"

I bite my lip. In all regards, it was a stupid question, but I can't take it back now. Cheeks burning, I say, "Maybe?"

Her eyes trail from my face, over my outfit, down to my backpack, then back up to my face. It finally seems to process who she let into her home. "You're not from here."

I shake my head. "No, I'm not."

Her thin lips purse. "This is not a safe place for you, then. The city is in an uproar over the monarchy, and the crowds have been hungry for revenge. Too often, they are indiscriminate."

I know there are questions to ask, but conversing with others has always felt awkward; and that's in a normal setting. Here, in the middle of the French Revolution? Where beheadings were commonplace? Certain questions could equal death. The fear of having my head cleaved from my body, mixed with lifelong introversion, means asking questions is actually physically painful.

But my purpose is more important than the fear locked onto my nerves. *Time to be a big girl, Saira.* Voice quavering, I ask, "Is this the revolution?"

Smooth.

She turns back to the counter, grabbing a tin can and popping the top off. As she piles cookies onto a plate, she says, "I'm not sure if it's *the* revolution, but there is certainly change afoot. Tomorrow, the king and queen will be executed by guillotine at the Place de la Revolución. After that ..." She looks back at me and shrugs. "Then who knows. It is a tumultuous time to be alive."

"King Louis and Queen Marie?"

The kettle squeals loudly. She plucks it off the stove, silencing the sound. "Are there any other kings and queens in Paris?"

This still doesn't make sense. There's clearly technology here in this alternative timeline. So what else makes this parallel universe different? "Why are they being executed?"

Water tinkles against porcelain cups as she says, "There's a lot of speculation, but the estimated tipping point was when the queen posted on *Place Publique* about a large soireé she held with those criminals

30

they call the monarchy. They flung cake at the camera, then licked it off their fingers. On the same day, the king raised taxes for the sixth time in two years."

"*Place Publique?*"

She turns back to me, holding two white teacups. She places them on the table and motions to a chair. "Come have some tea and biscuits."

My stomach growls, and I will my legs to work as I stand. The woman walks back to the counter and grabs the plate of cookies. She sits at the table and slides the plate over to where I'm sinking into a chair.

Her delicate fingers hook the handle of a cup, and she sips. "Yes. The electronic forum where people spend obscene amounts of time."

"So, like social media?"

The woman cocks her head. "That's a funny term, but yes, I think it could be called that."

Okay, I *have* to see this. "Can you show me?"

She watches me over the rim of her cup as she takes another sip. This close, I can see her eyes are a dark shade of blue. My question must be the wrong one, because she doesn't move to show me whatever version of social media this place has. Instead, her curiosity grows.

"Where are you from?"

Dad and I discussed how to answer this question multiple times. The thing is, we don't know how people would react upon learning that we're time travelers. Places like eighteenth-century France could burn me at the stake. In some places, people might not care. We can't know until we share the truth. It's why our biggest rule, above all, is to never take off our Scouts unless absolutely necessary. The hologram feature makes it easy to blend it into an outfit, and that way, it's always close enough to escape in the most dire of circumstances.

There's also the consideration that the concept of time travel might be too much for someone to understand. How do you explain closed time-like curves to the average person, let alone someone who lives where the plague is an actual threat?

Instead of explaining the truth and possibly joining Marie at the guillotine tomorrow, I carefully train my expression to stay neutral as

I say, "I'm not really from anywhere, but I'm a traveler trying to find a place to call home one day."

The woman seems to buy my story, although the curiosity in her gaze doesn't dampen. "Well, I do not recommend the city of Paris for home right now."

An abrupt chuckle escapes. "Yes, I agree. I plan on leaving in the morning."

Satisfied with my answer, the woman reaches into a pocket — her dress *actually* has pockets! — and pulls out a thin piece of glass. It's about the length and width of my hand. At the bottom is a small silver box with enough space to fit a part of the glass inside. On the silver box are a few buttons with symbols I don't understand.

She presses one with her thumb, and the glass lights up. I gasp as a video plays in the center, but a scrolling feed on the right side slowly moves upward, showing clips of other videos. The silver box must be some kind of projector. As her fingernail taps a video on the glass, I realize it's a touchscreen as well.

As she scrolls through videos, I grab one biscuit and take a bite. It's hard and tasteless, only flour and water. Not a trace of salt or butter.

My mouth goes dry, forcing me to grab the tea and take a sip. It's earthy, almost too earthy. However, because it's my first drink since lunchtime, I find its mediocre flavor delicious.

While the woman busies herself, searching for something specific, I grab another biscuit. This time, I put it into my jacket pocket to sample later. I should do it with the tea as well, but I don't want to be too conspicuous.

"Ah, here it is," the woman murmurs. I lean over the table to peer at the screen. She presses a button, and a video plays.

The display of opulence is otherworldly, with pastels, golds, filigree, and silk overflowing from every corner of the room. A woman, who looks eerily like the paintings I've seen of Marie Antoinette, has a face covered in white powder dappled with fake moles and pink blush. She giggles with the woman next to her, who looks just as gaudy. They take bites of tiny cupcakes, the frosting sticking to the outside of their mouths. Beyond the camera frame, there's wild laughter, and someone chants, "Throw it, throw it."

Marie giggles again and looks at the camera. "Do not worry, *mes chéris*. There is a shortage of meat, so just eat cake."

Then she throws the remaining bit of cupcake at the camera. It hits the screen, then slowly slides away, leaving streaks of white icing. The room lights up with laughter, then the video ends.

My jaw drops. "When was that taken?"

"About three months ago." The woman's voice is solemn as she turns off the screen and places it on the table. "It was the breaking point for the people. There have been food shortages, taxes upon taxes, and people could not find work or keep their homes. The aristocrats have become so far removed from the struggle of the people; they do not understand how callous their flaunting of a lifestyle could be."

How could a society so advanced become so poor? It reminds me of the issues my society experienced in the early twenty-first century. Technology can't buy evolution, no matter how many humans pretend it does. That also led to an economic collapse and a class revolution.

One big question remains, though. "With all of this technology, how did the government not squash the uprising?"

She scoffs and waves away my question. "The military was also hungry. There was no one left to protect them when the time arrived."

I take another sip of my tea, mulling over her words. Without a doubt, this is not the place to stay. It's important for me to rest, but I'll need to leave first thing in the morning.

A wave of exhaustion makes me sway. The woman notices and grimaces. "I'm afraid I do not have a second bed, but I do have extra pillows and blankets. We can make you a makeshift bed by the fire for tonight, so you may travel tomorrow more rested."

I smile. "Thank you. You didn't have to let me come in, but I appreciate you did."

She gives a brief nod as she walks to her bed, filling her arms with items for my makeshift cot. I help her organize it into something that will be comfortable enough for the night. As much as I want to take off the utility belt and boots, I can't bring myself to allow that level of comfort. Instead, I move around on the pallet of pillows until I find a comfortable position.

Before I drift off to sleep, I ask, "What's your name, by the way?"

The woman climbs into her bed, but looks at me. "Aimeé."

"I'm Saira."

She smiles and tucks herself into bed. "Good night, Saira."

Then we both fall asleep to the sound of the crackling fire and the far-off sounds of violence.

Chapter Five

Pardon Me, Monsieur

At the break of dawn, Aimeé wakes me up with a gentle hand on my shoulder. I jolt awake, heart racing.

"Saira, I've received a message from a friend, warning me of a mob coming. We must leave now if we are to get you out of the city."

I sit up, disoriented. It takes a few seconds for my brain to catch up. Dead family. Time traveling. Paris. Revolution. Danger. Stale biscuits.

Aimeé's already walked away, tinkering in front of the stove, scrolling on the same piece of technology she used last night. The fire has dwindled to embers, but the small house is still cozy and warm.

As she heats the kettle, I carefully fold the blankets. Sleeping was damn near impossible; at all hours of the night, the moth-eaten curtains couldn't contain the sounds of drunken revelry, screaming, and howling dogs. My brain feels scraped raw; my muscles feel weighed down.

Yet, curiosity stirs inside of me. I know it's wise to get the hell out of here, but the temptation of seeing Marie Antoinette beheaded is too strong. I studied this time period extensively as a teenager, fascinated with the parallelism between the French Revolution and the second American Revolution in 2029. This revolution is also in the time of social media, which is intriguing. Taking pictures wouldn't appear unusual. It's an irresistible opportunity.

So while I have every intention of getting the fuck out of here today, I'm reticent to leave without trying to experience history in real-time.

Projecting nonchalance, I ask, "Where is the mob going?"

Aimeé's shoulders tense as she places more of the stale biscuits on a chipped plate. "As I said last night, to the king and queen's execution."

"Is it a beheading by guillotine?"

She sits at the table and motions for me to do the same. She pours steaming water into my teacup. "*Oui.* It will stream everywhere, so there's no need to experience the chaos in person."

"And if I want to experience it in person?"

Her expression darkens. "The crowds are bloodthirsty, Saira. I am not sure this is wise."

"I just want to watch it, but I'll leave right after," I promise. There's no reason for me to stay beyond my morbid curiosity. The Mission comes first, always, but my inherent curiosity needs satiating, too.

She bites into a biscuit, chewing slowly. After taking a sip of her tea, she nods. "Alright, I shall take you there, then to the city's edge. We must not linger, Saira."

"Deal," I blurt. Through the curtains, sunshine pierces through moth-eaten holes. It's later than I thought. "Do we leave now?"

She gathers the dishes and brings them to the sink. "*Oui*, please give me one moment to dress."

While she changes, I double-check all of my supplies to ensure they are in order. Rummaging in my bag for the camera, I remove the slim piece of technology and slide it into a larger pocket on my utility belt.

When Aimeé finishes getting ready, she ushers me out the door, nervously glancing up and down the street as she locks the door.

"You must listen to me, Saira," she whispers. "I may not care that you are not from around here, but others will not share a similar sentiment. Follow me and do what I say, *oui?*"

I nod and match her brisk pace as we plunge into the maze of streets in the good ol' city of stinky love.

Except there isn't much love to be seen. Like yesterday, it appears people are hiding, watching televised streams in public areas, or joining various mobs. The most popular weapons of fury are pitchforks, swords, daggers, and the occasional sharpened broomstick. They scream and rage against the collapsing monarchy, although I've caught a few pausing in their fury to take selfies.

Human nature is human nature, regardless of the timeline.

There are a few cars driving around, most resembling late twentieth-century automobiles. Often, it's horses and carts doing most of the transportation.

At one point, a cobalt blue car that looks eerily similar to an American muscle car from the 1950s roars by. From the passenger-side window, a shirtless, bloodied man screams at onlookers as he waves the French flag. It's equally tattered and bloody. Just as I'm about to whip out my camera to take a photo, the man catches my eye and brings two fingers up to his mouth. I cringe as he spreads them and waggles his tongue.

Eww. Not in a million timelines, dude.

Sweat beads on my forehead by the time we reach the largest mob I've ever seen. It writhes like a living creature with bloodthirsty calls for beheadings. It's mid-morning, but the platform in the center of the mob shines with fresh blood.

A guillotine, the likes of which I've never seen before, shoots proudly into the sky, its silver maw spattered with shades of red. Some splotches are the color of deep rust, while other spatters are almost fluorescent in their freshness.

The energy is frenetic. Consuming. I have no tangible ties to anything happening here, and yet my heart pounds with adrenaline. Excitement. Shameful eagerness.

My feet propel me forward, driven by the manic whirlwind of emotions, but Aimeé grabs my elbow.

"Saira, don't."

I raise both of my hands and step back to her side. "Sorry, got a little caught up in it all. I've never seen a mob in real life. It's really ..."

"Disgusting? Deplorable?" she supplied, sneering at a drunk man stumbling by.

"Intoxicating."

She scoffs and hugs her chest. "Certainly, there are intoxications happening."

"That's not what I meant," I say dryly.

She ignores me, focusing on standing on her tiptoes, straining to look over the crowd. I don't even bother trying the same. I'm more of the type who needs to be on someone's shoulders to see anything in a crowd. Looking around, I spot a barrel. Motioning to Aimeé where I'm headed, I awkwardly crawl onto the barrel, probably resembling a seal on land.

The barrel's lid is wide enough for me to stand on, allowing me to take in the scene. Immediately, I want to jump off. This is easily the worst thing I've ever witnessed in my life.

Two men dragged a woman with greasy brunette hair onto the stage. As the crowd surges, the screams amplify. Her skin is a sickly shade of white, and even from here, I can see her whole body shaking. An executioner meanders up the stairs, covered head to toe in black. The tattered mask, obscuring his features, shows fathomless eyes peering through roughly cut slits.

The woman sees the guillotine and balks like a cow headed for the slaughter pen. She cries out as she's jerked forward and shoved down in front of the wooden bascule. They quickly lock the lunette. Sickness drops to the bottom of my stomach at the tangy taste of hate. The crowd screams and fists fly into the air. The woman slams backward, reminding me of a cat trying to escape a too-tight hug. Her movements are frantic. Blood seeps around her wrists, but she can't get her hands free. How can everyone cheer for this?

The two men step back and look away. The executioner walks up to the guillotine, his steps steady. Too slow, as if the drama exhilarates him. A man next to us screams, spittle flying from between his chapped lips.

A headache pounds at my temples. I was a fool to think this could be an interesting experience. I'm acting like a fucking tourist, watching history happen like this is a TV screen and I'm comfortable on my couch. This woman is about to die, and we're all standing here, like this is afternoon entertainment.

"Who is she?" I ask Aimeé, who just walked up to my barrel. Shock freezes her expression as she stares at the woman's face.

"Madame de Maillé de La Tour-Landry." She whispers the name like a prayer. To my shock, she walks forward. I bend down and grab her shoulder.

"What are you doing?"

The trance breaks, and her eyes meet mine. "She isn't supposed to be here. She isn't supposed to die."

"The woman about to be executed?"

At the word *execution*, she gasps and pulls away from me. "I must stop them. There must be some mistake."

"Aimeé!" I call out after her, hopping off the barrel and rushing to follow. She slices through the crowd like a knife, holding out a hand for me to grab. I lunge for it, gripping for dear life.

The mass of bodies presses in on me from all sides, even above. I'm elbowed in the head more than once. The stench is unbearable, but the sounds. Oh, gods, the sounds. I think people are having sex somewhere in the crowd. I hear farts and burps. Cruel laughter as the woman set for execution—apparently someone very important to Aimeé—cries hysterically.

Aimeé pushes forward, throwing elbows and curses. My grip tightens as a barrel-chested man shoves her back. She glares at the man and bares her teeth. The man's bravado sinks, and he steps away, skulking back into the crowd. A feral French woman is a sight to behold.

"Jeanne!" Aimeé cries out as the executioner reaches up for the rope. The woman, Jeanne, whips her head in our direction.

"Aimeé?"

"Jeanne!"

Jeanne's face contorts with agonized regret. "Aimeé! I'm so sorry!"

Aimeé screams toward the executioner. "Stop this instant! There must be a mistake. She couldn't have done it!"

"Aimeé! I love you!"

"Jeanne!" Aimeé shrieks as the blade whooshes downward, its journey ended by the sound of a *thunk!*

The crowd roars with satisfaction. They're all cheering this on. Cameras click and flashes of light illuminate the scene. Bright phone screens reach up past hats, trying to get the best photo possible. Shame fills me to the brim, the camera burning a hole in my pocket. Mere minutes ago, I thought it would be smart to document this moment.

What a short-sighted fool I was thirty minutes ago.

Vomit burns up my throat. Not caring at all, I throw up all over a man's shoes. He doesn't even notice, too busy screaming with glee. *I can't breathe. I can't breathe.* Tilting my head, I suck in lungfuls of air, trying to stave off more vomit. That just makes it worse, because it's fucking disgusting here. I throw up again, a smattering of half-digested biscuits landing on the cobblestones in front of me. Wiping my mouth with my jacket, I flinch as a pock-faced woman bumps into me. I shove her off, and she laughs.

How is this real? How are people like this? The barbarity of it all. It's one thing to read about beheading in books or watch them in a movie. But to experience it with all five senses?

It's nothing short of insanity.

Grief freezes Aimée in place; her eyes are wide and unseeing. Her gaze fixes on the head as it rolls to a stop at the platform's edge. Her grip slackens, and my hand drops.

"Aimeé?" I call out. She doesn't show any sign of hearing me. The crowd is deafening, and is it my imagination, or are they getting worked up even more?

"Aimeé?" I try one more time to get her attention, reaching for her hand. The grip is limp. All the energy has seeped out of her, sucked dry by the crowd. My fear rises. I can't just leave her here, but I can't stay either. I don't want to witness another beheading, and the way this crowd is acting? Anyone could be on the chopping block.

"Aimeé, we need to go." I tug on her hand and throw off her balance enough that she stumbles to the side. It jars her out of the reverie. Her head turns slowly toward mine. Tears soak her cheeks, and her mouth opens, then closes.

"Come on." I tug again, and this time, she follows. It's my turn to bully the people in our way, although I'm not very good at it. No one is going to take someone like me seriously.

It's an effort, but finally, we're at the edge of the crowd. I lean against my legs, trying to take my first full breath in the last five minutes. I look over and watch Aimeé staring blankly at the execution platform. They drag Jeanne's body down the stairs, and the executioner grabs her head, placing it into a cloth sack.

"Aimeé, I need to leave. Which direction should I go?"

The poor woman looks at me, dazed. Gone is the capable woman who brought me into her home last night. I'm not sure who Jeanne was to her, but I know there's nothing I'll be able to do to fix it.

She raises an arm like a zombie, pointing beyond the crowd. "Walk this way until you find a river, then continue until you're out of the city."

The time for questions ends abruptly when the crowd quiets. It's the most terrifying thing I've ever heard — the sudden, eerie silence of a bloodthirsty mob. Knowing I'll regret it, I turn to look back at the platform.

A regal, fresh-faced woman walks up the stairs. She's young, maybe in her twenties. Only a few slivers of pale blonde hair remain on her otherwise shaved head. No one guides her or even touches her. She looks out at the crowd, stoic and calm.

"Marie," someone calls out.

Others do the same, calling out her name or the horrible nickname, *Madame Déficit*. Marie ignores them all, walking past the executioner. Her pale eyes focus on the bascule, so much that she trips on the executioner's foot.

Remorse tightens her features as she looks at his foot, then at his covered head.

Her voice is soft as she pleads, "Pardon me, Monsieur, I did not mean to do it."

The executioner is silent. When she realizes he won't respond, she kneels on the bascule, then situates her head and hands to the lunette.

Phones rise to the sky, thumbs pressing the red record buttons. It's all done in a moment, Marie's head rolling ear over ear until it comes to an abrupt stop. Blood pools on the stained wood. Someone in the very front shoves their phone into her bloodless face.

The crowd cheers, and some people even break out in dance. It's a game to them. Two women died, and the woman next to me can barely contain her devastation. Yet, these people celebrate.

I don't know what it's like to live in a world of starvation and plague. I certainly don't know what it's like to shit in the street because public toilets aren't popular. It's not even twenty-four hours here, but I'm damn sure I have no intention of finding out any further what this place is like.

Looking at Aimeé, I say, "Thank you for helping me. Your generosity was unwarranted, but deeply appreciated."

She looks at me, a bit more alert and aware. "We need to get you out of here."

"Go home." I touch her arm gently, pointing in the direction we arrived. "I can find my way."

"Are you sure?" Her eyes flick toward her home. I'm overcome with shame for even talking her into coming with me. It was selfish and naïve. Now she'll never forget the moment she saw a loved one beheaded.

I nod firmly, looking more confident than I am. "Yes. I can get out of here quickly. Go home and stay safe."

She leans in and gives me a soft kiss on my cheek. "Safe travels, Saira."

We walk in different directions, toward two very different lives. I hope finds peace and lives to be a happy old lady. The odds aren't in her favor, but I can hope.

When I'm finally away from the crowd and find a quiet park, I leave the French Revolution behind.

Chapter Six

Carnage. Sharks. What The Hell.

When I land in the new reality, it's on all fours. The ground shakes like an earthquake. It's sensory overload with the instant cacophony of sounds. Around me are explosions and agonized screams, but it's hard to notice as I heave onto dark, wet sand. My fingers easily sink into the filthy slush.

My mask shows me the stats, confirming its breathable air. Yanking it off, I retch up bile. After the beheading, my belly has nothing left to give, leaving a hollow feeling in its wake.

I sit on my haunches. I've gone straight into a nightmare. Storm clouds pregnant with unshed wrath threaten to rip open. Screams cleave the air.

The ground shakes again, and my ears ring with another explosion. I scream as chunks of rock land on me.

Where the fuck have I landed?

Gritting my teeth, I stand upright, shifting the pack on my shoulders. The sound of angry waves crashes behind me. Turquoise waters batter the sand, touching the boots of dead men along the shoreline. In the distance are metal battleships of different sizes.

The regret of leaving France is immediate.

I've landed in the middle of a beach. It seems to be an island of some sort. In any other setting, it would be the perfect destination for a vacation. Minus the random rifles and handguns littering the ground.

And the moans for mercy in different languages. Torn and shredded body parts scatter in empty spaces with feeble hands reaching out for help.

The carnage steals the oxygen from my lungs.

Behind me, a man moans. Spinning, I spot sandy blond hair and filthy hands clutching a gutted stomach. A piece of silver shrapnel digs deep into his abdomen. The man's dark eyes fill with confusion when he notices me. It's immediately replaced with fear and pain.

"Help me," he croaks. Viscera poke through his fingers as he reaches out with another hand. "Please help me."

I rush over to him, trying to staunch the flow of blood with my hands. Immediately, there's blood soaking my arm. Lifeblood squirts into the air. Flecks splatter onto my cheeks. But so much more is coming out of this man, whose insides keep pushing outward.

"Please, you need to save me." The words are raspy, barely above a whisper. One of my tears falls onto his intestines, mixing with bile and shit. Sand is getting into *everything*.

"I'm trying," I sob. "I don't know what to do."

He reaches for my hand, squeezing with more strength than a dying man should have. "Call a medic. One of them will come save me."

I look around frantically, but all that exists is rubble, smoke, and bodies. "I don't see one."

A dozen airplanes cruise above us in formation. They look like old versions that collect dust in museums. Then, I examine his outfit. It's dark green, shredded in so many places. He has a round helmet strapped tightly to his chin.

"What year is it?" My translator doesn't activate — he's speaking English.

The man's eyelids flutter. The blood is pumping slower now. Knowing he only has seconds left, I let go of his wound and shake his bony shoulders. "What year is it?"

His vibrant green eyes, a color that doesn't belong in this gray-colored devastation, focus on me. "It's 1941."

Oh, my gods. "Where are we?"

"Wake Island, ma'am."

Wake Island. Where is Wake Island? Is this a battle in World War II? It was well over a hundred years ago where I'm from. Is this the same timeline as my original one? Either way, no one in my family will willingly stay in this time period.

The man's lungs begin to spasm. The whites of his eyes are the only things visible now, and his body shakes uncontrollably. He's going into shock, and there's nothing I can do about it. The helplessness fills me with shame. This trip was supposed to be about saving people, but so far, it's been nothing but dead bodies piling up.

"It'll be okay," I weep openly, brushing his stringy blond hair off his face. "It'll be alright. Just let go."

I can almost see his spirit escape the mortal cage of his decimated body. A rattle escapes from his throat, the final exhalation. It's the worst thing I've ever heard in my life. Maybe even worse than the machines in Mom's hospital room. Holding the back of a hand to my mouth, I let out a strangled wail. This is too much death. It's too much.

I stumble into standing, swaying from shock. On my left is another cry for help. Then two more to my right. There are more explosions, and a wretched sound of grinding metal comes from the ocean. A ship sinks as another approaches.

I can't stay here. This place is a death sentence.

After living in a carefully cultivated society, this reality is too high definition for me. A gull cries out above me. It lands on the chest of a man who's blown in half. It pecks at the innards sprawled on the sand.

That's gonna be a nope from me.

Suddenly remembering my purpose, I swing off my pack, and fumble for the analyzer. Typing in the password, I input pieces of sand. Cringing, I scoop up a bit of the man's blood and add it to the compartment, then do the same for bits of shells and ocean water.

When I feel like I've gathered enough evidence to stave off any future guilt, I put the analyzer back into my pack, wincing as another loud explosion goes off even closer.

Time to get the fuck out of here. Replacing the mask over my face, I press down on the button and let the nothingness rip me from this world.

The mask saves me from sucking in mouthfuls of water. The screen immediately lights up with red alerts. It's sensory overload. I'm struggling to understand what the alerts are telling me. I take in my surroundings, assessing for danger.

I'm floating in a warm cerulean ocean. The sky above me is soft yellow. There's so much light, it hurts. It isn't much of an effort to swim, though. The salinity must be high. Which is a miracle, because otherwise my boots and pack would drag me under. On the even brighter side, they're both waterproof. Bless the science gods and Dad's inability to chill in the lab.

The two suns easily explained the brightness in the sky, one half the size of the other. Puffy neon blue clouds dot the sky, some of their columns so high into the sky, it makes me dizzy. It's surreal realizing there's a version of Earth with two stars.

There's no land in sight. No movement. Only the sound of lapping waves and a breeze brushing against the shell of my ear. In any other circumstances, it could even be relaxing.

Well. I don't think we'll be living here. There's no godsdamned way I'll be swimming hoping to find land. Not when there's not even a speck on the horizon to hang a hope on. My legs are already growing tired from treading, even with the added buoyancy.

Wait. Something in the distance moves, catching my eye.

Shading my gaze with a hand, I squint. It's large and gray. The sunlight bounces off the slick material. My thighs cramp and I hiss, grabbing one while struggling to continue treading water.

The object is like a rocket headed straight for me. My heart pounds, fear spiking my blood. My intuition tells me this is bad. Really bad.

Shit. Wait, okay.

Samples.

I need fucking samples.

My breath quickens until I'm on the brink of hyperventilating. Fumbling for an extra vial in my utility pack, I pull one out and uncap it. It's a miracle it stays in my hand as I scoop in some of the water. My feet kick frantically as I twist the lid back on.

The thing is getting closer, and now I can make out a massive, dark shape below the surface of the water. The object is looking more familiar, but I don't want to consider the possibility of a shark coming to eat me.

Maybe I should try to get a sample of it.

Okay, that's enough of that. *There's a time and place for science, Saira.* I secure the sample back into my utility belt, then hold up the Scout. It's only been two minutes here. We'll pretend that's enough.

The black fin whips faster, the beast excited by its prey. Placing my thumb over the travel button, the five-second countdown activates.

Five.

The shark is only a hundred feet away.

Four.

A second fin appears, about twenty feet away from the first.

Three.

That's a tail. This thing is over fifty feet long.

Two.

The black head slips out of the water like a bullet. A golden eye with slits for pupils homes in on me.

One.

A mouth, the width of a city bus, widens. It's a bottomless pit, framed by rows of gray teeth.

Then, I'm gone.

This time, it's fire. Nothing but fire. The massive body of the shark comes with me. It'd been too close when I traveled, forced to leave its oceanic home for a fiery hellscape. If I weren't reeling from everything that's happened in the last couple of hours, I'd feel bad for it. It flops its three fins frantically, its jagged, toothy maw gaping open and closed.

The fire rages all around me, the heat biting at my skin. Sweat prickles my armpits. The sky is invisible. Nothing else is alive. A wall of fire springs toward me, its life-force the sound of roaring tornadoes. There's no time for samples. I'll burn alive if I stay any longer.

Onto the next hellish adventure.

Chapter Seven

The ESC Particle

Blinking rapidly, I dig my fingers into soft grass. It's warmed by what might be sunshine. The surroundings come into focus. I've landed in a forest. My ears stop ringing, and now all I can hear are songbirds. No bombs. No screams. No sharks. No fire. Only happy birds sing out their joy.

Coughing, I sit up. The backpack teeters me over again, so I unclasp the straps and wriggle out of my arms. Information about this world appears on my screen. The oxygen levels appear to be breathable, but to be safe, I need to check the Scout.

The material of my clothes is already dry. No rips or missing pieces of the custom outfit's material. It's the same as it was a second ago. Small blessings.

My training kicks in. Raising my wrist, I find the Scout still in perfect shape. Activating its camouflage capabilities, I turn it into a leather-like black band.

My fingers skim over the pouches on my utility belt, taking stock of the contents still inside. Dragging the pack to lean against my legs, I unzip a rectangular side pocket. Pulling out the analyzer, I press my thumb against the fingerprint scanner. The screen flickers to life instantly, a passcode prompt popping up.

After typing in the password, the home screen appears. I press the Nanites Status option. The screen centers an internal diagram of my body, with a status bar underneath. Taking a steadying breath, I scroll through everything, hunting for something to be wonky. Nothing appears.

This is an excellent sign, especially for this being my fifth stop.

Then I check the location point. Two dissecting loops appear at the location point; each represents one of the two intersecting closed timelike curves Dad and I are projected to follow. I have no way of knowing whether he made it to his destination. A pulsing dot marks my current location. This won't be particularly helpful knowledge for now — Dad just found something else to track. He's such a nerd.

Pressing the small compartment tucked into the side of the analyzer, a bright yellow piece of scooped-out silicone pops out. Pulling a small spoon from my utility belt, I dig it into the ground, lifting brown earth to the silicone.

Pushing it closed, I press on the Sample Output option.

An identification pops up.

Soil: Coniferous Podzol

Location: Forest

Oxygen levels: 23%

A duplicate world, oxygen-wise. The analyzer's information lines up with the information on my mask screen. There's no year available, though. Which could be good ... or bad.

As I remove the mask, cool air brushes against my cheeks, and the soft smell of pine fills my nostrils. After Paris, it's nothing short of a divine gift. I tuck it back into its assigned pocket. Closing my eyes, I take deep breaths, focusing on the sensation of my chest rising and falling. Unfortunately, a surge of devastation hiccups out as a sharp sob.

What the fuck, what the fuck, what the fuck? Maybe it's the quantum hormones or something, but in this very moment, I'm not sure I'm cut out for this. I was almost *eaten* and *burned alive.* Some of the soldier's blood still crusts my body.

It hasn't even been fifteen minutes since I left Paris.

The memory of Marie's blank stare, unseeing eyes peering into nothingness, opens the floodgates. Curled into myself, I let myself have a few good sobs. It's unproductive to feel sorry for myself, but my brain needs the oxytocin. I imagine flogging the cortisol out of my body, and it makes me laugh. The tears slow and then finally stop.

Wiping my cheeks roughly, I wiggle my tingling toes. All of them are intact. My body aches from all the trauma it just experienced, and my mind screams to sit still for more than a handful of hours.

It's unlikely that rest will happen anytime soon. There's nothing around here. No homes. No sound of a nearby road. Maybe this entire world is empty. At least there isn't something trying to eat me. Hopefully.

Pulling out a compass from my utility belt, I look for North. The arrow spins slowly, teetering indecisively, before settling its point to my left. Somehow, even after everything that has just happened to me, I need to find the energy to forge ahead. A safe place to rest is paramount.

Clipping the pack's straps together, I square my shoulders, inhale a deep breath, and take the first step forward into this strange new world.

It's my luck to be flung into what very well might be an endless forest. Trees, trees, and more *trees*. Every time I check the Scout for the time, I'm always dismayed to find it's only been minutes, not hours.

The only thing keeping me occupied is taking in the different plant life. I've taken samples of leaves, flowers, and types of dirt. So far, the samples seem similar to what's found on my Earth. That's promising.

Darkness cuts my sampling short after a couple of hours. A perfect excuse to stop.

The promise of relaxation spurs me to put together a tent. It's a top-of-the-line model, engineered to fold and unfold at the press of a button. When not in use, it resembles an oversized paper towel roll.

One second, it's in my hand; the next, I have a tent large enough to lie in and have my pack next to me.

Satisfied, I walk through the trees to find kindling.

Don't get me wrong — I'm not a professional survivalist. Sure, I've been to a wilderness camp for a couple of weekend stints, but my backpack has supplied me with gear most survivalists dream of.

My belt has a lighter capable of agitating any available molecules until it starts a fire. There will be no sticks being rubbed together here. My bag contains dehydrated rations. The thought makes my mouth water. All I've had in the last day are the dry biscuits and tea from Aimeé's home. Which probably still stains a pair of shoes in the French Revolution.

Pulling out a camping shovel from my pack, I dig a shallow hole in the ground and dump the kindling I found. Pulling out the lighter, I press it against some pine needles. The blue flame attacks the kindling with ferocity. The warmth seeps into my heart, thawing out the misery a little. Appreciating the little things is the only way to endure this trip.

Grabbing my cooking supplies, I say in a deep voice, "Up next: Becoming the first time-traveling chef."

Within ten minutes, I have meatloaf in a metal pan soaking in water, warming up at a snail's pace. Despite knowing it won't compare to Nana's cooking, it smells divine.

Squatting by the fire, I hold out my hands. The temperature dips, and despite my outfit being built for most circumstances, my fingers are stiff. The forest falls into darkness, silencing the birds. Trilling insects take their place.

The fire pops, spiking my adrenaline. Without the sun illuminating the trees, they look ominous in the firelight. Anything could be out there, watching me. Maybe it's ants the size of horses, ready to eat my elbows. It could even be sentient creatures ready to ensnare me for dinner, but not before dressing me up like a doll.

I'm too hungry for where my imagination wants to go. Checking the meatloaf, I'm excited to discover it's ready. Some might encourage me to savor the first meal as a time traveler, but the moment the beef touches my taste buds, it's hoovered in five seconds flat.

As the meal settles into my belly, I rinse out the bowl with a teensy bit of water. I wet my hands to scrub away the remaining blood on my neck and face. Since there's no way to know when a body of water will appear, not a lot of the water can be spared. My body still feels disgusting, but it'll have to do for now.

I pull the backpack into the tent with me and zip the flaps closed. The fire is already fading, but I don't want to put it out just yet. The glow is a comfort against the straining darkness.

Despite the cramped space, I've managed to position my pack to fit the sleeping bag I laid out. Reaching for the bag of Nana's cookies, I pull one out and relish the experience. Savoring the soft, sugary texture as it melts in my mouth.

Taking advantage of the brief respite and full belly, I sit cross-legged and take stock of the situation. So far, I've seen the French Revolution and a battlefield in a war well over a hundred years ago. Almost eaten by a shark the size of a luxury yacht. Nearly fried to a crisp in a world of fire tornadoes.

My family is dead, aside from Dad.

My best friend is now ash particles in space.

I'm the first time traveler ever, aside from Dad.

The meatloaf was good.

I desperately want a hot bath.

Okay, enough with this pitiful stewing. If I linger on these thoughts for too long, they'll eat me alive. I tuck myself into the sleeping bag, appreciating the attached pillow. Even though I'm as comfortable as one could be in this situation, my heart whispers an ache I can't acknowledge.

Instead, I close my eyes and drift off into dreamland.

The Scout doesn't look like anything special. It resembles a pitch-black watch with three buttons. One on each side and a slightly larger one at the top. It's made of a material stronger than titanium — a proprietary formula developed by Dad.

I'm clueless how he accomplished such a thing. I know you could drop the Empire State Building on it and it'd survive.

I turn it over in my palm, and the inky black absorbs the fluorescent lights in our work lab. On the back are the words "Through the folded stars."

Words from Mom's favorite poem. Leave it to Dad to be sentimental. Smiling, I place the Scout back onto the table. Swiveling on my stool, I turn toward Dad.

He's bent over the analyzer, wearing thick microscope glasses extending three inches from his eyeballs. In one hand is a screwdriver and in the other is a soldering station. A thin strap of worn leather, older than me, pulls back his long salt-and-pepper hair.

His worktable is littered with stickies, pens, equipment, notebooks, and other items dedicated to science. Behind me is my workspace, looking far more immaculate.

He's always been chaotic when it comes to organizing his work. Somehow, he keeps everything together long enough to be one of the greatest inventors in history. He makes Edison look like an amateur — especially since he's an actual *inventor. Nana tells stories about how he began inventing things as early as the age of five. Considering he's in his fifties now, he's had decades to hyper-focus on anything his brain can cook up.*

Over his ears are enormous headphones, from which rock music pumps out of the edges. I don't know how he hasn't lost his hearing.

"Hey, Dad." I wave my hands. He peers up, bug-eyed and irritated.

"What?" The single word is so loud, I flinch. He notices and grins. Placing down the tools, he pushes back the headphones. "Sorry. What's going on?"

I motion to the analyzer. "ETA on that being done? We kinda need it ready in a week, and a sloth could move faster than you."

He attempts to give a threatening glare. *"Don't rush genius."*

I scoff. *"Pfft. Then rushing you shouldn't be a problem, eh?"*

His eyes flick to the table, and in a flash, he tosses a different screwdriver at me. I duck, laughing. It clatters to the floor and slides under the table.

"So feisty," I tease. *"But really, what's the status? We need to test the Scout connection."*

He sighs with the kind of burden only a father can muster. *"Daughter, it'll be done in time. Why don't you go pack or something? Be useful."*

I cock my head in disbelief. *"I invented time travel, my dude."*

"As your male overseer, I'm allowed to take ownership of your genius."

It's my turn to chuck something across the room. He laughs and dodges the plastic pipette. Our ongoing joke will never get old.

He's right, though. I'm not even close to being packed. With a groan, I make a show of standing with stiff joints. It's not much of a show since I've been on the stool since dawn. A glance out the window shows twilight purples and blues.

"Don't forget to pack a yoga mat, you old fart," Dad teases.

Flipping him the middle finger, I walk over to the packs leaning against the wall. *"I'm going to sabotage your Scout. See if the patriarchy helps you survive on the surface of Venus."*

He chuckles and turns his focus back onto his task. The analyzer is almost done. He had everything working last week, so it's a matter of finessing everything just right. I'm not worried, regardless of my antagonizing. He's far more of a perfectionist than I am.

Grabbing my bag from the floor, I start packing. Lined up on the next table are my travel items of choice: an ebook reader, music player, a notebook for observations, a digital camera with a fresh memory card, a toothbrush, and my mother's wedding ring, glistening from its recent cleaning. Oh, and the vitally important solar-powered battery pack, to keep all of those electronics alive.

Shoving my hand into the dark bag, I pull out my utility belt and make sure all the necessities are there. *Compass, multi-purpose knife, lighter, and empty sample vials. There's a spot to slot in the analyzer if I ever feel like it.*

I check each pouch to make sure it's snapped shut before I move to my personal items. Each item tucks into its proper pocket.

Except for my mother's ring. The gold band slides onto my pointer finger easily. There's the tiniest of diamonds in it, all Dad could afford when he proposed to Mom.

My thumb rubs against the fleck of stone, the sensation as familiar as breathing. The emotions tied to it are as complex as layers of time. I like to pretend her essence remains in the soft metal. It's a comfort when things are tough or overwhelming.

Sixteen years is a long time for any remnants to linger.

Just like that, my life is stuffed into a backpack. Items from a soon-to-be nonexistent life. Or it will again, depending on how one looks at it. It's Schrodinger's Apocalypse: neither permanent nor avoidable. Only time will tell.

When I began to research particle theory with Dad, time travel seemed so abstract. It still does, even though Dad discovered and proved the existence of tachyons repeatedly. Manipulating them in the homemade machine Dad made based on the third-generation Antiproton Decelerator model from the start of the millennium.

When I was twenty-two, I discovered how to manipulate anti-matter particles in conjunction with tachyons. That's right: your girl discovered the key to time travel. It's okay to be impressed.

It was just a matter of time until we realized that when the antimatter and tachyons touched, it got a little weird. By weird, I mean things disappeared near the singularity.

We never did find that laptop ... It disappeared because it was closest to the collider as the antimatter and Tachyon touched. One moment it was there — then it was gone. We tested it with a few more items, and all of them disappeared.

Which is why Dad thought it would be hilarious to call this new particle the ESC Particle.

It was another three years before we successfully understood that when we introduced a set level of quarks, we could control the disappearance and reappearance of objects. All still in perfect condition.

The day we tested it on a rabbit, wrapping a band similar to the Scout model to its neck, was the greatest moment of my life. The rabbit reappeared an hour later, in perfect condition, on the same table. It didn't even seem to notice anything had happened, although a piece of grass was stuck to its butt.

When we did it again, this time with a camera on the band, we discovered the rabbit landed in a field. It was impossible to know where and when this field existed, but again, it was an incredible revelation.

Then we found out about the asteroid. Suddenly, the ability to time travel became more important than ever. It's sheer luck we were this far into our research, so it was a matter of Dad's genius figuring out how to take all of that science and pare it down into what's essentially a watch.

But there aren't enough materials. Since most of the world shut down when the news came out, it became instantly harder to gain access to what we needed to make more Scouts. Which is why we're aiming to come back about sixteen months before the asteroid hits, with enough time to order the supplies. So everyone can be saved.

Well, everyone in my family. It would be insane to try and move an entire society to somewhere else. Humans have colonized enough.

"It's ready!"

Dad's announcement breaks me from the temporary reverie. The words bring a skip to my heart.

"Excellent. Shall we see what your weathered old brain designed?"

"I should've let you have student loans."

Walking over to his table, I wave away his insult. "My scholarships would still have covered it all because my intelligence surpasses yours."

"You got those scholarships because you have your mother's good looks."

"Thankfully, her brains, too." *I stop next to him, leaning over his shoulder.* "Now show me the good stuff."

He holds the heavy-looking analyzer in both meaty hands. With a quick tap of a finger, the screen flares to life, illuminating both of our faces. Numbers and letters scrawl across the screen, the familiar words making me proud. The technology and coding for this piece of equipment were programmed by yours truly, for the small price of carpal-tunnel and eye strain. My life's work.

The greatest invention and biggest secret in human history.

Finally, the GUI appears with the simplest of menus. There are options for Nanite Status, Sample Output, and Location Point.

The latter, when we've traveled, will show the updated path for the closed timelike curve, stopping approximately sixteen months before the asteroid hits. It was the furthest back he could push his calculations with the information we currently have available. It'll provide us with enough time to order enough parts for everyone in my family who wants to go.

My travels between locations will auto-generate a map for our later reference. If either of us finds a perfect spot, we'll then be able to travel there.

"Check the nanite stats." I go to point around his shoulder, and he swats my hand away. He presses the simple button, and the screen flickers before showing a human body. Through it are hundreds of lines streaming in different directions. Each line is a vein or artery, carrying the little robots throughout the body.

In the top left corner is my name, showing my real-time status. The nanites injected a couple of weeks ago have behaved and stabilized at a steady one-hundred percent. They're intended to tell me what's going on with my body at all times. After The Mission is completed, the information will be used to further understand how interacting with singularities affects the human body.

"Everything looks good." He twists his head to look at me, a beaming smile deepening a dimple in his left cheek. "Now, all we need to do is create guidelines for where the family will be safest."

Pushing aside a pile of research paperwork, I hop onto the table, letting my legs dangle. I tap my chin, considering what an ideal world would look like. "Well, obviously, the air can't be poisonous. Or the food."

"Humans can't be at the bottom of the food chain, either," he says, grabbing a pen and pad. He writes the three qualifications, then chews on his pen as he thinks.

"Should humans exist at all?" I ask. "Or would it be okay for us to be the only examples of our species there?"

He considers the question. "We know it isn't feasible to bring everyone on this planet with us. It would be far too complex to bring strangers with us and suddenly colonize an entire other world. That's asking for problems." Dad leans back in his chair, peering up at the fluorescent lights. "We can't inbreed, either."

I blanch. "Absolutely not."

He grunts in agreement. "If it's possible, we need to seek a society where our DNA is compatible with the locals. I'd say we can't come home until we find this place."

I nod in agreement. Even if I'm not interested in having kids, it's good to at least have the option. "Okay, so write, 'must have compatible species there.'"

He makes a tally on the page, then scribbles down the requirement. He looks up, brow pinched. "Do you think it's too utopia-esque to hope for a place without violence?"

"Maybe." I shrug and drag a stool to sit beside him. "It's hard to say. What if humans are the most violent animals in the universe?"

He gives a sad half-smile and shrugs. "Wouldn't surprise me."

"Me either," I agree. "Maybe we can make it a requirement that a place can't have constant war. We can use our best judgment?"

He writes down the rule. "Anything else?"

I spin on my stool, thinking. "I don't think so. If we make the standards too stringent, we could alienate a solid option. The best we can do is take samples and observations, then make an educated decision when we get back."

He places the pen on the pad. "Then this is the current list: breathable, options for a fulfilling life, no major violence."

59

"Sounds good." I tap the pad of paper. "This is going to be interesting, isn't it?"

Dad's expression turns wistful. "Your mother would be so excited." He spins his wedding ring around his finger.

I nod, doing the same with the one I'm wearing. "Yeah, but at least we can take a little bit of her with us."

We sit in silence for a couple of minutes, each of us lost in our thoughts. Mom always supported Dad in his dreams and research. From the day they met at university, their goals aligned. Mom, like me, was a particle physicist. A great pairing for my mathematician father, who also had a doctorate in theoretical physics. Their relationship was based on compromise from the start — so much so that when they got married, they changed their last names to Andromeda as a symbol of aligning their worlds.

While they never even alluded to it, I don't think a newborn was on the agenda for them. They both defined the idea of, "Our baby will fit into our lifestyle." On the whiteboard by Dad's desk is a photo of me as an infant being rocked in a car seat by a mechanical arm Dad invented to save time when I was colicky. He thinks the photo is hilarious — I've spent too much time staring not at the tiny version of myself, but of him sitting beside my car seat, immersed in a textbook.

They raised me right alongside the technology developed for Dad's lifelong dream. The moment Mom squeezed me out into the world, my tiny shoulders felt the weight of potential. It increased when I continued to surpass each childhood milestone faster than most experts could fathom.

When Mom died, the weight became almost unbearable; endurance was the only option. I met Dad's expectations with the kind of fervor ignited only by grief. He needed a new lab partner, and I was more than eager to fill those shoes.

Dad's never said it, but I know he's contemplated trying to go back in time to save her. But even if he could go back in time, then what? It's not like we've found the cure for brain cancer. Going back would make things messy in unpredictable ways.

Instead, we're focusing on the one thing we can change: finding a safe place where we can take our family and exist without the threat of an asteroid.

It can't be that hard, can it?

Chapter Eight

Did Someone Say Bear Bait?

Not speaking to anyone is almost more than I can bear. It's been only five days in this world, and I'm ready to say *fuck it* and press the travel button. Pretend I've gathered enough information and move to the next place.

Dad and I talked about the ideal length and could never nail down a median amount of time. We eventually agreed to trust our own instincts.

gear,And my instincts tell me it isn't the right time.

Plus, I'm still more than a little traumatized by the last four stops. I'm desperate to find a place that not only gives a little hope that this time travel quest isn't idiotic, but that the universe as a whole isn't pure chaos, through and through.

Maybe I can find some pleasant, friendly creatures or people. Get samples and maybe have a conversation or two. Hopefully, they've never heard of sharks the size of boats or doing a trendy dance at someone's execution.

The thought of meeting others is exciting and terrifying, but after five days of isolation, I'm ready to beg on my inflamed knees for *some* kind of conversation.

For all I know, there aren't any lifeforms worth meeting. Dad based the locations on educated guesses, using a theory on closed timelike curves weaving into multi-verses. There are no guarantees.

Since I ended up in the middle of nowhere, this is either going to confirm the Grandfather Paradox and I'll run into a version of myself ... or I've never existed here before. I'm not sure which one I'm hoping for.

Loneliness is kicking into high gear, and being in the middle of nowhere is terrifying. I live in a world of sanitization, toilets, and air conditioning. There's nothing about me that screams Outdoorsy Girl. Half the time, my fight-or-flight instinct activates because a bird startles.

No matter how many times I remind myself that I'm, according to Piper, a Badass Bitch Scientist, the tears still appear randomly. I miss *everything* about home. Hot showers. Soft beds. Piper's laugh. Gas station coffee cakes. Dad's hum when he's focused on something. Did I mention hot showers?

It's difficult to steer my mind in a more positive direction. Each day, I trudge through the forest, and each evening, I cry over freeze-dried camping rations. Sometimes the tears are quiet, but other times the sobs threaten to split me in half. I never expected the grief to be like this.

There was a choice between dying with family or going on this adventure. It felt like a no-brainer at the time, but this ... this survivor's guilt might push me over the edge.

So here I am on day three, hoping I'll find something. *Anything.*

I take a sip from my canteen, surveying my camp in the dawn light. My brain hurts from the lack of quality sleep, and my eyes feel gritty. Wiping my mouth with a grimy hand, I tuck the water bottle back into the bag and double-check nothing will be left behind. The fire smolders a bit, so I kick dirt over it until all signs of smoke are gone.

Two hours later, I'm sweating my ass off. The humidity is increasing, enough for me to shuck off the jacket. Brushing back a sweaty strand of hair, I pause and scan between the trees.

That's when I hear it: the sound of babbling water.

It's coming from the left. With a renewed sense of energy, I jog toward the sound, my sore feet screaming in protest.

Hell yes. A narrow river. Sparkling and clean in the sunshine.

Exiting the edge of the forest, I walk up to the gurgling water. It's the perfect place to take a quick break. Dropping the pack, I sit down and untie my boots. A breeze wafts by, and my stink makes me cringe. This river is an unexpected treat.

My bare skin revels in the kiss of air as I peel off each layer. Before removing my bra, I look around one more time. Nobody but the birds in the trees. Good enough for me. Taking off the rest of my clothing, I step into the river.

It isn't super deep, maybe about four feet. With a good crouch, I can scrub the grime off easily. The cold water is uncomfortable, but not unbearable. Dirt washes off in rivulets, and soon I'm feeling refreshed.

I'm considering the pros and cons of scrubbing my clothes in the stream when a twig snaps. The goosebumps prickling my skin have nothing to do with the cold water and everything to do with the loud snort and snuffling coming from a large bush full of plump berries.

I make my way out of the river and to the edge of the stream when the bush shakes. A few berries plop to the ground, bouncing slightly. Then, a large brown paw appears, followed by three more.

Revealing the biggest animal I've ever seen.

I gasp, then slap a hand over my mouth. Too late. The sound catches the grizzly bear's attention as it comes into full view. Liquid brown eyes assess me as the bear's head twists from side to side, like it's trying to figure me out.

Or trying to figure out which part of my naked body will be the best afternoon snack. I try to think of everything I've ever learned about grizzly bears. There isn't much. It's been extinct for fifteen years, so I'd only learned about it during some obsessive stint where ten-year-old me was convinced I'd be a zoologist. Before the mass extinction began.

I scan around, and I'm relieved to discover it's alone.

The bear looks back at the bush, plucking berries from a branch. I take a risk and, with one eye on the bear, I'm able to grab my underwear and slide it on with shaking hands. It's still absorbed in its lunch as I pull my bra over my head. I'm reaching for my pants when the bear's round head turns back in my direction.

Gulping, I hold up my hands as if this bear will realize I'm not a threat. Or a meal.

"Hey there, Miss Bear," I croon. "Nice bear. Sweet bear. Beautiful bear. Let me put on some pants, and we can get out of each other's hair. Okay?" The bear takes another wide step forward, entirely focused on me. Blood thunders in my ears, muffling her grunt of irritation.

My soul leaves my body. There's no way I'm getting out of this alive. I'm going to die in the middle of the woods while trying to put on clothing. While wearing my practical, moisture-wicking granny panties.

The hell I will. There's no way my tombstone will read, "Died screaming while wearing a circus tent." Feeling a burst of fearlessness, I stand up straight and give a feral scream of rage, masking my pure terror. Our eyes lock, and Miss Bear appears to be nonplussed by my puny attempt at intimidation.

She takes two steps closer. We're now about forty feet apart, a distance she could close in three seconds. I take a step backward, and she lunges with a roar.

Screaming, I bolt, leaping into the stream, scrambling for the other side of the woods. Smooth rocks hide underneath the water, too slippery to find traction on. My left foot slips, and cold water slams into my face. Some of it shoots up my nose, burning.

I struggle moving forward, swallowing and hacking up water. Behind me is the sound of splashing. Panic wipes away clarity, whipping my thoughts into a frenzy. My fingers claw into stones and soft grass as my legs try to propel me out of reach. An impossible feat, but I won't have Saint Peter tell me at the gates I could've tried harder.

Are bears like sharks? Do I poke them in the eyeball? Maybe I'd win, and she could run around like a forest pirate, telling the tale of the battle with a human.

My heart feels ready to burst, its galloping beat throbbing through every blood cell in my body. Just as I'm about to pee myself out of unabashed terror, the bear grunts and roars in pain.

Confused, my eyes widen as the bear tumbles to the side, a large shadow slamming into it. Water spews into the air, cascading over me

65

like a waterfall. Miss Bear grapples with the shadow, and one of them snarls. There's a flash of teeth sinking into the bear's side and droplets of red flying into the air. Streaks of red slither down the stream.

The bear and shadow separate. It's not a shadow after all, but a big black wolf with glowing amber eyes. About ten feet away is a chestnut horse, patiently watching the scene.

The wolf glances at me before refocusing on the bear, baring viciously long teeth. It snaps its jaws in warning, but the bear stands its ground. It responds with another heart-stopping roar before swinging its attention back to me with predatory intent.

Squeezing my eyes shut, I think of Dad. Piper. My family. *Well, at least I tried.*

I hear the wolf give a warning snarl, and the ground quakes. The bear roars, then whines. Opening my eyes, I watch the wolf fall off the top of the bear and tumble to the ground, blood slicking its maw.

The bear peers at its shoulder and whines again. Finally deciding I'm not worth it, the bear turns tail and thunders away. The wolf stands and shakes off the blood.

Those glowing eyes are on me again.

Which sounds more heroic: being killed by a bear or devoured by a wolf?

A dense shimmer engulfs the wolf; as it dissipates, a woman appears, the wolf nowhere to be found. The gold eyes remain, but now a porcelain-skinned woman with wavy auburn hair is walking through the stream toward me.

Pretty sure the water is full of drugs because there's no way something shapeshifted in front of me. Rubbing my eyes, I blink rapidly. Nope, the woman is still there.

She's wearing a black linen blouse, the kind that characters wear in movies set in times before electricity. A waist cinch tucks it into gray riding breeches. I'm immediately obsessed with her black riding boots, with all the silver buckles.

Something about her screams warrior princess.

This is a bad bitch, no doubt about it.

Stopping near my feet, she says something in a language I don't understand, with hard consonants and low tones. After a slight delay, my transmitter chip translates.

"Are you alright?"

The horse snorts and takes a step toward me when I don't reply. Without impending carnage, I'm able to notice that the horse isn't wearing any tack. Not even a halter. I know some horsemanship disciplines don't utilize tack as much, but something feels off. A headache begins to pulsate at my temples; too much has happened in a short period of time.

"Are you alright?" The woman repeats the question, sounding worried. She holds out a delicate hand tipped with black nails.

After a beat, my brain finds words. Taking a moment to inhale, steadying my rapid heartbeat, I exhale and say, "Yeah, I'm fine. Thank you for"—I motion in the direction of the bear's path—"saving me from that."

She helps me stand, her grip firm. The chestnut mare chuffs and ambles to the river's edge, pawing at it with a hoof. Almost as if she's declaring she won't be stepping into the river. The woman glances at the horse, then back at me. The scientist part of me screams about *processes* and *testing* and *collecting samples*. There's so much potential to discover and learn about.

Her expression shifts, turning friendly. Oh, gods, her *smile*. It flips my stomach, just like the anticipation coiled in your gut right before a roller coaster plunges to the earth.

"My pleasure. I'm Kalliope Arnoux."

Smiling, I say, "Hi, Kalliope. I'm Saira Andromeda."

Kalliope gives my body a pointed look. "Would you like me to collect your clothing, Saira Andromeda?"

Oh shit. Our predicament sinks in. This is the nakedest I've been in front of anyone. Ever. Embarrassed, I tuck my arms over my chest. "Yes, that would be great. Thanks."

67

She crosses the stream, unbothered by the cold water. The mare's graceful head tilts in my direction. Is the horse a shifter, too? The way she's looking at me, it's the only logical answer.

Kalliope returns with my clothes. As I get dressed, I ask, "So you're a wolf?"

I try to sound casual, but my voice is an octave higher than normal.

The look she gives makes me feel like the biggest moron. "It's my preferred shift. Why? What's yours?"

My eyes widen. "Sometimes a couch potato or depression vegetable. But mostly human."

Her eyes narrow. "You can turn into food? Where are you from?" Then she sniffs the air. Her mouth parts in surprise. "You're a one-form?"

Did she just *smell* me? "Is that an insult?"

Kalliope shakes her head fervently. "Of course not. I didn't realize. And Ginger said nothing."

"Ginger?"

The mare nickers, shaking her head vigorously. Kalliope gestures toward her. "Yes, Ginger. She prefers to stay in shift, so please don't think her rude."

They're both shifters. Interesting. That's one of my favorite romance genres. As I tug my shirt over my still-damp hair, I ask, "So do you rescue people often in the woods?"

Kalliope gives me a lazy grin. "No, rarely. It's a coincidence that we even happened upon this area. We're deeper in the woods than we realized."

There's a shimmer, and on the other side of the stream, the chestnut mare disappears. In its place is a stunning redheaded woman. A *naked* redheaded woman.

Is this the land of gorgeous women? Because it's exactly what Ginger is. Luscious strands of red spill below her ample hips. Everything about her is generous, including her wide, mischievous grin.

"Nice to meet you, bear bait."

I scrunch my nose. "That's rude. I didn't try to bait the bear."

Ginger shrugs. "Does the fly aim to provoke the frog as it flies by?"

Kalliope chastises her friend with a dirty look, then returns her focus to our conversation. "Would you like to accompany us to town? I'm not sure the bear will stay away if we leave and you remain."

I finish lacing up my boots. This is the exact opportunity I've been seeking. Riding off into the sunset with a pair of strangers is more appealing than spending another night in this godsforsaken forest. "Yes, that would be great." I point at my pack. "I need to grab my stuff, and then I'll be ready to go."

Ginger walks over to my pack, her toes sinking into the muddied grass. She lifts it easily but raises a red eyebrow. "What do you have in this? A whole deer's carcass?"

I laugh nervously. "Just some stuff for camping."

Ginger walks to the stream's edge and easily tosses the pack. Kalliope catches it and hands it over. My arms bob with the weight as I grab it, slinging it over my shoulder.

"Would you like a ride?" Kalliope asks. I catch Ginger staring at me. She cocks a bushy red eyebrow, then shifts back into the chestnut mare.

Peering up at Kalliope, I shake my head. "No, I can walk with you."

Kalliope huffs out a laugh. "I will not be walking, Saira. You cannot keep up unless you are hiding shifting abilities and can discover four legs."

"What will you turn into? A horse?"

Kalliope cants her head. "Would that make you comfortable?"

"I'm a little rusty, but I should be able to stay on."

She chuckles. "I'll become a horse, then."

I breathe a sigh of relief and then grin. When I was eight, shortly after Dad first told me about time travel, I believed I would go to a land with flying Pegasi and needed to learn how to ride one. He invested in my weekly training sessions until I was sixteen. So, sure, it's been a while ... but isn't it like riding a bike?

I step back, giving Kalliope space to shift into a sleek, black mare. Long fringes of mane drop past her thick neck. She nickers and motions toward her back.

"Um, I don't think I can hop on. Is it possible ..."

Is it even polite to ask a shifter to kneel?

Kalliope must understand because she bobs her head, then slowly lowers her front legs. After only a second of hesitation, I swing a leg over her back, grabbing handfuls of her mane.

She's graceful as she rises, turning her head to eye me as if to say, *are you ready to go?*

I pat her withers. "I'm ready to get the hell out of these woods."

She nickers in agreement and plods through the stream. When we reach the other side, Ginger trots into the forest, disappearing past the tree line.

Kalliope eyes me one more time. Then, without warning, she breaks into a smooth canter. It's impossible not to be giddy. This morning, I was alone. Now? Now the real adventure begins.

Chapter Nine

I'm The Town Oddball

We ride hard until the forest thins. When we reach the tree line, Kalliope trots, heading straight for the road woven through tall emerald-colored grass.

The moment we reach the road, she slows to a walk. Ginger does the same, her head bobbing as she sniffs the fresh grass.

Me? Yeah, I'm about to pass out. Just because I know how to ride, doesn't mean I physically can anymore. You don't get a Ph.D. in nuclear and particle physics and maintain peak physical fitness.

I almost weep with relief when a quaint town appears in the distance. Soon, the shapes of people appear. Alongside animals of all kinds. As we draw closer, it's more obvious I'm not in Kansas anymore.

It's hard not to stare, but everywhere I look, body parts are too big or too small. Some of them look like Frankenstein's monster. Talons for hands in some cases. Even light fur covering bodies. The majority seem to be women, while the few men show no evidence of shifting at all. A man with skin as black as midnight sweeps dirt out of a house. Another, with skin the color of burnt desert sand, stands by a pen full of fat turkeys, tossing seed to the ground.

Nearby, a woman with alabaster skin, holding a basket full of fresh bread, calls out to us with a distinct coo. To my surprise, Kalliope returns the sound, delighting the woman and the surrounding townspeople. Everyone's pleased to greet her.

The town isn't big, and we're quickly in the center. Men stand quietly next to the women hawking their wares, keeping watch as loud, enthusiastic bartering fills the air.

Ginger stops in front of a building with a griffon on the sign, reading "Startkson's Pub." I swing off, grimacing at the noodle-like consistency of my legs.

Kalliope and Ginger shift. Kalliope is still wearing her clothes, but Ginger is still buckass naked. She peers up at me, rocking on her toes as she holds her hands behind her back. She resembles an innocent cherub.

Then she says, "My three-year-old niece rides better than you."

This abrasive redhead is testing my patience. It'd be stupid to be rude to my new hosts, but she's testing me. It's probably her intention, though. Instead of responding, I purposefully look over her bushy curls to Kalliope. "So, do they have food? Say yes."

Kalliope laughs. "Yes."

I clap my palms together and raise them to my heart. "My hero. I'm craving a hot meal that hasn't come out of a bag."

They give me an odd look, which I ignore.

My eyes take their time adjusting to the dimly lit space. I hear the fast chatter and lively music first. It's rather large, seating a hundred people or so. Long tables made of light-colored wood take up most of the space, and the benches are almost full. A group of musicians plays in the corner, enhancing the atmosphere.

The walls are pale terracotta, with dark wooden support beams. An immense fireplace roars, staving off the outside chill.

The cozy vibes allow me to take a breath and swallow my anxiety. I'd expected some movie-like moment when everyone stares at me. Maybe whisper a rumor the local witch had already spread. But there's nothing.

Kalliope leads us over to a table and sits, motioning toward a table where a burly woman is talking to another patron. She dips her chin in acknowledgement before pouring a drink for the guy wildly moving his arms as he tells a story.

I slide onto the bench across from Ginger and Kalliope. Shucking off my backpack, I place it beside me and rest an arm against the top. Then, looking around, I ask, "So do you come here often?"

It's a joke, but Kalliope shakes her head. "No, we haven't been here in quite a while." She jerks a thumb at Ginger. "This one hates being at restaurants, and she's the only one who can convince me to abscond and go frolic like younglings in the forest."

"So she never gets to go to restaurants anymore," Ginger chirps, twisting a strand of hair between her fingers.

"What a great example of a balanced friendship," I muse. My tone is slightly sarcastic, but Piper was always the one propelling my barest moments of socialization; literally no one else could convince me to leave the lab for a couple of hours. So, I understand their dynamic more than they realize.

"It can be," Kalliope agrees, then glares at Ginger. "See? Everyone else thinks you need to grow up and order hay at the table like a normal Amicum."

Ginger turns her nose up at the idea. "It comes out smelling like grease, I swear."

"Excuse me? I'll have you know I keep my greens away from the fryer," a commanding voice booms. All three of us swivel our heads to look up at the burly woman holding a metal pitcher. My eyes flick between her and Kalliope, waiting to know how to react. Her schooled expression tells me more than she realizes — she's adept at smothering any visible reaction.

All mirth disappears from Ginger's face. "I'm so sorry, Moira. I didn't mean any offense. Truly."

Moira narrows her gaze, her eyes receding under thick folds of skin. "Don't let it happen again." Then she looks at Kalliope, and her whole demeanor shifts as she releases a dazzling grin. "Lordess, it's a pleasure to serve you today. What'll it be?"

Lordess? What the hell is a lordess?

Kalliope motions to Ginger and me. "Three waters, please. Can we have the menus?"

73

"Absolutely." Moira beams. "Glad to see you again. It's been too long." She sends Ginger a pointed look before walking away.

"Oh look, the reason we don't come here," Ginger mutters. She looks away, pouting.

Kalliope taps a finger against the table. "You've never once eaten here in over twenty years. You sit outside, waiting. Any pub owner is bound to notice and get offended."

"Exactly." Moira has apparently teleported to the table or something, because a woman of her size should not be so quiet. She slides three menus onto the table. "I dare you to order my alfalfa and sprouts mix."

Ginger's mood shifts back to the jovial mare. "With some mash on the side?"

Moira dips her head in agreement. "Consider it done." She looks at me as I scramble to pick up the menu. My eyes blur as my brain attempts to decode the written language. Everyone's waiting for me, and I can't read a thing.

So, instead, I slide my menu back toward her. "Whatever's your favorite, I'll have some."

Moira's eyes widen with delight, her immediate smile revealing several missing teeth. She shakes a finger at me. "I like you." Then she looks at Kalliope. "Lordess?"

Kalliope hands her the menu. "I'll take the queso and bread, please."

I almost choke on my spit. "There's *queso*?"

Moira gives me a strange look. "What do you think this place is?"

I look around and take in the decor. Stacked cheese blocks. Pictures of fresh cheeses in frames. Fondue towers on tables. The smell of fried cheese.

"Does all cheese go to heaven? Because this feels like heaven."

Ginger mutters something along the lines of, "The bear would've won."

The mare shifter isn't making a great impression right now. Hiding my clenched fists in my lap, I plastered a placid smile on my face while seething on the inside. Hopefully, this is the only interaction I'll have with her going forward.

"Food will be right out," Moira promises before sauntering off, pouring more drinks for patrons calling for her.

Kalliope leans back in her chair, tapping a finger on the table. "So, Saira. Tell me more about you. Will you finally tell us where you're from?"

There's a steely tone in her voice, one that brooks no excuses. I've never been a good liar, so I'm not sure how to answer her question. It's not like I can say, *"Well, I'm not from this world. I can travel through time with this bracelet on my wrist, which is currently disguised as a leather band. No, that's not magic. No, you don't need to burn me at the stake. Please stop tying me up."*

Women were burned at the stake for far less outlandish things.

I take a deeper sip of my water to combat my suddenly dry mouth. Putting down the cup with more focus than is reasonable, I take a deep breath and blow it out. I'm stalling, trying to figure out the best way to word my predicament.

Kalliope tilts her head to the side, looking at me with curiosity. "Are you afraid the answer will be displeasing?"

"No." *Yes.* This woman is a stranger. She seems reasonable, but there's no need to create a connection with anyone. No need to establish mutual trust. I just need time to get samples, and then I can go. "I'm wary of people I've never met."

She narrows her eyes. "Alright. Well, can I ask you where you'd planned to go? Perhaps Ginger and I can escort you?"

It's better to stick with parts of the truth. Easier to remember. "I'm wandering from place to place, truth be told. Trying to meet people until I find a place that calls to me."

Kalliope opens her mouth to say something, but a woman with delicate iridescent scales tracing her arms walks up. Cropped short hair shows off round, furry ears, like a leopard. Wearing an outfit similar to Kalliope, she also wears an emerald green waist cincher and light brown leather leggings.

She gives a slight bow to Kalliope, earning a dip of Kalliope's chin in acknowledgement. Her eyes flick to me and Ginger, offering each of us a polite smile. Then she says, "Lordess, it's a pleasure to meet you and your companions. I hope I'm not intruding."

Kalliope looks up at the woman with endless patience. "Not at all ...?"

"Sable, Your Grace. I'm from Cape Schrute."

I glance at Ginger, who is braiding parts of her hair. It's still jarring to see her, sitting naked as the day — I presume — she was born. She seems nonplussed at Sable's interruption. This must happen often.

"I've been there before; it has beautiful coves and the best fresh seafood. I've been meaning to go there soon."

Sable nods her head eagerly. "I'm speaking on behalf of the town when I invite you to come visit. We'd be honored to have you."

Kalliope holds her hand out, and Sable seems to hold on to it for dear life as she shakes it. Kalliope smiles again. "I'll make sure to do so, Sable. Thank you so much for saying hello."

Sable offers another small bow before walking away. She rushes over to a group of friends, whispering excitedly as Sable regales them with what happened. In their group, only one man sits nearby. Where are all the men?

Glancing around, the general population of the pub registers. In fact, out of the few dozen, only five men are among the throng. What the hell?

It makes me think of home; decades ago — not nearly far enough in history — pubs didn't allow women.

And here I am, in a pub full of them. It's both incredible and shocking, especially when I spot different animal traits in almost all of them, except for the men. None of them appear different from what I'm used to.

I turn to Kalliope. "What is the ratio of men to women?"

"One for every five females."

Holy moly. "Is there tension around scarcity? Are there fights?"

Ginger turns her attention to me and snorts with derision. "We don't fight over them because that would be ridiculous."

Kalliope chuckles. "Could you imagine?"

"I would rather not." Ginger cringes, then shakes with disgust.

76

I frown, cheeks burning from my obvious ignorance. "What do you do with them?"

"It depends on the province," Kalliope says. "In Ilorna, we have a particular set of laws concerning males, their shifting, and other aspects of life. The majority of females forgo breeding in favor of pursuing a career or focus. Amicums also have lower birth rates for males. We don't understand why — that's simply how things are."

This is fascinating. I'm dying to ask more, but how many questions would it take to come off even more suspicious?

Moira sweeps in, interrupting. "Three ales on the house."

"Moira, you didn't have to," Kalliope says, eyebrows shooting up. "I'm more than willing to pay you."

Moira places the chilled mugs on the table and waves away Kalliope's words. "Nonsense. Your recent tax cuts for business owners have boosted my profits. It's the least I can do, Your Grace."

Ginger reaches for hers and raises in deference. "I'm sure it's the best ale in the world."

I stifle a laugh. Moira looks as if she doesn't buy the high praise, even as she politely says, "I'm sure as well."

Kalliope touches her forearm gently. "My gratitude."

The three flick their eyes toward me, and I freeze. The mug is cold in my hands as I curl my fingers around the edges. "My most intense thank you for this gracious delivery of beverages, Moira."

That sounded less awkward in my head. Anxiety spikes in my veins. This is far harder than originally imagined. Moira gives me an odd look before beaming at Kalliope. "Holler if you need anything."

As she turns away, Ginger raises an eyebrow. "Are you the town idiot?"

"Ginger," Kalliope says sharply. Ginger looks down at her drink, pursing her lips.

Somehow, I've messed up again. I gulp down ale, buying time. The translator may help me understand, but it can't take away my ignorance of the culture.

I try to brush it off. "More of the town oddball." I take another gulp, enjoying the intense flavor. It's unlike anything I've ever tasted. Like honey with a spicy bite to it. "So where are we going next? Since you've offered to be my escort."

Kalliope throws an ankle over her knee. In the warm candlelight, flickering firelight casts a glow on her dark auburn hair. Making a fist, I resist the urge to reach out and touch the strands.

"We're going back to my manor. If you'd like to stay, Meadow will find a bedchamber for you. If you'd like to attend in two days' time, I'm hosting an annual gathering of lordesses. I can arrange for your outfit and attendants, so you do not have to worry about that."

"A party?" There hasn't been a solid plan in my brain of what's next, aside from collecting samples. A party sounds interesting, though. It's an opportunity to examine this society further.

If I'm being honest with myself, a few days of relaxation are required. My whole body aches; the pounding headache currently throbbing in my skull forces me to admit it. As much as I want to save my family, it's unsafe to continue while influenced by this level of exhaustion. There's time to gain a solid perspective on this location and technically, I have all the time in the worlds.

Kalliope brandishes a wide smile. "Yes. It's a yearly event considered unmissable by some. There's dancing, food, and other activities sure to titillate. It's a chance to show off extravagant outfits and show off shifting skills. It's an unofficial competition, if I'm being honest."

Not sure what "activities" means, but getting gussied up sounds fun. The question is ... how welcome am I? Really? The ale's hitting my empty stomach hard, and I lean an elbow against the table to steady myself. "Are you sure you want the town 'idiot' involved in your ball?"

Kalliope looks at Ginger in disapproval, then back to me. "I do not think you are an idiot. Clearly, you aren't from here, and speaking differently than us does not signify a lack of intelligence."

Ginger snorts. "This is going to give plenty of fodder for gossip."

I'm about to ask why, but Kalliope speaks before I can get out my question.

"Let them." Kalliope sips her ale. "I'm not in the habit of giving a shit about what people at court think. Saira is welcome not only to attend

78

but to stand by my side." She cocks her head. "Would that please you, Saira?"

Would it please me? This morning, I was eating freeze-dried food in the woods. A week ago, Megaladon's cousin tried to eat me. Now I'm being invited to a party by a gorgeous woman who wants me to join her at a fancy party?

This might be a slippery slope, but also, how can I explore a culture without experiencing it firsthand? I'd be a terrible scientist if I didn't learn more about their culture. My anxiety morphs into excitement. The Mission can include my living a little. I'm making a scientific call — I hypothesize this will be a fun time. See? I'm still a scientist. Not just a woman looking for a little fun in a life full of work.

"Hell yeah, I'm *so* in."

Ginger scrunches her nose. "In what?"

Luckily, Moira shows up with a thick stone bowl of orange goo and a basket of something that looks similar to pita bread. In front of me, she places an oval wicker basket of breaded twists. They resemble curly fries, but oozy cheese peeking through a crack in the breading makes me think otherwise.

I pick one up, inhaling sharply as their heat. Snapping a piece, I grin wildly at the cheese pull. They're mozzarella sticks! Next to them are three tiny bowls of various sauces.

Cheese is always the best kind of distraction.

Kalliope swings her leg down and leans into the scent of hot, burned cheese. "Moira, you've outdone yourself. This looks delectable."

Ginger eyes the plate holding green piles of alfalfa and a small bowl of steaming mash. Moira crosses her arms and stares. Taking notice, Ginger grabs a handful and shoves it into her mouth. She looks like a chipmunk.

When she's done chewing, she eyes the mash. Grabbing hold of the bowl, she takes a sip. Then she sighs with delight.

"Forgive me, Moira, for I have sinned against you. This is delicious."

Moira purses her lips, begrudgingly accepting the apology. "Well, I don't serve slop." She stalks off, but I see a smile twitching between her thick cheeks.

Kalliope pushes the plate of pita bread toward me. "Guests first."

Tentatively reaching for the soft triangles, I dip one into the cheese. Scooping out a chunk and shoving it into my mouth, the melty concoction is like an explosion of flavor against my tastebuds. It's fucking incredible. Best queso I've ever had. I groan, loving the melty texture.

Kalliope chuckles. "Do they have queso where you're from?"

I swallow. I might eat the entire basket of bread if I'm not careful. It's addicting. "Yes, but the bread really makes it pop."

Ginger snorts, taking a sip of her mash. "What did you eat with it instead?"

I shrug, readying for another piece of pita. "Chips."

Kalliope grabs her own piece. Our fingers brush slightly, but it's enough to make my breath hitch. She furrows her brow. "What's a chip?"

Trying to ignore how her touch felt, I dip the pita into the cheese. "Just something thinner and crisper."

Kalliope nods and stuffs the cheesy bread into her mouth. Switching to the plate in front of me, I grab one of the oblong pieces of fried cheese. It oozes when I test out the cheese pull. We fall silent, filling our bellies. It hits me how wild my day has become.

Attacked by a bear. Saved by a gorgeous woman who's also a wolf. And a lordess — whatever the hell that is. And now I'm eating queso in a pub with a thatched roof in a land ruled by women. Being invited to a fancy party.

Cool, cool. It's fine. Not crazy at all.

All of us are hungry enough; we devour the meals in no time flat. Kalliope signals to Moira, but the barkeep waves her away again, our signal to head out.

I follow them outside, where they both transform. Kalliope's horse form walks to the nearby stairs as a makeshift mounting block. Then, with full bellies, we head out of the town.

Chapter Ten

That's A Centaur Making My Bed

I t's only an hour at a brisk pace before we arrive at a wrought-iron gate that opens to a long, wide road. Looming trees reach for one another, dappling the sunlight. In the distance, a manor waits for us. Ginger and Kalliope pick up the pace, eager to be home.

I've only ever seen manors and castles in movies. Seeing one in person is quite different. My jaw drops as I take in the magnificent cream-colored building.

At least twenty windows hole-punch the stone walls, with a massive balcony reaching outward above the front door. On each side of the building, green vines snake all over the facade, cradling the building in a gentle hold. Light blue shutters frame the windows, with flower boxes below each windowsill.

Robust piles of flowers spill over the edges, reaching toward the ground below. People tend to the greenery, looking up with smiles at the sound of hoofbeats.

It's a fairytale come alive. A sense of giddiness washes over me. I've been nowhere as beautiful as this place. In my world, this would easily be a five-star hotel. And I get to *stay* here?

Before we even stop, a stout woman bustles out, beaming. She's wearing a deep red dress with an even deeper red apron, the pockets bulging with items. Laugh lines surround her eyes and mouth, and she pulls her silver-gray hair back into a tight bun.

I resemble an unruly bag of onions as I slide off Kalliope's tall back. My knees buckle when I land on the soft ground. I crave a month-long nap, preferably right after a hot bath. Kalliope shifts into human form, looking immaculate.

The short woman runs up to Kalliope and wraps her arms around her waist. Kalliope makes an *oof* sound and returns the hug with a laugh.

"Your Grace, I'm so glad you're back." The woman holds the hug for another moment, then lets go.

Kalliope chuckles. "I was gone for less than a day." She motions toward me. "Meadow, this is Saira. She'll be staying with us for a while."

Meadow nods and curtsies. "Pleasure to meet you, Miss."

Someone curtsied to me.

This is surreal. Especially as Ginger shifts back into her nakedness, walking away with a wiggle of her fingers. "See you around, BB. Don't let the library bear get you."

My head whips to Kalliope. "There are bears in the library?"

"No, there are no bears in the library," she says, louder than necessary, a biting edge to her tone.

Ginger cackles as she disappears around a tall hedge lining a stone pathway. I need to keep my eye on that one.

I pretend to wipe away sweat from my head. "Thank the gods, because I don't want to be near a bear anytime soon."

Meadow looks between the two of us. "There was a bear?"

Kalliope grimaces and glances at me. "Yes, there was, but it scared off easily."

Meadow's eyes widen. They are bigger than normal, with thick, bushy eyebrows above them. "Well, you poor thing." She sniffs the air and bites back a grimace. "It seems as if you would like to wash up after your long travels?"

Did she just smell me? It's hard not to be offended, but she's not wrong. "Yes, that would be wonderful. Is there a way to wash my clothing as well?"

"Of course." Meadow beams. She looks to Kalliope for further instructions.

Kalliope nods. "Please escort Saira to a guest room. Find her some comfortable clothes as well. We will also need to find a gown for the gathering. She'll be here for the celebration."

Meadow's eyes skim me over, settling on the utility belt around my waist, then to the over-stuffed pack on my back. Something flickers in her eyes, and her nostrils flare.

Then she lifts her thick skirt. "Yes, Your Grace. Come, Miss Saira. I'm sure you're eager to get out of those clothes and into a hot bath."

Do not cry. The thought of both options is too good to be true. "If you can help me accomplish those two things, I'll be your simp forever, Meadow."

She gives me a quizzical look. "What's a simp?"

"She says odd things," Kalliope says, walking with us into the manor. I can't decide if her comment should offend me or not. Her tone is light, so she might be joking. Her expression reveals nothing as we step into the manor's foyer.

Cheerful female chatter replaces the sound of songbirds. The foyer is about a hundred feet wide with an enormous staircase made of elegant dark wood. It sprawls downward with delicate banisters.

On either side of the staircase are hallways with floor-to-ceiling windows that allow the bright sunshine to beam down on the dark hardwood floors. Creamy curtains complement the spotless window-panes.

At the bottom of the stairs is a large, round table covered in milky white vases filled with pastel-colored peonies. Two females lean over the bountiful collection of florals, trimming and arranging the beautiful flowers. They glance up as we walk in, cooing at Kalliope. Their eyes linger on my face for a split second, then flick back to their task.

Kalliope spares me a quick smile, already heading down another hallway to the left. "I'll see you later this evening, Saira."

A tinge of disappointment appears, but I quickly shove it away. Instead, I nod and allow Meadow to lead me down one hallway, past the stairs. As Meadow briskly escorts me through a maze, we pass various doors. Some are closed, but others are open.

I catch glimpses of posh-looking bedrooms with staff fussing over furniture and shiny sheets. Gold frames cover the walls, which are lined with marble statues. Pristine maroon carpets run the length of each hallway. From the ceiling, elegant chandeliers sparkle in the sunlight. It all seems to go on and on, one hallway after another.

The front of the manor was deceiving — this place must stretch further back than its width, like a rectangle. I'm so out of place here among the shiny and expensive adornments. Dad and I lived off grants, donations, and the sale of patents. I'm a ramen kind of girl — not a caviar kind of woman.

It's a struggle to keep up with Meadow's brisk strides even though she's shorter than me. Every step makes my already-painful feet ache even more. I'm a bit breathless when I ask, "Do lots of people live here?"

"No, miss," Meadow says over her shoulder. "However, we have a lot of visitors arriving this evening for the upcoming event. The manor is preparing for a large party, and it's rather hectic today."

Two males rush past, holding folded piles of sheets. They give Meadow a deferent bob of their heads before disappearing around a corner.

Meadow's words sink in. Obviously, I'm not an expected guest. "Have I kicked someone out of their room? I don't really need a lot or anything. I've been sleeping outside for days, so any old mattress will work."

"No," she assures me. "You're taking the smallest suite, and most guests refuse to stay in it, so we keep it open on the off chance we find ourselves with a guest who won't have a hissy fit at the room's size."

She weaves through short hallways, the busyness fading into the distance.

The wide hallway is minimalistic, with large paintings held in black brocade frames. All the furniture is black or white, with hints of silver trinkets on random tables. Deep magenta velvet curtains drape the ten-foot-tall windows.

The contrast adds a bit of drama to the aesthetic. The manor's full of bright energy. Even though a sliver of my brain is focused on where Kalliope might be, it's impossible to help but marvel at the beauty.

Finally, she pauses in front of two doors. Reaching for a gleaming knob, the door swings in silently, bright light warming my face.

The room is beautiful, with polished gold and different shades of green. There's a big four-poster bed, draped with forest green chiffon as a canopy. To the left of it is an immense fireplace and a beverage tray with different crystal bottles of liquid. Stained French doors lead to a balcony on the right.

Situated on either side of the doors are a desk and a chaise. A vanity table is next to a privacy screen covered in floral designs. The edge of a white tub peeks out from the side. All the furniture is deep mahogany with gold trimmings.

I love it.

By the bed are three servants tucking sheets under the mattress. One's a dark-skinned woman with large, owl-like eyes. The second has gold skin but feathers instead of hair, and the third is a *fucking centaur*. She has the body of a horse, but a torso dressed up in a shirt and jacket.

Her hair's pinned up, and her hooves hit the wooden floor as she walks to the corner of the mattress, tucking in a sheet.

The three females look up. Each shares a friendly greeting. The centaur waves and I wave back; surely this is a dream. Meadow bustles over to the privacy screen, and the sound of water filling the tub is music to my ears. *They have indoor plumbing!*

I've never had servants before, and especially not ones that are half bird or half horse. Do I tip them? I don't even know what kind of currency they use here.

The centaur motions toward a large armoire on one side of the room. "Hello, miss! We're almost complete. You can place your belongings inside the armoire, if you desire."

Eager to drop this backpack down and not pick it up for at least a day, I smile and rush over to the ornate piece of furniture. "Thank you."

Shucking off the pack, I let it drop to the ground. It makes a loud *thunk*, catching everyone by surprise. My cheeks redden as everyone looks at me.

"Sorry," I mutter. The female centaur chuckles, tapping one of the pillows to fluff it. The other females exchange glances and say nothing as they organize the rest of the pillows. Well, alright then.

"We're finished, Meadow," one servant calls.

Meadow rounds the edge of the privacy screen, wiping wet hands against her apron. "Thank you, ladies." As they close the door behind them, Meadow turns her attention to me. "Would you like to wash up, Miss?"

I nod eagerly. "You have no idea." I look down at my filthy outfit. "Do you have a place where I can wash this?"

Meadow scoffs and points at a nearby wicker basket. "You may place your clothing there, and I'll have it laundered. I'd never be able to live with myself if I allowed a guest to launder their own clothing."

Well, when she puts it that way. "Clothes in the basket. Got it." I look at the empty armoire. "Are there any other clothes I can wear while I wait?"

She nods. "While you bathe, I'll go retrieve some options for this evening. Do you require anything else?"

I unzip my jacket and shrug it off. "I'm fine, I promise. I'm exhausted and almost got eaten by a bear. I'm desperate for a bath and nap."

She dips her head in acknowledgement. "I'll retrieve some fresh clothes and leave them on the chaise. Please pull the bell if you require anything else. Otherwise, I will return in four hours to escort you to dinner."

I snap my utility belt off, placing it inside the armoire. "Thanks, I really appreciate it."

The door closes behind her, leaving me in silence. It's almost too silent after a week in the forest, where there was always the sound of wildlife.

I walk over to the privacy screen and peer around. A white marble tub filled with steaming water beckons. Next to it is a standing towel holder with a white, fluffy towel. A small table at the head of the tub holds various bottles, hopefully full of soaps.

Pinching the clips on the underside of the Scout's band, I slip it off and place it on the table next to the soaps. The ring of dirt circling where it's been is enough to convince me to put it down for a few minutes.

Stripping, I toss my filthy clothes into the basket. They're supposed to be black, but at this point, they're more like a dark brown. Gross.

I glide my fingers through the steaming water. The temperature is scalding. Taking my trembling muscles into account, I carefully step into the tub. It's like dipping into lava.

Absolutely perfect.

I take a moment as my body adjusts to the heat, then sink into the water up to my neck. My muscles soften like a dry sponge drinking up moisture. The uncountable miles walked this past week leech out of my exhausted body.

I dip my head back to soak my hair. Leaning over the tub, I look at the bottles of substances. Picking each one up, I inspect the contents. They're filled with creams and pearlescent liquid. I dab some on my finger. It's the texture of shampoo. Good enough for me.

I pour some into my hand. The smell of mint and fruit makes me close my eyes in pleasure. I rub it into my scalp, then spread it through my strands. I didn't notice what I looked like before, but I know my curls have been desperate for anything moisturizing.

I work my way through the bottles, using what I think is a conditioner. After a week in the wilderness, the process is luxurious.

By the time I'm done, the bath is a color I don't want to acknowledge. Grabbing the fluffy towel, I step out of the tub and dry myself off. Picking up the Scout, I wipe it down, too, then put it back on, and the little niggle of anxiety disappears.

Peering around the privacy screen, I notice someone has removed the basket of clothing and laid clothes out over a chaise across the room. Meadow is like a ninja, apparently.

I pad over to the clothes. The pants are supple black leather, and the shirt is made of maroon linen. There's no underwear or bra. Damn. I guess they free-ball it around here.

Toweling off the remaining droplets of water, I put on the outfit. The ensemble is more comfortable than I thought, with the shirt billowy and roomy. I'd still love a bra, but when in Rome, I guess.

Feeling like a whole new person, I grab a soft bristled brush on the vanity table near the balcony windows. Not the best for curls, but I don't want to go through my pack.

When the knots are gone from my unruly strands, I place the brush back and walk over to the bed. Running my palm over the satiny duvet, I pull it back to reveal shimmering green sheets.

Patting the nearest pillow — there's an imposing pile of them — I'm pleased to see my hand sink into the softness.

Jackpot.

I melt into the bed, moaning in sheer pleasure. It's unlikely, but my ideal future includes never sleeping in a forest ever again.

It's my last thought before the world slips into darkness.

Chapter Eleven

Sea Cucumber Curry Chowder

"Miss Saira?"

Like a reanimated corpse, I jerk up. My eyes try to adjust to the darkness, but my brain's so jumbled, it's difficult to catch up. "Huh? What? Who's there?"

Finally, I notice Meadow standing on the edge of the bed, wringing her hands. Her silver-dollar eyes are wider than before.

"Meadow," I rasp between quick breaths. "You can't do that. You scared the crap out of me."

Meadow takes a quick step back, her eyes scanning the bed. "Where?"

Finally able to take a deep breath, I tip my head to the side. "Where what?"

She lowers her voice. "Where is it? We can get it cleaned up."

"Wait — what?" For a second, her question makes me wonder if my translation chip's broken. Then it dawns on me. "Oh, *no*, Meadow. I didn't *actually* crap the bed. It's just a saying."

Her confusion is priceless. With a grimace, she says, "Miss, what an odd thing to say."

I flop back onto the mattress. "Yeah, I think I'm going to be hearing that a lot."

There's no place like home.

I turn my head toward her. She's still staring at the mattress with concern. It's almost charming. Almost.

"Why are you here, Meadow?"

"Apologies. I've come to escort you to dinner. But Her Grace has provided a dress for you to wear."

Oh yeah. Amicums. Shifters. Dinner tonight. I must've slept like the dead. "Dinners are fancy here?"

"No, miss, Her Grace thought you might like something nice to wear."

She steps back as I swing out of the bed, then leads me to the wardrobe. Hanging off a door is a royal blue dress that shines with dark iridescence. It'll be magical against my tawny skin tone.

The chiffon is soft between my fingertips. Meadow lifts it from the wardrobe and unbuttons the back of the corset built into the dress. It's a darker blue than the skirt with silver swirls stitched into it. It must cost a fortune.

"Are you sure Kalliope wants me to wear this?"

"Of course. Now, if you don't mind, please undress."

I narrow my eyes. "I can't put this on by myself?"

Her gray eyes glitter with amusement. "It would be quite difficult."

"Fine," I mutter. Clenching my teeth, I pull off my clothes, hugging my breasts tight. The saving grace of this embarrassing moment is how she carefully avoids looking at my body. I step into the dress as Meadow holds it up.

In the nearby mirror, our reflection appears. The woman who has a corset laced up her back doesn't even look like me. This kind of outfit would be unfathomable at home. The most flowy thing I own is a stained lab coat.

Grimacing, I raise a hand to my curls. Falling asleep with them wet wasn't the best idea. They're a bit wild and frizzy now. Like the mane of a lion. Will they even care around here?

Meadow gently pulls at the corset strings. Gasping, I ask, "So do you live here or something?" Another tug, this one rougher. "Not so tight, please."

It loosens a little. "Apologies. And yes, I live on the grounds with my partner, Rula."

"Does she work here, too?"

Meadow grabs my hips and gently pulls my hips side to side, inspecting the final look. "Yes. We've both been here for quite some time. Before Lordess Kalliope, I served Lordess Kailen."

"Who works with Lordess Kailen now?"

Meadow frowns as she straightens a string. "She has passed into the After. Ten years ago."

So Kalliope also has a mother who died. Curious. "What about her father?"

Meadow straightens. "Why all these questions, Miss? Did Her Grace refrain from sharing with you?"

"No," I blurt. "I'm curious, is all. I've never been to Ilorna before, and a lot of this is new to me."

"Ah." She comes around to my front, inspecting my curls. She grabs one and adjusts it. Up close, I spot fine lines edging into her soft skin. I wonder how Amicums age. Her eyes flick to mine. "Well, Her Grace is fairly transparent about her life. It's best if you inquire with her directly."

"Of course. Sorry if that's rude or something. It's not my intention."

Meadow smiles softly. "It's alright." She eyes the Scout, which still looks like a black leather band. "Do you wish to wear something more complementary to your outfit?"

Her tone is neutral, but it's clear she doesn't approve. I wrap a hand around it, holding it to my chest. "Sure, I think I have something in my bag. I'll go change it."

After making a show of putting my hand in my bag, I switched the disguise to a gold bangle before walking back to Meadow. She has a pair of black slippers in-hand. As I let her slide them onto my feet, she says, "We must hurry. The dinner gong has already been rung."

Following her out of the room, I place a hand over my belly, willing the fluttering nerves to calm down. *Everything is going to be okay.* This is all part of The Mission. There's no way to know if this place is safe if I can't experience the way the people engage with one another. It's for research. The whole point of this trip is to find a place to bring my family. The only way to make a thorough opinion is by mingling with the local population. Even if it requires wearing beautiful clothes.

Any other negative thoughts are quickly shoved away.

The brisk walk to dinner takes us through more hallways. So many look the same, with similar statues and art lining the walls. In the darkness, the hallways flicker with warm lamplight, but all I can focus on are the shadows that seep into the corners. It's spooky, as if some creature might spring out and gobble me up without warning. After living in a world full of fluorescent lighting, this feels more ominous than it should.

Meadow stays silent until we reach a set of thick wooden doors. As we approach, two men — males — step forward and swing the doors open, revealing a dazzling scene.

The room beyond is spacious, filled with one incredibly long table and at least a couple dozen chairs. On the table are endless piles of food and pitchers. Both males and females sit at the table, laughing and smiling.

Dozens of candles adorn the walls. Every three feet are single, double, and triple candle holders. Firelight glitters along the dark damask wallpaper. Three chandeliers, evenly spaced on the ceiling, dip low and sparkle with more fire. The whole room is cast in an orange, welcoming glow, with no shadows to be found.

Perpendicular to the table is another shorter table, with only three seats. In one sits Kalliope. Next to her is a gorgeous male sipping from a silver cup. She laughs as he says something, and his returning grin is a heart-stopper.

She's wearing a midnight-blue loose shirt with diamond stud earrings catching the light. The shirt is unbuttoned so low that the edges of her breasts show as she moves. One half of her hair sweeps up in intricate braids, with the other side cascading down her shoulder in loose waves.

When Meadow steps into the room, Kalliope stands, waving us over with a warm smile that lights up her irresistible features. The male rises when she does, towering over her tall form, mimicking her expression.

His skin is a glimmering golden brown with a rough-hewn bone structure. More lumberjack and less pretty boy. Wavy dark hair reaches broad shoulders. Very *muscular* shoulders shown off by a sleeveless black shirt. Half of it's tucked into his pants, revealing a sheathed dagger at his hip.

Heads pivot in our direction as we draw closer. The introvert part of me wants to curl up and die a little. When we're close enough, Kalliope pulls back the remaining chair.

"Saira, I'm pleased you could join us. This is my consort, Legend." She motions to the male, then gives Meadow's shoulder a friendly squeeze. "Thank you. I'll alert you when she requires an escort back to her room."

Meadow curtsies and disappears into the crowd. Kalliope motions to the chair, and I nervously walk over. As I sit, she scoots the chair forward behind my knees. The super-hot guy sits when she does, both relaxing immediately.

The male leans on an elbow, looking like the cat that ate the canary. "Nice to meet you, Saira. As my glorious and stunning lordess said, my name is Legend."

What a peculiar name. What makes him legendary? "Hi, Legend. I'm Saira."

His mouth quirks into a half smile. "So I've heard."

Don't be such an awkward nerd. My cheeks heat with embarrassment. Considering he's the most attractive man I've ever seen, let alone spoken to, this first impression is something I'll replay over and over again when I'm struggling to sleep. Because brains are chill like that.

Kalliope pours a red liquid into a silver cup and hands it to me. Grateful to have something to do with my hands, I bring the cup to my lips and take a tiny sip. The mix of tart and sweet is unfamiliar, but it's definitely wine. Excellent wine.

Satisfied, Kalliope reaches for hers and relaxes in the chair. She looks at the guests at the other table. They aren't looking at us anymore, which gives a sense of relief.

My eyes dance around the room, trying to take it all in. A small band of musicians — all of whom look like humans — plays an array of musical instruments. Lively chatter feeds the high-spirited vibe of the space. Groups of guests mingle together around the room, and many of them have animalistic features. Some resemble creatures I've only seen in fantasy art, including a few more centaurs, satyrs, and even a unicorn. How the unicorn can even converse is beyond my comprehension. It's curious that they're here in a realm just for them, yet on Earth, they're myths. Where did their depictions and mythologies originate?

A female passes by with her face shifted into a melding of human and tiger characteristics. Her mouth slopes away from a broad, striped forehead, ending in a snout. As she stops in front of our table to greet Kalliope, I notice whiskers flaring from her chubby upper lips.

When she smiles, it's like a tiger snarling. Her eyes flick over my features with curiosity, but that's the extent of her acknowledgement. Frankly, if she spoke to me, I'm not sure words could appear. My brain's cognitive dissonance is so strong, it's hard to get a mental grasp on what I'm seeing.

Turning my focus from the menagerie of strangeness, I take another sip of wine. Pretending to understand this world will be more difficult than originally anticipated. It's so surreal, I think a part of my brain is struggling to accept this isn't some form of delusion from a drug experiment gone bad — this is actual real life. No antidote offered.

"So, Saira, Kal tells me you are from,"—he waves an elegant hand in the air—"somewhere. At this somewhere, is everyone as beautiful as you?"

Legend's question takes me by surprise. I can't remember the last time a man called me beautiful. Swallowing thickly, I say, "Um, no? Yes?"

My response arches his eyebrow. Kalliope reaches forward and plucks a piece of fruit from a platter. She pops it in her mouth before saying, "Ignore him. He gets bored at these events, and he enjoys testing new people. Like a youngling fresh out of the playpen."

Legend tosses her a dirty look before casting me another brilliant smile. His fangs intrigue me. "It's true," he confesses. "These dinners are so boring. So much politics. But I'm also serious about you being beautiful."

A servant chooses that exact moment to sweep in with individual plates of food. I'm unsure if I should be relieved or annoyed by the interruption. The male servant leans forward and places plates in front of us.

Looking at the brightly colored meal, I can tell by the serving size it's an appetizer. I look up at the male servant. "What is this?"

His mahogany-colored curls dip as he looks to the plate, then back at me. "Seared heron with a peach glaze."

"Heron, like the *bird*?"

He gives me a strange look. "Yes, miss. Her Grace has the finest flock for hundreds of miles. Specially raised on acorns and mango over the first two years of their life, then slaughtered gently to not toughen the meat."

Alrighty then. "Thank you."

He nods and steps back. I reach for a nearby fork and knife. It's surprising to find utensils at all. Amicums are more civilized than an average pack of dogs, but utensils? Unexpected.

The dish smells sweet and earthy. I wonder what "slaughtered gently" means.

When I ask Kalliope, she makes a face, then explains, "I'm not a fan of how meat tastes pumped with adrenaline, so the butchers slaughter only a dozen per day, and separate the birds from the flock so as to not create a stir. Then their throats are cut quickly, too quick for the bird to grasp what is done. I do not believe it must be cruel for us to obtain sustenance."

I'm conflicted about this information. "But how do the butchers handle doing it with so much intention?"

Kalliope cuts into her dark meat with a wicked-looking knife. "Empathy is the key to society. My foremothers occasionally ruled with too cruel a hand; I wish to never do the same. When my mother passed, I vowed to infuse my land with as much kindness as possible. It is not always feasible, but I do what I can. It does not matter whether it is an Amicum, one-form, or an animal — everyone deserves kindness."

My knife slices into the meat, and at the first taste, I'm done for. I moan, closing my eyes against the lush flavor. When I open them again, I catch Kalliope boldly watching me with a piercing gaze. Legend looks equally enthralled.

With a voice made of smoke and honey, Legend asks, "I trust you find it delicious?"

I lick my lips clean of fatty grease. "It's amazing."

Kalliope's smile is wicked, all velvet and sin. "There are other things in my court that taste amazing."

She reaches for her wineglass again, this time taking a pointedly slow sip. Those sunset-hued eyes make me willing to burn to a crisp. Unfamiliar sensations coil in my chest.

"Yes, and they all begin with the letter L," Legend says, chuckling. Kalliope snorts but doesn't deny it. My belly does some backflips at the innuendo. This is already the most sexually charged conversation of my life. Piper was always the one out dating and having a good time. Fear makes me want to avoid engaging, but as usual, my curious nature wins. There's a version of me I want to be, and it includes being a sassy flirt. Might as well try it on for size.

After another glorious forkful of the heron, I quip, "My best friend told me that men who brag about their prowess can rarely back it up. I sure hope you aren't one of those. It would be disappointing."

Kalliope's head whips toward me, then she laughs. Legend's eyebrows raise with delight. His eyes shine with mischief as he takes a sip of wine, then slowly licks his bottom lip. My attention snags on the way his tongue pauses to rub at one of his fangs. Noticing, his grin widens.

"I assure you there is nothing about me that one would consider disappointing."

His confidence makes my mouth go dry. Kalliope's eyes ping-pong between the two of us, amusement crinkling the corners of her eyes. Normally, a man hitting on me this hard would earn him a scathing glare and a quick exit on my part.

Instead, his impish behavior coaxes out my atrophied sense of play-fulness.

I bat my eyelashes and offer Legend a saccharine smile. "Promises, promises, promises."

Inside, I'm wilting with self-consciousness. Has dark matter scrambled my brain? Am I actually flirting with him? My stomach flips violently, wanting to claw the words back. If he rejects me, I'll crawl under the table with a bottle of wine.

"Color me intrigued," he purrs, sipping from his wine again. It jars my sense of the world; he actually *wants* to flirt with me? Kalliope smacks him on the shoulder, and his eyes widen with fake innocence.

"What? I'm being a good boy," he grips, flashing me a lopsided grin.

A flutter of excitement buzzes in my blood. Piper would have a conniption if she heard me flirting. It's impossible to suppress a smile.

Whisking away the empty plate, the same male servant as before bends around to place a large bowl of orange, creamy soup in front of me. I thank him and reach for the spoon.

It looks like pumpkin soup with a drizzle of white sauce and flecks of seeds. As I dip the spoon into the concoction, Kalliope clears her throat. I look up, spoon suspended in the air.

She looks devilish as she says, "Do you know what you're about to eat?"

"Pumpkin soup?"

She tosses back her head with a throaty laugh. "No, it's sea cucumber curry chowder with potato and basil. It's a delicacy here. Ellie, our head chef, only makes it on special occasions."

I picture the dookie-looking creatures. "Like, from the ocean?"

Kalliope chuckles. "Yes, but they're farmed in Cape Schrute, raised in purified saltwater and harvested by locals."

I shrug. So far, everything here has been divine. When in other universes, right?

It's creamy and thick with bursts of varying flavors. The sea cucumber is soft and dissolves in my mouth. It's delightful.

We're all quiet as we sip the soup, but when it's all gone, Legend starts with the questions again.

"So Kal told me you almost got eaten by a bear?"

The change of subject throws me off. Clearing my throat, I say, "Um, yeah. It was intense. If she hadn't shown up, I'd definitely be worm food right now."

With a knowing smile, Kalliope pours more wine for us. Even the mention of the bear attack can't entirely dampen the good mood the wine has created. It's damn good wine.

Legend offers a sympathetic look. "Well, I'm glad Her Grace was there to help."

Kalliope and I lock eyes. Between the braided hairstyle and midnight-lined eyes, she looks like a Viking seductress. I know I didn't get out of the lab much, but I'm pretty sure this energy between us is something special.

Or maybe I'm a moony-eyed girl who simpers for anyone willing to give her attention. The thought sours my gut.

Regardless, she *did* save me. Kalliope gave me a place to stay, even if it's temporary. Her outright kindness is admirable.

My words are strangled with emotion when I say, "Yes, I'm glad, too."

Chapter Twelve

Meeting The Cohort

By the time a servant lifts the plates from the table, my stomach's full and happy.

Legend is catching Kalliope up on the latest court gossip, subtly pointing out guests. It's impossible for me to know who everyone is, but it's obvious Amicum courts are every bit as messy as the courts from human history.

From what I can gather, there are eight provinces on the continent Payla. Each province elects a lordess to govern, protect its people, and maintain its trade specialty. Ilorna specializes in training the Amicum military, the Guardians.

Even though it's a matriarchy, each lordess has a court filled with personalities, offering salacious gossip. Legend mentions the lordess of Raeland allows the males to shift freely — resulting in some violence that the Guardians will be required to quell.

According to Kalliope, while Ilorna is bound to send Guardians to each province, she has the ultimate authority on how many to send per circumstance. Because Raeland refuses to develop shifting mandates, she's reluctant to send a large group.

Half of the things they're saying, I'm struggling to understand. I'm dying to know more about shifting mandates or why the males are more violent. Unfortunately, every time Legend goes too in-depth, Kalliope stops him with a touch on the arm.

The lack of understanding increases my loneliness. I've always excelled at understanding how the world works, but not how society functions. It's one of the many reasons I love Piper; she never lets me feel left out or lost.

My fingers go to the locket again, the gold warm in my hand. Piper would've loved this. I wish we'd had enough time to make a third band. It would have been a waste, sending a third person on the same trajectory, but we would've had an absolute blast.

I wonder what she put in the locket. It could be something heartfelt — it could also be a clump of her hair. It's hard to say with her impish sense of humor.

Regardless, I can't bear to find out yet. The camera in my pack is still an absolute no-no; to see those images would rip me in half right now. I'm barely able to keep it together as it is. A zebra trots by me, wearing a yellow skirt flowing past its hind legs. Something I'll never forget for as long as I'm alive.

Shifting the conversation from court gossip, Kalliope watches me fiddle with the locket and asks, "From someone special?"

They both appear curious. Kalliope must see the answer on my face because her features soften with sympathy.

My teeth bite into my quivering lower lip. Nodding, I let it drop back against my neck. When I can trust my voice, I say, "Yes, it's from my best friend, Piper. This is the longest we've ever been apart."

"That's a pretty name." Legend's tone is free of flirtatiousness. "You must miss her so much. Is she your sister?"

Don't cry. Don't cry. Don't cry.

In spite of my efforts, my voice still cracks when I say, "I do." Kalliope refills my cup. "She wanted to come with me, but it wasn't possible. We're cousins, but we're only eleven months apart in age. Our parents traded babysitting for years, so we became super close. I wish she could be here right now." I motion to the room. "She'd love all of this."

Legend murmurs his thanks to the servant, placing a slice of dark cake in front of him. Grabbing a fork, he cuts off a bite. "Why wasn't it possible?"

The servant places a plate in front of me, and the smell of chocolate makes my mouth water. Not sure if there's any room left in my stomach, but it smells too good. Maybe just a bite or two.

It's similar to German chocolate cake with a bit of cinnamon and an unfamiliar spice that tickles the back of my mouth. It's utterly delectable.

Kalliope groans and closes her eyes at the first bite. "Ellie has done it again."

"Agreed." Legend's halfway done with his slice, eating with boyish exuberance. A smear of chocolate decorates the corner of his mouth; Kalliope reaches over and wipes it off. Legend pauses mid-bite to watch her lick it off her finger. Heat darkens his eyes as his lips curl salaciously. The sight stutters my thoughts.

Swallowing hard, I clear my throat, interrupting their sexy moment. "It wasn't possible because she had to stay with her family. Our family, I guess. This journey's only for me, for now."

Kalliope's sharp gaze tracks an extravagantly dressed woman walking past us. The woman pauses with hope on her face, but when she isn't invited over, she moves on.

Refocusing on me, Kalliope gives me a sympathetic smile as she says, "Was she too busy to come? Perhaps we can send a courier, and she can come join you."

"No," I say quickly. "She's preoccupied with her own life right now. Maybe in the future, but not right now."

"Mmm." Kalliope finishes the last bite slowly. Pushing the plate away, she sits back with a pensive expression. "And what about your mother? She couldn't join you on this journey?"

I look at the gold band on my finger. Even years later, the words are hard to say. "She died when I was a kid."

Kalliope's eyes tighten with empathy. She leans forward and lays a hand on my arm. It's warm and firm. Her voice is compassionate as she murmurs, "I'm so sorry to hear that, Saira. Legend and I have also lost both of our mothers." She gently squeezes my arm. "How did you lose her?"

The memory of heart rate monitors and rattling inhalations of oxygen is still fresh, even fourteen years later. "Cancer."

Legend looks confused. "What's cancer?"

My sorrow halts in its tracks. "You don't have cancer here?"

If this is a land without cancer, it could make this place an even more suitable spot for the family. Of course, there's no way to know if it's simply a difference in our species, but it's something to consider. Kalliope tilts her head. "I'm not sure what it is in the first place, so it's impossible to say. Can you explain it?"

It's difficult to not put a hand over hers. To squeeze it in return. "Toxic lumps growing in the body, slowly taking over until someone dies."

An oversimplification. They don't need to hear how bodies waste away and families are torn apart for months, even years.

Legend's jaw drops, eyebrows shooting skyward. "That's horrific."

Kalliope squeezes my arm again, and this time, I can't resist laying my hand on hers. After the week I've had, it's lovely to have conversation and empathy with another person. She glances down at the gesture, then back at me. Our faces are only inches apart, close enough to —

"Your Grace, I've been eagerly waiting for you to make your rounds this evening." The lilting voice interrupts my thoughts as a female struts up, pert nose in the air. She's wearing thick layers of taffeta, the color of bile. Her blonde hair contains braids decorated with pieces of jewelry. Iridescent scales fall from the base of her throat down her breastbone like an all-encompassing necklace.

Next to her is a dark-skinned male wearing an outfit like Legend's. He watches her with adoration, a wineglass in each hand. A quick glance around shows all the males wearing the same sort of outfit. None of them has animalistic features. With the little I've learned, Ilorna has stricter guidelines for males and shifting. That explains all of the males looking humanoid.

Kalliope's hand goes rigid, then she pulls away from me, sitting up straighter and smoothing out her expression. "Lordess Charlyn, it's a pleasure to see you again."

The lordess looks as if she smells something pungent when her gaze flickers over me. She casts Kalliope a demure smile. "It's a pleasure, Lordess Kalliope. We arrived earlier today. Your staff has been most accommodating."

"Pleased to hear it. I've been eager to discuss matters with you." Kalliope stands, and Legend does the same. Not wanting to look stupid, I stand. The wine makes me wobble a little. Alcohol has never been a staple in my life. Hopefully, no one notices.

To my chagrin, Lordess Charlyn does. Her brown eyes seem to miss nothing as they trail down my body, then back to my face. Her lips purse before saying, "I hear we have a new visitor from out of town. My maids were gossiping about it *all* afternoon. How Lordess Kalliope Arnoux saved a one-form and invited her as a guest to the manor." She titters. "*Quite* unusual."

Kalliope pushes her chair back. "I have many new visitors this week, Lordess Charlyn. Come, let's go find Lordess Gwaurvin and congratulate her on the upcoming youngling. I've only met her the once, at the gathering in Myea. Perhaps you can offer a reintroduction?" I watch Kalliope as she walks around me and up to the lordess.

Lordess Charlyn finally looks appeased. "Yes, of *course*. I'd be *delighted* to reintroduce you to her. I heard her gestation is predicted to go *over ten months*. Could you *imagine?*"

"Much better than thirteen months, like my mother," Kalliope says smoothly. She motions for the female to move forward. "Please lead the way." Over her shoulder, she gives Legend a meaningful look, then walks away. A tiny stab of hurt pricks my heart at her dismissal. She didn't even look at me.

He turns to me, touching my elbow lightly. My emotions must be written all over my face because he says, "Don't fret, gorgeous. The lordesses have their own games they must play. Kalliope means no ill will by leaving." My eyes slide to his, and for the first time, I feel like drowning in their jade depths. "Come. I'll bring you to Meadow."

Legend's honeyed voice sends shivers down my spine. It's unfamiliar and alarming. Instinct forces me to take a step back, the table hitting my back. I grimace, rubbing at the pain. There hasn't been a single moment I haven't made a fool of myself since the bear attack. Awkward might as well become my middle name.

His eyes shine with amusement. "Skittish, are we?"

I dismiss the words with a nervous chuckle. "I'm not worried."

Legend looks like he doesn't believe me for one second, but doesn't push the matter. He takes a wide step back, allowing me room to navigate around the chairs. We walk the length of the room, side-stepping party guests. Curious eyes trail behind us, the burning gazes drilling into the back of my head. My being a one-form appears to be a bigger deal than Kalliope leads on. It feels like a spotlight following me as I leave the metaphorical stage.

Legend opens one of the smaller doors, revealing Meadow, who's talking to another servant. Noticing our arrival, her conversation abruptly stops.

Concern furrows her brow. "Is there something wrong?"

Legend's hand brushes my lower back as I walk to her, enough to singe heat up my spine. "Not at all. Her Grace had other guests to tend to. Saira's had a busy enough day and needs to rest."

Conflicting feelings duke it out in my mind; he's not wrong, but no one asked me what I wanted to do. The only reason I don't object is the simple fact that he's not wrong.

Meadow smiles at me with sympathy. "Of course, you poor thing. Follow me, Miss."

She walks off, leaving me standing awkwardly next to Legend. Do we hug? Shake hands? Fist bump?

Saving me from embarrassment, he offers a shallow bow. "I'm sure we'll see each other again soon, Saira."

I hope so.

Nope. No *hope so*. I'm only here temporarily. No need to get attached. No need at all.

Waking up the next morning is like being reborn. All my aches and pains have faded, thanks to the soft mattress and pillows. I slept like a corpse all night, and the rest helped my mind sift through recent events. It's offered badly needed clarity.

This place has shown enormous potential. The people are pleasant; the food is delicious. So far, that's the extent of my understanding — which means more time is required. At least a few days, if not a couple of weeks. Today will help me understand things further, but I'll give it at least two weeks to start. After leaving the first four spots quickly, I need to stick with this place for a solid period of time.

Decision made, I hop out of bed, eager to start the day with curiosity. After inspecting my room again, I'm delighted to discover new clothes hanging in the armoire. There are so many beautiful options.

Allowing myself to have a little fun playing dress up, I try on some of the clothing before settling on black linen pants and a light blue shirt with a loose-fitting black linen vest. To match the outfit, I program the Scout to look like a black braided leather band. It all pairs well with my custom boots. Once I tame my unruly curls with a thick braid, I feel like a fantasy badass.

By the time Meadow arrives to escort me to breakfast, I'm rocking on the balls of my feet, eager to get my research started. In my pocket are small vials to hold samples.

She's all energetic cheer as she says, "Good morning, Miss. How did you rest?"

I close the door behind me. "Great. Having a bed to sleep on is something I'll never take for granted again."

She chuckles. "I've spent my fair share of time in the outdoors. It's not quite my favorite, either."

"You're an indoor girl?" I tease.

Ushering me down a hallway, Meadow hiccups out a giggle. "You could say that. I can't very well knit sweaters for younglings in the dirt." She pretends to shutter. "No, thank you. Me and my yarn will be in front of a fire with some tea on most nights, snacking with my partner."

Too focused on her face, I nearly topple over a statue, barely able to catch it in time as it wobbles toward the ground. Grimacing, I carefully re-situate the statue as I ask, "Does your partner knit as well?"

Meadow's eyes widen at the near disaster, but that's her only reaction. "No, it's my hobby. She loves baking little tiny cookies in the shapes of Amicums."

"Sounds cozy and yummy."

She sighs dreamily. "It is. With all the hubbub, there's a sweater waiting on my favorite chair and a plate of cookies nearby."

Looking down so I don't run into anything else, I smile. Even in another universe, women love to create and be cozy.

We stop at the same door as last night. She puts a hand on my shoulder. "Be careful of Daeva, Miss."

I frown. "Who?"

Sending me a warning look, she opens the doors. Beams of bright light blast us in the face. The room's been reset with a single long table stretching across the width. Last night, people occupied most of the chairs. Now only a handful sit at the far end next to Kalliope, who stands as I enter.

Meadow closes the doors behind me. I pat my braid and adjust the vest, then clasp my hands together. Too much fidgeting looks suspicious. Kalliope beckons me over with a wave of her graceful fingers. Like last night, Legend lounges next to her, nursing a glass of what might be more wine. To her right are two female Amicums.

The female closest to Kalliope has straight, white-blonde hair. Her pale ice-blue eyes are a bit too round and wide for her delicate features. She's wearing a crisp white shirt with silver braces wrapped around her forearms.

Her observant gaze makes my skin crawl. My attempt to look friendly makes her mouth pinch tight. Like she just sucked a lemon.

Next to her is an older female with dark brown skin and warm hazel eyes. Three patches of white cover her eyes and mouth. Wild sprigs of gray, tight curls frame her face. A red tank top dips to show a swirling, glimmering tattoo along her chest and over her shoulders, like armor.

She grins as I draw closer, and I can't help but smile back. She also wears a bandolier full of wickedly sharp and curved blades.

It's an effort to hide my nerves as I make my way toward them. The females stand, mimicking Kalliope's respectful stance, but none of them say anything in greeting.

Instead, it's Kalliope who opens her arms, bringing me in for a kiss on each cheek. She smells faintly of a smokey campfire. "Saira, you look rested. How did you sleep?"

"Like it was the first time I'd slept in a bed in over a week." She chuckles and points to the empty chair next to hers. Legend sits on her other side.

As I settle in, everyone else sits down. The silence is oppressive as four pairs of eyes examine me. The pale-blonde female's gaze rakes over me with a sour expression. There's something about her that gives me the ick. She looks at me like I'm a problem.

The tattooed female speaks first. "I'm Zenab. As Kalliope's ancient advisor and weapons master, I make sure things don't fall apart." She looks at the icy blonde. "This is Daeva, and she's the master at arms here. Don't mind her — she woke up on the wrong side of the bed."

"As usual," Legend mutters. No mirth shows on his face.

Daeva slices a nasty look in his direction before returning to our one-sided stare down. My anxiety kicks up a notch every second she remains locked onto me. What is this female's deal?

"Nice to meet you both?" It comes off as a question because I'm not entirely sure Daeva isn't about to shift and eat me. Trying to distract myself, I scan the table. "Do you have coffee here?"

To my utter delight, Legend leans forward to grab a carafe in front of him. He motions to a male servant nearby, and he's handed an empty cup. My patience is nonexistent as he pours it. It's a strain not to snatch it from his hands and take the first sip.

107

It's been far too long since I've had coffee, and to even call this coffee would be a sin — it's too damn smooth and flavorful to just be coffee. It leaves a nutty aftertaste.

When I moan, Kalliope and Zenab chuckle. Daeva snorts, but it's less amused and more derisive.

Ignoring her rudeness, I grin. "I haven't had coffee in days. This might be the best cup I've ever had. They certainly don't make it like this at home."

I immediately want to snatch back the words as Daeva eyes me with suspicion. "Where are you from?"

Kalliope cuts me off from trying to respond. "Perhaps we can let our guest enjoy some food before you grill her, Dae."

There's a flash of challenge in Daeva's sharp eyes, but she gives Kalliope a subtle nod. Taking a long sip of coffee, I weigh my options. I learned more about the continent last night, but if I say I'm from a nearby province, what if they ask me about someone specific I should know?

Continuing to be vague is also dangerous, but there really isn't much of a choice. It's been barely twenty-four hours since they found me in the forest, so I'm fairly certain there's a small window of leeway as I postpone honesty until the very last second.

Piper once told me that it's easier to lie when you stick closer to the truth. Lying has never been a strong suit, but I'll need to practice. After another sip of coffee, I say, "My family is the kind to enjoy traveling. We don't stay in one place for too long. So I'm not really from somewhere, so much as I'm from many places."

This answer doesn't seem to satisfy Daeva. "Surely you were born somewhere we've heard of."

Zenab pulls out a dagger from her hip and sharpens it with a stone. "Let it rest, Dae. I think the nomadic lifestyle is wonderful. I'm sure you've seen some fascinating things."

"You could say that," I hedge, taking a sip of the coffee. Zenab leans forward eagerly, but when it's clear no details will be shared, she swallows a frown and sits back in her chair. Daeva's suspicion only increases, if the way her gaze narrows into slits is any indication. While it'd be nice to share what it's like to land in a world filled with fire tornados, it's not wise.

Breaking the awkward silence, Kalliope turns to Daeva. "What are the updates on the recent village attacks?"

Daeva straightens, turning her glare toward Kalliope. "The Guardians have nothing to report along the Ilorna border, Your Grace. The attack on Tairn appears random, and the perpetrators are unconfirmed, since no Vulturian body was recovered. Guardians will continue to monitor for any potential threats."

Zenab sheaths her dagger and leans on the table. "We've begun rebuilding efforts. I've instructed the Treasury to provide fifty shillings per family as compensation."

Daeva scoffs. "At this rate, the province will go broke trying to compensate every family for these attacks. What we need to do is find the perpetrators and bring swift justice." She looks to Kalliope. "I recommend we send a missive to Vulturia and inquire with the king about the attacks. It's time to take this seriously."

"You think I'm not taking this seriously?" Kalliope's voice is flat, but there's an edge of violence in her tone.

Daeva's eyes are like two shards of ice. "Of course not, but it's foolish to think that the silence implies everything is alright."

"So now I'm foolish?"

Everyone freezes, including me. I'm afraid to even swallow the food in my mouth. My whole life has been in academia and science. When it came to research, I clung to Dad's genius coattails, avoiding the politics of corporate jobs or even wooing donors. He did all of that labor. This kind of back and forth is as foreign to me as everything else they're discussing. One thing is clear though: Kalliope's energy brooks no argument.

Daeva realizes her mistake and tries to backtrack. Sitting up straight, she gives a firm shake of her head. "No, Your Grace. I misspoke."

Kalliope taps a black nail on the table. Slow and steady. "Daeva, I'm aware of the rumors, but we've had peace for a decade, and I'm not about to insult the king by inquiring whether he has dissenting factions without irrefutable proof. We've already increased patrols, as you requested three weeks ago." She pauses to collect her thoughts, flicking her gaze to me before continuing. "For all we know, it's a band of raiders, and the traumatized townsfolk were mistaken. Once the Guardians witness a Vulturian attack, then I'll open a dialogue with the king. Until then, I will not risk another war when we've barely recovered from the last one."

Daeva's washed out cheeks bloom to the color of roses. "Lordess, as the master at arms, it's my duty to ensure we are prepared for —"

"Then stay prepared." Kalliope interrupts. Long black claws slowly appear at her fingertips. Everyone, including Daeva, takes notice. The warrior stares at Kalliope for a moment longer, then stands abruptly.

"Yes, Lordess." She bows stiffly before whirling around and stalking out of the room. Kalliope's claws retract, one by one, as she stares in the direction of Daeva's fading footsteps. Weariness pulls at the corners of her eyes before she quickly replaces it with a mask of indifference.

What the hell are Vulturians? Why is Daeva so concerned about them? The war ended only ten years ago? Is it possible to ask questions without drawing more attention to myself?

Legend sighs. "Dae needs a right romp with one of the consorts. Clearly, she hasn't gotten enough cock."

I nearly spit out my food. Zenab rolls her eyes and huffs a loose curl out of her face. "I'm not sure the cure for her behavior is found with fur and skin." She gives Kalliope a pointed look. "She needs reminding of her—"

"*Enough.*" Kalliope sounds tired and frustrated. "It is barely mid-morning, and our guest does not need to hear speculations and degradations within my Cohort. Instead, why don't we figure out how Saira would like to spend her day?"

Now everyone's looking at me. Swallowing my last bite of muffin, I say. "I'd really like to see more of the grounds today, if possible."

Zenab props her muscular body against the chair's arm. "The manor's gardens are the best in the province of Ilorna. You'll love them."

"Consort duty calls. I must go greet some males arriving today with their lordesses. Ensure they're aware of the rules around here." Legend stands, pressing a light kiss against Kalliope's cheek. She nods, leaning into the kiss. Catching my eye, he offers a wink. I refuse to examine how that makes me feel. Instead, I look away, choosing to focus on Kalliope as she stands. She sweeps an arm in the direction of the door everyone else has disappeared through.

"Shall we go on an adventure?"

Chapter Thirteen

No Chosen One Trope Here

We start the tour in a lush space full of trees heavy with fruit, bushes full of berries, and dozens of flowers. A herd of goats walks around, munching on the bushes, trimming them back into place. Two giraffes crane their long necks up to the tops of trees, using long tongues to break off branches and leaves. I really hope they wash everything before serving it at dinner.

Some human-looking Amicums walk around with baskets, plucking the produce off branches. They dip their heads as we pass, and Kalliope does the same. It's charming to watch her in action and witness how the Amicums interact.

"Lucinda, I love this coat you've chosen today," she says to a pure white goat. It bleats loudly and bends a knee.

She stops to admire a large lemon tree and the giraffe eating from it. "Griselda, do you think you can have the monkey Amicums bring those back about a foot? I want to make sure it's pruned enough for next summer's growth."

The large animal blinks slowly, munching with almost no sound. Apparently, the non-reaction is enough, because Kalliope continues bringing us through the garden. I'm amazed to see all these animals doing what I've only ever seen people do.

Kalliope walks next to me, letting me pick different plants and flowers, not batting an eye when I put them into my pocket. When I pick up fruit, she requests a basket for me to hold. She buys my explanation of wanting to try them all later.

And of course, I'll actually try every single bit of fruit after submitting samples. It's all part of the science, I swear.

As we continue through the garden, it's becoming clear she cares about the Amicums. She's patient with questions about the upcoming harvest. Another female approaches, gazing at her with adoration as Kalliope gives advice on fertilizer. When a male offers her a fresh peach from a full basket, she thanks him by name.

I peer up with surprise when she grabs my hand and loops it through her arm, holding my hand to her forearm. A small buzz of excitement vibrates through my body. My fingers tighten against her bare skin, the touch making my thoughts blur together.

I think she asked a question — those citrine eyes have snatched my ability to think. This isn't good. It hasn't even been a day and I'm developing a crush on a shifter? No, this is the exhaustion and homesickness making this happen.

But those eyes. They're enthralling, rimmed with dark eyelashes. The intensity threatens to overwhelm me.

Temporarily short circuited, I ask, "Did you say something?"

Her eyebrows draw together. "Are you alright?"

The amount of concern in her voice is too much. It makes my heart pang, and that's a big no-no. No attachments allowed. I'm on a mission to save my family, and any form of attachment is a *bad idea*. In a few days, I'll be gone. No time for entanglements.

Stay impartial, Saira.

I swallow hard and pull my arm from hers. "Yeah, I'm great. These gardens are really—"

There's a loud *twang* and a hoot of joy. I whip my head at the sound, and Kalliope chuckles, brushing fingers at the back of my arm, causing goosebumps to break out. She really needs to stop the physical affection. My body and mind are going to have a meltdown if it continues.

She leads me toward the hoots and hollers. "That's the archery training area. Would you like to see it?"

Still focused on the sensation of her skin on mine, I gulp again and nod. We stop and stand behind a dozen females holding bows with quivers at their hips. There are targets at different distances, some already full of arrows.

One female elbows another, and everyone whirls around to bow before straightening like a line of military men. Except instead of men, these are all buff warriors wearing shining black leathers.

Some have bandoliers of daggers, and a couple wear swords strapped to the opposite side of their quivers. I notice Zenab standing among them.

She steps forward with a proud gleam in her eyes. "Your Grace, I'm glad you are here. Shanen just scored three bullseye in a row."

A smaller female beams behind the leader, and Kalliope beckons her to stand forward. "Shanen, that is excellent to hear. Would you mind showing this skill again?"

Shanen looks nervous as she nods, eyes flicking toward me for the briefest of seconds. Turning with deliberate precision, she plucks an arrow from her hip and nocks it onto the long bow's string. It's so quiet all I hear are the sounds of bees in flowers.

Then the groan of wood and bowstring. A whistle, then the confident thwack of the arrow, driving true into the center of the target.

I think she's going to stop there, but instead, she swipes another arrow and does it again.

And again.

And again.

She empties a dozen into the poor target, the final landing snuggly between four others, chunks of straw floating to the grass. When her quiver is empty, there's a pause, then the group of warriors erupts with cheers. Impressed isn't a strong enough word for how watching that makes me feel. I may have helped invent time travel, but that doesn't equate to a super cool skill like archery.

Kalliope steps forward and claps Shanen on the back, congratulating her. She spins Shanen, then gently brings a hand to each of Shanen's cheeks, bringing their foreheads together.

Kalliope says something too quiet to hear amidst the excited voices around us. Shanen gives a nod, emotion trembling on her lower lip. It's an intimate scene, one that makes me want to bolt. Or find a way to earn something similar.

Finally, they step apart, Shanen wiping away a tear. Kalliope looks proud as she gives one more pat to Shanen's shoulder before turning back to me.

I'm taken aback by the fierce emotions on her sculpted features. She's such a handsome female, looking like a goddess come alive. For a split second, I can sense the wolf and the woman in one body.

It's super fucking hot.

Kalliope motions for me to come forward. The crowd quiets. Suddenly, all eyes are on us. Kalliope grabs an offered bow and presents it to me.

"Would you like to try, Saira?"

"Me? Absolutely not. I'm not some Katniss."

She continues to hold out the bow, forcing me to grab it so we don't look ridiculous. The smooth yew wood is warm and has some heft to it. A female dressed in deep brown leathers offers an arrow to me.

I grab it with a pleading look. "I've never done this. I wouldn't even know how. I'm going to shoot my eye out."

Kalliope chuckles, then sweeps her gaze to the crowd. The response is instantaneous. Within a blink, we're mostly alone, minus Zenab.

Kalliope steps forward and sidles up past my shoulder, bringing her mouth close to my ear. Her breath is warm as she murmurs, "It's relatively easy. First, bring the bow up."

Her hands slide down my arms, supporting my wrists as she helps me lift the bow. Her chest is now flush against my shoulders, and I nearly melt into her soft curves.

My breath hitches, the target going out of focus. Still supporting my left arm with hers, she brings her other hand to grab the arrow in my right hand, her fingers guiding mine as she shows how to nock the arrow.

She steps back, lightly drawing her fingers along my skin, and I bite back a whimper. I watch as she gently adjusts my fingers, showing me how to support the arrow. It's hard to breathe when she bats a foot against my ankles, widening my legs. Why am I suddenly feral? Was I really that sheltered in my scientific enclosure? Was there not enough enrichment and now, when a steamy warrior princess is in front of me, I become incapacitated?

She cocks her head. "Did you hear me, Saira?"

I shake my head free of naughty thoughts. "Sorry, I was ... what did you say?"

That perfect mouth curls upward, as if she knows I'm full of shit. "When you bring the arrow up, keep it angled to where the end is dipping toward your mouth. Take a deep breath in and let it go as the arrow flies."

My palms are moist. She's about to witness my making a fool of myself. "Right. Mouth, breathe in, breathe out. Got it."

Sighting the target's center, I do my best to align the arrow and manifest success. Sucking in air, I blow it out roughly as I let go. The arrow flies, landing three feet in front of the target, straight into the grass.

The target is only ten feet away.

Cheeks burning, I turn to Kalliope, expecting judgment. Except she's smiling broadly, giving a loud clap of her hands. I frown, lowering the bow.

"But I failed."

She shakes her head and reaches for an arrow stabbed into the ground by one of the warriors. "Not at all. You were still shooting straight — you simply need a bit more power to make it fly farther."

"That's all?" I say dryly.

I take the offered arrow and go through the motions. Mouth. Breathe in. Breathe out. This time, when I let go, the arrow sings as it slices through the air, slamming into the target.

Not the center, but *it's the target*. The tension held in my body releases, and I laugh. Like, really laugh, for the first time in, well, too long. I haven't felt this accomplished since the day I bent the dimension of time to my will for the first time.

Zenab claps her hands and hoots, "I knew you'd do it, Saira!"

Kalliope looks at me with the same pride she had for Shanen. A kernel of warmth unfurls in my chest as she says, "Excellent. You clearly have a skill. Would you like to go again?"

Hesitation has flown the coop, and I nock another arrow. This time, it's exhilarating to let it go and watch it get closer to the bullseye. Kalliope only watches as six more arrows creep toward the center. Finally, on the last arrow, it hits dead center.

Kalliope laughs with hearty enthusiasm. It's impossible to curb my joy, and I laugh again. My heart is so full, it might explode. Then I hear it — more clapping from behind us. I whirl around and gasp. The group of warriors had drifted closer and witnessed what I've done.

They saw me kick ass.

In a feeling of abject idiocy, I thrust the bow in the air as if I were a warrior armed with a sword. Zenab cackles, her auburn curls bouncing as she gives another whoop.

A warm hand slides across my back as Kalliope whispers in my ear, "I knew you could do it."

Something in my soul cracks enough to let her slip in and make a home.

Yeah, I'm the worst scientist in the history of scientists.

After the tour, Kalliope escorts me to a stunning barnyard. In the middle is a massive, pale purple barn with hot pink stall doors. It's very Barbie-like. I love it.

There are no paddocks or fencing. In front of the barn is a wide stretch of lush green grass. A pure white horse eyes me while it munches on a mouthful of hay. I wave in case it's an Amicum I'll meet later.

The barn door slides open, and a familiar female pushes against it with a huff. Ginger. Still naked, breasts swinging as the door hits the end of its track.

She gives me a wicked grin as Kalliope leads me closer. "BB! It's good to see you."

Kalliope sighs like she's the most burdened person in the world. "Ginger, I need to go greet some other lordesses arriving. It's chaotic right now, but I don't want Saira to get lost. Would you mind allowing her to keep you company for the afternoon?"

Ginger raises an eyebrow and makes an insulting show of looking me up and down. "Are you able to muck out the stalls with your hands?"

My hands make fists, and when I shove them into my pockets, she barks out a laugh. Kalliope sighs again and turns to me. "She's fucking with you. Don't let her make you do anything you don't want to do." She glances over her shoulder, then leans down to whisper in my ear. "Her neigh is worse than her kick."

"I heard that."

Kalliope straightens, touches my shoulder briefly, then begins to walk back to the manor. "Be nice, Ginger, or I'll tell your mother about the time you drank her vintage bottle of Croilin."

Ginger gasps with genuine horror. "You wouldn't."

Kalliope waves without looking back. "Don't give me a reason."

Ginger levels her gaze with mine. "She helped me drink half of it, you know."

I shrug meekly. "I don't even know what Croilin is."

Her red lashes flutter as an idea lights up her face. "Do you know how to braid hair?"

I bring a hand up to my braided hair and point. She purses her lips and turns on her heel back into the barn. She waves for me to follow her, and after a moment's hesitation, I follow.

It's dim inside and smells like horse sweat and manure. It's a welcomed familiar scent. Piles of hay take up half the walkway next to the doorless stalls lining the walls. The inside's painted similar colors as the outside, with the stalls being a deeper purple and the metal painted a brilliant gold.

A few horses munch on hay in the stalls, but the way they watch me shows more intelligence than the average horse. It's odd, like we have an audience.

Ginger leads me to a shower area that is still wet from someone else's bath. "Help me out, will you?"

I stare at her. "Help you with what?"

She gives a dismissive shake of her head, looking at me like I'm stupid. Then I catch the barest of smiles. "Kalliope says you have to do what I say, remember?"

I tilt my head, scrunching my brow together in confusion. "Pretty sure that's not what she said."

"It's illegal to turn down grooming a fellow Amicum."

I look around, bewildered. "Who the hell am I grooming? And how is that illegal?"

She tosses me a currycomb. I catch it and stare at the rubber toothed brush. I'm still confused until a shimmer circles her hips. Her torso floats up to the ceiling, half of a chestnut horse supporting the Amicum half.

Am I really about to currycomb a centaur?

Her heavy breasts sway as she twists her torso to glare at me. "Well, get to work, BB."

It's impossible to hold back an incredulous laugh. "You can't be serious."

She offers a saccharine smile. "Don't worry, I won't kick you."

"How comforting," I mutter. This is the weirdest experience of my life, but maybe this is part of their culture. It *could* be illegal, although something tells me Ginger makes shit up for fun. No matter what, though, I'll be able to say I groomed a centaur, and that fact will make Piper lose her shit.

Walking up to Ginger's withers, I run a hand over her spine, down to her tail. It's a familiar movement, born of riding for years. She shivers.

"You're going to have to treat me to a promenade before we get *that* familiar, BB."

119

My cheeks burn. "Sorry, I didn't realize that would be inappropriate. I won't —"

She laughs. "*I'm fucking with you,* BB. Now get to brushing."

I circle the currycomb through her fur. Dust swirls in the air. How she got so dirty when she just shifted is beyond me.

"So," I prod. "Why do Amicums live in barns? Can't they shift and live in bedrooms?"

"Can't you just wait a bit before asking annoying questions?" she whines. "I haven't been brushed for ages."

I lift the brush in silent threat. "I could go ask Legend or Kalliope."

She sighs and flicks her hand in irritation. "Oh, you're no fun. Fine. Some of us prefer to live a more simple life and live in our preferred shifts. I can't exactly crawl into a bed with four legs."

I gaze down the walkway at the stalls. "Are any of these stalls yours?"

She shakes her head. "No. I prefer to rest in the yard because I can't stand the feeling of being trapped. I'm not much for crowds or even large groups of people. It's why you'll rarely find me at the manor. Everyone makes shifting into a competition where there's no prize. It's boresome."

Sounds like she's a fellow introvert. I let myself sink into the familiar motions of grooming. It's quiet in the barn, with the occasional snuffling. Ginger busies herself by twisting her curls around a finger. I watch her from the corner of my eye, trying to come up with something to say. This female is nothing but a bundle of sass — will she be honest with me if I ask deeper questions?

There are lots of questions I need to ask to gain a better understanding of this world. Ginger might make me work for it, but she doesn't seem the type to be dishonest.

Taking a deep breath, I blow it out before asking, "So what's going on with the men being servants here? Are none of them really in charge?"

She slowly turns her head to peer at me over a muscular shoulder, then clicks her tongue in admonishment. "Saira. You really are obvious about not being from around here. *Really* obvious."

"So I'm told," I mumble. Strike two, I guess.

Instead of answering, she points a long nail at the ground toward a blue bucket with different grooming tools inside. I acquiesce and dump the currycomb in favor of a regular brush, then walk to her hind end.

"You better not kick me," I mutter. Her legs shift, and one of her hooves rises back in threat.

I jump back, and she laughs. "Just kidding, BB, I swear."

My glare only makes her smile wider. "You owe me an answer now."

She shrugs and giggles. "Fine, fine. Payla consists of eight provinces: Ilorna, Prinapalese, Cape Schrute, Raeland, Myea, Sealoury, Taelarue, and Vulturia. About a hundred years ago, it was a patriarchal society. The males made all the decisions. But they were terrible at it. Male Amicums are more predisposed to violence, and they wielded violence freely."

At the mention of Vulturia, my ears perk up. That must be where Vulturians come from.

With a steady tone, I ask, "How did it all change?"

"The Culling."

A chill creeps down my spine. "What's the Culling?"

She pauses in the middle of a braid. It's the first time I've seen her contemplate what she's about to say. "The females across seven provinces grew tired of the subjugation. And they ..." She turns to look at me. "Are you sure you want to hear this?"

I bite my lip. This is going to be bad. I nod anyway as I gently intertwine the strands of hair in her tail. Making sure she's not watching, I pocket a handful of her strands. The perfect Amicum sample.

Ginger cringes. "Somehow, all the females, or at least enough of them, planned a coup by culling all the aggressive males in power. Mates and acquaintances alike took it upon themselves to cull, at minimum, one male."

I do a double-take at her words. Did she really just say what I think she did? I choke out in shock, "Mates *killed* each other?"

Ginger's eyes bulge, and she waves her hands, dismissing the notion. "Oh, no, these were forced matings. Females didn't have the freedom of choice back then. Now, we can all freely love one another, but in that time, females were nothing more than vessels for males. Once the females regained power, they established the matriarchy we have now."

While home is better than when Dad was my age, men still take charge of a lot of things. The history books I devoured as a kid told stories about the folly of man. How they almost destroyed our planet. Somehow, enough men and women banded together to make a difference through aggressive policies. It was hard-won progress.

Satisfied with the braid in her tail, I affectionately pat her butt. "So now the males are slaves?"

Ginger laughs. "No, the males aren't slaves. We bred out most of the aggressive males through selective consent, and they naturally became more interested in supporting females. Each province has its own guidelines and laws for male's shifting. In Ilorna, it has been mostly banned, save for some exceptions. However, some provinces like Raeland have bare minimum guidelines — it's been messy recently."

In college, one of my biology professors was obsessed with a primate species called bonobos. They'd been extinct for a handful of years at that point, but he always raved about their relationship dynamics. How they refused to mate with aggressive males, thus having more submissive male offspring. Turns out, the professor had an unhealthy obsession with their sexual mating habits. Let's just say he lost his job due to content on his hard drives.

Shaking off the memory, I consider what to ask her next. On the topic of sex, it brings up my curiosity about consorts. "So Legend is Kalliope's sex servant or something?"

Ginger eyes me curiously, looking down at me. I wonder what I look like from her seven-foot-tall perspective. "Why would you think he's just there for sex?"

I roll my eyes. "Probably because it's all he implies."

Ginger shakes her head, making a smooth transition from having a horse's rear end back to her two legs in a rainbow shimmer. Now I'm the one staring down at her heart-shaped face.

"Legend is Kalliope's consort, but it goes deeper. They've been friends for almost their entire lives. Their mothers were both killed in the last Vulturian war."

"So they're going to be together forever?"

Ginger flings a strand of hair over her shoulder as she walks toward the door to the barn. "No, they won't be together forever because they aren't 'together' like that. We are a society built on the appreciation of bodies, sex, and living a life that feels true to us. If Legend decides to back out of his oath tomorrow, Kalliope will let him. But why would he? It's all he ever wanted. Kalliope is his everything."

I trail behind her, contemplating the revelations. "Is monogamy important here?"

Ginger slows to walk next to me and peers up at me quizzically. "What's moneyagamy?"

"Monogamy. When you're with one person only, ever."

Ginger's giggle is melodic as she slaps my shoulder with the back of her hand. "Oh, Saira. You say the funniest things sometimes. That sounds like such a bore. One person ever? No, thank you."

"But Legend sounds monogamous," I insist. "Like Kalliope is his sole focus."

She tilts her head, expression still alight with amusement. "Do not confuse loyalty with never wanting to enjoy the variety that life can provide. One could argue that this montronomy sounds restrictive and cruel."

"Monogamy," I correct her. "And some say it's romantic."

She snorts. "Well, I certainly could never. And I assure you, Legend has no compunctions about pleasuring others. Kalliope tends to focus on the well-being of her people and doesn't often join Legend in his escapades, but it's not an anomaly."

My imagination runs wild for a second, but I shove the dirty thoughts away. Instead, I think back to the way Kalliope walks among everyone, remembering their names and goals.

"Watching her interact with others, she makes it seem like everyone is important."

Ginger stops at the door I came out of earlier. The sun is past its apex, the warm afternoon light casting shadows across the barnyard. "Yes, that's Kalliope. Her mother left a large space in the world when she was killed. I think Kalliope is always trying to find ways to fill that space. To live up to some standard we don't know about."

"So how do you know if you're important to her?"

Ginger opens the door but pauses before going inside. Her gaze is assessing as she says, "I assure you, Saira. You'll know when you're important to her."

Chapter Fourteen

Yeah, I'm Doomed

G inger leaves me at the doorway, waving toward a long hallway on our left. "I need to go do some boring paperwork to get more hay delivered, but if you head down that way, you're bound to find something interesting."

The urge to hug her is strong, but I've never hugged a naked woman, so instead, I wave a hand awkwardly and say, "Thank you for the enlightening education, Ginger. It really helped me understand some things."

She smirks and bobs her head with self-satisfaction. "Don't tell anyone I gossiped, or I'll turn into a wasp and sting you until you cry."

"You can't take a compliment, can you?"

She sashays away, but says over her shoulder, "Oh, I can take a compliment. But no law says I have to do it with grace."

I snort with amusement and shake my head as I walk in the suggested direction. Ginger is an odd duck. At least she answered some of my questions. So far, Ilorna seems like a relatively positive place. There's still so much to learn, though, especially about these Vulturians I keep hearing about.

I get so lost in my thoughts, I stop paying attention to where I'm going. This manor is bigger than it looks. I think whoever designed the hallways was determined to make them a maze. Ginger wasn't specific about where she was sending me, so I'm not even sure what I'm looking for.

As I make my fourth right turn, I hit a wall of soft flesh. Stumbling back, I immediately apologize. "I'm so sorry, I'm lost and ..."

I peer up at Legend. He's wearing a loose tunic split down his sternum, tucked into form-fitting leathery pants. His eyes scan the hallway, then back to me. "You're wandering around by yourself?"

"Yeah, I was hanging out with Ginger, and she made me braid her horsehair, and I've never brushed a centaur, and that was weird, and I got lost in the manor. And now I've bumped into you and,"—I take a breath—"rambled."

The more I say, the bigger his smile gets. He must think I'm the town idiot, like Ginger said the first time we met. Will I ever stop being so awkward around everyone?

His voice has more than a hint of laughter as he says, "Ginger conned you into braiding her tail?"

"Yeah, and it was weird. She shifted, and the tail was gone, so what's the point?"

He steps closer. Close enough for his purely male scent to fill my nose. The urge to create more space between us is strong. He crosses his arms, and I get the distinct impression he's holding back from touching me. "It's a sign of respect from one Amicum to another."

"Braiding tails?"

He smirks. "Grooming each other. She now owes you a grooming."

The idea of Ginger trying to groom me makes me grimace. "With her sense of humor, I'm not sure I'd appreciate her grooming."

He chuckles. "Ask Daeva about the time Ginger butchered her hair."

I bark out a laugh. "Sorry," I say. "That's ridiculous."

Legend hooks a thumb into a pocket, the picture of ease. "Yes, it was. The two can't stand each other now."

Big surprise. "How weird, because they're both so pleasant."

It's Legend's turn to laugh. It's husky and makes my skin tingle. His eyes shine with mischief. "They have their redeeming qualities, I promise."

"Even Daeva?"

Legend scrunches his nose in distaste. "Yes, even Daeva." He looks around. "You don't have an escort? Truly?"

I look down at my feet, flexing my toes nervously. "I thought it was alright. I didn't go into any rooms or touch anything."

"Saira." His voice is so patient. Looking up, I find nothing but compassion in his eyes. "You aren't restricted anywhere. But this manor is a maze. Literally. Kalliope's great-aunt got some flea up her hind end, and she had extra rooms and hallways put in. For no reason."

Explains why I can't seem to make any progress. "So where are you going?"

Legend looks down at me. "You mean before you ran into me like a deranged jackalope?"

Grunting out a sound of protest, I scowl. "Excuse me? You bumped into *me*. I was minding my business, being lost. I have a right to do that, you know."

"You have a right to be lost?"

I cross my arms. "Of course. If I want to be completely lost and confused, that's my right."

A twitch tugs at the corner of his mouth. "Is this a law where you're from? It sounds stressful."

Well, he's got me there. "No, it's not a law. And you're not answering my question."

He spins on his heels and begins to walk away. I jog to catch up. He moves fast. Noticing me struggling, he slows down. "I was headed to your room, actually. To see if you'd like to have a late lunch with me and Kalliope."

His response renders me speechless. Who are these people, welcoming me with open arms like this? With such kindness? I can't tell if it's a good thing to be immediately suspicious of someone being nice to me.

"Uh, yeah. I'd like that. When is it?"

"Now," he says simply, "I'll take you to her private chambers. She'll join us shortly."

Panic flares. I've spent the day in the garden and the barn. Their sensitive sense of smell makes me paranoid. "Wait, shouldn't I shower or something? I stink."

He chuckles and leans forward. He takes a deep inhale near the nape of my neck. "You smell divine, Gem." He straightens and gives me a devilish wink. "Come as you are."

Gem? Has he given me a nickname? The double entendre is unmistakable. My cheeks flush, which only makes his grin broaden. This male is a bit too bold for my comfort, but I don't want to show it more than I already have. "Alright, lead the way."

Legend nods and places a hand on my lower back, steering me in the opposite direction. Within a minute, we're in front of a simple wooden door. He turns the nob, and the door swings open, revealing a plain-looking room.

Where mine is based on comfortable opulence, this room is focused on spartan comfortability. The walls are sparse, minus a beautiful painting. The bed, which reaches from wall to wall, has various sheets and blankets laying across it.

I want to go look at the painting, but the candlelit table catches my eye. Three chairs circle around a smaller table with platters of food already placed in the center. A silver pitcher sits on a side table next to three silver goblets. On the opposite wall, French doors open onto a wide balcony, overlooking undeveloped land warmed by late-afternoon light.

The door closes quietly behind us, and I turn to watch Legend strut across the room toward the pitcher. My stomach rumbles.

He motions to an empty chair and pours a golden liquid into a goblet. "Please have a seat. Would you like some wine?"

"For lunch?"

He flashes a grin. "Are you implying there's an inappropriate time for wine?"

I wrinkle my nose. "For breakfast?"

Legend places the full goblet in front of me and taps the table with a finger to emphasize his next words. "Wine is a state of mind, not a time of day."

While he fills the other two goblets, I take a tentative sip of my wine. It's sweet and light, tasting like a bright summer day. "This is delicious."

He gives me a knowing smile as he sits, placing Kalliope's goblet in front of the empty chair. "It's from my family's vineyard."

"Explains why you drink it for breakfast," I retort, grinning as I take another sip.

He tilts his head back and gives a full belly laugh. It's rich and smooth, like if melted chocolate was a sound. I can't help but laugh with him. Legend is just easy.

He raises his goblet. "To wine at any time."

I tip my goblet to his, letting them tap. "To embracing alcoholism."

As I continue to sip my drink, Legend begins slicing a crispy loaf of bread, and I watch as he adds a piece to each plate. Then, he plucks grapes from a cut vine, placing equal amounts on each plate.

Like with Ginger, I realize this is an excellent time to ask questions. Some of the things Ginger said have piqued my interest when it comes to the dynamics of the sexes here.

Taking one more sip of wine to gird my mental loins, I ask, "So what exactly do you do as a consort for Kalliope?"

Without missing a beat, Legend peels a fruit that looks like an orange as he says, "Subjugate myself to her evil whims whenever the mood strikes. And brush her hair."

I bite my lips together, suppressing a grin. When I'm positive I won't start laughing, I say, "That seems to be a very well-rounded task list."

His mouth twitches. "With Kalliope, a lot of things are very well rounded."

This time, the laugh escapes. "Is that all you do? Provide her sex and funny quips?"

Mirth-filled eyes flick to mine as he methodically peels the orange. "Being a consort can be many things for a male. Some are not sexual at all. My dynamic with Kalliope is always negotiable, as it should be."

Tossing chunks of orange onto the table, he continues. "Some days, I offer companionship through easing burdens and offering advice. Otherwise,"—he waggles his eyebrows suggestively—"I do whatever Her Grace desires. Evil whims and all."

This male is the embodiment of roguish sexuality. "And this is all you want to do for your whole life?"

He shakes his head, placing orange slices in a pattern on Kalliope's plate, making the arrangement look like a flower. "Most likely not. For now, this is what I choose. Males have plenty of choices. My own sire is a musician. My grandsire established the winery and still tends the land."

He pauses, making small adjustments to the presentation of Kalliope's food, tweaking the placement of fruit. "In a few years, I might pursue being a Guardian or open a shop offering the finest ingredients to the townspeople. I'm not restricted because of my sex. Serving Kalliope and making her happy is a privilege."

I think of the history books of the world I know, sharing a different experience inside the patriarchy. Maybe our civilization wouldn't have failed so spectacularly, time and time again, if we'd given women control.

"Where I'm from, the women are regulated to a more sexualized existence." My cheeks burn hot, and I look away. "Not that I have a lot of experience with that or anything. I'm not the type of person to ..." I don't want to come off as slut shaming, when all I want to say is that I'm a lame wallflower. Being a virgin at my age is ridiculous. Dating was simply never a priority.

One year fell after the other, one-hundred percent focused on school and research. For late nights, there was a cot Dad and I took turns sleeping on. The only person who could get me out of the lab regularly was Piper. She always made sure I didn't spend every waking second with my nose in a book.

Legend can't know about this, though. Someone like him doesn't want anything to do with someone like me. A virgin nerd.

Oh, god. That's what I am. *A virgin nerd.* The thought actually makes me want to cry. I've never regretted my hard work, and I never will, but it's like I've turned my life into a conduit of others' hopes and dreams. Mom. Dad. Even Piper, who always hoped I'd become a little more like her. More outgoing. A drinking buddy.

I feel like an adult infant, stumbling through life like a ping-pong, going where pointed. If I hadn't been born to two scientists, both existing with the same goal, would I even be a scientist? A *virgin* scientist? *Ugh.* Why am I suddenly so hung up on that? Until this moment, alone with an extremely attractive male who's trying to flirt with me, it never bothered me.

It's giving me pause because I never considered what could be gained from this adventure, other than the obvious mission goals. It's an opportunity to learn more about myself and maybe even step closer to who I want to be.

But who do I want to be?

Life hasn't presented an opportunity for me to consider this question. Everything was mapped out from the moment I escaped the birth canal.

So, who do I want to be?

I want to keep being the Bad Bitch Scientist, but I also want to live a little. To experience this journey with optimism and confidence. Someone not afraid to speak up.

This journey was not the end of something, or even the beginning. It's a continuation of everything I am or will be. Quantum theory says everything that has been or can be already is. You just need to choose your timeline.

I refocus back on the moment, lost in my head for a minute. Legend watches me think, chewing on an apple. Tentative confidence works its way up my body, relaxing my muscles.

Legend tilts his head with curiosity. "Looks like you had a lot of thoughts for a moment there, Gem."

Okay, this nickname is growing on me. Taking a deep breath in, then blowing it out, I admit, "This isn't the kind of life I normally lead. I've always been obsessed with work, so I haven't exactly appreciated the value of really living. I was thinking about how nice everyone seems." Daeva's sour face pops into my mind's eye. "Almost everyone."

Legend's mouth twitches. "How long have you been traveling?"

As he pours me more wine, I hedge my response. "Not long actually. A little over a week."

He whistles, sitting back in his chair. "Less than a fortnight and already avoided being a snack? That must be some sort of record."

Legend laughs at my stuck-out tongue. My voice is a bit whiny when I say, "Will that be the running joke now?"

"Depends. Does a bear shit in the woods?"

I pick up a roll and toss it at him. He snatches it up, grinning as he takes a smug bite. "Are you a dad joke person?"

He scrunches his nose. "Dad joke?"

"Yeah, like a really corny joke teller. The kind of jokes that are obvious and annoyingly funny."

Finishing the roll, Legend contemplates. "I guess the better question is, when is a door not a door?"

My chest warms. Biting back a grin, I ask, "When?"

"When it's ajar."

We stare at each other for a count of five, then burst into laughter. Okay, so he's a dad joke guy. Could be worse. He could be into collecting Kalliope's hair into little balls. Actually, the way he looks at her — that's not unrealistic.

When our laughter dies, we sit in silence for a moment, making eye contact that is slightly uncomfortable. It's weird to make direct eye contact with a too-handsome stranger. Especially if I'm not entirely sure actual hearts haven't sprung from my eyeballs.

Alarm bells tinkle quietly — I muffle them with a mental wet blanket. It's fine. This is still all part of The Mission. Even if I hope to shelve The Mission for an afternoon. Or two. Maybe three.

Trying to steer the conversation back to what I need to know, I ask, "So everything seems pretty great here, but I heard something called Vulturians mentioned this morning. What are those?"

Legend's eyes, sparkling only moments before, darken. His jaw clenches as his chest rises, taking a deep breath. I'm not sure what I've said that could be so upsetting. He didn't react like this at breakfast.

"I'm sorry," I rush to say. "I didn't mean to ask something upsetting."

His jaw unclenches, and he blows out a shaky breath. "It's fine. The Vulturians are a touchy subject around here. A lot of us lost loved ones, and the land suffered. We've only just recovered." He pauses, swirling wine in his cup. "The eighth province is Vulturia. While it's the largest province, it also doesn't have Amicums, nor do they engage in trade with any other province. It's an isolationist, patriarchal culture with a true monarchy."

His lush mouth sets in a grim line. "Eleven years ago, the former king started a war over one-forms. Their religion insists on consuming non-magic people because of reasons I've never cared to learn. However, they began raiding towns and villages, stealing entire families. The provinces came together and demanded the Vulturians either leave the one-forms alone, or the next attack would be considered an act of war."

Legend gives me a sardonic smile. "One guess what they chose."

Thoughts catapult against the confines of my skull. There's so much to digest. The war sounds brutal. The one question on the tip of my tongue is ... could it happen again?

The conversation comes to an end at the sound of a knock on the door. We both look over to watch the door swing open, and Kalliope pops her head around the side. Her aura's radiant, reminding me of sunshine on a warm summer day.

Would sex with her be like licking a sweet popsicle in a warm breeze? Or will it be like stepping into a cold pool on a scorching summer afternoon, both refreshing and shocking, all at once?

Okay, that's enough of that. It doesn't matter, because we're not having sex. I'll gather data and leave in a few days.

Blinking quickly, I shake the thoughts out of my head. To my chagrin, Kalliope notices my dazed response.

"Am I interrupting?" she teases, unaware of the thoughts in my head and the conversation we were having.

133

Legend stands and steps up to her chair, pulling it out. "Of course not. Come, I've been preparing lunch."

Kalliope closes the door and rushes to the table. A thin line of sweat beads on her hairline. She must've been running all over the place. "Thank Inanna, I'm famished. I swear, Lordess Charlyn is determined to win an award for the most stubborn female in Payla."

Legend helps her sit, scooting in the chair as Kalliope sinks into the cushioned seat. He kisses the top of her head before sitting down again.

"How did the trade negotiations turn out?"

Kalliope's eyes flick to mine before she says, "She wants to trade more of her land's minerals in return for an increase in sentry allocation, but no matter how much I explain we do not need the amount of ore she's insisting is a fair trade, she won't accept my refusal."

Legend contemplates her words as he takes a bite of bread. Eager to hear more about the dynamics of trade, I stay silent as I butter the slice Legend placed on my plate.

Finally, he asks, "Do you believe we could find a use for the minerals? Even if it means stockpiling for the future?"

Kalliope takes a sip of her wine, glancing at me again before saying, "Perhaps. It's always good to consider the long-term vision. I'm not keen on kowtowing to her demands, though."

Curiosity gets the better of me. "What kinds of minerals?"

Both of their attentions turn to me. Legend looks to Kalliope, deferring to her. She shrugs and flicks a hand dismissively. "Malignite. Pileon. Chalron."

Okay, no clue what any of that is, but new minerals could lead to more scientific discoveries. "Do you have any of that available for me to look at?"

They wear matching expressions of confusion as Kalliope slowly nods. "Yes. But what use are they to you?"

My shrug of nonchalance's stilted. "Just curious, is all."

They exchange a look, saying nothing. I've pushed too far. They know if I were from around here, needing to see these minerals wouldn't be necessary. For all I know, they're as common as coal or quartz.

Legend is the first to break the silence. "With Kalliope's permission, I believe some bits can be scrounged up."

Kalliope doesn't confirm or deny the request. Her eyes never leave my face. A bead of sweat trickles down my spine as I display an expression of innocence. Legend's attention flicks between her and me in an almost-comical manner. For the first time, it feels like she's not observing me as an unknown guest, but as a stranger.

The tension gnaws at my nerves. Unable to stand the silence any longer, I say quietly, "I'm sorry, was that considered offensive?"

"These are minerals used in the materials we use daily." Kalliope's tone is quiet and cautious.

Dread drags against my insides. "Everywhere?"

She nods once. "Everywhere."

Well, damn. Maybe curiosity kills the scientist sometimes.

Chapter Fifteen

"Material Unknown"

Dad and I knew we might stick out like sore thumbs in certain places. It can't be helped — we don't belong anywhere. However, as Kalliope stares at me, expressionless, I find my hand nervously fluttering to Mom's ring. Touching it offers a modicum of comfort.

Kalliope misses nothing and sees me twisting the wedding band. Her lips thin, and the blood in my veins ices over. This is it; this is when I'm burned at the stake.

Legend shifts in his chair, watching Kalliope uneasily, which only heightens my nervousness. Is this where they try to tie me up and throw me onto a pyre? Oh, gods, I can't burn to death. I'll die bald. I can't die bald.

Legend sees my panicked expression and leans into Kalliope, gently touching her arm. "Kal."

That's all it takes. One word. She jerks her attention to him as if breaking out of a reverie. The tension snaps. She smiles at me as if we hadn't just had a silent, yet tense standoff.

"Of course, Legend can have some bits of mineral sent to your quarters. Most people haven't seen them in their raw forms, so I can understand the interest."

A little voice in my head tells me this won't be the end of her curiosity, but I offer a grateful look, anyway. "Thank you. I appreciate it."

Kalliope plucks a berry off her plate, throwing it up in the air and catching it with her mouth. She's a picture of relaxation, but I'm not fooled. Something tells me she isn't a lordess simply because she's nice to everyone.

My hand shakes as I reach for the remaining bits of bread on my plate. If they notice, neither says anything.

Instead, Legend refills our glasses and says, "Apparently, our sweet Ginger convinced Saira to give her a good tail braid."

Kalliope barks out a laugh and flashes a wicked grin. "I knew she'd find a way to keep you busy."

My shoulders relax a fraction. "At least I didn't have to clean up manure with my bare hands."

She dips her head in agreement. "I never thought she would actually do that, but yes, she can be quite inventive when she wishes."

The rest of lunch passes by without any other tense moments, but for the first time since I arrived, I'm more guarded. Honestly, I feel naïve, too. Manipulation, especially in conversations, has never been my thing. I need to be asking questions, but outright seeking information has already proven to make me stick out even more. Hopefully, as this experience continues, it'll get easier.

That, or it'll get me killed. Only time will tell.

My earlier confidence is now crushed, and my thoughts darken. This is all too much. The deception; the lies; the loneliness. I want to be honest, truly, but I can't risk jeopardizing my purpose. Silly me, assuming that my introverted tendencies meant this wouldn't be a lonely experience. I took Piper's friendship for granted, never realizing how much pressure she alleviated as my live-in support system. I'd give anything to call her up and ask for advice.

But she's dead. And I'm here. Alone.

As Legend regales me with a story from their childhood, I nod and react at the right times, but secretly, I want to cry. It's the overwhelm of the last week catching up. The more Legend chuckles, the more I crave curling up into bed for the rest of the day.

137

The moment there's a lull in the conversation, I clear my throat. "Um, I'm pretty tired. Do you think it'll be alright if I go relax in my room?"

Kalliope's eyebrows jump. "Yes, of course. You've already had quite the day."

Legend nods. "I can walk you to your room if you'd—"

"I can do it," Kalliope cuts him off, taking one last sip of wine before standing. "Why don't you go greet the remaining consorts that have arrived?"

Oh. I'd really hoped they'd let me walk alone. I'm not sure I want to spend time alone with Kalliope right now. What if she keeps asking questions and Legend isn't here to step in?

But I can't say anything because to say I want to be alone would be rude.

Legend bobs his head in acknowledgement. "Of course." He steps up to me as I stand and offers the barest flutter of a kiss on my cheek before he's stepping back in front of Kalliope. He grabs her chin with just the right amount of roughness. She melts into the kiss he presses against her lips. Letting go, he gives her a wolfish grin. With one final look my way, he says, "I'll see you tomorrow, Saira."

Feeling awkward, I lift a hand in farewell. "I look forward to it."

With a wink in my direction, Legend heads out the door. Kalliope and I trail behind. Closing the door behind us, Kalliope motions for me to follow her. She doesn't appear to be angry or even irritated. Instead of asking more questions about my origins, she takes the time to point out pieces of art on the wall.

It's interesting to observe another culture's take on paintings and their portrayal of Amicums. There are pastoral scenes right next to scenes of battle. Some show large families with tiny cubs in their parent's arms, or singular portraits of female leaders. It makes me itch to bring out my camera.

One oil painting gives me pause. It's an enormous work of art, taller than Legend, depicting a scene of Amicums battling against enormous, demon-like beings. They fight on an emerald green field, with clusters of flowers here and there, each dotted with flecks of blood.

It's the creatures that capture my attention. They're gray and muscular, with a crown of horns jutting out of their square heads. Each holds a spear or blade, fighting Amicums of all kinds.

In the center of the painting, one of the demons is taking on a gigantic black wolf. Even though I have to crane my neck to peer up at the scene, it's large enough that I can make out the spittle from the wolf's mouth that the artist included. Blood covers them, most of it spilling from the gray creature's throat.

"This painting depicts the last Vulturian battle ten years ago."

Connecting the dots, I point to the raging black wolf. "Is that your mother in the center?"

She looks away, clasping her hands behind her back. "Yes. She died in this battle after fighting the Vulturian King." Her lips thin. "But not before tearing out his throat, which the artist decided to show here."

"That's awful," I murmur, taking in the scene again. It shows so much death and fury, even though the sky is a cerulean blue with puffy white clouds. A jarring juxtaposition. Maybe the artist intended that.

"Indeed. A lot of legacies and wisdom were lost in that war. Which is why I'll do everything possible not to engage if it isn't irrefutably necessary." Kalliope walks away, forcing me to give the painting one last glance before trotting to catch up.

The tour finally ends at my door. My forgotten anxiety resurfaces, making my hands shake. My begrudging crush has been evolving since we met in the woods. She's intimidating with her honesty, loyalty, and even friendliness. She's observing me like I'm a piece of art she's trying to learn; I simply don't know how to handle or process it. Her sunbeam-colored eyes skate over my face as if searching for clues.

I lean against the doorway, trying to look nonchalant, but instead, lose my footing. She shifts closer, following my movement. This close, I can make out her distinct floral scent with hints of campfire.

The urge to beg for a kiss is overwhelming. Is this how people feel when they're really into someone? I want her to kiss me so badly it hurts. Not just that — I want to seize a moment worth living for.

Plus, learning how Amicums kiss is strictly for science, right? There are definitely sciency things to explore.

The ridiculous trope of the crush slowly licking their lips and the main character swooning? Yeah, that's me. When she licks her lips, I let out the tiniest whimper. I cough, hoping to cover the sound. When she does it again, it's clearly on purpose.

Kiss me! Kiss me! Kiss me!

If I mentally chant it enough, I can manifest it into existence. She leans her head closer. My lungs turn to stone. This isn't my first kiss — if the awkward kiss with Melanie Buckson in the eighth grade counts — but I've never been so excited for one.

Except it never comes. Instead, her fingers brush against my temple as she tucks a strand of hair behind the shell of my ear. "Tomorrow, Legend will come and escort you to the party. Prior, a dress will be delivered, and some of my personal stylists will arrive and attend to you."

A dress? Stylists? What reality are we in? Brain scrambling like a dog on slick tile, I shake my head to refocus. Her words process and make me frown. "It's really, *really* fancy tomorrow?"

She smiles. "You could say that. Don't worry. This afternoon, I personally picked out your dress and accessories. Meadow will be there for support. You're in good hands."

"It sounds expensive." Will they turn me into an indentured servant? Washing dishes for chiffon? I don't even know if I like chiffon. Or the dress.

She gives a firm shake of her head. "Do not worry about it. Consider it a gift."

Confused, I say, "But you barely know me. That's such an extravagant gift for someone you don't know."

Kalliope looks unamused. "It's just money, Saira. Have you ever been to a party like this?"

"No, but I don't know what 'a party like this' even means."

When she leans in, I swallow hard. Strands of silky auburn hair tickle my nose as she whispers in my ear, "Then I suppose you shall find out tomorrow."

I swear I just time traveled out of orbit because *excuse me?* She has no business being this ... this *desirable*. With the briefest of kisses landing on my cheek, Kalliope turns and walks down the hallway, leaving me dizzy. I can barely find my senses to open the bedroom door.

Closing it behind me, I lean against the wood. No, there were zero plans to get frisky or catch feelings on this trip. I need to figure out how to try to stay even a *little* impartial.

Right. So, time to focus on The Mission.

Pushing off the door, I head over to the armoire and take out the analyzer. Pulling Ginger's hair from my pocket, I twist the hairs into a tight ball and place it into the small receiving drawer. Then laugh, because this is what I imagined Legend does with Kalliope's hair.

Pressing some commands, the machine whirs, analyzing the material. Within a minute, the data spits out, and I eagerly scroll through the information.

From Ginger's hair, I discover that we share about seventy percent of our DNA. It explains how they look like humans, but that's where the similarities stop. "Material Unknown" comes up in so many sections, I deflate.

I'd hoped that I could unlock the mysteries of their shifting and cancer-fighting properties, but it looks like I'll have to bring back samples on top of analyzing them.

One way or another, I'll figure out if this is a place my family will love.

Chapter Sixteen

Competing With Frogs For Flies

Today is the day I'm transformed into a pretty, pretty princess, and I'm not sure how to react. Should there be excitement? Guilt? Anxiety? All three?

All day, the sensation of butterflies on cocaine bounces around in my rib cage. I've read my fair share of romance novels. One of my favorite fairy tales is Beauty and the Beast. How she went from living a quiet life to being Stockholm'd by the beast. A rich, well-groomed beast.

In a way, if you squint hard enough, this is kind of like Beauty and the Beast — if he was a she, started off hot, then occasionally became the beast.

A prep team arrives mid-afternoon, sweeping into the room like glittery tornados. Full of questions. Not many one-forms come to the manor. From their friendly inquisition, I gather that while there isn't any current animosity, the two species tend to keep to themselves. They ask me some of the most interesting questions, such as "What is it like to never be anything different for your whole life?"

I didn't know how to answer that one.

My dress has yet to arrive, but everyone assumes it's okay. They don't know what it looks like either, so they decide to make my makeup a little more neutral in case the dress is flashy.

I had no clue it takes this long to get hair and makeup done. My back aches from sitting up for so long. The artists share court gossip, their voices filling the space, allowing me to stay silent.

The makeup artist, Bealina, is covered in an intricate pattern of leopard and giraffe spots running up her arms and over her shoulders. She's been chattering with Zinia, the hairstylist, who keeps tugging on my hair with brushes and braids. Their gossip doesn't add much more to what I've already learned about Ilorna.

Bealina finishes adding one more layer of lipstick when there's a knock at the door. It swings open without invitation.

It's Meadow, holding a plain-looking garment bag draped over her arms. A sleek dress made of iridescent black and silver material has replaced her crimson maid's outfit. It's simple attire, still covering her body up to her neck and down her arms, but it's beautiful.

She notices my anxious expression and clucks her tongue. "Don't worry, miss. We'll have you ready in no time."

"Wasn't worried at all," I lie.

She leaves the door open as she sweeps past the threshold, straight down to business. Bealina and Zinia pack up, each giving Meadow a quick curtsy. I call out a thank you, and they flash grateful looks before bolting out of the room, closing the door behind them.

Meadow bustles over to the wardrobe and floor-length mirror, hanging a garment bag on a wrought iron hook. She whirls to face where I'm sitting in front of a makeshift beauty station. She shakes her head in disbelief.

"Miss, I know you're shy, but Legend will be here any minute. I assume you'd prefer to be dressed by then?"

Standing awkwardly, I scurry over, cheeks flushing. Getting undressed in front of strangers is one of my least favorite things. Even for doctors. "Sorry," I mumble. She turns back to the garment bag and unzips it.

There are moments in life where you know things will be different forever. Like when Dad announced his invention of the Scout, or the

143

day Mom revealed her illness. The day I told Piper I was leaving her to die.

The fourth is right now. As Meadow peels apart the garment bag, allowing a cascade of shimmering gold twinkle in the firelight. She gently removes it, and I've never felt so insufficient in my life.

It's layers of sparkling chiffon attached to a corset-style bodice with sheer fabric. The corset plunges deeply, held up by delicate chains. The bottom of the bodice contains layers of gilded chiffon fluttering as she holds it up in the air.

Peering around the dress, Meadow frowns. "Miss?"

It's a struggle to breathe through the butterflies creating a racket in my belly. There's no way my body will be able to pull this off. She's too confident. But I undress anyway, avoiding the possible judgment in her gaze.

She's unfazed as I stand naked in front of her, my nipples squeezing painfully in the slight chill. Saving the universe requires me to be naked in front of strangers — yeah, I didn't expect this. Meadow unclips the back of the bodice and kneels in front of me. I step into it, and she slides it up. It catches on my hips, but she gently tugs, and it continues smoothly upward.

My arms slip into the gold chains, but to my surprise, they aren't there to support the dress. They hang loosely against my bare shoulders.

The boning in the bodice is supportive enough to stay up without help. The opening shows the curves of my breasts, but the sheer layers of material obscure my dusky nipples.

Meadow stands, prowling around me, examining the dress. There's a tug at my back as she straightens it, but it doesn't get pulled tighter. I can breathe while the corset still flatters my figure.

I'm afraid to look in the mirror. This dress already makes me feel beautiful, but there's no way it's *that* perfect. There's no way I somehow have a gold dress, going to my reverse UNO Beast's soireé. That would simply be too ironic. And iconic.

"Do you like it?" she asks, coming around to face me. When I don't respond, she grabs my arm and pulls me to stand in front of the mirror.

I squeeze my eyes shut. The hard truth may crush me, because I want this dress to be beautiful. I've never actually felt beautiful before. Truly beautiful.

"Don't hide from yourself." Meadow's soft command startles me, and they fly open.

The woman in the reflection is breathtaking. Her dark hair falls to one side in Hollywood waves. Lips the color of fresh blood. Kohl-lined eyelids. A dusting of glitter shimmered on her dark skin. When she moves, I move. This reflection is ... of me. This is me.

I've sprinted past beautiful and landed firmly in the goddess-realm.

Tears blur my vision as she places a diadem on my head. It's made of gilded leaves and swirling vines. They meet in the middle to hold a teardrop-shaped ruby. It probably costs more than I've ever made or will make.

Dressing up or even applying effort into my appearance has never been a priority. At home, I wore thrifted clothing and genuinely didn't give a shit if things coordinated. I've never owned a tube of mascara, let alone something with glittering gems on it. This feels monumental in a way I can't explain.

"Thank you," I whisper to Meadow. She waves my gratitude away with the flip of a wrist and walks back to the garment bag to remove a velvet box. Opening it, she pulls out a glittering pair of heels.

She leans down again and helps me step into each one. I'm taller by a couple of inches, adding length to my legs.

"I look beautiful." My voice cracks as I press my hands against my hips, admiring the way they flare and curve.

"Everyone deserves to look and feel beautiful, Saira." Meadow's voice is soft and contemplative. She adjusts one of my curls. Her matronly care softens my emotions even further. I'm about to thank her again until she says, "But you should thank Her Grace. She picked this dress out for you."

I look back at my reflection, mesmerized. Piper's gold necklace against my sternum, far too simple in comparison. She'd die of jealousy if she saw this dress. This outfit is so far out of my comfort zone, she wouldn't believe someone convinced me to wear it.

The Scout is now disguised as a simple gold bangle, matching the simplicity of Mom's ring on my finger. The necklace, ring, and bangle are simple, but maybe that's a good thing. This dress is so beautiful; it's a statement all on its own.

I'm so enthralled with my reflection, I don't hear Meadow leave the room until the door closes.

All there is to do now is wait for Legend to show up and escort me to the party. A rush of giddiness makes me clap my hands and laugh. Feeling silly, I busy my hands by double checking everything. I gasp with excitement when an idea appears. Rushing over to my pack, I dig until my hands touch a familiar object. Pulling it out, I lean it against a table and set the timer. Stepping back, I wait for the camera's countdown as I grab some chiffon between the tips of my fingers and flare out the skirt.

There's a flash of light, and I rush to the camera, then stuff it back into the pack. At least I'll be able to show Piper when I see her again.

I finish zipping up the backpack when there's another knock on the door. A spark of adrenaline jolts me upward. Staring at the door, I attempt to slow my breaths, but it's no use. Whatever's on the other side of that door is adrenaline worthy.

Taking a deep breath and blowing it out, I open the door.

I'm greeted with a bare chest with a lovely speckling of chest hair. Legend's wearing a thick black leather collar connected by straps laying across his broad shoulders.

At the ends of the straps, thin, black chains swoop back to the center of his chest, draping together in the middle. They each fall into progressively shorter chains, the shortest meeting up at the collar again.

He drinks me in with a lazy appraisal. And if I'm not mistaken, appreciation as well. "May Inanna have mercy on me."

Heat warms my body as I look down, trying not to bite my lip. The last thing I need is lipstick on my teeth. "Is it alright? Meadow seemed so sure it looked good, but I'm not sure."

His finger lifts my chin up. The softness in his expression smooths out my nerves. "You look like a goddess."

I knew it. My chin raises with newfound confidence, and the tweaking butterflies in my belly chill for a moment.

I take in the rest of his outfit. No shoes, but leather pants hug his powerful thighs. His hair is more polished than normal, tied back with a thin piece of leather.

"You don't look too shabby yourself."

Maybe it's my imagination, but I'm pretty sure he flexes as he offers an arm. "Let's go make some Amicums jealous, shall we?"

"Yes, let's shall." I loop my arm through his, closing the door behind me. His arm is bulky and hot to the touch. Unable to resist, I squeeze his bicep, earning an aggressive side eye. Worth it.

The hallways are full of servants running around while elaborately dressed attendees walk unhurriedly in spectacular, colorful outfits. Everywhere, there's something new. Some of the guests wear more clothes than others — if they have clothes at all.

Despite the array of nudity and opulence, my attention isn't on them. It's on Legend and his consuming presence. He smells like citrus, and his warmth makes my palms sweaty. Damnit. I swear if I smear sweat over this man and he notices ...

I'll figure out how to time travel back in time for the shark to eat me.

Faraway music comes closer as we weave through the crowd. We pause in front of enormous glass-paneled doors, which lead into a ballroom made of glass, large enough to fit hundreds of guests. Trees of all sizes and shapes line the glass walls, but the ceiling is open to a crystal-clear night sky.

A female wearing a white toga-like dress with wings for arms shoots down to the ground, landing gracefully. There are claps all around her. Others, resembling full grown fairies, translucent wings and all, do somersaults. People let out gasps and laughs.

So many things consume my senses. The laughter. Glasses tinkling. The smell of food. Sultry, but upbeat music plays, courtesy of a nearby band. The hallway and ballroom are full of smaller creatures flitting around like fireflies. It's a dizzying spectacle, and difficult not to stare in wonder.

In the distance, a female catches my eye. It's the way her glossy black hair snags the light. A shimmering black dress held up by silver chains around her neck wraps her powerful body. Like mine, the bodice plunges down to her muscular torso. Delicate cuffs decorate her ears next to canary yellow gems.

I'm undone. There's no more gorgeous creature in all the universes — of that, I'm positive. Flexing muscles that show not just strength, but danger. The way the wine glass touches her lips is a work of art. She pauses, looks away, and the mental image is in my mind forever. Piper will ask, "When did you know you really wanted her?"

This. This moment.

Kalliope senses my gaze. She looks over her shoulder, grinning with delight when we lock eyes. She beckons us over with black nails, long enough to look suspiciously like claws. Legend leads me over with purposeful strides, and the crowd parts.

As we approach her, I can make out the kohl lining her eyelids and deep maroon lipstick, the color of arterial blood. It matches the ruby nestled in the black diadem resting on her forehead.

When she smiles, I see elongated canines. Oh, sweet heavens. I'm a lamb ready for slaughter. She can suck me dry if it means I have that mouth on my neck. Those sharp gold irises strip me bare. She excuses herself from the conversation and slinks over to us.

The closer she gets, the harder my heart thunders. A ringing starts in my ears. I can barely hear her when she says, "Saira, you are absolutely delicious."

She's not delicious — she's a god-tier example of femininity. One I want to be worthy of. Squaring my shoulders, I boldly return the perusal. However, because I have all the social graces of a bull in a china shop, instead of saying something along the lines of, *I've traveled through universes, but I've never seen anything more beautiful*, I say, "Ditto, Your Grace."

Smooth, Saira. You nerdy nincompoop.

148

She arches an eyebrow, mouth twitching with amusement. "I'm not sure what a ditto is, but I do like it when you call me that."

Maybe all is not lost. Gaining confidence, I say, "What? *Your Grace?*" The word comes out slowly and seductively. Internally, I cringe. This entire exchange is so far out of my element.

My breath hitches as she takes a step closer. Kalliope leans in close, her cheek brushing against mine as she whispers into my ear, "Unless you'd like to become a midnight snack, I recommend you refrain from taunting me with sweet words from that pretty mouth."

Time stands still. This isn't real life. No one would ever say those words to me. Not the scientist nerd wearing lipstick for the first time.

Somehow, my heart continues to pump blood into my veins, but words fail. Instead, I swallow hard and smile nervously.

When it's clear she's made me speechless, Kalliope turns her focus to Legend. He brushes a kiss against her smooth cheek as she asks, "Any issues?"

Shooting me a mischievous expression, he quips, "Other than the sinfulness of this dress on Saira? None."

Kalliope hums in agreement, then holds out a hand to me. "Come, Saira. It's time to get all the pomp and circumstance started."

Legend loosens his hold, forcing me to let go of my muscular anchor. When he sees doubt flicker across my face, he gives me a grave smile and puts a hand on my shoulder. "Don't worry. You can't possibly be a worse dancer than Her Grace."

Kalliope hisses like a cat, swatting him away with a motion of her hand. "Don't scare the poor female." Whispering conspiratorially, she says to me, "That male has four left feet."

The joke eases my nerves — but barely. With one more backward glance at Legend's mirthful expression, I grab Kalliope's offered hand. It's firm and strong. To my surprise, callouses roughen her palm. Like she's no stranger to labor or weapon wielding. Wrapping my own soft fingers around hers, she leads me through the throng of bodies. Into the literal and proverbial lion's den.

When Kalliope mentioned shifting is a competitive art form, she wasn't kidding. While there are some fully shifted animals, like big cats, snakes, and even an ostrich — most decided to enhance certain body parts.

I'm pleased to spot a couple of centaurs, but I'm startled to find griffons, sphinxes, and a couple of satyrs. They might not use the same names, but those are the ones off the top of my head. No matter what people look like, they are all decked out in fabrics and jewels.

As for the males, they stand by their dates, some wearing fewer clothes than others. All of them are beautifully crafted — some with muscles for days; others rocking a dad bod like no other. There's so much to see; it's hard to process. Flashing metals. Gems shimmered in the candlelight, on bodies, clothes, and jewelry. Feathers, Fur. Spots. Stripes.

In the further left corner, a quartet of does with skilled fur-covered fingers play string instruments. A female engulfed in peacock feathers and draping plumage, with a shimmery blue and purple dress loosely hanging over her curves. A black and neon-blue frog the size of a miniature pony hops across the room.

The floor is sprawling white marble tiles, but instead of grout, moss grows between the ornate pieces. A large pond is in the center of the room, with various creatures and females swimming or lounging on the edges, talking to others.

It's like a fantasy book come to life. It's difficult to swallow the overwhelming urge to go grab the camera and take pictures of everything.

Kalliope nudges my shoulder and whispers, "You keep your mouth open any wider, and the frogs might think you're competing for flies."

Snapping my jaw shut, I pretend to zip my lips tight. When she laughs, I say, "I'll admit, this isn't anything like I expected. It's pretty magical."

Based on her expression, the answer seems to please Kalliope. Her fingers tighten around mine as she maneuvers through a group of females throwing out compliments to their lordess. All five of them are decked out in vines and flowers that barely cover their lithe bodies. When one of them attempts to begin a conversation, Kalliope graciously

150

excuses us, motioning to the pond. Understanding dawns on their faces, five pairs of eyes focusing on me. With more than a bit of judgment.

As we reach the edge of the crowd, the strung out butterflies batter against my rib cage, screaming for freedom. Everyone is watching us walk up to the pond, pausing as the aquatic guests hop out to perch on the edge. A glass panel slides from the aged stone edges, sweeping to the other side, making a clear dance floor. In the water, small fish glow, becoming a writhing mass of lights.

When it's clear she's going to step up onto the dance floor with me in tow, I jerk back, ready to dig in my heels. She feels the resistance and gives me a concerned look.

"Saira? What's wrong?"

There's no way I can dance in front of everyone. It's like my own personal nightmare come to life, being gawked at while my clumsy feet humiliate me. When Legend mentioned dancing, for some absurd reason, I thought he meant *she* would be dancing. Not me.

Whispers course through the crowd like wildfire. Terror licks up my spine, quickening my breath. This can't happen. I tug my hand again, but Kalliope grips it. Without a single glance at our onlookers, she steps close enough for her scent of smokey campfire to soothe the jagged edges of fear threatening to consume my mind. Not entirely, but enough.

"Are you alright?" Eyes the color of sunrays scan my face, seeking answers I can't quite give yet. My throat is tight. Behind me, someone giggles. My cheeks flush. They're laughing about the dumb girl who can't even dance. I just know it.

"No," I croak out in a whisper. "I didn't know you wanted to dance with me. Kalliope, I've never danced in my entire life. Ever. They'll laugh at me. And you."

Understanding softens her pinched features. "Ah. I see." Her gaze sweeps over my shoulder. At the gawkers. The gigglers. The judgers. Kalliope's hand squeezes mine tightly, refocusing on my face. "You don't have to, of course. Legend can easily come and take your place. But ..." Her voice trails off as she seems to contemplate something. Her jaw ticks, then she says, "I'd be honored if you allowed me to experience your first time dancing. Ever. I promise you won't look or feel like a fool."

How she can promise such a thing is beyond me. Yet, even only knowing her for a couple of days, a modicum of trust already exists. Her compassion for those around her shows through both actions and words, as well as her desire to protect and care. If she says it'll be okay, it probably will be.

Filling my lungs with much-needed air, I blow it out dramatically. She smiles, already knowing my response.

"Okay, Lordess," I say. "Let's pop my dance floor cherry."

Confusion flickers across her face. "Saira, there are no cherries here, but I'm sure we can find you some afterward."

Despite my fear, I giggle, motioning to the dance floor. "Show me what you've got, *Your Grace*."

Heat simmers in her eyes, full of promise. "Follow me, midnight snack."

Chapter Seventeen

Don't Sniff Your Armpits

Coming to a stop on the dance floor, we pause. All oxygen has vacated my veins, and it's impossible to hide the terrified shaking of my hands. There's no spotlight on us, but there might as well be. There's no time to freeze as Kalliope presses a hand to my back and raises my hand into the air. With the most delectable smirk, she jerks me into her body, flushing our flesh together.

We're so close; her warm breath heats the air between us. Reality's poised on too-tall heels and the warm press of our breasts. The world fades. All the whispers disappear. Check for a pulse, and you'll find nothing. I'm about to expire right here. The first scientist to die while time traveling.

"Breathe," she murmurs in a husky tone. A thumb brushes against my lower back, and my lungs obey her command. Life-giving oxygen spears down my throat, but it's not nearly enough. Not as the music begins — a haunting but quick beat. *Here we go.*

Kalliope moves, and I'm swept along, cradled in her competent grasp. Heat builds between us, and as the peacock female begins a crooning ballad, violins back up the yearning words.

"Focus on me."

My soul rakes against hot coals at the order. It's impossible to ignore. Our eyes lock, and I'm lost in the kaleidoscope of burnished gold. The energy between us is a tight wire, almost impossible to balance upon.

She tucks my hips closer as we float around the clear dance floor. The world is a blur, a sweeping mass of colors and lights. It's a simple enough dance, and even when I stumble, her firm hold never wavers. Never giving potential embarrassment a perch.

"Why me?" I whisper. "Why not Legend?"

Kalliope's eyes flick to the crowd, then back to me. With a wink, I'm flung away from her, snapping back when our grasp grows taut. My body spins inward, the speed sure to make us crash. She absorbs the momentum before spinning me away again.

With a flourished twirl that leaves me dizzy, she brings me back to her, holding my hip tightly. Her skin brushes against my bare chest, soft as silk.

Just as I'm about to repeat the question, she leans into my ear and purrs, "I'm intrigued by you, Saira."

"What?" I squeak. There's no way she's interested in me.

Kalliope flashes me a grin, wide enough to reveal the fangs. "You know, the diadem you're wearing. It's mine."

Her words sink in, shocking me to my core. "You let me borrow this today? Why?"

This close, I discover a white ring surrounding her black pupil. It makes the yellow glow brighter. "As I picked out my diadem, this one caught my eye. It hasn't been worn in ages, and I knew it would look magnificent on you." Her breath is warm against the shell of ear, prickling goose bumps. "And I was right."

What even is this life?

To my surprise, I'm actually disappointed when the melodic song fades into nothingness. With unparalleled grace, she brings our movement to a stop. Kalliope gives an affectionate bump of her head against mine before stepping back.

Still holding my hand, she faces the crowds and says in a loud, commanding tone, "People of Payla and my esteemed visiting guests, welcome to my home. Tonight is about Amicums coming together from all over, re-solidifying vital relationships and friendships. Eat. Drink.

Fuck. It would be quite disappointing if no younglings were conceived tonight."

The crowd titters. I'm more stuck on the fact that she told them to fuck. Are they going to fuck ... in here?

She continues, amusement in her voice. "Please. Enjoy yourselves."

The crowd claps politely as she leads me down the stairs, quietly accepting reverent greetings from those we pass. This time, the attention directed toward us is warmer and more curious. The tension in my shoulders softens. Kalliope's gentle but firm grasp of my hand is a steady guide as we head to the outskirts of the dense crowd of minglers.

To my delight, this wondrous female has brought me to the buffet table.

Hell yes.

Making a beeline for the sugary-looking carbs, I bite into a puff pastry overflowing with thick cream. I groan and reach for another.

Kalliope chuckles. "Hungry?"

I look at her with chipmunk cheeks. "Yefsh."

She reaches for a pastry and gently bites into it. Some icing smears at the corner of her mouth — my pulse skips a beat when her tongue flicks out to lick it up. She shares a wolfish grin. "Ellie's bakers are in excellent form this evening."

I swallow the mouthful, trying to suffocate the need growing in my core, and snatch up a cupcake. Kalliope watches with amusement, accepting two champagne glasses offered by a passing servant. She takes a sip while offering me the other glass. It tastes like summer days and roller coaster belly flops.

Eager to share how much I love it, I step closer to her, but draw up short when Daeva steps to Kalliope's side with a brief bow.

"Your Grace. A word?"

She's wearing an icy-white satin dress that shimmers with every shift of her tense, pale body. It wraps around her neck, offering the most modesty I've seen since I arrived. A waist cinch made of pearly white leather forces an hourglass figure, flaring her hips out wide.

Her matching shock of white hair is pulled up into a bun with glittering white eyeshadow punching the edges of her too-wide eyes. White feathers flare out from her cheeks down past the edges of her neck, meeting at her shoulders and cascading down her arms in a thick line. On her feet are pale combat boots.

It's a striking visual, like a snow owl preparing for battle. Though her dress is made of a fine, expensive material, a metallic leather belt hangs from her hips, flashing a gleaming dagger. Somehow, the effect is intimidating as fuck.

It takes every ounce of self-control not to guzzle the drink in my hand. Something about her is dangerous.

Daeva's nostrils flare as if smelling my spike of fear. Her leering gaze inspects my outfit, pausing at the bangle on my wrist, a clever disguise for the Scout. Her observation stirs up unease, making me fidget.

Kalliope gives a cool look. "Hello, Daeva. I've missed your presence today."

Daeva gives an innocent, slow blink. Shifting her focus off me, she looks at Kalliope as she says, "Forgive me. I had security detail to attend to. There is quite an influx of visitors."

Kalliope scans the room with a thoughtful nod. "Yes. Is the Lordess of Prinapalese here yet?"

Daeva gives a curt nod. "This is why I'm here — she requests an audience with you."

My heart sinks. Kalliope frowns with an apology as she says to me, "Saira, please excuse me while I go meet with a fellow lordess. It is a long journey for her, and as such, is due my respect." Apprehension pinches her features as she glances at Daeva, then back to me. "Find Zenab or Legend if you need assistance. Until then, enjoy the ball."

It doesn't escape me that Daeva's not included on the list of helpful people. Before I can respond, the crowd swallows up Kalliope, leaving me with an angry female bird.

Looking at Daeva, I finish off my champagne, placing it on a passing tray. It's too much to hope for Daeva to leave me alone because she's clearly not going anywhere. Boots planted firmly on the marble, she crosses her arms.

"Are you enjoying the ball? I saw Her Grace choose you for the first dance."

Maybe I've been around too many Amicums already because it makes me want to bare my teeth. She's decided she doesn't like me, so it's easy to return the sentiment.

"Yes, it *was* a lovely time." I respond coolly. My words imply she's changed the experience, but if she catches the inference, she doesn't show it.

Instead, she looks to Kalliope, who has finally reached the visiting lordess. With what I now recognize as her diplomatic smile, she offers a greeting to the lordess, immediately absorbed into whatever is being said.

Daeva looks back at me. "She does enjoy her flavors of the week." She takes a step forward. It's a small one, but there wasn't a lot of distance between us to begin with.

My feet ache to step back, but I refuse. She's clearly trying to bother me. Bullies aren't unfamiliar to me, and that's all she is: a bully.

Her voice drips with condescension as she says, "My job is to keep these lands and everyone within those borders safe. I don't like you, Saira. I don't trust you. Everything said about you makes me think you're hiding something. I'm going to find out what it is."

Alright, I'm over it. "What is your damn problem?"

Daeva leans in and takes a loud sniff. "Did you know one-forms have a particular scent to them?"

Don't sniff your armpits. Swallowing hard, I make a show of rolling my eyes. "Let me guess: I smell like shit?"

A shoulder bumps into mine, and I stumble forward, further closing the gap between me and the upset chicken.

Daeva stands firm, her large eyes narrowed into slits. "Watch it. The lordess might find it acceptable that you're here, but I don't. You aren't just a one-form, and we both know it. I'm keeping an eye on you."

A woman with six-foot-long legs walks by and leans over with a tray of champagne flutes. I grab two and immediately swallow the contents of one. The bubbles slipping down my throat are in good company with the still-panicking butterflies rattling in my chest. I'm not a drinker, so the bubbles are already floating to my head. Anxiety and booze are a terrible combination.

Offering a bland smile, I say, "Aren't you tired of being the insufferable movie villain?"

To her credit, Daeva doesn't even blink at the obscure reference. Instead, her focus switches to something behind me.

Without a parting verbal blow, she spins around and marches off. I finish off the glass of champagne and dive into the second.

"She knows how to bring down the festivities, doesn't she?" Legend appears by my shoulder. I heave a breath of relief. My unexpected shield. He offers a glass of champagne, but pauses, looking at the empty and full one in my grasp.

Offering him a wide, grateful smile, I place the empty glass on the table, smoothly grabbing the one he's offering. "Nothing can bring me down from all of this." I sweep out an arm to the crowd. "This is incredible."

He lifts the flute briefly before taking a sip. Resting an elbow on his other arm tucked against his chest, he watches the revelers with interest. "It's absolutely breathtaking, isn't it? Kalliope always ensures her guests have a wonderful time."

"Yes," I murmur. "I've never seen anything like it. It's better than anything I could've imagined."

"I'm glad you're enjoying it." He takes another sip before saying, "Did Daeva give you any issues?"

"No, she's a ball of joy," I say dryly. "Clearly the personality hire for the Cohort."

His lips press together, clearly swallowing a laugh. "Not sure what that means, but it sounds sarcastic, so I'm inclined to agree."

I laugh and wrinkle my nose. "What the hell is her issue, anyway? Why does she seem hell-bent on hating me?"

Legend dips his chin as a small group of females walk by, but answers, "Daeva is what one might call a traditionalist. She comes from a tiny town in Raeland, hundreds of miles away, close to Vulturia's borders. They're suspicious of outsiders. It makes her good at security, but poor conversational company."

He looks toward where Kalliope stands with a group of Amicums. One of them's dressed in deep purple ruffles, wearing strings of pearls with a matching pearl diadem curving and dipping to the tip of her brow. She must be the other lordess. To be sure, I try not to be too obvious as I point in her direction. "Who's that?"

Legend follows my finger's direction. Spotting the subject in question, he sighs. "The Lordess of Prinapalese, Narcissa. Not the friendliest, but not the worst. She's also been trying to negotiate a trade deal with Kal."

Trade deals. Vulturians. Daeva is constantly watching for me to mess up. I miss the peace of a lab and headphones.

My good mood evaporates. For a split second, it's too much. Deciding if it's a good spot or not. Saving my family. Developing unexpected emotions.

Although it would be glorious to watch Nana take Daeva down a peg or two, the court intrigue and politics are overwhelming. Dad and I want a place where everyone can be safe. As "one-forms," the threat of Vulturians means we'd never be safe. Although there probably isn't a place in the whole universe completely safe.

I'm about to ask more questions, but Legend raises a hand to acknowledge someone behind me. Sparing a quick glance, he smiles. "I must also greet some other consorts and answer any questions they might have. You'll be alright here at the buffet?"

I wave him off. "Sure, go do your thing."

"See you soon, Gem." I receive my own kiss goodbye on the cheek. Now it's just me, the buffet, and the inevitable next glass of champagne.

Chapter Eighteen

Soulmates Could Be A Spoon?

After Legend leaves, I'm left alone to my own devices. I drink another glass of champagne, knowing full well it'll cause regrets in the morning. I've drunk more here in Ilorna than I have collectively in my whole life. Even stuffing a few more appetizers into my belly doesn't ease the discombobulating sensation taking over my poor brain.

When I'm finally fed up with the loneliness, I push through the guests, heading toward the nearest set of doors leading outside. It's odd, having the sensation of dress fabric, fur, and feathers press against my arms.

No one pays attention to me. Everyone seems to be drunk, communicating in various animalistic sounds. I pass by too quickly for my translator to catch up, but I'm not trying to talk to anyone, anyway. Daeva came in and shredded my happiness. How could I let her do that?

Finally, a fresh breeze brushes against the light material of my dress. Cold air fills my lungs, making it easier to breathe through the whirlwind of emotions coursing through me.

She does enjoy her flavors of the week.

I hate that Daeva's words bother me. It took a moment for them to land, but now they dig into me like claws.

Does Kalliope find new "flavors"? Is that what I am? A flavor?

Why does it even matter? I'm here for mere weeks, at most. This is a science expedition, not an interspecies dating experiment. All of this is overshadowing the most important fact. I'm being a moon-eyed imbecile for being upset about the possibility of a shifter female possibly not *valuing* me?

So much for staying objective.

Looking around the garden, I'm relieved to find it empty. The moon bathes the bushes and trees in pale light, enough for my human eyesight to make out shapes and shadows.

Taking off my heels, I pause at the wetness. A thin blanket of dew coats the grass, squishing between my toes.

Holding the front of my dress up, I walk toward a bench. The song inside changes to a more frenzied beat. Laughter gets louder, and there's something about the tone of someone's laugh that brings me back to my last night at home. Playing cards with my cousins and reminiscing. Hugging Piper. Saying goodbye to Dad one last time.

What am I thinking? Spending time with strangers instead of collecting samples? I should be focused on my family — on The Mission. This experience has barely started. Already, I'm so lost and lonely. This is the fifth stop, and I'm not sure how many there will be until the closed time-like loop delivers me back home. Will I be torn like this the entire time?

I look down at my dress in disgust. Does this make me a traitor? Enjoying an evening while my family is technically dead, waiting for me to save them?

What if I never see them again?

What if I wasted the opportunity for a true goodbye?

What if I'm in denial about my ability to save the family?

My nerves are already raw, so when the unexpected wave of emotions arrives, they overwhelm my inebriated senses. I choke on the first sob, but the following come freely. My heart aches so deeply, I want to dig into my rib cage and yank it out. Homesickness feels like something vital has been cored out of your chest. It's a gaping mass, shiny and sticky.

Piper's locket is warm in my palm as my fingers play with the chain. It's tempting, knowing something is inside the locket. Have a little home right here in the garden.

I dip my nails into the clasp. Right before it pops open, an unmistakable voice says, "There are rumors that if you cry in the garden at night, bears will hear you and come in search of a midnight snack."

I choke out a laugh, looking toward Ginger. Delicate glittery ribbons weave through her bushy red curls. For the first time, she's clothed, decked out in a dress the color of shimmering starlight. The thin material flares out at her hips and cascades to the grass. The bottom's already lined with dirt and flecks of grass.

"You're ruining your dress." I point at the offending stains.

Ginger glances at the bottom of her dress and grins. "I promised Kal I'd be dressed for the first portion of the night — I didn't promise the dress would stay clean."

With grace I'll never achieve, she sits next to me and brings one of her soft hands to cover one of mine. "I'm not sure what has made you so upset, but any of us are willing to talk to you about it. I know I can come off as a bit of a bitch, but it's just for fun."

I give a watery smile. "Thanks. I needed a good cry, is all. I'm homesick right now."

Ginger nods. "I can appreciate a good cry. It doesn't happen enough. Sometimes, I'll hold up an onion to my face and try to force a good cry session."

The joke makes me snort. I dab at the edges of my eyes with a finger, stemming the tears. I've ruined my makeup at this point. "It sounds like a lot of Amicums are having fun in there."

Ginger huffs out a chuckle. "I'm not sure you're prepared for the devolution of the evening."

My curiosity piques. "What do you mean?"

Her laugh is light and lyrical. "We're a bit free around here when it comes to the pleasures of life."

Now that she mentions it, the music has picked up, and there's less laughter and more ... primal sounds.

My cheeks are flaming hot. "It's like an orgy?"

"Yes."

I look around. The garden's still empty. "Everyone?"

Even Kalliope and Legend?

"No, not everyone," she admits. "I know Kal tends to go back to her chambers before the vamping up of celebrations."

Which means Legend does as well.

This should not give me comfort.

Ugh. It does, though.

I nibble on my lip, doubting myself, before asking, "Does Kalliope have flavors of the week?"

Her thick red brows scrunch with confusion. "Like for breakfast?"

The confused comment evokes a real laugh from me. "No, for the people she sleeps with." I frown. "Although I guess technically, that can mean breakfast, too."

Ginger's mouth parts with surprise, scanning my face. "Who told you such a thing?"

I look away, my cheeks burning in the shadows.

Ginger sighs. "Daeva."

Not a question. Why is she allowed in the Cohort if everyone is always on the alert about her behavior?

"Yeah. She just said it out of the blue."

Ginger scoffs. "Kalliope has Legend. It's almost always completely the two of them. There are occasional experiences — even I have joined on occasion — but Kalliope tends to keep a boundary between herself and the court."

I'm not sure how I feel about the freeness of friends sleeping together for fun, but it's not my place to judge. "Smart."

"Yes." Ginger nods. She pauses, messing with some grass with a toe. "Why does what Daeva said bother you?"

Before I answer, the sound of something crashing and laughter makes me chuckle. "Sounds like that devolution is happening."

Ginger hums in agreement, but says nothing else. When I realize she isn't going to let me get away with not answering, I say, "Not sure why it bothers me. Maybe because this is the first time I've even had a small crush on someone. Maybe it's because I don't want to be treated like I'm just another body."

"You've never had a crush on someone?" Ginger sounds appalled.

Feeling awkward, I shrug a shoulder. "No. I've had a really busy life that mostly involved studying, working and sleeping at work. Before this trip, I'd never even left my city before."

She squeezes my hand. "Well, I'm glad you're here." She leans in and whispers conspiratorially, "Even if it's just to distract the bear so I can get away."

The joke breaks the melancholy. I laugh. "You're incorrigible."

"That's the hope." She stands, holding a hand out. "Would you like me to help you back to your chambers?"

"Nah, I'm okay. It's peaceful out here, and I need the fresh air."

"Sounds good. I'm going to go sample some of the visiting males, if you know what I mean." She makes an exaggerated wink while swishing her dress. "Toodle-loo."

"Have fun." I watch as she heads back toward the manor with the soaked dress trailing behind her. I catch a flash of spots and bare skin — yeah, I'm not ready for that.

After spending a few more minutes in the garden, restlessness spurs me back to the steps and into the manor. It takes a moment longer until I find a door leading to the hallway outside of the ballroom. I slip inside and look around for Meadow. Guests mingle in the hallway, but none of them look my way. Not willing to stand here and wait, I walk down the hallway. If I wander long enough, something will start looking familiar.

I turn a corner and run right into a lush body. Looking up, I'm stunned by Kalliope's beautiful eyes.

The smile fades as her glowing eyes size me up, the inspection pausing on the wet hem of my dress. She tilts her head. "Are you alright?"

I jerk a thumb toward the gardens. "Having a grand ol' time outside."

"Did you roll in the grass, or have you been crying?"

I laugh it off, hoping she'll drop it. "Okay, maybe I got a little bit emotional. It's been a long week." I pause, confused. "I thought you were talking to other lordesses."

Kalliope sighs. "I needed a breather. It can be a lot, being a lordess. Taking a walk down the hallways sounded nice." She looks up and down the empty hallway. "Would you like an escort to your chambers, or would you prefer to rejoin the party?"

As if on cue, there's the sound of a roar from the ballroom. I look toward the door nervously. "Look, I'm no prude — at least, I think — but my brain might melt if I go in there."

She tips her head from side to side with an amused look. "Perhaps." She holds out an arm. "Shall we?"

I take the offered arm, leaning a little to alleviate the ache starting to swell in my feet. "Thanks."

She's silent as we make our way through the empty hallways. It's the quietest it's ever been, and it's odd. I say as much, and Kalliope nods her head in agreement.

"It's been a busy week, but things will die down over the next couple of days as the guests leave."

"Do you have parties like this often?"

She shakes her head, necklaces clinking with the movement. "No, thank Inanna. This particular event is once a year, a tradition for lordesses to commune. Normally, I prefer the quiet. So many arrive expecting to be entertained and consistently ask for an audience with me. Forgetting I'm merely one lordess with thousands of Amicums to care for."

Yet, she's made time for me. Maybe not just a flavor after all. "That all sounds like a lot of pressure."

She looks down at me. Even in the dim light, her irises have an inner glow. "It can be. Being a lordess is a privilege, but it can be lonely as well."

I frown. "Don't you have Legend?"

"Yes, of course." She looks away, leading me down a wide hallway with art on the walls. Portraits of females in stunning sets of fighting leathers and armor. "But it can still be lonely. Always having to stay one step removed from things."

"Like the party?"

"Yes, like the party. Until my mother died and I was chosen to follow in her footsteps, I enjoyed similar parties. However, it's important to

165

maintain objectivity with the people you lead. A bit difficult if you've had their genitals in your mouth."

A laugh erupts from me, echoing against the walls. "That's definitely one way to put it." The need to maintain objectivity rings too close, though. "I get the needing to be objective." I look up at her, my focus lingering on her red lips. "I'm not good at it."

She gives me a sad smile. "Full lives aren't meant to be lived objectively."

"So you aren't living life to the fullest?"

Kalliope chuckles. "When it comes to Legend, I throw all objectivity out the window. Always have and always will."

Curiosity gets the better of me. "Is he your soulmate?"

She peers down at me, stopping at my chamber door. "Amicums believe in multiple soulmates. A soulmate is one energy recognizing another from a past life."

"Or universes?"

She cocks her head. "I suppose."

"So soulmates could be anything?"

Kalliope shrugs. "That's what we believe."

"Even a spoon?"

This elicits a full belly laugh. Her whole face lights up with joy, and I can't wait to make her laugh again. I could listen to it all day.

She shakes her head. "Perhaps not a spoon, but I won't claim to be an expert on these things."

She guides me to lean against the door. My knees weaken as she steps closer, invading my senses. Is she about to kiss me? *Gods, I hope so.* It wouldn't be my first kiss, but it might be the first one I've really wanted. My breath shudders as my eyes trace her high cheekbones and full lips. The red lipstick still looks pristine.

"I should go." Her voice is hoarse, and there's unmistakable desire in her expression.

It gives me hope. I'm drunk enough to say, "You can always come inside?"

She closes her eyes, takes a deep, shaky breath. "It's getting late, and you've been drinking."

I frown. Those are terrible reasons. "I don't mind."

Slowly, she straightens. Her boss bitch energy appears. She gives me a stern look. "I do." Sucking in a deep breath and blowing it out hard, she looks to the door. "You should go inside. *Alone.*"

With one last parting glance, I turn the knob and step into the room. "Last chance ..."

"I'll see you in the morning, Saira."

There's a shimmer, and I'm looking down at the black wolf. She nuzzles my hand with her snout, then bolts down the hallway.

Leaving me feeling like I'm on fire and in a downward spiral at the same time.

Opening the chamber doors, I step in and lock them behind me. The fire roars with fresh wood, casting shadows around the room, frolicking against the walls. It's tempting to crawl straight into bed, but my thoughts are on an endless merry-go-round. Sleep will be impossible.

Padding over to the beverage cart, I pour myself one of the liquids, not giving a shit what it is. Pressing the glass to my lips, I hiss at the burn on my tongue. Whatever it is might very well put hair on my chest.

Satisfied, I float toward the couch, eager to sit down. The soft cushions are a balm to my sore muscles. Taking another sip, I ignore the disgusting taste as I contemplate my ridiculous predicament.

All of it's too much, like being dropped through the looking glass, plopping straight into a fantasy romance novel. Don't get me wrong; I love my fantasy novels. But this is still a scientific mission — not the time to get my metaphorical dick wet. There are still responsibilities to focus on.

Allowing myself to be distracted by gorgeous shifters is unprofessional. Would I have been so wooed by Kalliope and Legend if I hadn't been studious my entire life? I'm not sure. There's nothing to measure it against. This could be a simple case of arrested development, where my teenage hormones finally get to shoot their shot. It could also be entirely in my head. Kalliope clearly let me down gently because she's polite.

There's no way someone like *her* would be into someone like *me*. I have the game of a drunk slug; tonight she was just being kind to the nerd.

My eyes trail across the room, stopping at the full-length mirror. In its reflection, I see a woman costumed in a beautiful outfit. Everything about her appears perfect, but I know better. She's betraying her family, one yes at a time. Her father would be ashamed of her inability to be an objective scientist. The woman in the mirror left her family to die so she could play dress up and pretend it's all for science.

Maybe it's the scotch, perhaps it's the truth; all I know is that the woman in that reflection is consumed by doubt and shame. She's a fake.

My knuckles blanch as I squeeze the glass, half-hoping it'll shatter in my hand. My family deserved better than what they got.

And what they got was me.

The shame of it might consume me alive.

Chapter Nineteen

Going Full Throttle Stupid

The sound of a door closing wakes me up. Sunlight shines through the open French doors, the curtains blowing in the breeze. A pounding headache thumps against my temples, making the light stab into my pupils.

Next to the bed rests a steeping pot of tea and a teacup. The door closing must've been Meadow. I'm surprised she didn't rouse me from my drool-laden sleep, but the earthy smell of the tea tells me it's going to help with this hangover.

Something stabs into my back, and I groan as I turn on my side. Sleeping in this dress was a bad idea. The boning digs into my torso as I sit up. Leaning over, I pour a cup of tea. It steams as it hits the porcelain. Bringing it to my mouth, I take a tentative sip.

It tastes like dirt, but in a strange, comforting way. It's the perfect temperature, making it easy to drink the whole thing. Almost instantly, my nausea subsides, and the pounding headache eases.

A miracle hangover cure? That's a check mark in the *Is This A Good Place To Live?* mental checklist.

As I sip the tea, I try to recall the last bits of my night. It turned into a spiraling pity party, ending in a pool of self-loathing. Some of it was justified, but when I began considering throwing away the Scout to "save" my family from my bullshit, I knew it was time to go to bed.

It was a momentary lapse of judgment. That's all. Today is a fresh start. It's only been two days; I promised myself a couple of weeks here for research. If I avoid any romantic entanglements, it'll be okay. I'm a Badass Bitch Scientist — objectivity is my metaphorical middle name.

By the time I've changed into something far more comfortable and washed off the smeared makeup, I'm feeling good as new. I drink a second cup of tea for good measure while simultaneously taking a sample of the liquid. The ingredients are unidentifiable. Damn. Maybe if I ask politely enough, I can bring some with me to the next stop.

Ready to take on the day objectively, I throw the bedroom door open and peer down the hallway. Racking my memory, I walk to the left, looking for anything familiar that might lead me to breakfast. I pass the brutal painting and refuse to let my eyes linger on the violence. It means I'm close, though.

Finally, after a couple of wrong turns, I find myself in the dining room. Kalliope, Legend, and Zenab already sit at the table, chatting.

Legend sees me first, face lighting up. Surely not for me, right? *No, not for me.* He's just being polite as he motions for me to come closer. "Good morning, Gem. How did you sleep?"

Ignoring the pet name, I pull up a chair beside him and grab a muffin. "Not too bad. Someone left wondrous tea for me, though. It cured my hangover."

"Oh, it's a miracle," Zenab agrees, throwing an ankle over a knee. "It's Meadow's special concoction."

"Do you think she'd share the blend?" I ask.

Kalliope scoffs. "She'd rather fight you to the death."

Well, there goes that hope.

Instead, I shift the conversation. Maybe I should have more of a preamble, but the sense of urgency to help my family makes me blurt out, "I'm looking to experience more of Ilorna. Do you think someone can point me in the right direction to visit a local town or someplace interesting?"

Kalliope bites into an apple, looking out the window thoughtfully. Zenab does the same, tapping her chin.

Finally, Kalliope says, "There is a small town nearby, Eastam. I've been meaning to visit for a while now. That could be a good place to go."

Excitement buds in my chest. I know she's just being polite, but the prospect of seeing more is irresistible. "Can we go today?"

Kalliope nods slowly, sipping her coffee. Her expression turns mischievous. "Of course, the fastest way to get there is the most fun way."

The look on her face makes me wary. "What do you mean 'fun'?"

Legend chuckles. "Aren't you in for a treat?"

Kalliope and I have different ideas of fun.

The giant gold eagle in front of me snaps its beak, then jerks its feathered head to its wing. It's partly a demand, partly an invitation. Apparently, the fastest way to the nearby town is as the crow flies. Or in this case, as the eagle flies.

Legend stands beside me, grinning like an entertained fool. He pats me on the shoulder, probably assuming it'll encourage me. It doesn't. I'm not interested in being so high in the sky, where a simple mistake will flatten me into a pancake. Cramps squeeze at my gut.

Legend either misses or ignores my hesitation. "It's okay, Gem. Hold on tight. And she'll catch you if ..."

He pauses. Realizing what he's about to say, I finish the sentence for him. "If I fall over and plunge to certain death."

The smile he gives is far more of a regretful grimace than anything. "To be fair, I did say she'll catch you before that happens."

The eagle snaps its beak again. Objectively, I know Kalliope won't let me die. At the very least, I'm ninety-five percent sure.

Looking at Legend, I ask, "Where will you be?"

With a weary sigh, he says, "This is a time for the two of you. After all the damn entertaining this week, I'm looking forward to a nap." Legend pats my shoulder again. "Go on. It'll be alright."

Kalliope lowers her body to the ground, and I bite back a laugh. She looks like a roosting chicken. Something tells me she wouldn't appreciate the comparison, though. I'm not about to insult the bird taking me into the sky.

Stepping closer, I put a hand on the curve of her wing. The silky feathers consist of different shades of gold and brown. "You're going to catch me if I fall off, right?"

Kalliope makes a soft coo in her throat, and I melt. "Fine. But if you drop me, my death is on your hands."

Another coo, louder and longer. Choosing to interpret it as an affirmation of my survival odds, I dig my fingers into her feathers, gripping them. One of her big golden eyes watches me patiently.

I bite my lip. "Will I tear these out?"

Kalliope snaps her beak. A warning.

"No promises," I mutter, carefully pulling myself onto her neck. She helps me by jostling her shoulder until I'm in position. It's easier to settle into a comfortable seat because of her width. Tentatively pulling on feathers to get a better position, I'm grateful to find them resist being plucked.

"Does that hurt?"

Kalliope shakes her head. I gasp as she stands. It's like sitting on a small building during an earthquake. Clutching the feathers tighter, I squeeze my legs around her body.

She turns her head again, eyeing me and the position I'm in.

Looking down at Legend, I try to appear brave. "I think I'll be alright. Enjoy your nap."

He winks and steps back. Kalliope looks upward, and the world explodes in a hurricane of air and feathers. My stomach bottoms out, and my eyes clamp shut. Every inch of my body vibrates with terror, palms already sweaty with fear. I should've never agreed to this. Who could've guessed — other than everyone on this planet — she could turn into a huge eagle, perfect for riding?

Our vertical ascent evens out, and the surrounding air is finally calm enough to breathe in. Kalliope chirps, encouraging me to look.

I don't want to.

I need to.

A sliver of a glance.

And when I do, it's ... indescribable.

From this height, a few thousand feet up, everything is smaller. More miniature, like a tilt shift image. Tiny homes dotting green and yellow pastures. Brown roads wind through the fields and trees. Little wagons and Amicums travel on them.

Copious gold and green forests rise into the sky. In the distance, the ocean sparkles in the bright sun. The wildness of Kalliope's land is striking. All around me are familiar shades of color, yet so much more.

I can objectively confirm it's breathtaking.

"Oh, Kalliope." The wind swallows my words, but as she gently banks to the left, I know she's enjoying this as much as I am. What's it like to have the power to turn into anything? If I'd had the power to escape into the skies when I needed to think, I would never be stressed.

Kalliope dips down, and my stomach lurches with excitement. When she begins lazy circles toward the ground, I can't help but laugh with happiness. This is the most free I've ever felt. I'll be asking to do this again.

I'm grinning like an idiot until, out of nowhere, Kalliope takes a steep dive. It's like a roller coaster drop that keeps going and going.

What the hell?

Wind rips at me, at my chest, at my shoulders. My fingers strain to hold on to the silken feathers, losing their grip thanks to this unexpected velocity. Without a saddle, my legs slip along the silky feathers.

"Kalliope! Slow down!" I try to scream, but the wind fills my throat, punching back the sound before it can exist. What was a previously beautiful landscape now hurtles toward us, offering an unyielding landing if she continues at this speed.

"Kalliope! Please!"

Her body disappears as she rolls upside down, leaving me in a free fall. Her hawk form rises past my falling body, gliding above me. My hands frantically grab at the air, my instincts screeching in terror. My bladder threatens to release when my brain processes the fact Kalliope has dumped me into the sky.

Fear is a funny thing. Less than a month ago, I stepped into the unknown, the possibility of death almost certain. Now that I've reached the thick of this adventure, an ache of regret pangs against my breast-bone.

I still have thousands of feet left, long enough for my life to flash before me. Piper's smile. Grandmother's stern glances. Dad's joy at figuring out time travel. Mom hooked up to IVs and monitors. The moment I received my diploma in front of a clapping crowd. Mom tucking me into bed and kissing my forehead.

Tears stream down my face and into the air. A quiet acceptance. If this is how I go, at least I can say I tried my damndest to save my family. To embrace adventure.

Something clicks inside me. Peace, like nothing I've ever felt, slides over the terror, smothering it.

I spread my arms like they're wings and let go. If I'm about to die, I'm going to greet death with the respect it deserves. I've done my best, and this trip was always a —

Ginormous talons curl around my spread arms, and my free fall comes to a jerking halt. I scream at the pain in my shoulders. Surely, they're going to tear at the seams — how can they hurt this much and not rip apart?

A big gold eye levels with my gaze, and Kalliope gives a high-pitched chirp, dipping her head to the ground. She's homed in on something below us. A small town is on fire. People the size of ants scurry around while being chased by creatures I can't identify.

All I can make out through the smoke is a town center with merchant stalls knocked over. Blotches of red speckle the dirt, and little dolls lie next to them. But those aren't dolls. They're corpses.

We're heading straight for it. Now, a new flavor of dread slithers down my spine, replacing the fear of death by falling. What are those *things*?

Within seconds, the ground is swallowing me up as Kalliope glides down, slow enough I can get a running start when my feet hit the grass. It's still a bit too fast, and I stumble, falling onto all fours. Pain explodes throughout my body, taking my breath away.

Gasping, I watch the beautiful eagle disappear, turning into a familiar black wolf. Kalliope's wolf is three times its normal size, the obsidian fur absorbing the sunshine like a black hole.

She pauses and looks over her shoulder, checking if I'm alright. I know for certain she never meant to hurt or scare me. Her people are dying, and she still wants to make sure I'm alright.

Panting, I wave her off. "Go. *Go!*"

Digging my fingers into the soft soil, I heave in breaths, trying to calm my out-of-control heart rate. The adrenaline coursing through my veins spikes at the sound of destruction. If I stay here, I might be safe. There's no reason to get involved. I *must* stay objective. Scientists observe and record; they don't bolt into the fray.

Piper's face floats through my thoughts. She wouldn't just sit in the grass, waiting for the danger to disappear. She'd go help people. I can almost imagine the look of disappointment drooping her expression if she found out I let an entire village burn to the ground without doing something. All in the name of "staying objective."

The indecision is like a serrated blade against my cognitive dissonance. Morals against objectivity. Safety against failure. Life against death.

Who do you want to be?

The answer appears, propelling me to stand and begin running toward the mayhem. My legs are like jelly, the adrenaline from the free fall evaporating. Determination propels me forward. Or abject stupidity.

Since we landed so close to the burning town, it takes only thirty seconds to reach the edge. The chaos of the moment threatens to overwhelm me. Sure, I've seen movies with similar scenes. But movies could never capture the suffocating smoke of burning homes. The fearful cries of babies. The smell of iron.

Without the carnage, the town would be quaint. Stalls from the market litter the town center. Toppled carts spill their contents across the dirt. Piles of fruit, clothes, and gleaming jewels.

It seems the attack came out of nowhere. Bodies lie prone in pools of blood. Some wear faces of fear, while others look like they're taking a nap.

My stomach heaves, and I rush to the house right by me. Leaning against it, I vomit up breakfast; the acid burning my mouth. When nothing else comes up, I wipe my mouth with the back of my hand and turn back to the chaos. While the town center is empty, I catch flashes of movement between the buildings.

I make my way through the bodies, wincing as I trip over an out-stretched arm. It belongs to a young woman with chestnut hair, her dark brown eyes staring off into the distance. My stomach cramps again, but there's nothing left for it to give. How many bodies do I need to see before it stops making me queasy?

Coughing from the smoke, I look around. To my left, a building collapses, embers of fire floating into the air, catching on the thatch roof of the neighboring building. It whooshes up in flames.

It's the wail of fear that raises goose bumps along my arms. There's someone in the building, its roof engulfed in flames.

With a sudden burst of energy, I bolt toward the sound. The world around me narrows as I hear the scream. "Help!"

The voice is weak. Young. I skid to a stop in front of the thick wooden door. Without thinking, I grab the metal handle and push. It squeals open, revealing an orange and yellow lit room, the shadow of flames dancing along the walls and floor.

It's a modest home with a bed in one corner and a small table in the other. A fireplace sits against the wall, ironically containing a roaring fire.

"Help me, please!"

The voice is weaker, a staccato of coughs interrupting the plea. My focus homes in on the bed and the two eyes peering at me from underneath. Without a single thought about myself, I rush over. Pieces of straw and mud fall from the ceiling, and a blanket near a washbasin catches fire. We have mere seconds until we're swallowed up by flames.

Dropping to all fours, I lean over and hold out a hand to the young girl, her russet skin marred with smears of soot and dirt. Her sepia-colored eyes glisten with tears, wide and frantic.

"Come on, let's go," I urge, shaking my hand impatiently, hoping she'll grab it. There's another crash behind us, and the crackle of something burning makes a cold sweat break out down my spine.

The girl looks at my hand, then beyond my body. Just as I think I'll need to drag her out, she grabs it. Her small palm holds on for dear life as I drag her out.

She's younger than I thought, around five years old. She barely comes up to my hip. Hoping for the best, I scoop her into my arms. She's heavy, but the door isn't too far away.

My thighs tremble as I rush out of the burning home, the smoke almost too thick to see through the doorway. Stumbling past the threshold, I'm able to bring her a few more feet before I fall down. My knees slam against the ground, my arms barely preventing a face-plant. She cries out as she tumbles with me, clutching my neck. Behind us, the house collapses into a bonfire of memories.

"Meegan! Oh, thank sweet Inanna, you're alive."

Still on all fours, trying to breathe, I look up to watch a dark-skinned woman rushing over to us, her arms already out. Meegan lets go of my neck and scrambles toward her mother, bawling.

"Mama!" The two collide, hugging fiercely. The mother's covered in mud and blood, although she doesn't appear to be injured. Her loose braids decorated with beads tinkle as she covers Meegan's face with frantic kisses.

I cough and sit up, leaning against my heels. "She seems okay. Just scared."

177

The mother looks at me, her head still tucked into Meegan's neck. Her voice cracks when she says, *"Thank you. Thank you. Thank you."*

She focuses back on Meegan, pushing her away enough to scan her body. The burning building catches her eye, and a look of unfiltered anguish flickers before every emotion's wiped away.

She looks back down at Meegan, showing a look of strength only a mother in survival mode can offer. "We need to go, honey. Okay?"

Meegan nods, grabbing her mother's hand as the woman stands. My lungs still ache, but I push myself to stand. The rescue took only seconds, but it feels like years have passed since I last used my legs.

They both look at me. Meegan brings a dirty hand up to her mouth to cup a cough. A tear tracks down her cheek through a layer of soot. Behind me, the screams come back into focus, and my heart pounds wildly. This isn't over yet.

The woman croaks out, "Thank you again for saving my little girl. You should come with us. There's nothing left here but death."

The howl of a wolf wrenches the air, a beacon for my original intent. I shake my head. "You go. I'll be fine. The lordess is here to kick butt."

She hesitates for a split second, looks down at Meegan, then whirls away, tugging her daughter to keep up.

As the mother and daughter disappear, I turn back to the sounds of fighting. If I'm going to do stupid things today, I might as well go full throttle stupid.

Chapter Twenty

Must. Stay. Impartial.

The walkways between each row of buildings are littered with more bodies and pools of blood. I can witness death being delivered in high-definition.

It's delivered in the form of beasts covered in gray, scaly skin. At seven feet tall, each of them holds wicked-looking spears that slice through bodies like butter. On their heads are tall, curling horns. When they roar at their victims, fangs flash in the sunlight. Most of them wear pants with leather boots, but are otherwise bare chested.

I'm fairly positive these are Vulturians.

They look like the vicious creatures in the painting — brutal and bloodthirsty. Their weapons swing freely, destroying anything in their path. Men attack them with rough-hewn weapons. Some succeed in inflicting superficial injuries, but too often, they don't.

One of the monsters takes a massive hand and wraps it around a man's throat, lifting him off the ground like he weighs nothing. His kicks are futile, as are his attempts to claw at the large hand. The Vulturian just laughs in his face.

Newfound adrenaline surges, filling me with rage. These people probably woke up this morning, worrying about mundane things like gardening or peddling their wares. Now these assholes show up, murdering and pillaging?

My toe stubs against something. It's an orange covered in dirt and as big as my fist. I pick it up, my hands shaking violently. The smooth skin is warm in my palm. In this situation, I might be a mouse, but I'll be damned if I let the cat get a free meal.

Digging my fingers into the piece of fruit, I jog toward the creature. The man in his grip is turning purple, and his movements are weakening.

"Hey! Over here! Over here!!"

The monster ignores me. Instead, its face leans closer to the man, seeming to feast on his terror. I'm used to being ignorable, but this is literally a matter of life or death. The man's face is turning an alarming shade of purple. *I need to make it stop.* Reeling my arm back, I throw the orange with as much power as I can muster.

With every atom of stupidity available in this universe, I scream, "Hey, asshole! Your brother fucked your mother last night."

Surprisingly, my aim is true. It lands against its head, catching on a horn. It dangles for a second before plopping to the ground.

The monster stills, pitch-black eyes focusing on me. I look down and grab another orange. There's a loose pile on the ground, spilling from a nearby basket. I throw it again. This time, it lands between those soulless eyes. It snorts with surprise and shakes its head.

I'm just as surprised as he is, to be honest. I didn't know I had that kind of aim.

The man gasps as he's released, falling into a heap on the ground. It takes a second, but he's finally able to suck in air, clutching at his throat. He cast me a grateful look before stumbling to stand and running away.

My relief is short-lived. The monster stalks toward me, murderous rage clear on its scaly features. I scramble back, stepping behind a wagon. He bats it away, and it flies across the market, shattering against a brick building.

Shit.

Before I can run, he backhands me hard. I fly through the air ... and not in a cool way. More in a "that frisbee hit the wall and redirected" kind of way.

The earth greets me with cold apathy, rattling my bones as I land like a sack of wet flour. A wheelbarrow hits my spine, and pain forces a cry from me as the wind leaves my lungs. My eyesight disappears for a second, increasing my fear.

There's no time to assess anything. When my vision clears, I scan what's around, spotting a jagged piece of wood with the ends still smoldering. It's not a wooden sword, but maybe it'll help? Lunging for it, I swipe at the monster as it steps closer.

Out of its mouth comes a grating chortle. Like an orca playing with its food. Although my body screams in protest, I try to stand. I will *not* die lying down.

Instead of having a brave moment myths are made of, my body gives out. I've pushed it too far. There was no way to train for something like this in such a short time, and now, I'm unable to greet death on my terms.

The monster senses weakness and steps closer. I try to lift the piece of wood, but this time, my shoulders refuse. It's all I can do to get air into my lungs, and even that's turning into a struggle. The world's tunneling, and clearly, this is the moment I'm going to die.

For the second time in less than ten minutes, I'm facing my death. As the creature outstretches its dagger-sharp claws, I fiercely wish it was the earth that had flattened me.

Bracing for the blow, I wait for all of it to end. The terror's interrupted by a mighty howl. The creature's removed out of sight by a train wreck of black fur. My head lolls to the side to watch Kalliope slide to a half stop, kicking up dirt, spittle flying from her fangs.

Her fur's matted with blood and mud, the snarling maw coated with brilliant blue liquid. The blood of whatever these creatures are.

The male's barely fazed, still standing. They square off, circling each other. The wolf's hackles rise, and a feral snarl rends from her jaws.

The Vulturian hoists up its weapon and swings. She jumps out of the way easily. The weapon swings again and thus begins a dance of swiping and missing. Kalliope dodges each swing. When the creature swings slowly, she takes advantage of the mistake and lunges.

181

There's a roar as Kalliope's teeth slice into the scaly skin easily, ripping apart the flesh. Blue blood sprays in the air, and even though I'm an inch from death, I smile. I'm officially, happily, Stockholmed.

"You weren't supposed to be here," the creature hisses in a deep, grinding voice. The words shock me. For whatever reason, the idea that they could speak didn't cross my mind.

He swings again, and she hops out of the way. "These one-forms are ours to harvest as we see fit. Our forefathers owned this land, and it's not yours to take."

Kalliope growls so low, the sound rumbles in my ribs. No words are needed to translate her thoughts on the matter. He responds in kind, taking another swing at her.

She looks at me and winks. She fucking *winks*. This whole time, she's been playing with him. With a howl that rattles the nearby windows, she lunges so fast, he doesn't even have time to raise the weapon.

He lands on his back with her paws on his shoulders. I hear bones cracking. In a flash, her teeth are around his skull, crushing it like a watermelon. Pulp and blood ooze out. It's absolutely disgusting.

And so godsdamn hot. Because I'm a half-dead horn-dog virgin nerd.

With one more glance toward me, Kalliope bounds off. There aren't a lot of them left, and within a couple of minutes, she's back at my side. She transforms back into her base form, falling into a heap at my side. She's covered in blood and dirt — shifting didn't remove the carnage created by her wolf.

"Saira, are you okay?"

Her hands rove over my body, checking if the blood is mine. I try to sit up and fail.

"Give me five minutes, and I can go for another flying lesson."

She hisses through her teeth as she lifts my shirt, looking for wounds. "Now is not the time to jest. Where are you hurt?"

I weakly raise a hand, trying to wave her away. A long nap sounds wonderful right about now. "Go help everyone else. I'll be okay here. I might live here now, to be honest."

All around us are wails and the sounds of terrified animals. Kalliope bites her lip and looks around. "The Vulturians are gone, for now. I need to fly back to the manor and give word to the surrounding towns and have reinforcements sent." She looks back at me. "I need to know you're safe. Can you stand?"

"No." I'm not about to act tough. "But don't worry about me. Go help everyone else."

"I'm not leaving you here, Saira," she says fiercely. "Give me a second."

She stands and runs off before I can respond. I turn my head until my cheek is flush with the dirt. The beads of sweat coagulate into the mud on my face. All I want right now is to crawl into my big soft bed at the manor and sleep for weeks. Months. Decades.

Closing my eyes, I force myself to focus on the breath entering my sore lungs. A rib cuts into the left one, causing unfamiliar sharp pains.

When I try to move my arms, an electric shock of agony streaks down my spine. Probably from when I'd landed on the wheelbarrow.

The longer I'm on the ground, the softer it becomes. A nap sounds like a great idea. I could sleep for a decade right now. The muscles in my body relax without permission, and the sounds around me fade.

"Saira." Kalliope's voice comes from far away, but I'm too tired to even open my eyes now. Kalliope repeats my name several times, but I don't respond. Darkness comes and wraps itself around me.

The room's cast in deep shadows when I wake up. Familiar sheets are pulled up to my shoulders, tucked in tight around my body. Someone brought me to my bedroom. Was it Kalliope?

Stifling a groan, I roll to my side and peer into the darkest parts of the room. A crackling fire offers nothing but orange light and deep shadows. Empty shadows.

No one's here.

My heart falls. I didn't expect anyone to be anxiously waiting by my bed, but it would've been nice to wake up with someone caring about me.

Sitting up, wincing at the stiff muscles, I huff and let out a growl of frustration. "Saira, get your shit together," I mutter. "Being alone is only temporary."

There's no point in feeling sorry for myself. Biting back a whimper, I reach for the edge of the comforter, bracing for the inevitable agony.

I hear a voice below me. "I wouldn't do that if I were you."

I shriek, and my entire body jolts with fear. Adrenaline numbs my pain enough to allow me to crawl to the other side of the bed like a startled cat. "What the fuck?"

Kalliope's form rising from the edge of the mattress. She contorts her limbs, stretching them. Her hair is tousled, desperately needing a brush. She yawns, ignoring my obvious fear.

The sense of loneliness from seconds ago vanishes. She'd been sleeping on the floor. Watching over me. Protecting me.

"You better lay back down." Her tone holds a warning. With predatory grace, she walks over to my side of the bed, eyes locked onto me. "You seriously hurt your back, Saira."

Sitting back on my heels, I bring my hands to the small of my back. It's bruised and stiff, but nothing else seems to be wrong.

She stops alongside me, peering down. There's something indecipherable in her expression. My head swims, and I sway. In a flash, Kalliope has my head in one hand and my back in the other. She lowers me down tenderly, making sure my head isn't jostled.

"Like I said," she murmurs. "You should lie back down."

"Sounds awful like an 'I told you so.'" Exhaustion sweeps over me as the adrenaline of my initial shock fades.

Pulling back the sheets, working around my prone body, she smiles. It's wolfish, her sharp canines so foreign yet familiar. "I don't believe in such a phrase." She pauses. "But I will say my predictions were correct."

It's difficult to muster the energy to stick my tongue out at her, but I succeed. She chuckles, bringing the blanket up to my chest. It feels like being tucked in by my mother. The thought makes my throat tighten.

Unaware of the sudden surge of emotion overtaking my thoughts, Kalliope sits at the edge of the bed and grabs one of my hands. Dark smudges mar her face. The scent of soot and iron hit me. Has she not even showered?

"Saira, you almost died." Her voice is raspy, catching on the last word. *Died.*

With a nervous laugh, I wiggle my fingers. "I look pretty good for someone who should be dead."

She squeezes my hand and stands. "Well, I'm glad for your quick healing."

Exhaustion is settling in. "Me too. But I'm already ready for a nap."

She places a chaste kiss on my forehead. "I must go tend to matters. I'll send Meadow in to assist you with whatever you need."

She walks toward the door. Desperate to keep her here a little longer, I ask, "Where's Legend?"

She pauses at the door, one hand already twisting the knob. "He's been helping at the village we saved. They need as much support as possible. Daeva isn't sure how the hell they made it that far in our domain, so she's gone on a border inspection. This can't ever happen again."

The charred scent of the buildings still lingers in my memory. "How many people were lost?"

A haunted look darkens her expression. "Too many. Far too many."

"Did any Vulturians escape?"

Anger pinches her brows, a tinge of red flushing her cheeks. "It's uncertain. Daeva has Guardians scouring the nearby forest for trails, but there's been nothing yet."

It's unsettling to know those Vulturians are out there, possibly planning another attack. Kalliope opens the door, offering one last meaningful look before closing it behind her. Snuggling into the soft blankets, I blow out a frustrated breath. Things have become infinitely more difficult. Without knowing if the Vulturians are going to continue being an issue to non-Amicums, it's hard to justify recommending this place as a safe haven.

The thought of leaving this place and never returning creates a sense of unease. Minus outliers like Daeva or the Vulturians, everyone has been generous with their kindness. Plus, there's indoor plumbing ... fancy parties ... incredible food ...

And Kalliope. Legend.

Nope. This decision, this recommendation, can't be based on whatever emotions are growing. The scientific part of me has to take everything into consideration, with nothing but objectivity. Dad will be disappointed if I can't provide impartial facts and recommendations.

Those facts don't make the thought of leaving and never returning any less disappointing.

Hopefully, it doesn't become even harder to say goodbye.

Chapter Twenty-One

Petting The Manticore

The next day, Legend comes to visit. In his arms is a wicker basket overflowing with items.

"What do you have there?" I ask, eyeing him as he walks over to the bed. He's wearing a maroon shirt and tan breeches, but entirely barefoot.

Legend slashes a grin. "I'm sure bedrest is boring. When I was ten-and-three, I fell off of a cliff and broke a leg. My mother forced me to lie in bed for two weeks. It nearly drove me mad."

"I am *not* staying in this bed for two weeks," I insist, panic blooming.

He places the basket at the end of the mattress and waves away my concern. "Of course not. However, I'm sure this is still boring."

Sitting up in bed, I watch him perch on the edge of the mattress and unload everything. My eyes lock onto the set of cards kept together by string.

Reaching for them, I untie the string and inspect the design. The design comprises purple, green, and blue shades. Various types of shifted Amicums decorate the smooth card stock. Unfortunately, I can't understand any of the characters.

"Do you like playing cards?" Legend asks.

I shrug. "I've played poker with Piper a few times. She tried to make it strip poker a couple of times with her friends, but it never sounded appealing."

He tilts his head, interest clear on his face. "Strip poker? As in stripping off clothing?"

Laughing, I flip over the individual cards. "Yep. Piper has always been a bit more free in that way. She likes being the life of the party."

"She sounds like a good person to have around for a good time," he says, placing the basket on the ground. "I don't know what poker is, but there are some games I can teach you." He pauses, eyes scanning my face. "If you'd like, that is."

A shy smile splits my face. "I'd love the company."

The next hour's spent with Legend trying to teach me how to play a card game Plorate Prime. Since this is the first time I've tried to learn their written language, it's overwhelming. Solve the problem of singularities and wormholes? No problem.

Learning the numerical symbols for a batch of cards? Less impressive.

It doesn't matter though — we spend the time laughing. Legend regales me with stories of growing up on a vineyard and the pressures his parents placed upon his shoulders to join the family business. I learned the adult age for Amicums is twenty-one, and they don't join any formal training until they're seventeen. Before then, younglings learn self-defense skills and hone their shifting abilities. Younglings from all over the continent come to Ilorna for this training.

It's a fascinating insight into their culture. The bonus feature of this experience is the privilege of watching Legend's face light up when he talks about his family. He's an only child; his parents also had high hopes for him, something I can deeply relate to.

"My father thought I'd stay, simply because of how scrawny I was," he jokes, throwing down a card. He crows with delight, so it's probably safe to assume he's winning.

I rear my head back, then make a show of looking him up and down — or side to side, since he's sprawled out on his hips, resting his head in a hand. "Scrawny? You?"

Legend flips three cards, then places one on top of the other. No clue why. "Unfortunately, yes. Adolescence was kind to me. It was fortuitous, because the bigger I became, the larger shifts I could manage."

I nod as if I understand. "What is your preferred form?"

He throws me a crooked smile. "A manticore."

This male is full of surprises. "Why the hell a manticore? Do they actually exist?"

"Yes, not too far from here," he says vaguely. Almost a little too nonchalant. "When I reached adulthood, my true-form filled out, granting me the ability to shift into much larger creatures."

"But why the manticore?" I try to imagine the mythical beast in my mind's eye. It's a struggle.

When he picks up five cards randomly — at least, it seems random — he says, "It's a triple threat. Four paws for ground attack. Wings for scouting. A stinger for the most gruesome of deaths." He winks. "Or if I'm feeling particularly dramatic."

"Can I see?"

Legend considers the request, then swings off the mattress in one smooth movement. I appreciate the view as he walks to the middle of the room, pushing the chaise aside. Turning to look at me, he says, "Males may not shift publicly without a permit. Because Ilorna is home to the Guardians, and male shifts are more aggressive, it's tightly controlled after a male reaches adulthood." There's that crooked grin again. "So please refrain from sharing with anyone but the Cohort that you've seen me shift."

I cross my chest with a finger. "I promise."

A shimmering cloud appears, then an immense manticore sits prettily, watching me with intelligent eyes. With a lion's body the color of burnished gold, its jet black mane frames a gold leonine face. From between its shoulder blades flair a pair of light-gold feathered wings, almost as tall as the ceiling.

Something crashes to the ground, and I peer around the lion's body to see a twitching scorpion tail right next to a shattered vase. The onyx carapace narrows into a wicked stinger that glints in the lamplight.

Its eyes are Legend's eyes, though. Irises the shade of early spring watches me with an intensity I'm not sure how to handle. Heat sparks

189

in my belly. This massive predator could kill me in three seconds flat. I'm pretty sure my head could fit in its mouth.

The manticore slowly blinks, then pads over to the bed. My heart rattles the bars of my rib cage as the largest predator I've ever seen comes to sit next to my side of the bed. Oxygen refuses to spear through the tightness in my lungs, the adrenaline and fear shaking my bones.

A deep vibration turns me into a human tambourine. It takes a second to understand it's the manticore purring. Fingers shaking, I reach forward, pressing a hand to its snout.

Legend nuzzles my palm. Grinning, I rub into the soft fur of his cheek. "You're just a sweet kitten, aren't you?"

Legend purrs louder. Even shifted, he still smells of citrus. The manticore groans when my fingers find the back of his ear. I recruit both hands to rub my thumbs into the shell of his ear — it's as big as one hand. The manticore snorts, pushing its snout into my chest. I laugh, playfully swatting at him.

"Naughty kitty. Mind your manners."

I swear Legend laughs through a breathy chuff. Now that my fear is dissipating, it's a fantastic realization I'm petting one of the most revered mythical creatures. Somehow, I need to get a photo of this.

The air drops a few degrees in temperature as the manticore disappears, replaced by Legend kneeling in front of me, arms crossed on the edge of the mattress. His head's propped up on his wrists, giving me puppy-dog eyes. It makes me laugh again.

"That was pretty impressive," I admit. "Bigger than I expected."

He sighs, crawling onto the bed, laying on his side again. "If I could, I'd be like Ginger, shifted into the manticore all the time."

"But you can shift around friends?"

Legend nods, recollecting a handful of cards. Don't ask me why. "Yes, and around other Amicums in specific situations: training, on private land, and in dire emergencies. It cuts down incidents drastically, although accidents happen."

"What happens if there's an accident?" I breathe.

He grows somber. "For each offense, they send males who break the law to a refreshment course and take away all their privileges for six months."

"Harsh," I say, grabbing some cards, pretending to know what's going on. "Is it actually peaceful here? Amicums respect the law?"

"Mm-hmm," he hums. "The law went into effect fifteen years ago, in part of our foremothers laying the groundwork. Those who agreed with the restrictions were welcome to stay. Of course, the war granted an exception for those long fourteen months."

"What was it like? The war?" I ask, the words a whisper.

Legend's expression darkens, his brows furrowing. He places the cards on the duvet, but I'm positive it's not related to the game. Running a hand down his face, he says, "Horrific. Most of Ilorna's Guardians left and never returned. It decimated the population across all provinces, but most of all here since our province focuses on Guardian training."

His voice grows hoarse as he says, "Kalliope and I were lucky in the way we were barely adults, so our parents' passing wasn't devastating as it was for the younglings suddenly without family. The situation thrust Kalliope into the position of Lordess, replacing her mother before the embers of her corpse cooled."

The words catch in his throat, and tears silver the rims of his dark lashes. "We were barely into adulthood, Kalliope and I. While my father was permitted to stay on the vineyard — he didn't have enough power to shift into useful forms — my mother dedicated every part of herself to protect one-forms. She died protecting them. Kalliope's father passed shortly after she was born, so losing her mother was compounded by suddenly becoming an orphan."

My heart aches deeply for them both. Knowing what it's like to watch a parent die and lose everyone in your family ... at least I have the option of saving most of mine. They have no option but to live with the sorrow. Empathetic tears blur his grief-stricken face as he continues.

"Those first few months were ..." he struggles to find the words. "... catastrophic. We were fortunate to have Zenab return as a valuable resource and advisor. Without her, I'm not sure what would've happened.

Kalliope rose to the challenge beautifully, and I gladly stood at her side, offering whatever support possible."

The words dry up in his throat as he swallows hard. I scoot forward, placing a hand on his arm. "You don't have to share anymore. I'm sorry if my curiosity caused you pain. It wasn't my intent."

Emerald eyes drill into mine, still wet with tears. "I'm glad of it. We don't discuss these things anymore. Everyone is eager to move on from the devastation, so aside from the Cohort's discussions, most Amicums prefer to avoid the topic."

His smile is soft and appreciative. "So thank you for asking. While we're still learning one another, it's clear how good your heart is, Saira. It's my favorite thing about you."

A blush creeps up my neck, spreading across my cheeks. The compliment is overwhelming, and it's easier to ignore. I'm trying so hard to stay objective, but at this point, I'm just struggling to lie to myself. "Of course. I'm always willing to listen. I'm sure Kalliope listens, but I'm also here if you need."

We hold eye contact for a moment longer before he looks away, down to the cards. "You know you've lost, right?"

I laugh, grateful for the topic change. My heart can't take anymore devastation. Blinking away the unshed tears, I say, "I'm still not sure how this game is even played. Want to go over the rules again?"

Legend chuckles, transforming his face to one of amusement. "It would be my pleasure, Gem."

The next few days are spent lounging in bed while my body slowly heals, with Meadow fussing over me. Legend visits every day, either playing cards or telling me Amicum fairy tales, which are not too different from Mother Goose stories.

When no one is looking, I pop in my headphones and listen to some of my favorite songs and read books on my e-reader. Not realizing I have books of my own on a device, Ginger stops by to offer a handful of books to read. None of them are in a language I understand. The chip simply won't let me process words. Something Dad and I are going to remedy somehow.

Kalliope hasn't visited once since I woke up. I hate that it bothers me. After days of tension building between us, this distance is painful. Post-Vulturian attack, she needed to consult with other lordesses and towns to ensure future security and protection. I get it — it's a leadership thing.

Doesn't mean I have to like it.

Having comforts from home helps ease the constant homesickness. Even though Meadow brings me delicious food, I miss greasy chow mein and enchiladas; I asked Meadow if the chef could make any of it and received only slow blinks of confusion.

All this time in bed has given me ample opportunity to consider how I want the rest of this experience to go, especially here in Ilorna. I'd be lying if the first four stops didn't make me nervous to go somewhere new next. Even my backpack filled with amenities can't make up for certain things.

The other day proved how out of shape I am. At home, I wasn't the most active person. Research ate up my free time when I wasn't studying. On the rare days off, my preference had been takeout, movies, and sleeping in until noon. Quick, reliable nervous system regulators that didn't actually regulate me. It just made me feel less like an agitated cactus as the stress ate me.

Safe in my lab, I imagined trekking through lands without weather, meeting people without biases, smiling as I shoved samples into the analyzer, and then reappearing in the lab feeling refreshed.

I was a fucking idiot, and it's time to get real with myself.

That life is over. The sooner I come to terms with this, the easier things will be. Ilorna is a suitable spot to learn how to defend myself. Maybe I can become some fantasy heroine with epic bow and arrow skills. Or, at the very least, learn to use more than an orange as a weapon.

It's a complete one-eighty from my thoughts after the party, but being attacked was a wake-up call. Objectively, it's more dangerous to cling to my dedication to objectivity like armor. I can't very well hold up a finger at an attacker and say, "Well, actually, I'm trying to remain neutral, so if you could not, that would be great."

I'm sure that'd go over well.

So far, I've had a shark and a bear try to eat me. Tossed around like a volleyball by a Vulturian. I'm not sure what kind of defense skills could've saved me in those moments, but it's highly improbable those will be my last brushes with death.

This is an opportunity to arm myself with skills. While there is an urgency to get home, it's not like rushing through this experience will save them any faster, technically. But if something successfully kills me because I couldn't run any meaningful distance or defend myself somehow, I'd die a stubborn fool.

By day four of bedrest, I conclude that it's more short-sighted to rush through the experience than to take advantage of the opportunity to learn more defensive skills and improve my physical capabilities.

Which is why, when Meadow shows up with a tray of breakfast, I'm already dressed and on my way out the door.

Her mouth drops open. "Miss Saira, you should still be in bed." Placing the tray down on a table, she rushes over. "Please let me help you —"

I hold a hand up before she has a chance to try and steer me back to the four-poster bed. "I promise I'm alright." I do a messy pirouette as if it proves my point. "See?"

A wrinkle pinches between her brows. "I'm not sure. The lordess might not—"

"Is she at breakfast?"

I'm eager to be near Kalliope. Meadow must see resolve on my face because she sighs and heads out of the bedroom.

"Yes, I'll take you."

This time, I recognize the pathway and almost charge ahead of her out of sheer enthusiasm. When we enter the dining room, I'm pleased to find not only Kalliope at the table, but the Cohort and Legend.

They all look up with surprise, then joy — except for Daeva, who scowls. I hold back an eye roll. Shocking.

Without an invitation, I march down the room, passing the empty chairs until I'm beside Legend. I sit beside him and grab a carafe. He slides an empty cup over, and I fill it with coffee.

Kalliope watches with silent appraisal, and it's surprising to find dark circles under her eyes. Exhaustion strains her features. Is it my imagination, or is she also frowning at me?

Zenab, on the other hand, grins. "There's our new warrior. I heard you took on a Vulturian by yourself."

I snort. "It was disastrous, is what it was."

"Doubt it," she shoots back. "It might've been embarrassing, though. Should I now call you the Vulturian Victor? Victim? Vindicator? Perhaps Ginger has recommendations?"

"I like the Vulturian Vindicator," Ginger quips.

Zenab catches the roll I throw at her face and takes a bite, grinning.

Legend angles toward me, leaning against an elbow. His green eyes twinkle with a hint of diablerie. "How are you?"

"Like I've spent days in bed and I'm going stir crazy."

Zenab unsheathes a dagger and sharpens the edge with a stone. "If you're looking to avoid disaster in the future, we could begin training, if you'd like."

It's like she read my mind. I grin. "I was actually thinking about asking for training." I punch the air dramatically, like I'm in a fistfight. "Gotta give those Vulturians the ol' one-two, you know?"

She holds back a laugh, then looks to Kalliope for confirmation. The entire table does.

Kalliope takes a sip from a cup. It's hard to ignore that she avoids making eye contact with me. "I don't see why not, but take it easy. You just endured your first battle."

195

I shrug. "Thanks, but no thanks. Frankly, that battle went poorly because I'm still not in the best shape."

Daeva curls a lip, sneering. "Maybe you're not built to defend yourself. One-forms aren't known for their survivability."

"Are you threatened by the idea of my becoming more capable?" I shoot back. This chick is getting on my nerves.

Her eyes turn to slits as she hisses. "As if you could become capable of being a *threat.*"

"Come on, Dae. Don't tell me you're opposed to someone learning how to defend themselves?" Zenab sounds like she's teasing, but there's an undercurrent to the words. I remember her comments at the first breakfast, about Daeva needing to be reminded of her place.

Daeva shoots a sharp look at Zenab. "You can mind your own business, Zenab."

It's a mystery why Daeva's in the Cohort if she's the problematic one. A question better asked when she isn't around.

Kalliope's water glass slams on the table, interrupting whatever Daeva opened her mouth to say. "Stop. Daeva, your concern is touching"—Zenab snorts, and Kalliope shoots her a reproachful glare before refocusing on Daeva—"*but*, unwarranted. If Saira believes she is ready to continue training, none of us are in a position to tell her otherwise."

Daeva looks away, her jaw muscles pulsing as she grinds her teeth. Zenab responds by stuffing a handful of berries into her mouth. Legend sits back in his chair, slowly sipping a coffee.

The idea of a Cohort would imply a more cohesive team, but there's nothing cohesive about them. Daeva is clearly the most outspoken — and the most unhappy.

The coffee in my belly sits heavy as angry red splotches mottle Daeva's cheeks. She glares at everyone at the table, her gaze settling on me. "You're a liability. A distraction. So if you need to get training like some weak youngling, who am I to deny you?" She bolts upright. "But if you'll excuse me, I have to go do my *job* and figure out why the Vulturians made it past our borders."

With a frustrated snarl, she stalks out of the room. She doesn't shift, but dark leopard spots speckle her icy skin. The black cloud of energy I hadn't noticed before lifts and leaves with her.

The rest of us watch her walk out of the room. Looking at Kalliope, her expression now blazes with frustration.

Zenab sighs. "Well, it wouldn't be a real breakfast without some sort of disagreement."

Ginger snorts. "It's becoming tedious."

"Why is she always so angry?" The question pops out before I can pause and think better of it. Three pairs of eyes shift to me. I shouldn't have asked, but the words can't be taken back.

Kalliope twirls her water glass on the table. "I enjoy having Daeva in the Cohort because she isn't afraid to disagree. She's extremely protective of these lands, which is worth appreciation."

"But it also means she can be a bit of a bitch," Zenab adds.

Kalliope shoots her a razor-edged look. "Mind your words before I mind them for you."

Even though she has at least a couple of decades on Kalliope, Zenab looks chastened. "Apologies. That was uncalled for."

Legend stands, pushing his chair back loudly. "Well, respectable females, I must tend to my duties. It was an eventful breakfast." He looks at me. "I hope your training goes well."

Kalliope reaches for an apple, taking a bite as she stands. "I have a council meeting in an hour I must prepare for." She glances between Zenab and Ginger. "Please ensure Saira is safe."

All I receive is an unreadable glance before she marches out of the room. My spirit deflates. I thought we were getting somewhere, but apparently not.

Zenab and Ginger must think the same thing because they frown. Zenab furrows her brow, quirking her mouth with confusion. But the expression fades away, turning friendly.

"Meet me at the training grounds in an hour."

Chapter Twenty-Two

They're Vicious Piranhas

The training grounds are far behind the manor, surrounded by evergreens. It's a circular area that appears to be split into quarters.

One quarter hosts a jungle-gym-like setup with some lifted platforms higher than the nearby trees. Wooden posts are connected by ropes, bridges, and other tactical development challenges.

The second quarter is a big pond of water, with younglings sitting on the edge and shapes swimming underneath the cobalt surface.

Next to that section is flat, with soft sand covering the ground. Baby animals frolic in the sand, including an energetic, feisty colt trying to bite the butt of a tiger cub.

Zenab stands in the middle of the final area, surrounded by a group of younglings, all of whom are wielding wooden swords. It's comical to watch seven-year-olds fumble with the fake weapons, even going so far as to stab one another while laughing.

Multiple pairs of eyes latch onto my form as I make my way over, swinging myself ungracefully over a short wooden fence. The younglings move away from Zenab as I draw closer. She pauses in whatever she's saying to look over her shoulder. Smiling, she beckons me to come closer.

As I come to stand beside her, she gives the younglings a stern look. "Stop gawking and begin with the footwork."

They scramble to obey, squaring off in pairs, back to smacking one another with squeals and laughter. It's impossible not to chuckle at their antics.

Zenab watches them with a mix of amusement and exasperation. "I swear, this batch might be the death of me." She looks me up and down, assessing. "Tell me a little about your physical abilities."

I blanched. "Well, I've never lifted a sword before, if that's what you're asking."

She raises an eyebrow. "That's not what I'm asking. How far can you run without stopping?"

My body prickles with embarrassment. "Does jogging to the kitchen in between commercials count?"

Zenab's mouth parts as her eyes widen. "What ... is a commercial? Is it a type of workout?"

Cringing, I shake my head. The most running I've actually done recently was at the lab on a treadmill, setting baseline stats for comparison when I return. I wheezed through the entire ordeal and tweaked my knee at barely a mile. It took a whole week of ice and rest to heal it.

Pretty sure this information will send Zenab into a fit though, so I say, "I've never really been much of the type to workout, period. Things have been a tad crazy at home."

Normally, Zenab is as cool as a cucumber. So when her jaw slackens with shock, it's clear that my words were unexpected.

Her voice is breathless when she finally says, "So you've never worked out?"

I shake my head. She steps back to reassess her opinion of me, mouth twisting in thought. Maybe the ground will open up and swallow me whole; save me from this humiliation.

Finally, Zenab must come to a decision because she abruptly nods her head once and motions for me to follow her.

"Training just began, so we're still in warm-ups. Today, we can get you familiarized with the footwork."

"Wait, you want me to train with these,"—I motion to the group of younglings eyeing me curiously—"*kids*? Won't I hurt them?"

199

This elicits a hearty laugh from her. "Most of these younglings could outspar you any day. Don't let their smaller stature fool you. They're vicious piranhas."

"I'll fight her!" a small boy chirps. He has dark blond hair and eyes the color of the full moon.

Zenab snaps her fingers, and he winces. "Asher, focus on your own training. Saira needs to catch up first."

Not saying another word, Asher begins an awkward dance in the dirt, looking down at his feet so many times, he trips every couple of steps. Walking over to the nearby fence, I pick up one of the wooden swords. It's light in my hands; the wood is worn and smooth. Easy day.

"Come on, let's go over here." Zenab guides me off the side, not so far that I'd be alone, but not so close to tempt the younglings with trying to sword fight me.

When she stops, she reaches for the wooden sword. I hand it over, and she promptly tosses it over her shoulder. "You need to earn that."

Earn a wooden sword?

Well, that's insulting. I'm out of shape, but not *that* out of shape.

She squares off opposite me and commands me to do different things. Balance on one foot. Do squats. Run to the fence and run back. The whole time, her expression remains serious. A leader figuring out exactly how much work a soldier needs.

Sweat pours down my temples and soaks through my shirt. My body aches, and, well, I hate to admit it, but she was right. My arms already feel like they're falling off.

More than a bit winded after running laps around the training yard, I stop in front of her and rasp out, "Gimme the truth, doc. Am I a lost cause?"

"Well, you certainly won't be fighting battles anytime soon," she responds dryly. "You carry your weight on your left foot, exhibit horrific posture, and have the balance of a three-legged giraffe."

Wiping sweat off my brow with my shirt, I try to imagine how a three-legged giraffe would walk. It's not promising. "Aren't you supposed to tell me I'm the Chosen One meant to save the world or whatever and that I just need a ten-minute montage to get good?"

This time, she guffaws, bending over at the waist and slapping a thigh. "An excellent jest. You can't even carry the wooden sword for more than two minutes, but you're going to save the world?"

"Thanks for breaking it to me gently. So what can I do about it?"

"Well, being here every single day is a good start. We can train in the mornings before breakfast. Meet me here in the same space. Wear something comfortable."

I motion toward the wooden sword. "When will that come into play?"

She walks back to the younglings, who have now begun wrestling in various animal forms. "Honestly, you'll need to work up to the sword. Run a mile without wheezing, and we'll talk about letting you swing objects around."

It's humbling to look at the younglings and know that they could grind me into the dirt. "Bright and early. Got it."

She gives a curt nod, shifting her attention back to the group. "Alright, cubs and pups. Whose idea was it to shift?"

Chuckling, I find my way back to my room, but it's slow going. All the books I've read talk about how exhausting getting into fighting shape is, living it is a whole other experience. Muscles that have never revealed their existence before burn and throb. I'm not beyond begging Meadow to draw me a hot bath and drowning in it.

My hand shakes as I grab the doorknob. Grimacing, I twist it and almost curse as my first two fingers cramp. Stepping inside, I hiss and shake my hand, forcing the muscles to relax.

"The cramps are the worst."

The familiar voice jerks my head up. Kalliope is sitting on a chair in front of the fire, watching me with interest. Dark crescents cradle her eyes. Her feet perch on the coffee table, fingers crossed in her lap.

"Yeah, well, Zenab is ruthless as hell." I hesitate, then say, "You're a much nicer teacher."

She chuckles. "She makes excellent Guardians, but I remember well what it was like to suffer under her tutelage."

201

Chuckling, I sit across from her, trying to mimic her relaxed demeanor. The claw-foot tub is calling my name, and I love the company, but a bath almost sounds better than whatever conversation this will be. I'm not even positive I'll be able to stand back up without assistance. "To what do I owe this pleasure?"

Her expression is inscrutable. It's draining how much she hides her thoughts and emotions. Although even thinking that makes me a hypocrite.

She goes straight to the point. "I came to apologize. Things with the Vulturians have left much to be handled, and this responsibility has kept me away from you."

"I appreciate it. I've been feeling like I did something wrong."

Her face sours. "Absolutely not. My apologies if this is what you've been thinking." She looks away.

"Zenab says you're a brooder."

Kalliope scoffs and runs a hand down her face. "My Cohort is everything to me, but sometimes, they need to learn the virtue of silence."

A laugh escapes. "I'm not sure they got the memo." I recognize the look Kalliope gives when she has no idea what I've said, but I'm not about to explain what a memo is, though. "You wanted to apologize for being busy?"

She stands abruptly, startling me. I watch wide-eyed as she paces. Clasping her hands behind her back, she stares at the carpet as she says, "No. I came to apologize for the unforgivable act of putting you in danger."

Tension radiates from her in waves. While I can't claim to know Kalliope well, this new side of her is alarming. Normally, she's chill as a cucumber — this is decidedly *not* chill. "What are you talking about? Are you talking about the village attack? Why is that your fault?"

"Because I took you there." Even though she doesn't raise her voice, it's hoarse with emotion. Her pacing increases. She's going to burn a hole in what I'm sure is a very expensive carpet.

I stare at her, stunned. "Kalliope, that wasn't your fault. You couldn't have known the Vulturians would attack."

Everything she's been hiding under the cool facade is leaking out. It hurts my heart to know she blames herself for what was ultimately my poor choice.

She pauses mid-stride to face off toward me. "I should have listened to Daeva. I dismissed her concerns, and it killed people. On top of it all, *I put you in danger.*" Her tone drips with self-hate. "Yes, their attack isn't my fault, but I had the capability of dropping you off further away from it all to keep you safe. Instead, I terrified you with the drop, then essentially inserted you into the danger."

The guilt has been eating at her, and I'd no idea. She isn't responsible for any of it. I've spent this whole time assuming she knew this, but apparently not. I shake my head vigorously. "No, this isn't your fault. *I* ran into the village. If I hadn't, a little girl would be dead. So would have been whoever the Vulturians would have kept attacking. Your fast thinking saved lives, and I'm *glad* I was there to help."

"If something —" Her mouth snaps shut, and she grinds her jaw before saying, "If something had happened, I would have never forgiven myself. Do you understand? You trusted me, and look how I repaid that gift."

It's a heroic effort not to whine as I stand. My muscles aren't currently up to the task. She watches me with gilded eyes as I shuffle closer. Good gods, I need a hot bath and massage. Stopping in front of her, I look up at her face.

There's a tightness in my chest, growing worse as the inches between us fade. These emotions are as unfamiliar as anything else in this world. Why would she care about me?

Putting a hand on her arm, I say, "It wasn't your fault. And I'm okay, alright? Minus my body being in a lot of pain right now, but that's Zenab's fault."

The corner of her mouth twitches. She brings a hand up to cover mine. My pulse quickens at her gentle touch. Voice softening, she leans closer. "Saira, I don't know what it is about you, but since I saw you running from the bear, I've wanted nothing more than to know you. Watching the Vulturian throw you scared me. Those *feelings* scare me." Her face is so close, my cheeks warm with her breath. "Tearing off his head wasn't enough. He deserved far worse. Will you forgive me for not making it more painful for him?"

My heartbeat gallops, pumping blood loudly in my ears. She's so close, we're almost brushing noses. The scent of lavender and fire smoke fills my nose. I bring my other hand up to hold one of hers. It's firm, calloused by years of weapons training. Between the two of us, energy crackles. Touching her feels like a summer day, a delightful buzzing flowing through my nerves. This sensation is familiar. I can't quite place where I've felt it before. Like familiarity and ... home.

She's like home.

Which is impossible.

"Kalliope." My voice is hoarse. "You don't have to apologize for not torturing someone. I'm cool with how he died."

Finally, our foreheads touch. Her hands come up to cup the backs of my arms. Her nose tickles mine. Electricity pings between us, electrifying my skin. "I'm still apologizing all the same."

The tension between us is a rope ready to snap. "Well, now that you've apologized for not torturing someone, what now?"

Warmth spreads through my core. My hips thrust forward of their own accord. She breathes in sharply, tightening her grip on me.

"Saira."

My name is a prayer on her lips. I close my eyes, reveling in the touch. It would be so easy to lose myself inside this moment. With a future so uncertain, it would be a gift to do so.

Lucky for me, she doesn't wait for thoughts to muddy whatever this is, because her lips crash into mine like a hurricane slamming into land. It's frantic. The way she kisses me — there's nothing gentle about it.

Our hands come up to each other's faces. Despite her force, the way she holds my face is reverent. Her thumb sweeps against my cheek. Our tongues dance like familiar partners, swirling and swooping like the planets and stars.

My sore muscles loosen; this kiss reinvigorates me better than any hot bath ever could. There's undeniable magic here, and it scares me. No, it *terrifies* me. This is the fifth moment in my life where I know nothing will ever be the same. I'm ruined and remade as our atoms collide, becoming something entirely new.

Pulling away, my lungs can barely suck in enough air as I say, "Guilt-fueled kisses are incredible."

She growls, slipping one hand to the nape of my neck. Voice rough, she commands, "Be quiet and kiss me again."

Our mouths are back together, and this time, our hands roam. My hands are finally touching everything I'd been admiring. The curve of her ass. The firmness of her breasts. The muscles that ripple down her back. Her fierceness burns through me like a wildfire, frying up every moment of self-doubt that's ever existed. It's all glorious. It's so completely—

You can't fall in love with her.

The unexpected thought causes me to stumble.

You're leaving her here. Forever. You'll break her heart. She doesn't deserve your selfishness. Dad will be so disappointed.

The excitement burns to ashes, and I pull away. It's like ripping off a limb.

Kalliope frowns, scanning my face with confusion. "What's wrong? Are you alright?"

It's the perfect time to reveal everything she needs to know. To spill the beans and put the whole story out in the open. But something inside me refuses to let the words come. Fear has become a steel door, blocking any possible honesty. So I do what needs to be done: I lie.

"I'm tired. I'd hoped to have a bath because everything hurts. Do you think Meadow could come help me out?"

The tight wire of emotion between us snaps. The energy's severed completely, like a hacked-off limb.

She clenches her jaw and looks away. "I'll have her summoned."

She walks to the door. Everything inside me screams to grab her. To say something. To beg for patience. Instead, I stand there in the dark as she leaves; the door closing with an ominous click.

Chapter Twenty-Three

Eavesdropping Is Never A Good Idea

T raining is far more challenging than expected. I wake up early every morning and let Zenab torture me. There isn't much else to do. It's been a week since the awkwardness of the post-kiss with Kalliope, and while she hasn't been outright rude, she's been keeping her distance.

Even Legend seems determined to stay out of it, answering vaguely when I ask for any insight. There's no blaming the guy, but it is frustrating.

What did I expect, though? For her to withstand my hot and cold behavior? It's unfair to hope she'll rebound and just get over it.

Today, I'm going to try and get her to talk to me, though, even if she won't.

All I need to do is get this stupid shirt over my head without my arms falling off.

Gritting my teeth at the tightness in my triceps, I gingerly shrug on a loose shirt—the fashion style is growing on me — and slide on a pair of soft, tan leather trousers. Throwing my hair up into a messy bun, I inspect my reflection in the full-length mirror.

These past couple of weeks being outside have darkened my skin to an even deeper shade of brown. A few new freckles have appeared across the bridge of my nose. My body looks leaner, although my curves still soften my figure. This is the best I've ever looked.

Yet, it's the worst I've ever felt.

Glancing at the fireplace, I remember how Kalliope felt in front of the fiery heat. Of her skin against mine. The way I rejected her.

You're doing her a favor. You'll hurt her.

It's the undeniable truth. It's icky to escalate our relationship at all without full honesty. Otherwise, she's attracted to a farce. The question is: do I bother with honesty? Soon, this place will just be another world I've hopped to. Kalliope will move on, and so will I — universe to universe, until I make it back home. Then, Dad and I will decide what to do, *together.*

That doesn't mean things need to continue being awkward with Kalliope. I crave seeing her happy. I *need* to find her and make things right.

With a heavy sigh, I step out into the hallway. It's empty, so I head to the dining room. Maybe I'll stumble into her like I did last week.

I realize this might not be the best idea. This manor is so big, I still get lost in its many hallways.

Today is no different because I find myself at large glass doors leading to a greenhouse stuffed to the brim with greenery. Flowers I've never seen before bloom on lush bushes. This is a perfect place to gain samples of the local flora.

The sweet smell of flowers beckons me forward, but as I'm about to step in, I hear familiar voices, including Kalliope's patient tone.

Against my better judgment, I pause. I wouldn't be a scientist if I didn't have a bit of curiosity about the unknown. Pressing against the door, I strain to hear what they're saying. Daeva speaks, anger lacing her words.

"... we need to respond immediately. The Vulturians slaughtered the Guardians stationed there. It's how they could destroy the village without warning. We need to go on the defensive. They violated the treaty. We need a show of force, so they think twice before doing it again."

This is terrible timing. There's no way Kalliope will want to have an awkward conversation with the frigid witch around. I turn and walk in the other direction, then I hear Zenab speak.

"Your Grace, as much as it pains me, I agree with Daeva. If we let this slide, who knows what they'll do next?"

It probably makes me an asshole, but I pause, my never-ending curiosity piqued. It's an opportunity to learn more about the Vulturians without having to ask questions. I *need* more information about this conflict with the Vulturians before I can confidently recommend this place as an option. Tucking myself against the wall, I tilt my head to hear them better.

"I will not step into the possibility of another Vulturian war without a strong enough cause." Kalliope's tone brooks no argument.

"Three dozen villagers isn't *enough* for you?" Daeva seethes.

Kalliope snaps, "Of course it's a travesty, General Stryder, but you seem to forget our mothers died for the cause. We lost an entire generation beating them back. We're still waiting for King Rhyaxis's response. As far as I understand, he's dedicated to introducing a matriarchy in Vulturia."

She sighs heavily. "It apparently didn't go well when he installed his daughter as the heir. These could be rogue rebels trying to start a war. If we immediately retaliate, we could step right into the shitstorm they're trying to start. Three dozen lives is unacceptable, but so would be the thousands of Guardians and civilians if we start a war."

"Fuck diplomacy," Daeva growls. "Kalliope—"

"Lordess," Kalliope corrects.

Daeva grits out, "*Lordess.* These attacks will most likely continue. I cannot protect every town. The Vulturians have always been a potential threat, but if we go on the offensive, we can prevent future deaths. You need to take a stand, or the people will think you're not qualified to be a lordess."

The following silence is thick, and I wish there were a way to see Kalliope's face. What they're saying makes my head spin. There's the real possibility of another war — which could be the end of this world being an option for the family.

"General, you are in charge of our security and military forces. As such, your opinion is valuable and necessary. However, diplomacy should always be a priority. Do you want more of our fellow Amicum to die?"

"Of course not, *Your Grace*." The disrespect in Daeva's tone surprises me. She's always deferred to Kalliope's judgment, but maybe that's not always the case. I've only been here for a few weeks. Maybe this is normal. Kalliope *did* say she likes Daeva challenging her.

"You're dismissed," Kalliope growls. "And I don't want to discuss this again until we receive King Rhyaxis's response. Which will be any day now. Go make sure the Guardians are prepared to be deployed, but do not make any other move. Understood?"

"Yes, Your Grace." Zenab's tone is respectful and reveals nothing about her thoughts.

"Yes, Your Grace." Daeva's voice is nothing but impudent fury. Footsteps stomp off in a different direction. I'm about to sneak off until I hear Zenab's voice again.

"Your Grace, I'd like to discuss the matter of Saira."

Kalliope sounds so weary when she says, "What now?"

There's a moment of hesitation before Zenab says, "Kalliope, I see your growing attraction. I see how she makes you happy. But I would be remiss as your advisor if I did not speculate whether she's a potential liability?"

Kalliope doesn't correct her for overstepping like she did Daeva. I hear her blow out a deep, exasperated breath. "Elaborate."

"We still don't know where she's from. Yes, she has proven to be relatively helpless and friendly, but what if she's a spy?"

I wince at her bluntness. It's true, but to hear they think that about me behind closed doors stings.

Kalliope huffs out a laugh. "You think she could be a spy? For who? The Vulturians?"

There is a beat of silence before Zenab says, "Maybe. I'd be a piss poor advisor if I didn't entertain the possibility."

"The Vulturians eat any one-form they come across. Besides, the amount of ignorance she's shown strikes out this possibility."

Their voices travel closer as Zenab says, "You're attached to her."

It's a statement, not a question. My heart skips at the words, then flutters pitifully when Kalliope says, "I maintain focus on my duties, Zenab."

"Of course, no one questions your dedication."

"Yes, they do."

Zenab lets out an amused chuckle. "Okay, yes, some are. Some of those in the court might not appreciate your becoming involved with a one-form over an Amicum. You know many are eager for you to breed and present an heir. You can't do that with a one-form distracting you."

"No. That's why Legend has reserved the rights, Zen. He can breed. Who I spend my time with is no one else's concern. Let them gossip."

Kalliope wants to have a baby? Does she plan to do this soon? This is another reminder that I'm still so ignorant of the way things work here.

"And he will make an excellent pairing," Zenab agrees. "Still, I would be remiss not to bring up the court rumors and personal concerns. Personally, I trust you to execute your job as always. She's eager to train and tries hard, even when it hurts. It's admirable. I'm simply doing my job, but I agree — she is most likely not a spy."

"Is there anything else?" The words are clipped. Frustrated.

Zenab's tone softens. "How are you, Kal?"

There's a pause before Kalliope says wearily, "I'm tired, Zen."

Their voices are drawing dangerously close. Now would be a good time to walk away, but I'm too invested now to pretend I'm not eavesdropping.

Zenab's voice is empathetic when she says, "It's a lot. With no easy solutions."

There's the sound of something being put down, then a groan with the scuffling of shoes. Something creaks, like chairs being sat on. Kalliope pauses, then says, "The first day I met her, she was half-naked and sopping wet. A bear had tried to eat her, and instead of falling apart, she stared at me with fascination. No fear."

"Ginger mentioned that," Zenab adds quietly.

Kalliope hums in agreement, then says, "In the village? She ran in to save a little girl from a burning building. The mother has sent a letter informing me of the good deed. She's funny and clever. Yes, she's a one-form. But she's unlike any other I've ever met. She's not from anywhere around here, and I don't care. I want to teach her everything. Protect her." A pause. "Maybe even love her."

What? My head spins. Love? She loves me? Or wants to love me? Which is it?

There's a beat of silence, long enough I'm about to scurry off before I'm caught. Finally, Zenab speaks. "Nothing is stopping you from doing so."

"You pointed out that some in the court are displeased. It's my job to balance my choices with their needs. I can't fail. If my mother knew what I was doing, she'd scruff me."

Zenab chuckles again. "Your mother was my best friend until the day she died. I assure you she would agree with me when I tell you that loving a one-form, even one as much of a stranger to our customs as Saira is, would be a gift. Love is a precious thing, Kalliope. She'd more hug you than scruff you, any day."

I'm desperate to hear Kalliope's response, but the sound of footsteps from a nearby hallway jerks me away from the conversation. I can't let anyone discover I'm eavesdropping — they already think I'm a spy.

Adrenaline surging, I turn away from the greenhouse, hurrying back the way I came. Maybe I can find the dining room before anyone else finds me. I'd love a moment alone to consider everything I just overheard.

Kalliope's admission makes my head spin. Love was never on the time travel agenda, but it's impossible to deny the feelings budding inside me ... even if I refuse to acknowledge them.

Does Legend feel the same way? Does it matter? Is it worth bringing it up?

I'm so wrapped up in my worries, I miss the sound of another set of footsteps.

So it's a complete shock when I run smack dab into Daeva.

Chapter Twenty-Four

Neighver Do It Again

Daeva glowers down at me with ice-chipped irises, nostrils flaring. Probably scenting my adrenaline and fear. Her gaze draws to where I came from, and she snickers with understanding.

"Eavesdropping, one-form?"

My hands tremble, and it's a struggle not to rub the clammy sweat onto my legs. Knowing she can probably scent my fear makes it worse. "Um, no. Got lost. Still not sure how to get around this place. Can you help me find the dining room?"

She tilts her head, assessing me. The hairs on the back of my neck raise, and a voice in my head demands *Run, run, run*. Instead, I lift my chin, showing off fake confidence.

Then Daeva smirks. "Of course you're still lost, despite being here every day for weeks. Pathetic."

I bristle at the insult. Sure, I'm helpless without a GPS for anything bigger than a closet, but it's still rude of her to say. Knowing she can't do anything to me, I snort at her agitating words.

"Are you going to be helpful?" I clip, making to move around her. "If not, I'll just be on my way if you don't mind."

Stepping in front of me, she sneers, "In fact, I do mind. Strangers don't need to be skulking around the manor, going into random rooms. Follow me, one-form. I'll get you to where you should've been."

Biting back a scathing retort, I fall a step behind as she leads me down the hallways. Servants step out of her way, eyes dipping to the ground, as we pass. She doesn't acknowledge any of them, unlike Kalliope.

Speaking over her shoulder, she says, "Kalliope might think you're harmless, but I'm not so sure. It's suspicious for you to appear, and suddenly, the Vulturians are attacking again. After a decade of peace. Don't you find it curious, one-form?"

Okay, the timing might seem a little suspect. I'd think the same thing. It will be a disaster if she continues trying to convince people of this, though. "Well, Kalliope found me in the forest. Being chased by a bear. I didn't seek anyone out."

"Enemies have created far more elaborate tricks throughout time. Even a youngling can be trained to be in the right place at the right time. Perhaps mysteriously appearing in the forest, refusing to explain where they're from."

She has me there, but I won't let her intimidate me. "Kalliope doesn't seem to think I'm a spy, and from what I've learned, Amicums follow her lead and trust her judgment."

Daeva whirls around, eyes blazing with fury. "Are you implying I don't trust her judgment?"

"I implied nothing," I snipe, my heart throbbing against my sternum. "If you took it personally, maybe that's something you should examine."

Her canines elongate and thicken. Spots ripple along her neck, appearing and disappearing. Like she's barely restraining from shifting and ripping out my throat. Shit, my big mouth got me in trouble again. I take a step back, eyes darting to the hallway behind her. Empty. With no witnesses to the shredding that she's probably imagining with those growing claws.

"Hope I haven't interrupted anything important." A smooth, honeyed voice immediately eases my growing fear. Daeva peers over my head, sneering at Legend. How is he always at the right place and time?

"No," she snarls. "Not at all. You're welcome to take this *one-form*,"—she looks down at me with disgust—"and bring her somewhere out of my fucking way."

213

She spins and stalks away. Huffing out a sigh of relief, I turn to my handsome reprieve. Words fail after taking the murderous look twisting his face. His hateful eyes follow Daeva, features full of wrath.

I've never seen him emanate so much dominance. Suddenly, I'm extremely aware of the muscles that wrap around his imposing figure. The way his fist clenches with bloodless knuckles. In the whole time I've been here, he's been a cinnamon roll. This version of him didn't seem to exist. Like he could choke the life out of her without missing a beat.

When he focuses on me, the expression evaporates. A look of genuine concern smothers the fury. "Are you alright? Did she hurt you?"

My knees are jello, and I'm trembling, but I flash a smile. "Good thing you came, because I was totally about to kick her ass."

The responding chuckle is deep and comforting. I peer up as he puts a hand on my cheek. "What are males good for if not meat shields? Or as back-up to a good tail-kicking?"

I pretend to brush off a piece of invisible lint on my shoulder. "Or other things, maybe."

Those sensual lips curl deviously. The pad of his thumb brushes lightly against my cheek. "I can be very good at other things."

"Like giving directions?" I quip, immediately backtracking from my innuendo.

Legend peers down at me, eyes shining with mirth. "Where are you trying to go?"

Swallowing hard, I say, "Breakfast, please."

He holds out an arm for me to hold. "Sounds like the perfect plan."

We walk for a minute in amiable silence, slow and steady down the hallways. Warmth seeps from his body into mine, burning away the leftover anxiety. Something tells me he just saved me from Daeva, in a way I don't want to consider. Was she really going to hurt me? His reaction causes me to wonder if I've been a fool, not taking her seriously enough.

Legend breaks the silence by asking, "How has your stay been here? I hope things have been going well." He cuts me a sly smile. "Minus, of course, being bedridden for the past week and subjected to losing every card game against a handsome male."

The joke makes me laugh, but the question leaves me somber. I can't just say, *The science experiment to save my entire family is a disaster because hearts are black holes, obsessed with consuming every atom of connection. These feelings deep inside my soul scare the absolute shit out of me, and sometimes, a scream bites up my throat because I'm terrified of, and utterly captivated by, this place.*

No, those are inside thoughts. Instead, I beam and say, "As from that, it's been a really welcoming experience. Minus Ginger consistently trying to conscript me into daily tail braidings, that is."

Legend snorts. "That mare is certainly of a different breed." His Adam's apple bobs, and to my surprise, he chews on his lip. Finally, he says, "So, is there a special someone, at all, where you're from?"

Curious, I peer up at him, scanning his expression for clues. Why would he even care? Sure, it's wise to be honest to balance out the obfuscation about my purpose of being here.

But the truth stings to admit. He'll absolutely think I'm a loser if it's revealed how little of my life I've lived. He's confident. Handsome. Clever. Masculine. I've seen how others look at him — with envy and desire.

Maybe he's actually interested, though. It's delusional to consider, but ... is it really *that* delusional? At home, society dissects women's bodies like it's a sport. Here, females reign; their autonomy and beauty are an absolute inspiration. Perhaps in Ilorna, for all of its wonders, not having to worry about what people think about my body could be the best part.

Minus talking to the demi-god holding my arm.

Finally, I admit, "No, there isn't. You'll probably think I'm a loser, but my whole life's focus is learning and research. Before this trip, my life was an introvert's dream. Sometimes, Piper would get me out of the house to have margaritas, but usually, my free time was spent reading spicy romances."

My mouth goes dry at the truths tumbling out. In for a penny, in for a pound, right? "This place is pretty special. What you and Kalliope have, most people would kill for. It's not something I'll probably have, but it's great to see."

Legend frowns, pausing us in front of a group of Amicum statues. The hallway's empty, although the din from nearby kitchens confirms breakfast is in full swing. Putting his hands on my shoulders, Legend bends to catch my eye, our faces mere inches apart.

"Saira, I'm not entirely sure what a spicy romance is or a margarita, but I did understand the last part. Why on Inanna's fruitful soil would you believe you could never have something special?"

"I... I..." Words become too hard. It's unwise to explore exactly why those feelings exist right now. Furtively glancing down the hallways, it's a relief to reconfirm it's still empty. Refocusing on Legend, who actually looks a little ticked off, I continue. "Dating is hard where I'm from. Men are ..." I laugh nervously. "Not like you."

He chuckles. A stray hair tumbles across his forehead. The urge to tuck it back is strong. *Do not touch the demi-god.*

Warmth from his face radiates against mine as he says, "Would you like to know how special I think you are?"

"Wha-what?" I sputter. Has the translator failed? Cause surely he's not saying what I think he's saying.

Said demi-god brings his hands to my face, invading my senses with his consuming presence. The smell of citrus and leather alters my brain chemistry. Oxygen stalls in my lungs as irises the color of rich rolling fields zero in on my soul.

"I said, do you—" His nose grazes mine, our lips centimeters apart. "—want to know how special I think you are?"

"Yes," I whisper, bringing my hands to his wrists. They're anchors to every swooning molecule in my body. Legend becomes my new gravity, raising my body onto my tippy toes.

Firm, velvety lips brush over mine. Taking shallow sips of air, I let my eyes flutter closed. Stubble scrapes against my chin. A growing firmness presses into my body as Legend takes a step closer.

"You're kind."

Warm lips feather across my jaw.

"You're brave."

Deft fingers trail down my neck, tilting my head.

"You're full of curiosity."

Fingers shift curls away from my neck, threading through my loose strands.

"What I have yet to discover, though..."

Hands command my head to tilt back, exposing my mouth to the heavens.

"...Is if you're as good in bed as you are clever."

A gasp escapes as knuckles graze my ribs.

"Because if so, you're going to be the most exquisite lover."

My soul escapes my body, right along with my sanity. His lips crash onto mine, fierce and consuming. His tongue invades my mouth, demanding as good as he gives. It's like he's starving, feasting after a week of starvation.

There's no time to think about anything but the tiny, breathy moan he lets out when my tentative hands find their way to his chest, brushing over broad shoulders. Gods, that *sound*.

You're doing it again. Leading them on. Lying to them.

The thoughts bring me to an abrupt stop. Sensing my shift in mood, Legend freezes, removing his hands from my body.

"Are you okay? What's wrong?"

As usual, my brain ruins what could've been an amazing moment. It's wrong to get involved with them if they don't know the truth. And maybe it doesn't matter to them, learning my truths, but it matters to me. It's a misrepresentation of myself.

I take a step back, bringing my hands behind my back. Immediately clocking the change, Legend mirrors the movement. Now we're awkwardly squared off, after making out next to a bunch of Amicum statues. I swear one of them snarls at my cowardice.

Clearing my throat, I look in the direction we'd been heading. "Are we almost there? I'm starving."

Legend doesn't miss a beat. With a smile made of a thousand beaming suns, he holds out an arm. "Of course, Gem. Coffee or tea today?"

Linking arms, I fake a scowl. "You know I'm a coffee girl."

"Who knows? People change their minds all the time." He gives me a wink, leading me down the hallway. Something that shouldn't exist flutters gently in the mostly dormant organ nestled in my rib cage.

Legend is quickly gaining both my admiration and respect. The ease with which he interacts with the world is like sitting on a cliff side, dangling your legs while you watch the most colorful sunset. His laugh makes me want to leap into the clouds, just for a taste of the sky.

A deep ache roots into my chest, forcing me to clench my fists to prevent rubbing at the pain. This shouldn't be happening. This is dangerous.

Yet, it's everything I could've dreamed of and more.

Thankfully, the dining hall is the next room. When we step into the room, I'm surprised to find Ginger. In front of her is a huge metal bowl full of greenery.

She waves frantically when she sees us. Even though no one else is in the room and it's impossible to miss her. "Hey, guys! Over here!"

We sit in chairs across from her. Ginger's hand, full of greens, pauses halfway to her mouth. She makes a scene of scenting the air. Her grin transforms into a self-satisfied smirk. "Did you two fuck?"

My cheeks burn as I rush out to say, "No! Of course not."

At the same time, Legend says, "That's none of your business."

I shoot him a glare. He responds with an impassive look, like he doesn't want to air our business or even allude to it. I can appreciate the discretion. At least someone at this table has it.

Instead of insisting on an answer like I thought she would, Ginger throws the greens down onto her plate with a disappointed huff. "I owe Zenab five shillings now."

"You had *bets?*" I shriek. Legend doesn't look the least bit surprised. Increasing the power of my glare, I ask, "Did you know about this?"

"No," he says blandly. "But Ginger is a nosey busybody with a penchant for gossip and bets."

Ginger stabs an empty fork in our direction. "I was going to invite you both to town. I need to pick up feed. But not if you're going to be mean."

I slouch, crossing my arms. "You're one to talk," I mutter.

Legend snorts in agreement as he pours a cup of coffee and slides it over. Unperturbed, Ginger stuffs another forkful into her mouth, red eyebrows raised in question.

Well, I guess that's the end of her nosiness. Three can play at that game. I shrug. "It would be nice to get off the grounds and see more of the land." *And hopefully not run into another Vulturian attack.* I don't voice the thought, though.

Legend bites into a pastry, chewing slowly as he thinks. Swallowing, he says, "Let me clear it with Kalliope, but I'm sure it's fine." He slides a glance to me. "I'm not sure how she'll feel about taking Saira elsewhere without her."

Ginger bats her eyelashes. "Isn't a big, bad, strong male all we need?"

Flexing his arms like a meathead, he says, "Pretty sure you'd be able to kick my ass if you wanted to. These things are just for show."

Ginger preens at the comment, her expression turning haughty. "There's no 'pretty sure' about it. I'd wallop your ass all the way across Ilorna."

"And why exactly are you doing that?" Kalliope says, breezing into the room, Zenab walking closely beside her, examining papers in her hands.

Legend sits back in his chair, slinging an arm across the back of mine. It makes me want to lean into his hard muscles. Take in more of his citrusy scent. My lips still tingle from his claiming kiss, overriding any logical thoughts grasping for perch.

Kalliope sits next to Ginger, bumping the mare shifter's shoulder with her hip first. Ginger gives an outraged look and stabs the fork in the air toward her with an empty threat. Kalliope blows a kiss. Zenab sits on the other side of Ginger, pouring a glass of water, ignoring their shenanigans.

"Ginny here wants Saira and me to join her on a jaunt out into town."

Ginger's creamy complexion darkens with rage. "Don't you call me that, *Paul.*"

Did she call Legend "Paul"?

Legend doesn't miss a beat as he takes a smug bite of a roll. Then says, "I will *neighver* do it again."

"I've changed my mind. You're uninvited. Only BB can come with me." She levels a glare at me. "You won't tell me terrible jokes, will you?"

I pretend to be interested in my mug of coffee. "I'm staying out of this."

Kalliope laughs. "Smart." She looks at Ginger. "We can go whenever you're ready." She spears Legend with a glare. "I'll make sure Legend keeps his puns to himself."

We? I still haven't even processed what she said about me in the greenhouse, and now we're spending time together? A part of me thrills at the prospect, but the other part ... is begging me to remember my mission. To stay objective. To guard my heart.

Oh, who am I kidding? There's no guarding it anymore. In the last few weeks, I've quietly given away chunks of it to these people with no return policy in place.

Ginger stuffs the last bite of salad into her mouth and stands. "Sounds fine. Meet me at the stables in twenty."

"How are we hoofing it to town?" Legend calls out. She stalks off, flipping him the bird over her shoulder, not looking back.

Kalliope gives him an unimpressed look. "Knock it off. She will kick your ass."

Legend grins wickedly. "I'd be interested in how a mare can handle a manticore's sting."

Zenab says dryly, "She'll probably become a unicorn and stab the shit out of you."

He makes a little *moue*. "My big bad lordess would never let that happen."

Kalliope reaches toward a platter of sticky buns and grabs one before reaching for a carrot. Standing, she tucks it into her pocket. Most likely as a peace offering to the mare shifter.

"I'd pay good money to watch you both duke it out."

Zenab stands, following Kalliope out of the room. "Same."

"Traitors," Legend mutters.

I finish up the cup of coffee. "I'm going to head to the courtyard now. Coming, Paul?"

He raises an eyebrow. "I'll have you know, Paul is a legacy name. My father would be insulted."

I shove his shoulder hard. He barely budges, his eyes dancing with amusement. "So where did the name Legend come from, then?"

He leans forward, looming over me. For a split second, it looks like he might kiss me. Instead, the bastard whispers, "Because I've changed entire destinies between the sheets."

"Oh jeez," I grumble. "Why are men like this?"

He doesn't move away, keeping his sharp green gaze on my face. There's that magnetic pull between us again. I jump when his knuckles brush against my arm. The touch zings with an unfamiliar, but welcome, excitement through my whole body.

A rough thumb scalds my skin as he softly slides it over my cheekbone. My eyes flutter, and the air is suddenly difficult to inhale. The hitch in my breath is too loud because the smile he unfurls is pure male satisfaction.

My eyes widen as he leans down. Only minutes ago, his lips were on mine. Naturally, I ruined the moment, but that doesn't mean I'm not craving more. For a split second, I think he's actually going to kiss me again until my ear tickles as he whispers, "Last one to the courtyard is a squishy peach."

Then he's speed walking to the door.

Asshole.

To my surprise, Ginger isn't the horse pulling the cart. Instead, it's a black-and-white paint draft horse, looking similar to a Gypsy Cob I rode when I was younger. It nods at us as we approach the cart.

Ginger sits atop the cart's seat, motioning for us to hurry. Kalliope is already sitting beside her. Legend stands below, holding a hand out for me. I grab it with a grin, unable to resist another verbal stab for the way he just teased me.

"Thank you, Paul."

Legend gives Ginger a deadly glare as he helps me keep balance as I climb into the seat next to Kalliope. "You just had to say it."

Ginger gives him a rude gesture and hitches a thumb toward the back of the cart. "Males in the back. It's the law."

"Is it the law?" I ask, swiveling to watch Legend walk to the back of the cart.

"Yes," Ginger chirps cheerily.

"No," Kalliope says at the same time.

Yet, Legend obeys, hopping onto the edge of the cart, dangling his long, muscular legs. Ginger calls out to the draft horse. "Forward, friend." The cob begins a slow pace along the dusty road.

Even though the ride is bumpy, it's exciting to leave the grounds. The last time I left, we ended up in a burning town. Hopefully, this time is different.

The entire way, Ginger hums an upbeat tune. Her red hair is like flames in the sun, the curls wild and unbrushed. A smudge of dirt smears against her button nose, but I doubt she'll care if I point it out.

Next to me, Kalliope hums along with Ginger. The few Amicums we pass wave at us, and feeling brave, I join Kalliope in waving back. Their smiles toward me are genuine.

Closing my eyes, I imagine how Piper would react. She's a city girl, through and through. I think she'd like Ginger. Piper would match the snark, word for sassy word.

The thought squeezes my heart tightly.

My butt's numb by the time we get to the bustling town. The roads are thick with people and shopkeepers shout out their wares and prices. The smell of something sweet with a touch of spice catches my attention.

The Amicum crowd parts as the cart ambles forward. Ginger has the cart stop in front of a large store with the word "FEED" in red wooden letters at the top. She hops off the cart with fluid grace, turning to face us.

"Should be done in an hour."

Kalliope climbs off and holds out a hand, helping me not make a fool of myself. There's nothing about me that screams Amicum grace. When my feet touch the ground, I stumble forward. Kalliope catches me, her grip strong but gentle.

"Careful there."

Legend walks up behind her, assessing the crowd. "Want to go visit some shops?"

When I nod eagerly, they walk along the road. Ginger's already disappeared, the draft horse already dozing in the warm sun.

Legend is taller than Kalliope by a few inches but dwarfs her with his sheer size. The three of us in a row look like a gradual incline, from shortest to tallest. A ridiculous sight, to be sure.

He uses it to his advantage, too. Out of the corner of my eye, I see him looking around. Like he's there to protect Kalliope, even though she's perfectly capable of taking care if anything happens.

It's sweet, the way he has dedicated his life to her. There's no doubt in my mind he'd die for her if it came down to it. As we close in on a row of open-aired shops, filled with shiny baubles and fresh fruits, he lags and takes up the rear. Kalliope doesn't notice his movement, as if it's normal.

Kalliope stops under the shade of a tent, and the shopkeeper moves forward eagerly. He's a skinny male with wiry arms and a long, graying beard. Laugh lines carve into his face, emphasizing his elated expression.

"Your Grace. What a pleasure it is to see you. It's been a while since you've been in town."

They exchange pleasantries, then he points to the rows of beaded jewelry in front of us. They come in all shapes and sizes, made of stones I recognize and some that I don't.

"Your Grace, please, it would be an honor for you to wear some of my wife's jewelry."

Kalliope frowns as she inspects a turquoise bracelet, rolling the beads between her fingers. "Where's your wife?"

The man grows solemn. "Your Grace, she's fallen ill, I'm afraid."

Kalliope looks up sharply, sorrow drawing lines on her face. "I'm sorry to hear that." She turns to me. "Which one do you like?"

Putting up my hands, I shake my head. "Me? Oh, I don't need anything."

"You don't need pretty things, but they're nice to have, anyway," she murmurs, motioning to the collection. "Pick one you might like."

Her generosity is touching, so I brush my fingers along the beads, stopping at one appearing to be made of tiger's eye.

The shopkeeper's eyes gleam. "Excellent choice, my friend."

He gives Kalliope a price, and she pulls out a coin from a small pouch on her belt. The way his jaw goes slack, it's far more than the bracelet is worth.

"For your wife," she murmurs. "Please give me her best."

"Ye-ye-yes, Your Grace. Thank you, Your Grace."

And so it goes, from shop to shop. Once the shopkeepers realize her steady patronage, they pull out their best items. Heady, colorful spices. Handmade leather belts. Coin purses. Even the luxuriously designed capes are made of soft material.

When we're given random flowers or food, I discreetly pocket items for the analyzer. It's the most unscientific way to collect samples — shoving everything into a pocket — but it's the best I can do given the circumstances.

By the time our hour is up, Ginger's waiting at the cart when we return, piling feed bags and hay into the cart. Legend places satchels full of our purchases into the back and helps her finish loading. When he's done, he slaps his hands together; dirt particles float to the ground.

Kalliope walks over to Ginger and says something I can't hear over the noise of the crowd. Ginger glances at me with a mischievous smirk.

This can't be good.

Ginger hops onto the cart and commands the horse forward.

"Where's she going?" I ask. My heart rate spikes at her departure. The look she threw my way before leaving ties my stomach into knots. If it were a problem, I don't think she would've smiled at me, but with Ginger, you never know.

Kalliope shrugs. "You know how she is about crowds. In and out. But I thought maybe you'd like to stay a little longer. Take you to my favorite place in town."

My shoulders relax a fraction. They don't have an ulterior motive — they're trying to spend time with me. "Yeah, that sounds great."

We approach a quaint building with a thatched roof and pale orange terracotta walls. To the left and the right of the building is a garden springing into the air with spindly vines and out-of-control flower bushes wrapping around tall trellises.

Lit braziers lie scattered around the space, surrounded by benches full of Amicums. The air's filled with the clinking of glasses full of beer and other concoctions. The lively hum of conversation comes from within the pub and the garden itself.

On the pub's sign reads "The Flowered Goddess."

Communal joy hits like a radiant burst of energy when we step inside. Unlike the first pub we went to, this one focuses less on dim coziness and instead integrates as much sunshine as possible. Huge windows wrap around the back and sides of the building, opening to the biergarten.

Kalliope heads to the bar, made with branches of wood, still holding sticks of leaves. The barkeep, a female with owlish eyes and dark brown hair, grins as Kalliope orders whatever she's decided we're drinking. The barkeep nods and turns to the barrels of booze behind her.

Kalliope motions for me and Legend to follow her out to the garden to a quiet spot away from everyone else. She sits around a simmering brazier and reaches down for a poker to stoke the embers. It crackles, and flames lick at the air again.

Around the brazier are comfortable Adirondack chairs. Settling into one, I watch Legend take the chair facing more toward the crowd.

Within a second, he'd be able to stand and interfere with anyone trying to interrupt.

I lean back in my chair, enjoying the way the soft cloth hugs my body. A barmaid rushes over with a tray of our drinks, gold liquid sloshing over the steins. Legend stands, stopping her from getting closer to Kalliope and me.

"Thank you so much." He grabs two of the drinks and hands one to each of us, then grabs the third for himself.

I take a sip. As expected, like everything in this world, it tastes delicious. Fruity and sour. It bubbles down my throat, warming me up from the inside.

We take sips of our drinks for a moment, but Kalliope's gaze locks onto my face. Unreadable yet intense. I look toward Legend, and he's looking between the two of us. Waiting.

Finally, Kalliope speaks.

"So, Saira, tell me where you're really from. And if you try to deflect from answering, you'll be dis-invited as my guest and left to fend for yourself."

Chapter Twenty-Five

A Goddess Of Flickering Flames

I nearly spit out the sip I'd taken. I'm not sure why this was an unexpected ambush. They've let me stay here for free for weeks without an explanation. In that time, we've grown closer, and I've still refused to share.

My mouth opens, ready to pour out words, when I stop and think. The Scout looks like a leather band right now, but that doesn't mean I can escape if they take me prisoner. Not without the supplies.

Plus, what if they don't believe me?

What if they do?

What if they think it's unacceptable, and she decides I'm a liability?

But this is the true test, right? Kalliope has shown nothing but kindness. Legend has been supportive in a way I didn't even know men could be. Both Zenab and Ginger have continued to offer their support and expertise. I've all but outed myself as someone who isn't from here, and it hasn't upset them. Maybe this is a chance to make them both see reason and understand why we can't possibly become something more.

"It's going to sound crazy," I warn.

She waves me forward. "Try me."

I stare into the fire in front of us, choosing my words carefully. "I'm from a different place. Not here, in these lands, but somewhere else entirely."

Legend leans forward, intrigued. Kalliope frowns. "Like from across the ocean?"

How the hell do you explain time travel?

"You know how there's a door between walls?"

"Yes."

"Imagine both sides of a closed door. I'm on one side, and you're on the other. I have the power to open the door and walk onto your side."

Her brows furrow, and the frown deepens. "But we're in the same home?"

This is making me realize how, at home, you inherently learned about time travel from movies. Most people could explain the concept of wormholes and other universal magic.

Here, they keep things more practical. "It's actually as if the room and the hallway were in two different homes, but the doorway can connect them."

"And how does that happen?"

Magic. This is already becoming complicated. "My dad and I created a piece of equipment that allows me to open doors."

She nods, her expression thoughtful as she scans the crowd. "So you truly know nothing about Amicums, Vulturians, or the sovereignty of females?"

I chuckle. "Where I come from, society views women as less than. It used to be worse, but it's definitely not perfect. This place has been quite eye-opening."

She wrinkles her nose. "It sounds terrible."

I nod in agreement. She has no idea, but I'm not about to reveal all the travesties throughout the millennia.

It's Legend who asks, "Aside from Piper, what did you have to leave behind?"

The answer becomes a lump in my throat, so complicated and not complicated, all at once. "Everything. Everyone. My world. Technically, no one and nothing. It's complicated."

Their faces show nothing but curiosity, so I give them the entire story.

It takes multiple drinks, and twilight greets the skyline by the time we're done. It's incredible finally telling *someone*. They ask questions throughout the story, mostly curious about my family and the technology. They seem impressed when I explain what I've studied in school and how hard I worked with Dad to make time travel possible.

When I'm done explaining everything, Kalliope seems wholly satisfied and clearly believes me. Legend's beautiful mouth quirks to the side.

Finally, Kalliope says, "You're very brave. We already knew this, but finally understanding where you're from and where you're going ... it all makes sense. I would've been reticent about sharing this as well. If you had told us in the beginning, I'm unsure how we would've handled it." With a serious expression, she says, "But you're welcome here, Saira. More than welcome. You may stay as long as you'd like."

Her words swell a rush of relief in my heart. My vision waters, and I wipe away a tear.

"I'm not brave," I confess, the words miserable on my tongue. "I've abandoned everyone and everything." My voice catches before I admit, "I'm also terrified I'm going to hurt you both. Because I can't stay. You understand that, right?"

I motion to the three of us. "Whatever this is, it could be something. But I have to leave when I've gathered enough data and trained a bit more. There's *no way* I can stay. I *have* to go save my family. Find them a place to be safe."

Tears fall in clumps now, and it's impossible to keep up with wiping them all away. Legend leans over and puts a hand on my trembling arm. It's a warm comfort, bolstering my wilted confidence.

"Gem, it's been a pleasure getting to know you. We aren't asking for anything you won't and can't willingly give. Your family is the priority, and we respect that."

Kalliope's own face reflects my grief, but in subtle ways. It shows in the tightening of her lips and crease in her brows. People can't witness her crying in a biergarten, but she clearly understands.

In a voice almost too low to hear, she says, "Saira, we're happy to have time with you. Neither of us expected you to stay. You said you travel around, so we never thought this would be permanent. We've invested in you, regardless."

Her response cracks open my heart completely, and the parts she hadn't already reached are now completely hers and Legend's.

"Thank you," I whisper, wiping away the remnants of the tears.

Legend and Kalliope exchange glances. Communicating something. Legend gives a quick nod.

Kalliope shifts in the chair, mouth twisting in thought. Then she asks, "Would you be interested in becoming romantically involved with us? No expectations — simply fun, at any level you're comfortable with."

Flashes of the intense experiences I've had with each of them have my blood heating. They haven't hidden their intentions. I've spent weeks contemplating how involved I want to be. I've sworn to squash the identity of "virgin nerd" as soon as possible. This is my opportunity — so why is there any hesitation at all?

That's when it hits me. These two beautiful creatures want me. Romantically. *Sexually*. Little ol' me, a studious nerd without an ounce of—

Don't panic. It'll be okay. Everything's fine.

"I'm a virgin," I blurt out. A bit too loud, gauging by the looks we receive. Legend chokes on a sip of his almost-finished beer. Piper would congratulate me on my smoothness. Or pommel me with a pillow.

Kalliope's eyebrows shoot up, and her mouth drops open. "I'm sorry, *how* old are you?"

Well, this went from one of the best moments of my life to the most humiliating. My whole body flushes with embarrassment. I look down at my hands, picking at a cuticle. "I'm twenty-six. But I've been so busy being the Badass Bitch Scientist, I didn't date. You don't get to invent the single greatest piece of technology in human history by having an avid sex life."

I gnaw on the inside of my cheek and look up. It's hard to look either of them in the eye, but I put in my best effort. "I went on a couple of first dates when I was in college, but no one kept my interest. The males in my world aren't what one might call exceptional. They're judgy to the short, pudgy girl."

"I'm not sure what delusional asshole called you pudgy, but perhaps we can remedy this," Legend grins, standing and stretching his muscular arms out wide. Kalliope follows suit, offering me a hand, which I take gratefully. This went better than I could ever have expected. Relief is a balm to the anxiety coursing through my mind for weeks. For the first since I've arrived, true freedom to be myself appears.

Without another word, she leads me through the biergarten, not letting go of my hand. Legend walks behind me, a comforting presence.

My thoughts are so jumbled, it feels like mere seconds pass as we make our way to the edge of town. Kalliope brings me to a clearing and shifts into the eagle.

Too depleted from so many confessions, I don't even hesitate to get on. Beside us, Legend shifts into the manticore, and together we take to the skies.

The crescent moon barely offers any light, and while I'm sure they can see just fine, all I can do is look upward and take in the night sky. Stars twinkle above us, some constellations exactly like home. At least I can now answer Piper's question when we're together again.

Kalliope makes a smooth landing, barely a jolt when her talons hit the ground. Legend has already shifted, arms up and waiting for me. He helps me dismount, but instead of letting me walk, he scoops me. Like I'm some sort of maiden about to be brought over the threshold. It's a little ... weird. But also fantastic.

They take a different route than normal. Kalliope opens a side door opening into a darker hallway. We stop in front of a plain wooden door, and Kalliope turns the knob, revealing a bedroom I've never seen before.

It's a mix of rich blues, golds, and blacks. Like Kalliope's, the bed is enormous. Enough to have half a dozen people sleep side by side. Gold sheets drape across the mattress, glittering in the pre-lit fire.

This must be Legend's room. I never even thought he had his own room, with him and Kalliope joined at the hip. It's more opulent than her room, which makes me wonder if she prefers to stay in here.

Legend deposits me on the lush black velvet sofa in front of the fireplace.

To the right of the fireplace are shelves filled with hundreds of books of all sizes. If he's such a prolific reader, he might appreciate exploring some of mine.

Behind me, I hear clinking glasses and liquid pouring. I peer over the edge and watch Kalliope pouring wine into glasses. And ... Legend is taking his shirt off.

I've seen him shirtless before, but not in the context of having those muscles under my hands in the next few minutes. From broad shoulders to a tapered torso, Legend's built like a predator. Not an inch of his gorgeous body is wasted. His bronze skin glows in the firelight as he collects his hair and ties it back.

Kalliope turns to him and hands over a glass of wine, then grabs another one and walks over to me. It's an opportunity to appreciate the way her body curves in all the right places. Even in a loose shirt and leather pants, it's impossible to hide her feminine figure.

After handing me a drink, she sits down opposite me, leaning against the pillows. Her hair is wild from the day, the long strands loose and wavy. She watches Legend come around the couch and lean against the armrest. When their focus is on me, it strips me bare.

Kalliope takes a sip of her drink, then says, "Is there anything you may not want to partake in?"

"I've never even watched porn, so I have no idea what I won't like. I'm probably not into pain, though."

To their credit, neither asks me what porn is. Instead, Legend sticks out his lower lip in mock disappointment. "Even choking? Just a little?"

The idea is intriguing. "I'm willing to try it and see."

"What would you like your safe word to be?" Kalliope asks, resting a hand on Legend's thigh.

"Safe word?"

"Yes," Legend says. "A clearly unique and potentially outrageous word that won't make sense during sex. When you feel unsafe or overwhelmed, you can say this word and everything immediately stops."

Quirking my mouth, I look upward, trying to come up with a word. "Eggplant?"

They both chuckle. Kalliope takes a deep gulp of her wine, then places the glass on the end table. "Eggplant it is."

She stands and holds out a hand, wriggling her fingers in invitation.

This is it: another evolution of who I want to be. To say I'm nervous would be an understatement. I don't even feel worthy of being in the same room as these two. Who am I to them? A plump, out of shape nerd who can't even wield a sword? For a moment, my self-doubt and hate curdle in my gut, freezing me in place. This is ridiculous. None of this is real. There's no way they want me.

Yet, they do. The proof is in the way they watch me, waiting for me to work through my thoughts. Their patience is a gift I refuse to squander.

Grabbing her hand, I follow as she leads me to the bed. Each step forward increases my heart rate. Legend trails behind as she silently commands me to sit on the edge of the bed.

The mattress sinks as I lean against the edge, unable to figure out what to do next. Clearly, the tension here is mounting. But is tonight the night I'm losing my virginity?

Kalliope tilts her head. "You don't have to do anything you don't want to do tonight. We can all go to bed because it's been a long day. Or ..." She gives Legend a devilish look, then winks at me. "Or we can start things slow with a show for you."

Legend flashes a wicked grin. "I vote for that." He looks at me with concern. "If you're into it. It's up to you. I'll tuck you into bed if you prefer."

I look at his bare, muscular torso, then at her sensually curved mouth. They're giving me an opportunity to choose, while making it clear they want me. It's clear things can be called off immediately, and I don't think they'd even show a flicker of disappointment. Is this what I want? It will make everything so much harder when it comes time to leave.

Yet ... I don't want to be the shy, unsure scientist anymore. I want to be the actual Badass Bitch Scientist Piper has always claimed I am. And she'd kill me if I passed up this opportunity.

A salacious smile spreads across my face as I say, "What kind of show are we talking about?"

Grinning, Kalliope speaks first. "Legend, would you like to get started?"

Legend's face darkens with desire. "Nothing would please me more, *Your Grace.*"

The way he purrs out the title is like silk on my skin. No wonder she enjoys it when I say it to her. Kalliope turns away from me and walks over to him, her hips swaying from side to side. Not sure what else to do, I stay sitting on the edge of the bed, watching.

Legend's hungry gaze locks onto hers, amusement curling his lips. His head dips incrementally as she grows closer, watching every movement.

Stopping in front of him, she runs a hand up his stomach, then his chest. Elegant fingers run over the plains of his pecs up to his collarbone and down one of his shoulders. Legend's focus never leaves her face, but his body slightly sways into each movement of her touch. Like he can't get enough of it.

Her hands come to his belt. She yanks at it, but when it doesn't unbuckle fast enough, she holds up a hand. A wicked claw forms on a finger, and the sound of ripping leather makes my blood pump harder.

"May I finish undressing?" Legend's voice is husky and strained.

I can't see Kalliope's face, but she tilts her head to the side and sweeps back her hair to expose her neck. "Do what I like first."

He licks his way upward, from neck to ear, giving her earlobe a nip. She gasps, then moans as one of his huge hands roughly grabs an ass cheek. Palming the flesh, his eyes trail to me, expression full of promise.

It's been thirty seconds, and I already feel like I'm being set on fire. Lust is a tidal wave through every nerve ending as Kalliope hooks her thumbs into the sides of his pants and tugs down. No wonder people do stupid things for mere seconds of this sensation.

The material drops smoothly from his hips, revealing ...

Oh.

Oh.

Either shifter males are built differently, or I've never seen a lot of dick, because his girth looks positively animalistic. Smooth and long, twitching at Kalliope's gentle grasp. She tugs on him a few times, and he jerks forward with a sharp inhalation.

Only something created by a god could be this beautiful. I'd never had the pleasure of seeing his happy trail travel down his flat stomach to his groin. The most beautiful example, if there ever was one. I'm so focused on the lewd display, I almost miss his playful wink in my direction. It stokes the blazing heat roaring in my belly.

Kalliope drops her hold on him and turns to face me. Legend doesn't hesitate to reach around and begin tucking fingers under the hem of her shirt, one by one. A tantalizing dance of movement that has oxygen freeze in my lungs. Then both hands slide up and under the shirt. She moans and pushes her hips back into him.

"What would you like?" His voice is raspy, barely above a whisper.

Kalliope looks at me, eyes lidded with lust. "Would you like to join us yet?"

I gnaw on the inside of my cheek, not sure what to say. My body is screaming *yes*, but words are cemented in my throat. My confidence is teetering on the edge of the cliff, not quite ready to let go.

When I don't immediately answer, an eager gleam lights up her face. "That's fine. Legend loves to give a good show." One of her hands comes up to his face, fingers digging into his hair, then yanks his head down. She whispers something in his ear, and he nods slowly.

His hands fall to his side as he steps back. Moving to her side, he slowly lowers into a kneeling position. Kalliope looks down at him as he prostrates on the wooden floor, expression filled with adoration. Like a penitent worshipper looking for absolution.

"Good boy," she croons. He beams. She runs black nails through his dark strands of hair, twirling one of them around a finger. "Now beg for the privilege."

"My lordess —"

"Ah, ah, ah," she admonishes.

His hand reaches for his formidable length and begins with languid strokes. "My lordess, I offer every inch of myself for you to enjoy and use as you see fit. I want to worship your body and wring every inch of pleasure possible from you until you dismiss me. Or choose to use me again."

I'm slack jawed. This man, so confident and kind, is willingly submitting in every way possible to Kalliope. It piques both my curiosity and desire. Sitting up straighter, I lean forward, enthralled.

With a benevolent smile, Kalliope caresses his cheek and jaw. "That was so good. You're always so good, Legend."

He whimpers with pleasure, and I stifle the same noise. I'm suddenly desperate to hear those words directed at me.

She notices my movement, and as she continues to pet Legend, she turns her attention to me. "Do you like this, Saira?"

I nod. In the firelight, the way it jumps along her curves and shimmers in her hair, she looks like flickering embers and smoke. She gives a devilish grin.

"Too bad, because I want you to watch him fuck me first." She walks toward me slowly, pulling off her shirt and tossing it to the side. She shimmies out of her pants, kicking them away.

Leaving her completely naked. A goddess of shadows and flickering flames, the light dancing along her muscular curves. Her breasts are heavy and full, with rose-pink nipples that make my mouth water.

Leading Legend to the bed with a single crooked finger under his chin, he stands and follows, eyes now firmly locked onto her ass. He licks his lips as if imagining what it tastes like.

When she stops in front of me, she points over my head. "Lay against those pillows. You can look — don't touch. Understand?"

Resisting the urge to say, "Yes, ma'am," I position myself against the down-filled pillows. As I get situated, Kalliope slides back onto the bed, leaving Legend standing obediently between her thighs.

He looks down at her naked body with pure lust, one of his hands still slowly pumping, the other twitching at his side. Like it can't wait to get a fistful of flesh. At this angle, the firelight rims his frame. He looks ethereal.

Kalliope stretches out like a cat, her head resting in my direction. I could reach out and touch her, but I won't. This is a spell not worth breaking.

With her legs hanging over the edge, she lifts one. Legend uses his free hand to grab the offered thigh, letting it fall over a broad shoulder. She leisurely drags a hand down between her thighs, two fingers dipping into the patch of black curls.

Her head bows back. I'm captivated by the way her mouth slightly opens with the exhaled moan.

Legend pumps faster, stepping a fraction closer, instinctually aching to slip inside her. But Kalliope is in her own world, fingers sliding in and out. When she pulls them out, they're slick with her desire.

She snaps her fingers, and Legend kneels, abandoning his cock in favor of grabbing her thighs and pushing them forward. Exposing her entirely. She gasps when his mouth descends onto her core, lapping up her taste.

It makes me wonder what kind of education he received as a male. He'd chosen the career of being a consort, so that means he must have received actual training. Or maybe he earned the name Legend for the exact reason he said.

Kalliope grabs one of her nipples and twists, letting out a moan. Legend returns the sound, muffled by servicing his lordess.

Her panting increases, the moans growing louder. He brings a hand between her legs and slips in two fingers. She cries out and brings both hands up to twist her nipples. My hand twitches with the need to take their place.

Legend's arm pumps furiously while he continues to consume every inch of her pussy. Her toes curl, and she throws her head back, crying out. Legend doesn't change his pace or pull back — he's a champion.

Finally, his pace slows as her spasms subside. His head lifts, mouth covered in her cum and grins.

"Did I do well, my lordess?"

She huffs out a laugh. "As always, my love, you deliver."

He sits back on his haunches, looking quite pleased. She props herself up by the elbows, craning her head over a shoulder. "Are you ready to watch the second appetizer?"

The ache between my thighs has me clenching them tightly, already yearning for them. "There are multiple appetizers?"

Legend stands, giving a lopsided grin. "She's voracious in this mood."

Kalliope flips onto her belly, then shoves her ass up into the air. The perfect positioning for him. Over her shoulder, she commands, "Fuck me."

Chapter Twenty-Six

Worshiped By A Man

Legend steps forward and leans down to spread Kalliope's thighs wider. She gazes at me, leaning on her elbows, as he enters her.

Her mouth forms an O as he groans. My desire tingles up and down my limbs, my mouth mimicking her expression as if I can feel him sliding into me, too. He grabs her hips possessively, using her body to provide himself pleasure. It's intoxicating.

The sound of their frenzied joining is indecent, creating a desire that becomes a wildfire in my core, pounding between my thighs. My need is so intense, I whimper, catching Kalliope's attention.

She smirks. "Would you like some attention, Saira?"

All sense of insecurity has fled the room. All I want right now is this female and this male. And everything they're willing to give.

My head bobs eagerly. "Yes, please."

Kalliope grins and looks over her shoulder. "Legend, you can pause." He obeys, heaving, body already slick with sweat.

She points to my clothes and snaps her fingers, smiling. "Quick. Undress so I can taste you."

Taste me?

In a wink, I'm undressed, tossing my clothes aside. Thoughts have fled so rapidly, it takes a second for me to blink clarity into my mind.

JENNA AVERY

They look at me like I'm a delicious dessert after starving for a week. It's a strain not to hold my arms up to hide my breasts, to distract them from my belly.

"Oh, Gem," Legend croons. "You're so beautiful."

Kalliope says nothing, although lust paints every feature of her face. She pats the space in front of her. "Come here."

I go to crawl over to face her, and she shakes her head. "No, love. I want you in my mouth."

Anticipation has me scrambling, scooting my hips forward. Her fingers dig into my waist, yanking me even closer. Positioning me directly under her head. Placing a hand on each of my thighs, she presses them wide.

My instincts want me to slap them shut, but she presses into them gently but firmly.

Then she begins.

Her tasting starts slow, blowing warm breaths on my thighs, grazing over my throbbing core. Propped up on my elbows, I get the perfect view of her bending forward, beautiful ass in the air, with Legend filling her from behind.

He and I lock eyes, and his fingers grip her hips tighter. As her tongue flicks against my ultra-sensitive bundle of nerves, he slowly pulls out, then slams into her.

The desire becomes an inferno, almost painful. Legend whimpers as he watches my reaction. "Saira, you're so fucking perfect."

Kalliope groans in agreement between my thighs.

Just as an orgasm begins, Kalliope pauses, bringing her head up. "Would you like to see how Legend compares?"

"*Yes,*" I groan. She grins, and Legend steps back. Sliding back, she grabs my ankles and drags me to the edge of the bed. With my legs dangling, this beautiful man gets on his knees in front of me.

His chest glistens with sweat, and on impulse, I sit up and brush my fingers along his jaw. It's warm with rough stubble. "You're beautiful, too, Legend," I breathe.

He gives me a lopsided grin and jerks his chin. "Lay back, Gem, and let me show you what it means to be worshiped by a man."

Kalliope stalks around him, breasts swaying heavily in the dim light, and settles onto the bed beside me. Sliding to lie parallel to me so she has better access to my aching nipples.

Intoxicating waves of euphoria wash over my nerves. Simultaneously, Legend leans forward and savors my slickness. It's gentle at first until he groans, pressing into the flesh, teasing the peak of my pleasure.

As Kalliope titillates my nipple, Legend brings one of his thick fingers and slides it into me. It's like being electrified with lightning, and my hips buck of their own accord.

Kalliope shifts to the other nipple, tilting her body over mine. The sensation of her breasts brushing against mine is transcendent. Her soft hair brushes gently against my already sensitive skin. I've spent too many days wondering how soft her skin is. I drag my fingers along the curve of her spine. Reality is better than my imagination.

An orgasm begins to tighten my insides. Sensing my core tensing, Legend slides in a second finger. His slow and steady pace increases while he sucks directly on my clit. It's like I'm slowly being split in half, the pleasure so severe, I release a moan.

"Let go, Gem," he murmurs before refocusing on my pleasure.

And I do. The orgasm rips me to shreds, burning my reality into ashes. I'm nothing but everything, in all of it, and nowhere. Time and place don't matter anymore, as bliss pumps in my muscles, flexing and relaxing.

"Such a good girl," Kalliope murmurs, trailing kisses down my belly. She nuzzles the ample flesh, taking a small nip of it. "I love every plump part of you."

Embarrassment, ingrained in me from a society full of fat phobia, cringes. My legs draw up, trying to hide the curves, but she stops them with an arm. She looks at me, incredibly serious. "Don't hide yourself from me, Saira. You're perfect."

Legend kisses and sucks the insides of my thighs, but pauses in his ministrations to say, "I'm on Team Saira's Thighs from dusk till dawn."

They kiss every inch of the body I've had a complicated relationship with. These two worship me like I'm a goddess.

Damn, it's fucking incredible.

Their kisses soon slow, and finally, they sit back on their haunches. Kalliope looks at Legend, whose face shows hope. She grins and raises an eyebrow toward me.

"He's worked hard tonight, yes?"

I don't even recognize my husky voice when I say, "Yes."

"He deserves to cum. Perhaps you'll grant him the pleasure of cumming on that delicious ass of yours?"

At this point, I'll do anything they want. I nod eagerly, and Legend flashes a wicked grin before flipping me over easily. Like I weigh nothing.

A girl could get used to this.

I peer over my shoulder and watch him scoot forward so he's hovering his cock over one of my ass cheeks. His balls lightly graze the skin, and my hips instinctively rise.

He groans. "Not today. But soon."

The promise in his voice makes me moan with frustration. With one muscular arm, he slides it under my hips and lifts my ass like an offering to the heavens. Looking over my shoulder, I watch him grip himself and pump it furiously, staring at my ass longingly.

In seconds, ropes of hot cum spurt onto my ass. He roars, sounding more animal than man, and I spot a flash of sharp canines. Legend's lost control of his form, and I love every bit. He's lost control because of *me*.

Nothing has ever felt so empowering in my life.

The first thing I notice when I wake is the press of a leg against mine. I open my eyes, and my smile sparks to life when I see a sleeping Kalliope, black hair spread across the satin pillow. Her warm breath skates across my hand, steady and deep.

Shifting, it's impossible not to wince. Everything aches a little, especially my core. That was just with fingers. What will it be like if I ever have Legend inside me?

Speaking of, I look over my shoulder and grin when I find him sleeping peacefully beside me. He's still naked, and I enjoy taking a moment to admire his form in the morning light.

I'm a happy Saira Sandwich right now. In fact, that's how the rest of the night went, and you won't find me complaining. It was easily the best night of my life.

I'm trying not to think about how temporary it all is.

Legend stirs and opens an eye. His curls are a mess, and sleep still holds his features as he offers a sleepy smile.

"Good morning, beautiful."

I wait for some level of shame to rise, but there's nothing. I'm barely covered by a sheet, with my voluptuous glory in the light, and all I want to do is offer him more of it. His gaze trails along the slope of my breasts and hips. He shifts forward, cock pressing against my thigh.

"Already?" I tease.

One of his hands comes up to my shoulder. He runs his knuckles down my arm. "Always."

A soft hand with long nails caresses my breasts. I arch my back in surprise, but wince when my back muscles spasm. Legend chuckles, and the hand on my ass pauses in its exploration.

Kalliope teases, "Did we wear you out?"

I pout. "Yes. You're absolute animals."

The nails on my ass sharpen into claws, and I squeak.

Kalliope laughs, sitting up. "Don't grab a tiger by the tail and get surprised by the bite."

Legend swings out of bed, and I swipe to hit his shapely butt and miss. The statue of David has nothing on his tush. He pads over to the bedroom door and turns to look at us. "Breakfast in bed, lovers?"

"Coffee, please," I beg. "And some pastries. As long as they're covered in icing or sugar."

Kalliope nestles into the blanket, leaning against a pile of pillows. "I'll have black tea."

He nods and walks out of the room, buck naked, with half a boner. I look at Kalliope wide-eyed.

"He's going out there naked?"

She laughs. "We're Amicums, Saira. We love the expression of clothes, and in our true forms, they can be elements of protection, but we have no shame here." She pauses, then says, "And neither should you."

"I'm realizing," I say. Turning on my side to face her, I prop a cheek in my palm. "I've never had a man worship me. Did he receive a lot of training, or is it some natural talent?"

She fingers the knots in her hair. "When he applied to be a consort, he attended a year of training at a local university focused on training males for this skill set."

I waggle my eyebrows. "Can I volunteer to help train the males?"

She arches an eyebrow. "You're sore from last night and want to help train dozens of males a week?"

On second thought ... "Maybe a part-time gig?"

She chuckles. "You are welcome to do whatever you please, Saira." Sitting up, she swings off the bed and pads over to one of the many bathrobes I've never used. Slipping into it, she says, "We're going to Cape Schrute today. Would you like to come with us?"

I perk up. "I've never seen the ocean."

She braids her messy strands, then wraps them in a knot at the top of her head. "We'll leave after lunch."

The door opens, and in walks Legend with a tray containing a steaming kettle, three mugs, and a heaping plate of food. "Your food has arrived, lovers."

My stomach grumbles, as does Kalliope's. We sit up as he lays the tray on the mattress. Leaning forward, I snatch up what looks like a turnover.

Stuffing it into my mouth, I moan.

"Don't do that unless it's an invitation," Legend teases. He pours Kalliope a cup of steaming water and dips a tea bag into it, bobbing it before handing it to her.

"Thank you," she murmurs, taking a sip without waiting for it to steep.

Legend sits on the mattress, munching on a muffin. "So what were you discussing while I was off finding food and libations?"

"I was telling her about going to Cape Schrute." She takes a sip of her tea again.

It takes a second until I can remember where I've heard that name before. The female at the first pub we visited invited Kalliope to visit. "That sounds great. I'll come with—"

The whole manor shakes from a resounding *boom*. Books fly off the shelves, and Legend almost falls over. Kalliope is up in a flash, teacup crashing to the floor. The wolf inside her shimmers into existence, snarling. She snaps her teeth at Legend, and he runs to the door, slamming it open. She bolts out the door.

Panic bolts through me like a lightning strike, forcing a cold sweat to break out across my body. Their reaction only increases the racing beats of my heart. The manor is under attack; that much is certain.

Legend's body pulses with frenetic energy as he reaches for me. "Hurry, Saira. Get dressed."

It's a safe bet Cape Schrute isn't happening today.

I tug on my clothes and make sure the Scout is still secure around my wrist. Legend pulls on a pair of pants and pulls me toward the door. He looks out into the hallway. Chaos echoes all around us. Wails of agony shatter against the stone.

My supplies. There's no way of knowing who's attacking the manor, at least not yet, but I can't leave everything behind.

Legend whirls to face me with a distraught expression. "Don't go far. Stay with me. And *don't* do anything brave," he hisses.

"Legend, I need my things. I can't —"

But he's already shifting. The air shimmers, and the manticore appears. I stumble back, making room for the six-foot-long scorpion tail.

245

It thumps to the ground impatiently, and he growls, jerking his lion's head toward the door.

He tucks in the wings, then nudges me forward, implying that he won't entertain my request to pick up my supplies. I scurry to stand in front of him, with his face looming over my shoulder as we make our way down the hallway. Chaos reigns as servants and guests run down the hallways, frantic and calling for help.

Legend ignores them and snarls at anyone stupid enough to get too close. Kalliope is nowhere to be seen. Adrenaline rushes through my body, and my heart is about to burst through my chest from the sheer terror.

Another *boom* rocks the walls, and paintings crash to the floor. Some rip in half from the force of the blast. Legend growls with frustration as Amicums rush around us. Most are in animal form, bolting in fear.

It's bedlam like I've never seen.

We aren't going toward the courtyard. Instead, we go down hallways I don't recognize, each one increasingly empty. Finally, we're making our way down one with no one around. I'm not sure if everyone has escaped or if this is an alternative route they aren't supposed to follow.

We stop in front of two tall doors. Legend nudges me with his muzzle again, pushing me toward them. I obey and twist the knob of one, shoving the heavy door open.

It leads to an unfamiliar area, with high hedges blocking the view of the grounds. A perfect place to take to the skies. Alright, I'm about to ride a manticore. That should be ... interesting.

Legend trots past me, guiding me to the center of the courtyard, lowering and stretching a wing. I walk up to his shoulder and grab some of his soft mane for balance.

I'm swinging my leg over when he stumbles to the side. The roar he lets out makes my ears ring, and I bring my hands up to cover them. A wing sweeps up and slams into my back, bringing me onto all fours.

Instinctually, I tighten into a ball, the scorpion tail breezing over my body as he whirls around to face whatever is behind us. He snarls, moving to cover me with his body.

"Oh, how disappointing. It would've been nice to try you out for once."

The crooning voice roils my gut with dread. Between Legend's golden legs, I watch Daeva swaggering toward us. She's holding a bow and nocking another green-tipped arrow, aiming it at him. I look up and discover one lodged deep in his flank. Blood spattered the fresh-cut grass. The smell of iron makes me gag.

"I'd tell you to step aside, but only a fool would think you'd let Kalliope's pet out of your sight." She raises the bow and draws the string. "This is going to hurt me more than you."

Legend steps forward and roars in defiance as the next arrow flies. He stumbles again, and I scramble to avoid being stuck under his collapsing form. The ground shutters as his huge body crashes. The new arrow sprouts from his chest, the wound completely covered by the shaggy mane.

"Legend!" I cry out. My fingers linger on the smooth wood of the arrow. Should I pull it out? He whines and tries to stand. He's only able to come to a lying position, still trying to shield me with a wing. Daeva walks toward us, smirking.

Smug bitch.

When she gets too close, he strikes in the air with his scorpion tail. She barely dodges the curved stinger.

She clicks her tongue in admonishment. "Bad boy. Kalliope has let you on a loose leash out of affection, but you would have been better served in the Guardians." She leans forward, bracing her hands on her knees. "Serving *me* instead."

His growl rattles my bones, but she looks nonplussed. Ignoring him, she waves me over. "Come, one-form. It's time to go."

"Fuck you," I seethe.

"*Fuck you*," she mocks. "I've slain one-forms with more creative comebacks. But I wouldn't expect creativity out of a one-dimensional brain such as yours."

247

"How about 'Fuck you, you mangey whelp of a flea-ridden bitch,'" I sneer. Thanks to one particular afternoon with Ginger involving mead, I've learned some rather offensive phrases.

Her eyebrows pop, looking impressed. "Well, I see you've spent enough time around foul-mouthed Amicums. I'm sure the Vulturians will beat it out of you before they salt you up and slowly turn you on a spit. Alive."

The Vulturians? *She* betrayed Kalliope to the Vulturians?

Legend's breath becomes labored. The arrows must be dipped in a fast acting poison. Panic races through my thoughts, making it hard to figure out what to do next. "Please don't let him die."

Daeva raises the bow. "He might still survive ... unless I shoot him one more time. A guaranteed death sentence, even if I don't shoot it through his eye. Which I will, if you don't get off your ass and come with me."

Legend whines. He's fading fast. Unable to continue laying upright, he slides to his side. But the wrath in his shamrock-colored eyes doesn't fade. They say *I'm going to kill you* perfectly fine without words.

Daeva sees it, though, and snickers. "Best of luck. Come, one-form. We have a date with some males."

When I don't immediately move, she draws back the bow, aiming toward his face.

"Okay, okay. I'll come with you," I blurt out. It's an effort to stand and rush over to her. "Just don't hurt him."

Legend growls again and tries to dig his claws into the dirt to find leverage. His muscles fail him. His eyes never leave me as I walk toward the betrayer.

Mine doesn't leave him either, not until Daeva roughly grabs my arm and directs me into a side door, leaving me with the image of him, laboring to breathe.

Chapter Twenty-Seven

My New Benevolent Jailers

Daeva drags me alongside the manor, pausing around corners and scanning the skies. She's slung the bow over her shoulder and is now holding a green-tipped dagger. Her skin is cold against mine, reflecting her bitter heart. If she even has one.

She leads me through the garden, heading toward the forest. Her long strides force me to jog, but I'm able to witness the destruction. All around the manor, Vulturians and Amicums battle.

It's a large group, spread out with their spears piercing anything nearby. Smoke fills the air; something is burning down. I see a Vulturian skewer an Amicum tiger right through the throat. Shock numbs most of my emotions, but I can't help but cry out when I see a black wolf ripping the face off one of the Vulturians.

Kalliope.

If I scream her name, will she hear me? Would it just put everyone in more danger? I'm not worth more than anyone else fighting for their lives. But if she can get to Legend faster, maybe he has a chance of surviving. Finished with her kill, Kalliope's wolf turns its focus on an oncoming Vulturian warrior who holds two spears.

If I can just call out her name ...

"Don't you fucking dare," Daeva hisses, jerking me forward. "Or I'll turn right around and kill that mangey mutt."

I can't bear to watch the carnage any longer. Looking away, I glare at her pristine features. Her beauty is sharper than any blade. "Why are you doing this?"

She ignores me. I yank my arm, but she grows sharp claws that slice into my skin. I dig in my heels, ignoring the puncture wounds beginning to bleed.

She finally looks at me. There's nothing in those moonstone eyes. "*Shut the fuck up*. Unless you want me to go back to that pathetic excuse of a protective consort and execute him."

"You poisoned him. That's not fair," I say hotly.

"You're observant."

"Is he going to die?" My question is barely a whisper. The memory of him coveting me last night ... and the image of him lying on the ground dying ... it's almost too much to bear.

She shrugs. "If someone finds him fast enough and gets the antidote fast enough."

Her tone implies it's an improbability.

"*You stupid bitch*," I hiss. "What the *fuck* is your problem?"

She lets go of me, but the relief from pain is temporary as she backhands me. The world goes black for a second as I collapse. Stars dance as I bring a hand up to my throbbing cheek.

"If I weren't positive Kalliope will come save you, I'd kill you and leave your body to rot. One-forms have no right to speak to their betters like that."

She yanks my arm so roughly, it almost dislocates. I have no choice but to stumble behind her, trying to unscramble my brain.

It only takes a minute until we reach two matching creatures I've never seen before, standing about twenty feet apart. They're built like bulldogs, with thick shoulders and a tailless hind end. When one roars, its mouth shows razor-sharp teeth.

Their hairless skin is the color of a corpse, with purple noses similar to a lion's nose. Short, squat, and square ears point out from the sides of their boxy heads. The closest one watches me with reptilian yellow eyes, its thin slits assessing me. It has a simple saddle strapped to its back with the other remaining bareback.

My knees shake as its attention homes in on me. It sniffs the air, then rumbles a growl. Daeva is undeterred as she marches me forward. I balk, pulling back. It's a testament to Zenab's training because I'm able to force Daeva to stumble. She snarls and yanks me forward. I trip on a tuft of grass and almost face-plant.

"What the fuck is that?" I whisper, panic becoming a living thing inside me, scraping its sharp claws against my sternum.

Daeva jerks me roughly, and I struggle to catch myself before I run into the creature's side. "A Morgoth. Get on."

"I'm *not* getting on that thing."

"Yes. You will."

"No. I will *not*."

She walks up to me and punches me in the stomach. Air whooshes out of me, and I collapse again, retching over the grass. She pulls my head up, forcing me to look at her. She's still as impassive as a statue. Hurting me doesn't bother her in the slightest.

"I've wanted to do that since I met you, and each day I'm forced to inhale your putrid scent. If you don't get on that Morgoth right now, I'm going to spare some time to yank out a few teeth and make you eat them. Understand?"

The sounds of screaming animals fill the air. Smoke plumes over the manor, a thick pillar of black. I hear the sounds of weapons and shrieks of pain. She organized all this death. There's no doubt she'll yank out some teeth to make sure this plan succeeds.

So I turn to the Morgoth and mount up into the saddle, swinging a leg over its barrel-shaped back. Daeva walks forward to its head and says, "To the clearing. No stopping. If she fights you, rip off an arm." She glances at me, amusement lighting up her pale eyes. "Or two."

The Morgoth chuffs in acknowledgement. She steps toward me, pulling out a piece of rope and binding my wrists.

Before I can pull my hands back, she whips out a dagger and slices my forearm. The pain is blinding, and I whimper, trying to jerk out of her grasp. With a ferocious grin, she wipes her palm against the leaking blood, then smears it on the ground.

"What are you doing?" I gasp, watching my blood drip down my palms and onto the grass.

With a scowl, she tosses away my hand. "Her Grace must believe you're kidnapped. A little blood will motivate her further."

She steps back and orders the Morgoth, "Go."

The Morgoth snarls and lopes away, while the other goes in the opposite direction. Why on earth is it going the other way? Peering over my shoulder, I was Daeva turn into a snowy owl and take off to the skies. Where the hell is she going?

I can't focus on my confusion for too long because riding a Morgoth is like riding an earthquake. Its big shoulders, matched with pounding strides, make it difficult to stay on.

The blood continues to drizzle down my arm as the Morgoth charges through the sprawling fields of crops. The cut burns, but there's no way to staunch the bleeding unless I rip up my shirt. Something tells me I'll want to be clothed when we arrive wherever we're headed.

An idea sparks. What if I pull a little Hansel and Gretel to help Kalliope find me? Squeezing against the cut, I encourage more blood to appear. Every few meters, I let drops of blood fall to the ground. Perhaps Kalliope will find me this way. Really, it's the only hope I have.

That isn't true, though — I look down at the disguised Scout. It's barely a comfort knowing there's an actual escape plan. Without my supplies or the analyzer, the entire purpose of this trip will be forfeited.

Plus, disappearing from Kalliope and Legend won't do my mental health any favors. They've wormed their way into my heart, even as I've tried to create distance.

It'll be okay. There's no need to time travel right now. I know Kalliope will come for me. Daeva has a plan to lure her somewhere with me as the bait, so it's just a matter of time.

But what about Legend? Will he be okay? He tried so hard to protect me, and I hope he knows I don't hold it against him. Those were poisoned arrows. I suspect if they took him down, they would kill lesser Amicums. So many of my friends could be dead right now.

These worries eat me up as the Morgoth barrels through fields and trees like a demonic creature straight from hell. How much further until I can get off this thing?

The answer appears not too long after. By the time the Morgoth slows to a trot inside a forest clearing, sweat stains cover my shirt. My heart thunders from the physical effort of staying on for so long. The cut dried up a while ago, even though I attempted to keep it bleeding to leave a trail. I can only hope it was enough for Kalliope to find me.

The Morgoth stops in the center of the clearing, panting hard like a dog. Standing at the edge of the clearing is a group of Vulturian warriors, all of them watching me with hungry expressions, their four-fingered hands gripping thick spears. The largest one steps forward, motioning for the Morgoth to come closer. It obeys, dropping its head to the ground. Is it a sign of submission?

The Vulturian's onyx eyes watch me intently. With a sneer, he reveals fangs. "So you're the one-form that Amicum bitch sent us?"

"Who, me?" I make a show of looking around, then point at my chest. Their language feels so odd to speak, with a lot of rolling r's and the back use of my tongue.

He looks confused. "Yes. You?"

Is it dumb to antagonize the beast? Yes. Can I stop myself? No. "Are you sure? You don't seem sure."

The male snarls, then snaps his fingers, and the beast lowers to the ground in supplication. The Vulturian stomps through the soft blades of grass, then reaches up and jerks me off the saddle.

I tumble to the ground. The grass offers zero cushion when my shoulder is the first thing to hit the dirt. Crying out, I lay there, discombobulated.

The Vulturian says something in a guttural tone I don't quite catch, and the Morgoth disappears. Leaving me with the Vulturians.

Pushing myself up to stand, I hold my sore shoulder, glaring at the Vulturians. "So I take it you're my new benevolent jailers?"

The Vulturian who pulled me off the Morgoth steps forward and sneers. "One-forms are to be seen, not heard."

"Or slow roasted." Another snickers.

Before I can retort, my legs buckle, and I fall forward. I've lost enough blood and adrenaline, I barely have energy to stand. Maybe these guys will have some fresh fruit to spare. Unlikely, but hey, a girl can dream.

"While I'm honored you want to eat me,"—I look down at my body, then back to them—"and who can blame you? I'm delicious looking, but I must decline."

The one that snickered raises his spear. "I don't mind my meals being raw and screaming."

"Enough," the tallest one commands, grabbing my arm and jerking me closer to the group. "We must wait and be patient."

I eye the dagger strapped to his bulging thigh. Will my training with Zenab be enough?

It's also not a good idea to wait around and let these guys eat me. There's no telling what they're waiting for, but it's all but guaranteed that I'm ending up as someone's meal soon. I'll be damned if I don't at least make myself a difficult meal.

The Vulturian releases my arm and faces the group. "She said she'd be here shortly before — ARGH!"

His words cut off with a roar when I stab the dagger into his thigh. Blue blood gushes out, coating the gray scales. I yank it out and plunge it back in again. More blood spills onto the grass.

Dropping the blade, I turn to bolt. I'm yanked back by my braid. Air whooshes out of my lungs when I slam to the ground. The Vulturian bellows with pain and fury as he bends over to grab me by the throat.

Air might not reach my lungs right now, but somehow, I wheeze out a laugh. Finally, I could *do* something. Even with the stars dotting my vision, it was worth it.

"I think I'll save one of your legs and make you watch me eat it," he sneers as he drops me. My ankle collapses awkwardly, shooting pain up my leg.

"At least buy me dinner first," I cough out, my lungs struggling to expand. Panic clouds my thoughts. My fingers flutter around my throat, grazing the swollen skin. It's going to leave quite a necklace, and not the pretty kind.

He snaps his fingers. A warrior steps forward, offering a strip of cloth. The Vulturian wraps it around his thigh. The blood soaks through it immediately. I grin, with the taste of blood in my mouth.

He takes a menacing step toward me, favoring the uninjured one, but another warrior stops him. "The Amicum betrayer approaches, Prince Frostbane. Perhaps we should wait before harming her."

Prince?

The prince whirls on the warrior, punching him squarely in the jaw. There's a crack, and the warrior stumbles back, spitting out a tooth. "Do you dare question your prince on his methods with one-forms?"

The warrior looks down in submission, cupping his split lip. "No, of course not, sire."

This is probably why females willingly died to prevent the Vulturians from being in charge. They're barbarians.

The prince turns back to me, some of his fury faded. He gazes over my head, then refocuses on me. "My second is right — we have some business to take care of first." A purple, pebbled tongue strokes one of his fangs, and he picks up his bloodied dagger.

I follow his gaze upward and bare my teeth at the large white owl landing next to us. I don't think I've ever hated anyone as much as I hate Daeva. She shifts into true-form, closing the remaining distance with a swagger.

"I'm going to kill you!" I scream, rage blocking out any sense of self-preservation. She laughs heartily as she walks toward our group, palming the daggers hanging at her hips. "You couldn't hurt an Amicum fly, let alone hurt one of the most powerful Amicums of our time."

"Kalliope is going to shred you to ribbons."

The threat is ineffective. "She's welcome to try. I've been preparing for this since the bitch stole power. It should've been *me* as lordess." She slams a palm to her chest as a wild look enters her pale eyes. "*I'm* the better leader. *I* train the Guardians. *I* keep these lands safe. She goes around entertaining villagers while I work my tail off to protect each and every Amicum."

Daeva looks at me like I'm the shit between her toe beans. "She's not as clever as she thinks. Didn't suspect a thing, so she'll fall into the trap."

There's no telling if anything she's saying is true, but I have a sick feeling she's not off the mark. Not entirely, at least.

Daeva focuses on the Vulturian prince. "Prince Cedric Frostbane, your king still has no idea?"

The prince shakes his head. "No, he's too focused on his new daughter. Thinks she might be the 'new future.' I've told him —"

"Wait," I interrupt, unable to resist. "Your name is Cedroo Frost-nipper?"

They pause and turn their heads slowly, incredulity in their expressions. It's satisfying to witness Daeva at a loss for words.

Surprisingly, the prince is the first to catch up. "I'm Prince Cedric Frostbane, soon-to-be King Frostbane. You'll mind your sharp tongue, one-form, before I mind it for you."

Redirecting my fear into something that will help stave off sobbing hysterically, I mutter, "Geez, Frostcrumble, I'm just confused by everything going on right now. Cut a one-form a break, will ya?"

Daeva sucks her teeth dismissively. "Well, *King* Frostbane, like me, you are qualified to bring back the old ways." She looks down her nose at me with disgust. "The *right* ways."

I bare my teeth at her again, but the sentiment doesn't land. I'm too meaningless to register as a threat. I bet that wouldn't be true if I could stab her in the gut with the dagger on her hip. I'm feeling stabby right now. My eyes slowly trail to her dagger, my hand itching to grab and stab.

Noticing the focus of my attention, Daeva steps back. *Good.*

To the prince, she says, "Keep her hostage. Prepare for the lordess to arrive. While you take care of her, I'll be at the manor, picking up the pieces she's left behind."

"Why don't you just kill me now? Save Prince Frontcrinkle a swing of his dagger," I taunt. Frostbane snarls, but Daeva holds up a hand. He obeys the silent command.

I make sure my smug look shows him exactly what I think of his obedience. I'm delusional with exhaustion and blood loss, but taunting him is satisfying as hell.

Daeva unsheathes her dagger. "Don't tempt me, one-form. This needs to be a clean coup. She thinks we're both kidnapped. If she wants proof of life, we'll need to offer it. Can't do that if I sever your head from your shoulders too soon."

Before I register what's about to happen, she kicks me in the gut. Pain explodes, knocking the wind out of me.

"Stay vigilant and stick to the plan," she reminds the prince. The air shimmers, and a snowy owl rises into the sky.

"Get up," the prince growls.

There's no point in arguing. Another beating will only make things worse, and their hunger might eventually overshadow my potential worth. They don't seem like the type to listen to an Amicum's orders.

Especially as the prince sniffs the surrounding air, noting how yummy I smell.

Swaying as I stand, I suck air through my teeth. There isn't an inch of me that isn't throbbing at this point. The prince limps forward, and his second, still palming his bleeding face, points ahead with his spear, showing me where to go.

And so, we march into the darkness.

Except when he isn't looking, I make sure my palm keeps dropping blood along our path. If it worked for Hansel and Gretel, it might work for me.

Unless I end up as the meal in the end.

Chapter Twenty-Eight

Failure. Failure. Failure.

Legend

Reality is not what it seems. Searing pain burns my skin and blood. Unsure of what has happened, my body tries to follow Saira. My instincts scream, rattling against the cage my weakened body has become. I can't remember why I'm trying to go after, just that I *need* to.

Every attempt to move is beaten back by an incapacitation I've never experienced before. Even as the strongest male of my age, it's too much. It's also most likely why I'm still alive.

My thoughts are slop, but the last look Saira gave me, full of fear — for *me* — plays over and over again in my thoughts. I'm too weak to protect her. That's the only reason I exist — to *protect*.

I failed.

Who took her? Why am I so desperate to save her? Her face haunts me, but why?

My scorpion tail goes flaccid as my strength continues to ebb. My glorious wings hang limp at my sides. All around, shapes and creatures crawl around. Some of them jump onto my face. I must be hallucinating. It's improbable that a family of raccoons is trying to make a home in my mane.

The world is technicolor, with melting blobs plopping off anything within sight. My mind curls in on itself to avoid focusing on any of the hallucinations for too long.

A male's life is defined by his choice of service. My father, with his gentle spirit, serves the land with music and drink. My mother, while she was alive, balanced her priorities with a fierceness few females can embody.

Somehow, she accomplished curating home and hearth, while serving Ilorna with steadfast duty as a Guardian. Both of them assumed my future also held music and the vineyard, or at least the vineyard. It was a shock to both of them when I became a consort. Specifically, the personal protection consort for Kalliope.

There was no other choice. Kalliope is my chosen mate. There is no greater honor than to guide and protect one of the greatest warriors this land has ever seen. My servitude will only end when I eventually die.

Which, turns out, might very well be today.

The door to the manor slams open, and the sound of running feet comes my way. I'm too sick to see who it is. Perhaps it's someone to put me out of my misery.

"Legend!" Kalliope drops to my side, terror widening her beautiful golden eyes. If they're the last thing I see, then so be it. Her gentle hands push me over, and I grunt as the pain intensifies. The wounds are hot to the touch, too hot for me to feel her prodding the arrows.

"Who was it?"

Unable to shift, I say into her mind, **Poisoned. Saira's gone.**

That's all I know. All I remember.

Her mouth forms a thin line. Over her shoulder, she barks out orders to someone I cannot see. Grabbing my head, she shuffles until it's laying in her soft, warm lap. Yes, this is a good place to die. In her arms. Fingers dab at one of the wounds. She raises the green residue to her nose, then pales. She screams at someone to hurry up.

I love you.

259

"Be quiet, you," she hisses. "Stop sounding like you're going to die. You aren't. Do you understand? If you die, I'll chase you to Inanna's Afterworld and pluck each hair from your mane one by one."

My thoughts drift. Memories from long ago resurface, playing in my mind on a loop. The first moment I saw Kalliope as a youngling. With her auburn hair in messy braids and dirt smudged on her cheek. She handed me an apple to share. An evening when we were mere adolescents, chasing one another through the woods, practicing our shifting. Under the full moon for our first messy, tentative kiss. The first time I slipped inside her lush body and met our goddess inside the pleasure.

Even the one time we actually fought, during the war, when her mother ordered that I locked her in a room so she couldn't follow her into battle. Kalliope hated me then, but the forgiveness was swift. Her fierceness and loyalty cemented my need to serve her until the day I die.

The memories stall on fresh ones. Saira. She's unlike any one-form I've ever met. There's something about her sassiness that has always enchanted me. When she arrived, her bright eyes would dart around every room and every Amicum, observing and absorbing.

Yet, not an inch of judgment has ever existed. Even when afraid, she's pushed through, coming out stronger each time. Some days, I watch her from afar as she practices with Zenab. The ferocity she brings to the training is admirable. She might fall on her cute ass, but she always gets right back up. Knowing she's not from this world doesn't affect the way I admire her or love her.

Because I *love* her.

She's so much like Kalliope, yet so different. Where Kalliope is forged with steel and patience, Saira is both thoughtful and impulsive. Always with a sharp quip ready to be released like a flying dagger.

The memory of both Kalliope and Saira in bed with me last night was nothing short of transcendent. I've cavorted with plenty of other females, but last night ... Saira was spectacular. Eager to learn. Excited to experience it.

It's a shame I will never know what it means to join with her. To feel her covering my body with her soft heat. To —

Something hits my furry maw, jolting me out of my thoughts. I lift a lip, growling.

"Wake up!" Kalliope sounds frantic. Something cold presses against my lips. "Drink this, you fucking male. Or I'll banish you. I'm sure Lordess Charlyn would love a taste."

Disgusted at the idea, I peel open my mouth. Cool liquid coats my mouth. It's an effort to swallow as much as possible. Now, all there is to do is wait.

Low voices wake me. Everything's stiff. I'm on something soft, and it doesn't smell like outside. It smells like me, Kalliope, and a faint scent of Saira. My bed chamber.

Shifting on the soft mattress, the cool sheets comfort my hot skin. In my sleep, I've shifted back to true-form. That's a good sign. It means I'm finally strong enough to do so.

Peeling one eye open, I look around the dark room. Kalliope sits on the edge of the bed, discussing things with Zenab and Ginger. The three of them look distraught.

Ginger is the first to notice me awake. She points excitedly. "Look! He's awake!"

Kalliope's head whips around, tears of relief immediately falling. She crawls over to my side, grazing her hands over my bare torso. "How are you? Are you okay? Are you hot?"

Licking my dry lips, I say, "Water."

Zenab rushes over to a nearby pitcher, pouring a glass. Kalliope helps me sit up. My abs are weak and sore. When I look down, I'm dismayed to find two healing wounds, both of which will most likely scar. My brain's sluggish. Memories are hazy, hiding behind a wall of hallucinations. All I remember is Saira being dragged away by someone.

After taking sips of water, I'm able to ask, "Where is Saira?"

The three of them frown. Kalliope brandishes a letter from a pocket. "We found this letter a little way away from the courtyard. It says Daeva and Saira are kidnapped by the Vulturians and I need to turn myself over to save their lives."

We turn to look at Ginger, who lets loose a deep growl. "We'll slaughter them all."

A dry cough catches me by surprise, and I wince as my abs flex. Taking another sip of water, I clear my throat. A memory tries to resurface, but it slips away before I can snatch it.

"I remember Saira leaving, but the drugs also made me hallucinate." I put a hand over my heart, where the ache of her missing throbs in time with my heartbeat. "I just know she's gone, and someone took her."

Kalliope watches me for a beat before saying, "We need to go search the forest. Zenab and I picked up two Morgoth trails, but only one with some of Saira's blood on it."

"One must be a decoy," Zenab says. "We could get a group of Guardians together to —"

"No." Kalliope scoots off the bed and begins pacing. "Just the Cohort. No one else. If this is an ambush, and it most likely is, then we need to focus on stealth. A group of Guardians is not stealthy."

"I'm going. For Saira," Ginger snarls.

"Me too." Zenab declares.

I shuffle my body to the side of the bed. Kalliope rushes forward, trying to push me down. "Not you. Rest."

It's rare for me to question her. Mostly, there's no need to. She's wise beyond measure and always balances being a lordess and being herself. So when I level her with a scathing glare, her hands jump back as if scalded.

"I'm not staying here like some helpless fucking male while Saira is out there with those brutes who will just as soon eat her than keep her alive."

I've seen what Vulturians do to one-forms. The thought of anything in that realm of possibility happening to Saira? I can't bear it.

Kalliope knows if I ever challenge her, she can't change my mind. She also knows how much Saira now means to me. Instead of giving me an order I'll refuse, she holds out a hand. We clasp forearms, and she helps me stand. The world wobbles for a moment, forcing me to take a breath. *I can do this.*

While Zenab calls for Meadow to bring me an additional healing balm and pain suppressant, Kalliope finds me clothes to wear. It's a journey, pulling on pants and a shirt. Every movement pulls at my injury. Gritting my teeth, I lace up my boots.

It's easier to stand this time. I look over to find Ginger watching me; her worry creases lines on her heart-shaped face. I hold open my arms, and she rushes into them. It's difficult to hide my groan of pain as her chest hits my wounds.

"I thought you were dead, Paul."

The joke elicits a chuckle. "Well, they don't call me Legend for nothing."

She snorts and pulls away. "Didn't you decide to call yourself Legend when you were ten and three years of age? When you snuck into that manticore nest to steal an egg? And instead, you fell off the cliff when the mother returned?"

I patted her on the head, earning a curled lip. "My origin story remains a mystery for many. Let's keep it that way."

Without missing a beat, we fall into our regular dynamic. She swats my hand away. "Pat me on the head again and see what happens."

Ginger is vicious in her revenge. She'll chop off hair, turn into stinging insects, replace sugar with salt, and do many other inconvenient retaliations to make anyone think twice. Including me. Dropping my hand, I sling an arm over her shoulders and tuck her close.

"Let's go save Saira, shall we?"

She looks up with saucer-round eyes. With feigned innocence, she asks, "Even Daeva?"

I pause, pretending to contemplate. I've never liked Daeva. She's cold and relatively unfeeling. Taking life too seriously, with too much suspicion. Her prejudice against one-forms has always been alarming as well. "If the Vulturians have not killed her just to shut her up, then yes. Daeva, too."

"Okay," she says with a glum tone.

Together, we walk to the woods and shift. Picking up Saira's scent, the smell of her blood is like chum to my protective instincts. It makes me want to shred every enemy that exists in this entire fucking world. The last I saw her, she was scared, and I was too helpless to do my job.

It won't happen again. We'll find her, and she'll be safe. I refuse to exist in a world where that is not the truth. She's been gone for twelve hours so far. It's twelve hours too long.

Imagining the strength and deadliness of my manticore form, the wings sprout from my ribs. My healing wounds ache, but I don't care. The scorpion tail bursts out of me, its needle-sharp curved point ready to spear anyone in my way. I'd like to see them try to get between me and the female I love.

Chapter Twenty-Nine

That's Not a Chunk Of Meat

Saira

We walked through the woods for who knows how long. The deeper we go, the darker it grows. The canopy is thick and intertwined, creating a false twilight.

If it were any other situation, I'd love the purple-green glow of the light and the beautiful hue it casts. Unfortunately, it also highlights the bright gray skin of my captors. They look ethereal, and I hate everything about them.

With careful observation, I can spot slight differences between them. Each of them has a crown of horns, black hair falling between them like spooky waterfalls. They each hold a spear but only have four sausage-sized fingers. Everything is thick, from their forearms to their legs, which are wide enough to be tree trunks.

After what feels like hours, we stop. The prince grabs my wrists and drags me forward into the middle of a small clearing.

Pushing me down onto the ground, he snarls, "Don't think your leader will get past us. You'll sit here as we rest. If you try to escape, I'll start dismantling you joint by joint. Then force you to watch me eat them. Do you understand?"

The entire description is, frankly, over-the-top. So much so, I'm unable to stop myself from asking, "How will you cook them?"

His eyes flare. "What did you say?"

I shrug, plopping down on my ass. "I mean, will there be a fire? Do you eat fingers raw? Cover them in dirt like animals? You seem the type to —"

The hand comes out of nowhere, slamming into my face like a sledge-hammer. The world goes dark for a second. Licking the corner of my mouth, I blanch at the taste of copper. Okay, maybe I really should keep my mouth shut. Another punch and it might leave me concussed.

He leans down, the twilight enhancing the pale bone of his crown of horns. When he bares his teeth, bits of rotten meat are stuck between them.

"You don't need your tongue. That, one-form, I'll eat raw while you scream. Or try to." The other Vulturians laugh as they take up posts on the perimeter.

One raises his spear, smiling like a gleeful demon signing up for torture. "I ask for the throat."

Another, shorter with fewer horns, huffs out a sound of irritation. "You always ask for the good parts, Elorzo. Give someone else a chance to enjoy a meal."

Elorzo shoves the smaller Vulturian. "Silence, runt. When you can break off one of my horns, you can try to have the good parts."

The prince glares at them. "Be quiet and keep watch in case that psychotic bitch was wrong, and the lordess finds us."

They settle at different points in the clearing, ignoring me. Which is fine because I'm not interested in losing my tongue, but I'm not sure I can be civil if they ask me anything else.

My face throbs in time with my heartbeat. Sighing, I shift to my side and place my tied-up wrists under my head for a pillow. Tucking my legs to my chest, I close my eyes. The ground is cold, seeping into my bones and forcing a full-body shiver. I'd do anything for a fire, but I know it'd be stupid to ask for one. A fire would signal our position.

Somehow, defying all odds, I fall asleep.

The first thing I notice when I open my eyes is trees. Their swaying branches and rustling leaves. In the pale light of dawn, birds are beginning their songs. A warm breeze caresses my skin, offering minor comfort.

For a split second, I'm confused about my surroundings. A pungent scent follows the breeze, bringing reality front and center. It's the smell of unwashed, bloodied Vulturians. Oh, right. I'm a captive.

Disappointment oozes into every corner of my brain that isn't already exhausted and scared. No one has come for me yet. Daeva was so positive the Cohort would come for us, but it's been almost a day. What's taking everyone so long? Do I really not matter?

Peering around, I observe that most of the Vulturians are still curled up on the ground, hugging their spears like blankies. Are Vulturians given their first spears in their cribs? If they weren't so disgusting, I'd chuckle at the sight.

My lips are dry and cracked as I nibble on them. Water would be a gift from the gods right about now. I haven't seen a single Vulturian drink anything, though.

There's movement in the corner of my eye, and I look over to find the prince sitting against a tree, watching me while he slides a stone against the sharp sides of his spear.

Creeper.

Pretending not to care about his glowering, I roll my ankle in circles. It's stiff, but usable. My fingers touch the delicate skin of my neck, causing me to wince. Gently twisting my body around, I can feel the bruises settling along my torso, but nothing's broken.

"Enjoying your accommodations, one-form?"

He shoves off the tree, towering over me as he stands. If he's trying to intimidate me, it's working. But he doesn't need to know that.

I pick up a leaf and pretend to inspect it. "Spiffy, Prince Fangbanger. Ten out of ten, would recommend."

His lack of response makes me look up. His dark, empty eyes are slits as he tries to parse apart my words. "What ten of ten are you recommending?"

Tossing the leaf, I look up at the swaying tree branches. "Never mind. You wouldn't understand."

He morphs into a tower of wrath, stomping toward me. "Do you mock me?"

Shut the fuck up, Saira. Ignoring the wise inner voice, I retort, "Of course not. I'm not sure your tiny brain could handle something as simple as a rating system for things."

The Vulturians around us stir. Some sit up to watch the prince stalk over, the ground trembling under his steps. Why is everyone so big around here? They seem to create tiny earthquakes.

I try to wriggle away, but my tied wrists make it hard to balance and stand. In a flash, he's on me, meaty hands wrapping around my neck, squeezing so hard I almost pass out. The regret is immediate, with my neck already so bruised.

"Why ... are ... you ... so ... kinky?" I squeeze out between attempts to inhale. Panic blooms in my chest, constricting my lungs even further. In response, he squeezes harder, but with more pressure, he might snap my neck in half. I bring my bound wrists down onto his face.

The only thing hurt is my pride, because that was an enormous judgment error. The guy's face feels like pure bone; it's like hitting a wall. My palms throb from the impact, and leave zero marks on his scaly skin.

The prince grins, grinding his hips into me. Revulsion mixes with my terror. I don't even want to consider what presses onto my belly. The last thing I ever want to see is Vulturian dick.

With zero effort on his part, he pulls me upward as he stands. Now I'm dangling a respectable distance from the ground as he brings me closer. Close enough for me to see the serrated edges of his teeth. Something is stuck in his blue gums. It looks like uncooked meat.

"One-form, I have been quite hungry. And your sharp tongue has convinced me of your uselessness."

Said tongue lodges on the roof of my dry mouth, extinguishing any words. Air wheezes down my windpipe. My lungs burn, pressing into themselves like deflated balloons.

"We haven't gotten the signal yet."

The voice comes from Elorzo, whose eyes dart around as he steps up to the prince. The impassive revulsion on the prince's face flickers. He makes a sound of frustration and tosses me roughly.

"Bah, there better be a signal soon. We've no breakfast."

My hip bone screams in agony as I land on my ass, and my hands go to my throat. The swelling is worse now. By the time I get back to the manor, I'm going to resemble a punching bag.

The prince turns to the others. "Let's go. We need to be at the camp by the time the sun is directly above."

My sarcasm's firmly locked down for now. Breathing hurts so much; it's a constant reminder that sometimes, it *is* better to be seen rather than heard. I somehow bring myself to stand and let them lead me through the trees. It's a slow march, thanks to all my injuries. For whatever reason, they don't harass me too much for dallying.

What would Dad think of the situation I've found myself in? Maybe I should've left the moment I realized the Amicums had mortal enemies. On the other hand, there's no way of knowing if a "perfect" society even exists. Statistically, so many things would have to go right for a place to be perfect — it's virtually unattainable, even with the trillions of options in the universes.

It'll be okay. Kalliope will come for me, provided she doesn't fall for the trap. I have to believe the Cohort will come. So instead of panicking, I make a mental note to get samples of the Vulturians.

Mission first, everything else second. Dad's voice in my head brings out both longing and anxiety. Maybe I've stayed here too long. A few weeks ago, it was easy to convince myself I'd stayed to collect information and leave with zero complications.

It's time to stop lying to myself. I've fallen in love with Legend and Kalliope. I've made friends. There's yummy food. Beautiful landscapes. What more could I want in a new place to live?

Aside from being kidnapped by people-eating assholes, of course.

We reach their camp less than an hour later. It's an acre of open-aired buildings with some tents dotting between the structures. An enormous bonfire sits in the center of it all. Around the bonfire are tinier bonfires, each serving a different purpose. One for a blacksmith, the sooty male pounding away at something as sparks fly. Others sit under steaming pots, blackened from continuous use.

Beside the center bonfire is a slightly smaller one, holding a sizable chunk of spit-roasted meat.

Oh. That's not a chunk of meat. That's …

My body folds in half as I throw up bile. The crispy vision of a person quartered and roasting is too much for me to handle.

The prince makes a sound of disgust and shoves me forward. "You're going to sit with the females while we wait for the signal. Don't get into trouble and maybe we'll find some *special use* for you."

The way he says "special use" makes me wonder if being burned alive might be a tad more preferable. Elorzo claps a hand on my shoulder, guiding me to a tent. Shoving me roughly toward it, he says, "Stay in there and shut up."

He pushes the entrance flap aside. I tentatively step inside and look around. It's a large tent, big enough to hold five Vulturians, presumably females. They're more pale and instead of large horns, they have boney nubs. Each of them wears loose material resembling burlap sacks. A quick inhalation of the stale air confirms the lack of access to showers.

They all shrink back, fear stricken at my appearance. I put my hands up and try my best to look non-threatening. They're probably less afraid of me than I am of them. They eat people, after all. But as one scrambles back, I'm thinking that might not be true. The scared part; not the person part. There's definitely a person being cooked right now.

One of them holds an infant to her breast, covering it protectively. In a corner, two younglings play with some sticks. They both rush up to their mothers, clutches to their legs.

"Don't worry, I'm only here for a bit," I say, shuffling to the side and taking a seat on a worn, dark green blanket.

They exchange looks, and one speaks rapidly. It takes my translator a moment to pick up.

"... do you think she'll be able to help?"

The one she's talking to sizes me up before responding. "She's clearly the size of a youngling. It's unlikely."

I'm pleased I can understand them. I'm not pleased with the comment about my height. I'm five-foot-four, for fuck's sake. I'm horizontally challenged — not stupid.

"I'm not *that* small," I argue.

Their eyes grow wide. The first one gasps. "You can understand us?"

"Yes," I drawl. I look around the tent closer and take in how spartan it is. Some blankets on the ground, a bucket of dark-colored liquid, and some cups. Not even enough for each of them to have one. "Can you tell me why you're in this tent?"

The smallest one, holding the baby, tucks it a little closer. "We've been kidnapped from our families. The prince captured us a few weeks ago as he attempts ..." She motions into the air with a disgusted look. "Whatever it is he is trying to do. We are mostly ignored here in the tent."

"Have you tried to escape?" I ask, curious to know if there's a way out.

"Yes," the female says sharply. "Every attempt ends in violence."

The way she says the word "violence" tells me more than I'd like to know.

Great. Now I'll have to break it to Kalliope that she needs to save more than just me. It'll be fine — she can never resist saving someone.

271

JENNA AVERY

We're all silent for a while. I hug my legs to my chest, resting my chin on my bound hands. I'm tempted to drink the liquid, but the way flies perch on the edge, rubbing their legs together, it's easier to resist the temptation.

The females continue to watch me, now unwilling to talk around me. The toddlers return to playing quietly, not paying attention to me at all.

The tent becomes a stifling oven in the afternoon heat, and more bugs buzz around us, which I swat away. My stomach grumbles. I haven't eaten or had water in over a day and a half. The headache throbbing against my skull is becoming unbearable.

Finally, unable to continue the silence, I point at a cup. "I'm sorry, but I have had nothing to drink or eat since yesterday morning. Can I please have some of that?"

More exchanged looks. The first one who spoke with me nods and fills a cup with the liquid. I grab it from her and guzzle it down.

Big mistake. It's sour and salty. Definitely not water. At least my lips aren't dry anymore. They all give me looks of pity.

"Thank you ...?"

The female looks wary as she says, "Ulvita."

"Thank you, Ulvita." I look at each of them with a questioning tilt of my head. They each introduce themselves as Brutoxin, Sylvanda, Artlina, and the final one, the one holding the baby, is Tylain.

"Nice to meet you." My smile is genuine. None of them seem to be like the males. If anything, they flinch at every loud noise outside the tent. Which is *very* loud. Every order's screamed and swords clashed as they presumably practiced. All of them male.

And to my utter disgust, the smell of something cooking is so enticing, it makes me even more nauseous. It's not nearly long enough since my last meal for that small to be truly appetizing.

So the hours march on. The females continue to be reluctant in sharing details, but I'm able to glean they're kidnapping victims from the king's own entourage a few weeks ago. Kept as potential breeding stock and collateral. The baby is the son of a noble, as are the toddlers, who have now crawled into their mother's laps for naps.

272

The shadows grow longer on the tent. At least the heat is abating. They've let me have more of the liquid — which continues to be nasty — but have no food to share. None of them seem eager to eat the meat from outside, either.

Soon, it's pitch-black inside the tent. The males can't even be bothered to offer a candle. The need to sleep drags over me like a heavy blanket. Curled up in a ball like last night, I lean my head against my bound arms. My wrists bleed from the friction, but somehow, I'm still able to sleep.

The comatose respite lasts only for a short time. A shout from somewhere in the camp wakes me up. Then more shouting and the sound of running. The females whisper fearfully, and one of the toddlers begins to cry.

I shoot up, looking into the dark like there's something to see. A large beast roars in the forest. A disgusting squelch makes me grimace. More screams and shouts. A massacre is happening out there. Adrenaline courses through my veins, heightening my senses. My ears pick up the sound of cracking bones. A male shouts commands, but from the frantic cadence of his words, it doesn't sound like it's going so well for him.

A wolf's howl abruptly cuts off, followed by a yelp.

Kalliope!

The flap to the tent jerks back, and all the females grab their children. A scowling warrior motions impatiently toward me. When I'm close enough, he grabs me roughly, jerking me past the tent flaps. The momentum trips up my feet, and I stumble forward.

The scene is chaotic. Vulturian males run back and forth, the fires casting eerie shadows on their fearful faces. A spear flies over one bonfire, lodging in a tree. A flash of brown darts through the trees, easily dodging the weapon.

Elorzo pushes me toward a group of males, all holding spears, wearing gleaming armor that reflects the bonfire's spitting flames. Their eyes widen, wincing as bodies slam into tents. In front stands the smug prince, who seems nonplussed as another one of his men's screams are silenced. His toothy grin widens when he sees me. He's far too cocky for someone whose camp is falling apart.

"Ah, little one-form. Your lordess is now falling for our trap. She'll now watch you die, then we will kill you. Then we get to have a quick bite before we take over what is rightfully ours."

From the sound of things, it doesn't sound like Kalliope has fallen for jack shit, but my throat hurts so much, every inch of sarcasm needs to be worth it. By the faltering grin and disappointment in his eyes, my lack of response upsets him. Staring it is, then.

He's on his villain monologue though, so he puffs out his chest and boasts, "Once we kill Lordess Kalliope, everything will fall into place. That Amicum traitor is so short-sighted, she doesn't see how she's outwitted. She's never going to be as strong as the dead lordess. Her people adored her. Daeva's coup will fail. And we'll be there to feast on the carrion."

Behind him, a pitch black lion charges through a small group of soldiers. A few streaks of white break up the inky mane. *Zenab.* Joy sings through my aching body. They all came for me!

Somewhere from behind, I hear a furious horse squeal and roar. *Ginger.* Where's Kalliope? Is Legend here?

It's going to be okay. Everything is going to be okay. I'm not about to be slathered in butter and spit-roasted. I lift my bound hands up and fake a yawn. With a raspy voice, I say, "So cliché, Fro-fro. A villain monologue? Really?"

He points over my head and says to Elorzo, "Bring her to the spit."

The prince's grin is wicked as I'm dragged backward by my arms. So, I do the only thing I can do.

I flipped him the bird.

His grin fades, and confusion twists his features. Oh. Right. He has no idea what that means.

"It's offensive, fuckface!" I holler, doing it again. The scream costs me and I end up coughing.

The asshole points at me and mimics using a fork and knife to cut into the air. Implying I'm about to be his next meal.

Okay, maybe he won that round.

The heat of the fires beads sweat all over my limp body as my feet create trenches in the dirt. I look around, trying to get out of this. I might be weak, but that doesn't mean I'll willingly climb into the fire.

The males toss me to the ground, and I hiss at them. "I didn't consent to being tenderized first, asshole."

Elorzo reaches for a smooth wooden bowl. His fingers reach in and pull out white granules pinched between them.

He has the gall to sprinkle it in my hair. Not a lot, but enough to make a point. I'll be damned if I make this easy for them. Pretending to go limp with defeat, I watch their feet as they walk around me, tossing more wood into the fire. When they're a few feet away, I bolt upright and sprint away.

Only to skid to a stop when a spear pierces the ground in front of me, missing my torso by inches. I gasp, a hand flying to my galloping heart.

"Try again and I won't miss," the prince calls out. I glare at him as Elorzo grabs me again. Bringing me back to square one. Except this time, the other male stands right by me while Elorzo preps a long, *sharp* poker.

The prince walks up to me, a dagger in hand, looking too victorious for my liking. "I told you I'd like that tongue raw first, didn't I?"

275

Chapter Thirty

It's Been A Real Vacation

P rince Frizznozzle reaches down and grabs my chin hard.

"Open up!" he demands. I clamp my mouth shut and shake my head away, but he holds me firm between those meaty fingers. It feels like my face is stuck in a vise.

"Open up, or you'll make this worse for yourself."

His fingers squeeze even harder, and on reflex, my jaw unhinges, unable to bear the pressure. Two of his fingers shove into my mouth, and I gag at the taste of dirt, blood, and who knows what else. He pinches my tongue between two fingers and yanks it out. It garbles my cry of pain.

"This is going to be so delicious," he purrs.

"Fook yu," I scream, unable to even jerk away now. Not without it tearing loose on its own. The regret of goading him is intense. I'm going to lose this tongue because I can't keep my damn mouth shut. For someone with a genius IQ, I'm a real slow fucking learner.

"Let her go or I'm going to shred your balls into slivers and feed them to you over the course of a week. I'll make you eat everyone else's balls, too."

Tears flood my vision at the sweet but deadly sound of Kalliope's voice.

"Can I watch?" Ginger quips.

The prince lets go of my tongue, and my jaw snaps shut as I frantically search the shadows.

There she is. Kalliope walks into the clearing. Murderous intent darkens her features. The prince follows my gaze, then bares his teeth like a feral dog. He turns to face Kalliope. All the remaining Vulturians raise their spears, leveling them at her as she comes closer.

Behind her, Zenab prowls forward with molten gold eyes. Ginger is naked, as usual, covered in blood. Like Lilith come to life, stepping out of Lucifer's playpen. She grins, her white teeth stained red. I've seen nothing more disturbing in my life.

She waves her hand furiously, looking deranged. "Hey BB. Or should I say VV?"

I look between her and the prince. In a voice like sandpaper, I say, "Uh, not the best time, Ginger."

She shrugs, twirling a curl and popping a hip. The remaining Vulturian soldiers are stunned, turning to stone, their eyes locked on her naked form. It doesn't seem to bother her.

Refocusing on Kalliope, a rush of relief relaxes my muscles. She came for me. The terror I'd carefully smothered rises to the surface, and I cry in earnest.

"Kalliope," I whisper. Parts of her leathers and shirt are in tatters, and blood splatters different parts of her body. Her face is gaunt, as if what she just endured has already taken a toll. It speaks to her strength, not buckling under the weight of anguish.

She's never looked so beautiful.

Her golden gaze scans me up and down as she continues to ignore the advancing Vulturians. "Are you alright?"

I nod. It takes extreme effort to say, "Never better. It's been a real vacation." The words jumble against my thickened tongue. Air singes my throat, coming in small gulps.

The corner of her perfect mouth quirks. "Still making jokes at inappropriate times, I see."

"Be quiet." The prince's voice is thunderous. "My warriors failed, but I think you'll make a nice entrée after this appetizer."

I roll my eyes. Like I said; so cliché.

Kalliope stands there, hands on the hilts of shining daggers. "Is that so? And who are you? I'm only familiar with high ranking Vulturians."

The prince sneers at the insult and puffs out his chest. Smacking it with a hand, he declares, "I am Prince Frostbane, the soon-to-be King of the Vulturians."

"Delulu," I mutter.

Kalliope looks him up and down, amused. "Oh, I remember you. You're the spare after the spare. No wonder you seem so unfamiliar. Does King Ryaxis know of this? Or is this a desperate, yet failed, grasp for power?"

The prince bares his teeth and reaches down to grab his spear. Pointing it at her, he promises, "*I'm* king. Ryaxis knows nothing of this because he's too weak to do what needs to be done. When I'm done with you and your Cohort, I'll consume your one-form with some salt and vinegar. It goes well on the soft flesh of the eyeballs."

His words raise bile up my swollen throat. The visuals are almost too much for my empty stomach. It's a struggle to swallow the bile threatening to burn my throat.

Unimpressed, Kalliope inspects a dirty nail, rubbing it on her pants. "Spare me. Let's get this over with, shall we?"

All the Vulturians snarl, stepping forward. The prince growls, making fists with his meaty hands. I'm shoved aside as Prince Freshkipper makes Kalliope his sole focus. His soldiers turn their attention to Ginger and Zenab.

Ginger tosses her hair, skips forward three steps, then shifts into a small, ruby-red wyvern. No bigger than a cow, but big enough to inflict some actual damage. Striking like a snake, she lashes out at a too-close Vulturian, ripping off his arm. I look away, unable to watch more of the massacre.

Zenab rushes forward and swipes at soldiers, baring six-inch long fangs. The Vulturians, armed with only spears, stab and miss repeatedly. One soldier howls as ribbons of flesh are rent from his chest. My legs wobble with a fresh wave of nausea. I could really use some water right about now.

Kalliope draws both daggers. She rolls her shoulders and cracks her neck. They all rush her, spears aimed at chest height. My throat aches when I whimper in fear. She looks at each one, assessing. Pulse pounding, I begin working at the ropes around my wrists.

The one Elorzo called a runt is the first to reach her, his arms raised to spear her. She looks up at him, his bulk casting a shadow on her face. The second he's within arm's reach, she slices upward so fast, I barely see it. He lets out a gurgling scream. Blue blood gushes out of his neck, pouring over her. The soldier's eyes bulge, shock coating his face.

As he falls to the ground, clutching at his chest, she's a blur of movement as the unoccupied Vulturians attack. She spins and roundhouse kicks Elozo right in the groin. As he collapses, she parries with another. Her arms fly like wasps, stinging every inch of flesh, having the audacity to get in the way. Even with eight of them, she ducks and dances out of reach of each spear thrust. The Vulturians are quick, but they're still mountains trying to hit a buzzing fly.

Prince Fruitsniper hangs back, watching the murder machine that is Kalliope. His face is impassive, revealing nothing, while his eyes dance at each movement.

Blood pounds in my ears, muffling the screams of pain coming from all around. This is a level of violence I've never seen before. Even in the village attack, it wasn't this gruesome. The smell of everything ... is unbearable. Reality swims as I grow lightheaded; the only thing keeping me upright is adrenaline and terror.

Behind Kalliope, Ginger pops the head of a Vulturian like a ripe grape. Zenab flies over a fire, catching a Vulturian trying to bolt. She lands on his back, claws sinking into his muscular form like a hot knife through butter.

They're destruction incarnate. I don't know about Zenab, but I know Ginger is enjoying turning one of the Vulturians into a crispy marshmallow with her wyvern fire. I swear she chuckles as she pokes the smoking

JENNA AVERY

leftovers. Me? I'm ready for a week-long coma and a long talk with a therapist.

There's a guttural cry, and Kalliope leaps into the air. She shoves her feet off the chest of one Vulturian, then launches into the air. The dagger in her hand lands right in the throat of Elorzo. A finishing blow. The sweet irony.

He drops his spear, clutching at the blue blood pouring down his neck. His eyes go to mine, and I give him a mocking fat lower lip, showing how sad I am about his demise. When his eyes show regret, I look away.

The clearing's covered with several bloody corpses. Leaving the would-be king, who is now looking ill and perhaps even with a satisfying level of uncertainty. There's a crash through the woods and I catch sight of both Ginger and Zenab giving chase to the remaining Vulturians.

The prince looks between me and her, about ready to lunge for me, when Kalliope raises a dagger at him."And here I thought you valued your balls."

He freezes. With a frustrated snarl, he shoots me a scathing look before dropping his spear as a sign of surrender. "You win this round, lordess."

Kalliope doesn't drop the dagger. Her voice is cold and unyielding as she says, "There are no more *rounds*. You've killed my people. My mother might have offered you mercy for your inherent nature."

She *tsks*, shaking her head sadly. "She offered a peace treaty with your dead brother before tearing off his head. It cost you a king and me, a mother. Her kind heart led to her demise." Kalliope looks at me, eyes like gilded flames. She hesitates, and I know she's thinking about living up to her mother's legacy. How important that is to her.

Maybe she's afraid I'll judge her for deviating from that goal, and I've never appreciated her moral compass more. I nod encouragingly, hoping she understands I won't judge her for doing what needs to be done. Even if the sight makes me sick.

With a resigned sigh, she looks back to Prince Frostgiblet. "But I am not my mother. I will not request peace with a usurper. And I am not playing any more games."

His brows raise with indignation. "You're making a grave error. Someone will replace me. There will be war."

She lets out a disdainful laugh. "The only grave in this situation will be yours. I'll deal with the rest when required."

There's a shimmer, and the wolf I love and admire appears. Hackles raised, Kalliope snarls, spittle flying in the air. The prince picks up his spear and gives a deafening roar in return.

They run, each a missile locked onto the other. I'm frozen in awe and fear as they collide. The prince's spear flies out of his hand from the impact. They're a flurry of movement, blood and spit flying into the air. Pressing my hands to my heart, I feel it rattle against its prison of bones.

Kalliope latches onto one of his hands and gives a rough shake of her head, leaving his skin in bloody ribbons. He brings the free hand to grab her by the scruff and tosses her toward the trees. Exhaustion stumbles me forward, instinctually aching to help her. I keep glancing at the forest, hoping Ginger and Zenab will come and join the fray.

Kalliope skids on all fours, claws digging into the dirt. With a vicious snarl that hitches my breath, she's on him again before he can grab the spear. This time, she bites into the back of his shoulder, using her back legs to dig into his spine. Her claws sink into the gray flesh, causing more blue blood to leak out.

He grabs her by the neck, yanking upward, and slamming her into the earth. She yelps, unable to move fast enough as he slams a fist into her ribs. I scream, scanning the woods, hoping *someone* will come save her.

You can help.

The voice is a caress to my senses. I've been training for weeks. What was the point of sparring with Zenab and strengthening my body if not to fucking *help*? I'm not the useless girl who bumbled her way into Ilorna based on sheer luck. My body is exhausted, my hands are literally tied … but there's enough strength left to help Kalliope before he kills her.

The prince is pummeling her with vicious focus. She barks out in pain again, and it spurs me into action. He's not paying attention to me, which makes it easy to lurch up onto my feet and sprint for his abandoned spear.

Picking it up, it almost falls out of my bound hands, the weight overwhelming. My shoulders burn as I raise it; the rope around my digging into the raw skin. A spark of pride surges extra energy into my muscles. *I can do this.* I heft the spear over my shoulder, bracing the weight as I run to him. Kalliope's still struggling to move out of his fists, the Vulturian's colossal bulk too overwhelming.

The Vulturian's broad back is to me, exposed. Raising the spear above my head, arms wobbling, I bring it down onto his spine with every inch of strength possible. The tip catches on his thick skin, and for a second, I think I'm not strong enough to penetrate it. Crying out with frustration, I shove harder. It slides into flesh, sinking deeper and deeper.

The would-be king rears up, hands going to his back, grappling with the spear. I freeze, my brain too drained to process the oncoming danger. He stands, whipping to face me, the spear still lodged.

"*Stupid cunt.* I'm going to eat you alive for this."

He charges, hands outstretched, and I back up, tripping over a rock. He's only inches away, bloody fingers ready to crush me, when he's knocked backward by a mass covered in feathers and sharp claws.

A familiar manticore hooks him with a scorpion stinger, plunging it into his chest before yanking it upward, splitting the Vulturian's torso from navel to throat. Legend jerks the tail again, and the corpse tumbles to the ground. Legend roars in his face with endless fury. It rattles my bones and the ground under my hands.

He's alive. Legend is *alive.*

Chapter Thirty-One

Lordess Tenderheart

Legend's at my side in a flash, catching me as I collapse — the dehydration and hunger finally winning. He lands on his knees, cradling me gently. It's overwhelming, feeling his healed body embrace mine. Those warm, powerful arms are a haven to my aching body. The past thirty-six hours are too much to process.

"I thought you were dead," I rasp out, muffled by Legend's chest. He's real. Here. Uninjured. Not poisoned.

Legend strokes my hair. "I know, but Kalliope found me in time."

A warm hand presses against my shoulder. Through the tears, I see Kalliope crying happy tears, kneeling next to us as she looks over my injuries. Her eyes deaden when she sees my neck. Legend's hands skim over the tender skin, and I flinch.

"Oh, Gem," he says, voice filled with regret. "I'm sorry it took us so long to find you." He brushes sweaty hair from my brow. "Are you okay? Where else are you hurt?"

It takes a moment for my sobs to lose their intensity. When the tears slow, I'm finally able to whisper, "Can't talk much. Stomach hurts. Really hungry."

Legend holds me tenderly in his arms, a thumb gently skimming my arm. "Let's get you home. Do you think you can ride on Kalliope's eagle?"

"Not sure," I say. "Do you have something to drink?"

"Here's some water," Zenab says, placing a waterskin against my lips. I hadn't seen her walk up — she's filthy, her armor covered in blue blood. I unapologetically drink every last drop. My stomach cramps, but I don't care. It soothes my throat, making it easier to talk.

"Where's Daeva?" Kalliope asks, scanning the camp. It's deathly quiet now. "Is she in one of the tents?"

I forgot that smug bitch lied. I shake my head. After clearing my sore throat, I say, "No. She kidnapped me and worked with these assholes to set a trap for you here. They were supposed to kill you here."

Legend's face pales. His eyes jerk up to Kalliope's, widening with shock. Zenab's expression twists with devastation. It's jarring to witness a female normally so strong crumble.

Ginger snorts, poking a toe at a dead Vulturian. Her pale skin is almost entirely covered in blue, as if she'd bathed in Vulturian blood. "If by traps you mean those crude nets made of worn fibers, yes, there were technically traps." She blows me a kiss. "Always saving your sweet ass, BB."

I roll my eyes good-naturedly. Kalliope shifts to balancing on her toes, squinting into the carnage. "Are you sure? They didn't take her to a different location?"

"I'm sure," I say firmly. "Check my stomach and you'll find bruises courtesy of her dazzling hospitality." I peer up at Legend's chiseled face. "She poisoned you. Don't you remember?"

"It made me hallucinate," he says, tone grim. "I only knew you'd been taken, but it incapacitated me otherwise."

Legend's hold tightens around my body. "Are you okay to ride back?"

I nod. "I think so. How did you find me?"

Kalliope surveys the surrounding bodies. "There was a supposed ransom letter left over the scent of Morgoths. The letter stated they had kidnapped both of you. I was to come and turn myself in to spare your lives."

Her expression darkens. "I don't take kindly to blackmail. So me and the Cohort came to deal with business in the way we know best. I followed the trail of the Morgoth, then the scent of you on the ground.

We figured Daeva was incapacitated with an anti-shifting venom or shackle, and had to be carried. There was no reason to suspect she wasn't with you."

Kalliope sighs and uses her dagger as a saw, severing the ropes around my wrists. When my arms are free, she inspects my plethora of wounds. "We'll get you home and find Daeva. Then we'll drag her in front of a tribunal for sentencing."

Zenab steps forward, looking troubled. "You're positive Daeva is behind all of this? She's always been an angry one. Got it from her mother. But she's loyal to Ilorna. She and Kalliope were practically littermates."

I nod, rubbing my sore wrists. "Yes. In fact, she's waiting for you at the manor. Said once she received a signal of Kalliope being dead, she'd take over. That the people wouldn't mind."

Zenab swears and kicks the dirt. No one stops her when she stalks off, needing to be alone. Even Ginger's cockiness deflates, watching Zenab disappear into the shadows with a tortured expression.

I reach out to touch Legend on the arm, and he grabs my hand gently. The warmth of his body is a comfort. "I really thought you were dead."

Legend looks at Kalliope with adoration. "As usual, my lordess came to my rescue. Took one sniff of the poison and knew the antidote."

"It was that easy?" I ask, surprised.

Kalliope snorts with derision. "She's not as smart as she thinks. My mother was a renowned herbalist, but Daeva must have forgotten this key fact."

The three of them look around the camp. It's silent, even though I know one of the tents has occupants. Just as I'm about to mention the females and child, Kalliope asks, "Why did Daeva give you to the Vulturians? She could've killed you."

"No clue. She and the prince seemed buddy-buddy. They kept me alive in case you demanded proof of life. I don't think they were going to wait much longer, though. You saved me from being a shish-kabob."

All three of us eye a suspicious lump of meat blackening on a spit. I shudder and look away as I wiggle. Legend releases his hold, helping me stand. My balance is wonky, forcing him to stick like glue to my side.

Leaning on my handsome crutch, I ask, "So the real question is: where is Daeva now?"

Legend growls. It's a deep threat rumbling in his throat. "Now that I know what she did was real, I can only imagine. She probably assumed either the Vulturians killed us and went to claim the diadem, or she ran, like the rat she is."

Kalliope's voice cracks. "I knew she didn't always agree with my choices. It's her job as general to challenge my decisions, to keep all perspectives available." Kalliope pauses, steadying her voice before she continues. "But I never thought she was this ambitious. This ... this *hateful.*"

I raise my hand. They give me quizzical looks. Guess they don't do that here. "So what now?"

Kalliope's expression turns murderous, all of her pain gone and locked up for another day. "Now we go back to the manor and right some wrongs."

I hold up my hand again. They look at me like I'm deranged. I point to the tent full of females behind me. "Um, we have something else we need to take care of first."

Kalliope raises her brow. "This should be good."

I scoff. "Come on, Lordess Tenderheart, you'll love this one."

The four of us step over the dead Vulturian bodies, and I lead them to the tent. There's the sound of shuffling and whispering from inside. When I flip the tent flap, the females gasp.

"Ulvita," I call out, keeping my voice soft. "It's alright. They're here to help you."

Ulvita's head appears past the shadows, eyes round. "Saira? What happened? We heard all the fighting."

Kalliope pushes past me into the tent. She squats on her toes, taking in the dumpy conditions. Her focus freezes on the children.

"Gods," Legend mutters. "They were savages."

When Zenab walks up — eyes puffy and wet — I catch them up on everything the females told me. Ulvita explains where all the females are from.

When she's done, Kalliope leans against her knees, hands out in supplication. "We did not know you were here. Of course, we'll make sure you're returned to King Rhyaxis. I'm sure he's incredibly concerned about where his niece is."

Ulvita dips her head. "Thank you, lordess."

Kalliope nods. "Of course. He hasn't reported you missing to us personally, but we will certainly escort you home."

Ulvita looks up and sneers. "Cedric misled his brother about where he was taking us. We were his trophies when he won the coup. The ultimate insult. We would be grateful to go home."

Tylain starts crying, looking down at the infant in her arms. "You hear that, Tryaxis? You're going *home*."

Kalliope's voice wavers. "If you're okay with it ..." She takes a deep breath, collecting herself. "Ginger can stay with you while I head back to my home and send wagons. I'm sure you'll appreciate transportation over walking the entire distance. We'll also send a missive to the king immediately."

"Yes. That is alright," Ulvita says confidently. "We've been here for weeks — a few hours is nothing."

"Thank you." Kalliope stands and looks around. "Do you need anything? Can we help you find anything?"

"No." Ulvita shakes her head. "We'll be fine. Thank you."

Kalliope steps out of the tent. To Legend, she says, "Let's go. The sooner we return, the faster these females can go home."

Pausing at Zenab's side, she leans in to whisper something to the matriarch. Zenab wipes away a tear and nods. They bump foreheads, then Kalliope turns away. Zenab looks distraught, but a new steely look hardens her features. There's a shimmer, then the obsidian lion takes off into the night.

After checking in with Ginger, Kalliope holds out a hand for me, and I take it, letting her lead me outside of the camp. For the first time in almost two days, I'm safe again. There are people here willing to put themselves in danger for me. Sure, they thought Daeva was still here, so maybe that's why they all came.

A little part of me thinks otherwise, though.

Kalliope shifts into an eagle and lifts a wing for me. It's difficult to hop on, and Legend carefully props me up as I struggle to put a leg over her neck. Finally, I'm situated, as safe as possible.

It's time to go home.

Chapter Thirty-Two

A Tub The Size Of Four Jacuzzis

Riding Kalliope's eagle form doesn't scare me anymore. Up here in the dark sky, among pearlescent clouds, it's easy to forget that this conflict isn't even close to being done.

Legend flies next to us in his manticore form, a shadow against the night sky. Their wings flap slowly, soaring the thermals when possible. They can move way faster than this, but I think they're using the time to think and plan.

What I need to figure out is whether I need to jump time before this continues to unfold. My fingers graze the Scout. The faint feel of its metal is reassuring. I have a choice to make, but I haven't decided yet.

I look over at Legend, who senses my gaze and looks back. I break the stare first, my emotions too jumbled to dive into whatever's about to happen.

Our descent to the manor is gradual enough to take in the destruction. Smoke still snakes out of the ruined parts of the building. Amicums are hauling bodies away on carts, and even from up here, the wails of grief are impossible to miss.

Vulturian bodies litter the ground, ignored and left to rot until someone finds the energy to dispose of them. Kalliope lands in the same clearing in the garden where Legend almost died. There's still a manticore-shaped indent in the grass. I try not to look at it as Kalliope lands, and I dismount. When they shift back, Kalliope supports me as we head to Legend's room. The moment the door locks, all the tension coiled in my body evaporates.

A wave of exhaustion weakens my muscles. Sensing an imminent collapse, Legend scoops me up and deposits my tired body onto the couch.

"I'll go start a bath," he murmurs. Kalliope heads over to the hanging blue rope at the door and pulls it on her way to the alcohol cart. Shoulders drooping in exhaustion, she pours some into a glass. Knocks it back. Pours more into the glass. Swallows it in a big gulp. Filling it up a third time, she shoots it back before pouring the liquid into two more glasses.

She brings a glass to Legend, who is setting up the bath behind a large partition. He murmurs his thanks as she hands me the other one.

I thank her and take a tentative sip. There's a knock at the door, and Kalliope unlocks it, opening it only enough for her to poke out her head and say something to someone, too low for me to hear.

Closing and locking the door, she turns back to me.

The silence is comforting and alarming. Kalliope is clearly deep in thought. Like me, neither of them has had a moment to process what has happened in the last two days.

"It's ready, Gem." Legend walks back to me and grabs the drink out of my hand, then places it on an end table. Smooth as butter, he leans over and scoops me up like I'm as light as a feather.

Kalliope follows, footsteps silent. I glance over his shoulder and watch her undress. There's no emotion in her features, minus the dark circles that rim her equally dim eyes. The bright gold is now tarnished with betrayal and sadness.

Legend rounds the partition, and I gasp. It's not the same size as the one in the other room. No, this one is the size of four jacuzzis. Big enough to fit the three of us easily.

Legend sets me down, making sure I'm steady on my feet before focusing on helping me take my shirt off. When he sees the still-healing bruises that spot my torso, his eyes darken with fury again.

He kneels and helps unlace my boots, letting me brace against his muscled shoulder as he slips them off. I shimmy out of my pants, feeling exposed, yet protected. There's not an inch of lust on his face as he strips, then helps me into the tub. I notice the wounds on his stomach, but it's wrong to bring them up right now. All that matters is that we're safe.

Kalliope's already sinking into the water. The haunted look on her face hasn't changed. She leans against the edge, water up to her sternum, staring off into the distance. I wish there was something I could do for her, but there's nothing to say that would fix the betrayal of a dear friend. It's an impossible situation, and I'm not sure what she can do from here.

Legend holds my hand as I carefully step in and sink to sit on the built-in seat. The water is nothing short of bliss, its heat welcoming to every ache and pain that has lingered since yesterday.

He grabs a bottle of shampoo, then motions for me to come closer. I scoot over and can't help but grin when he leans me against one of his thighs. Grabbing a cup, he fills it and pours it over my head. I tilt my head back and close my eyes, reveling in the gentle ministrations.

He spends the next few minutes rubbing me down, washing my hair, and finishing up with the best foot rub of my life. He says nothing the whole time and stares off into space, just like Kalliope. The fact that he's even mindful of caring for me, while his best friend sits over there, almost catatonic, fills my heart.

Finally, there's a knock at the door. Legend grimaces and stands. Water pours off him in rapid streaks, following the hard lines of his body as he steps out and grabs a towel. Wrapping it around his waist, he makes quite a mess as he walks to the door and unlocks it.

The door opens, and I hear the exchange of words. Gathering bubbles around my body, I look up to see Legend leading Meadow past the privacy screen. The sweet maid holds food and a tray table. Unfolding it, she places the platter on top.

Her expression is concerned as she kneels next to me. "Can I get you anything, Miss? We were so worried."

I shake my head. "Feed me anything, please."

Reaching for a plate, she grabs a little of everything and hands it over. Well, she tries, but Legend smoothly intercepts her. Taking it instead, he sinks back into the water and holds it above the bubbles for me.

He watches me eat, still silent.

Meadow curtsies to us all, then walks out of the room. The lock turns when she leaves. The room is eerily quiet, minus the absent-minded undulation of Kalliope's arms in the water. Her gaze is unfocused as she peers down at the rippling water.

Legend touches Kalliope on the shoulder. "How can I help?"

She startles and glares at him, jaw clenched. I know it isn't actually toward him, and apparently, he knows too.

"Can I hug you?"

She nods, icy demeanor thaws in seconds, face crumpling. He moves toward her and gathers her in his arms. She looks so small, so broken. And so he holds her while she comes apart.

While she cries, he washes her hair and scrubs her down with a soapy sponge. When he's done, she curls into his chest. Legend murmurs words, cradling her gently. The sobs come out louder and faster. They echo against the walls, as if the manor itself is weeping.

There's nothing I can do. I'm not even sure I'm qualified to comfort her like that. He knows exactly what she needs — I'm simply not experienced enough.

So I sit there quietly, giving space for this intimate, heartbreaking moment. That's the best I can offer. Space and silent support.

Soon the water turns tepid. It's getting uncomfortable, and I must shift one too many times because Legend looks over, then down at Kalliope, whose tears have faded to nothing. For now.

"Come; let's go to bed," he murmurs. Kalliope nods into his chest. Her grief-stricken face finally turns to me, and it's horrifying to witness this powerful female reduced to such pain.

The right isn't mine, but I'd kill Daeva for making this happen.

Legend stands, every glorious inch of him, and helps her out of the tub. He turns to me and does the same. He's the last to step out, and before drying himself off, he turns to her and wraps a big fluffy towel around her. Then he does the same for me, pressing a kiss to my forehead.

Kalliope and I follow him to the bed, the sheets still rumpled from yesterday morning. This time two days ago, we were all entangled in passion here. Now, we're going to rest in grief.

She climbs in first, taking the middle. I admire Legend's sleek movements as he crawls over her, letting me sleep on her other side. He brings the blanket over the three of us, and without another word, we snuggle together and pass out.

Chapter Thirty-Three

Virginity Is Just A Construct

The sound of birds chirping outside the window is the first thing I hear. It's the steady breathing of Kalliope that brings me fully awake. Allowing all the memories of everything to come crashing down. It wasn't a bad dream after our night together. This is still real.

Turning toward Kalliope's prone body, I see Legend peering over her face, watching me. Dark circles frame his eyes, as if he stayed up all night to guard us.

"*How are you?*" he mouths.

I bring a hand up and teeter totter it to show that I'm so so. I point at him. "*How about you?*"

His mouth twists with uncertainty, brows dipping together. "*I'm okay.*"

"You aren't as quiet as you think you are," Kalliope drawls. Legend's face lights up. I nuzzle my forehead into her shoulder, enjoying the warmth. She turns to look at me first. It's relieving to see some of that familiar spark back in her eyes.

"Hi," she whispers.

A sudden sense of shyness has me murmuring, "Hi, you."

She turns onto her side to face me, making her hands a pillow on her cheek. "I thought I lost you yesterday. And I wasn't sure if I'd be able to handle it. And finding Legend there, in the courtyard, barely hanging on by a thread ..."

The words choke off, and one of Legend's hands comes to her hip, running his knuckles along the curve in slow, comforting sweeps. Tears shimmer in the sunshine of her irises. She blinks them away and brings a hand to my cheek. "The thought of you dead out there nearly broke me in half."

Now would be a good time to admit my feelings, but the words are ash on my tongue. It's a line I'm not sure I can cross without severe levels of guilt.

All there's left to do is nod and sink into the kiss she presses to my lips.

She's tentative at first, like she's also trying to reacquaint herself with the taste of me. My lips part, allowing her to sweep her soft tongue into my mouth.

Desire is like lightning to my core, and my spine arches. Her mouth savors my moan as the kiss deepens, growing in urgency. One of her hands comes to the small of my back, caressing the soft skin. I suck in a sharp breath, the spot so sore that if she's any rougher, I might cry.

She pulls back, puzzlement creasing her brow. The confusion melts into anger as she finally sees the bruises along my torso and arms. Her eyes shoot to mine, fury stoking the flaming embers ringing her dilated pupils.

"I'm going to fucking kill her," Kalliope promises. Her tone brooks zero doubt.

"Looking forward to it," I retort.

Her mouth is on mine again, more urgent. One of her hands grabs my ass possessively, tenderly tugging my hips closer to hers, pressing our bellies together. It's incredible having her against me, silken and hot. With a gentle hand on my shoulder, she coaxes me onto my back, straddling me.

Her dark red hair hangs around our faces like a curtain, capturing our panting breaths. Muscular thighs cage in my own legs, and as she undulates her hips, I feel her slickness against my skin.

My head falls back in bliss as she trails kisses down my throat to my chest, to one of my breasts. I whimper as she licks my nipple, sucking tentatively.

"More," I gasp, arching my back. She obliges, clamping down firmly. My core throbs at the sensation. When she nibbles, I cry out, bringing my hands to her silky hair.

"Fuck me," Legend groans. I turn my head to look at him, grinding my hips into Kalliope. His eyes are heavy lidded, burning with unbridled lust. A movement catches my attention; he's touching himself with lazy strokes. Drawing out his own pleasure while letting Kalliope ring out mine.

Kalliope shifts, trailing kisses down my belly and past my navel. Her hands come up to my breasts, kneading them. My body is desperate for her mouth between my legs, but she pauses.

For each blooming bruise, she kisses it tenderly. Reverently. There's a flash of guilt in her expression before she dips her head and goes back to where I'm desperate to have her.

Kalliope tortures me as she lazily explores my center, flicking her tongue playfully over my clit. My back arches again so hard that it makes me wince. Her head lifts, and she frowns.

"You're going to hurt yourself." She looks to Legend. "Can you help?"

He looks at me with so much earnestness. "Please say yes." His breath's ragged, and his strokes speed up.

"Well, how can someone turn down such a polite request?" I tease.

He's hovering above me in a flash, his rock hard cock poking into my hip. It twitches, making me giggle. He grins, and it's so beautiful that when Kalliope gently prods my core with a finger, I almost come right then and there. My back arches again, my hips thrusting upward. It's impossible to hide my wince.

"Ah, ah," he chastises. I suck in a breath as he trails the tips of his fingers over my belly, leaving goose bumps in their wake. He cautiously spreads his fingers across the span of my belly.

Kalliope works her finger in and out, crooking it slightly to hit the most delicious spot inside my core. Her mouth descends on me again, and my body arches with the zing of pleasure down my spine. He trails kisses along my jaw, bringing his mouth to brush against mine. The teasing kisses eradicate any logical thoughts. It's a maddening combination of the two.

Kalliope pulls out the finger, and I whimper at the loss. My disappointment is brief as she slides in two. She pumps them with increasing speed and sucks with that glorious mouth of hers.

Pleasure tightens between my hips, my core throbbing with the desperate need for release. When Legend kisses me, it's worshipful.

Kalliope increases speed, moaning as she continues to swirl her tongue against my clit. Just as I contemplate begging for a break, when it becomes too much, Legend breaks the kiss. To my dismay and pleasure, his mouth finds one of my nipples. He isn't gentle either, clasping the peaked bud between his teeth.

The orgasm rips through me like a tidal wave, my core throbbing against Kalliope's fingers. She groans with satisfaction, as does Legend, who comes back to kiss me. As I call out to the goddess, he's there, devouring my cry of pleasure.

The wave recedes, leaving me panting for oxygen and sanity. Limp and spent. They slowly pull away from me. Kalliope's mouth is ringed with wetness, and like a cat, she wipes it away with a salacious grin.

Legend cock's engorged without release. I'm surprised at the urge to have him in my mouth. The ache for a taste is overwhelming.

"Can I try ...?" I point to the potential snack in question.

His eyebrows shoot up. "You sure?"

"I mean, I've never done it, but I'd like to try. If you're okay with it." I'm babbling, afraid he's going to tell me no.

Kalliope chuckles. "Females don't do that very often."

"But I'll never turn it down." Legend says, stroking himself slowly.

My eyes dart between them. "So ... what do I do?"

Legend scoots off the bed. "Well, Gem, there are so many ways. Why don't we start with something simple?"

"Simple is good," I exhale with relief. He motions with his hand for me to move forward. Kalliope slides off the bed and rounds to where he's standing. She leans over and grabs some pillows, placing them on the floor.

She points at them. "Kneel right here, baby."

Biting my lip, I do as she says. It brings me a little lower than eye level, so I have a front row view of his hand making lazy strokes from base to tip, using his thumb to rub a bead of wetness at the tip.

I audibly gulp. "What if that doesn't fit in my mouth entirely?"

"It won't," Kalliope assures me. "Legend's quite blessed, even among Amicum standards. But I can show you how that won't matter."

I peer up at him, and my fingers are desperate to touch myself again, to find release. The way he looks down at me, it's like a god finally noticing me. His mouth parts as his breath hitches. His pecs strain against his brown skin, flexing as he pumps his arm.

Next to me, Kalliope kneels. She brings a hand to my chin and turns my head to face her. Against my mouth, she asks, "Are you ready for a taste?"

What can I do other than nod? She quirks her lips with amusement and taps his hip. He turns, lined up perfectly with her open mouth. Legend drops his hands, at the utter mercy of whatever she pleases.

"Fuck, Kal," he groans as she flicks her tongue between the small slit where a bead of wetness just came out of. One of her hands wraps around him. Legend's knees wobble when her grip tightens. I'm mesmerized, watching her draw out his pleasure with skillful licks.

She pumps him at an agonizing pace, taking the tip of him into her velvety mouth. The memory of what that mouth feels like makes me whimper. Her eyes go from his to mine. Kalliope grins, the tip still between her lips. She closes them around the smooth head and sucks hard enough he gasps. His hips buck forward as she pulls back, making a popping sound.

"See, Saira," she says lackadaisically, bringing her palm forward and back at a torturous pace. "The head of a male's cock is the most sensitive. Some of them don't even care if you use your hands, if you can do this."

At that, she rolls her tongue around the head, stopping at the underside, then running it over and above the slit. Without pause, she takes as much of him into her mouth as possible. Her cheeks hollow, and only half of him disappears.

His knees visibly buckle, and one of his hands comes up to the back of her head, grabbing a fistful of hair. He grits his teeth and bites out, "You're being cruel."

"No," she says simply. "I'm teaching." She moves away from him and tilts his cock toward me, like she's offered an ice cream cone. "You try."

I bring a tentative hand up, slowly wrapping my fingers around him, one by one. He's hard as stone and hot in my fingers. It twitches in my hand, making me drop it in surprise. They chuckle.

"That's him saying hi," Legend jokes.

Giggling, I bring my hand up again, then open my mouth. Bringing the tip to press against my lips, I flick out my tongue. Expecting there to be a flavor of some sort, I'm surprised there's none.

My tongue lingers against the warm skin, trailing along a ridge of veins. He sucks air through his teeth, and I look up, worried I've already hurt him.

He's looking down at me with a pained expression.

Concerned, I jerk my head back. "Are you okay?"

He says measuredly, "Saira, if you don't put my cock in your mouth, I'm pretty sure I'm going to die."

Kalliope snorts. "Drama queen."

He shoots her a dirty look. "You're going to pay for this."

She shrugs. "Don't threaten me with a good time."

While they banter, I find my courage, and without warning, I slide him into my mouth. He cries out, and his hips thrust forward, shoving him even deeper. Soft flesh hits the back of my throat, and I gag.

"Relax," Kalliope says. "Or else you're going to hurt yourself."

I do as she says and focus on relaxing my throat muscles. Legend is panting like a dog, fists clenching and unclenching. Instinctually, I move my head back and forth.

It's odd, but also so natural, to have him in my mouth. I taste the bead of wetness at his tip. It tastes tangy with a touch of salt. I move my hand back and forth in tandem with my mouth.

"That's it," Kalliope encourages. "Show Legend how much you want him, how much he deserves to cum."

"If you don't shut the fuck up," he growls. "I swear to all the gods ..."

She snickers. "What's the point of knowing you for so long if I can't use the information of what gets you off in situations like this?"

I'm gaining confidence and speed at the same time. I try the technique she showed me, then try moves from my imagination. Roll my tongue while he's in my mouth. Angle so I can get him a little deeper down my throat. I bring up my hands, pumping him like my life depends on it.

"Kal," he warns, his breath jagged.

Kalliope shifts a little closer. Her mouth lines up with mine. I stop for a moment to figure out what she wants. She opens her mouth wide and motions with a finger for me to do the same. When I do, she brings the finger under my chin, moving my mouth close enough our lips almost touch. Creating a space between us. For him.

"Ready whenever you are, my love," she purrs, opening her mouth again. He groans, and the tip presses against the corner of my mouth. His hand comes to the back of my head.

"Is this ... okay?" He can barely talk, and it sends a thrill through me. I nod, and his hand grips my head in place. He does the same to her, creating a steady hole for him to fuck.

Then he's pressing his cock between our mouths, sliding in and out. I press my tongue against the underside, letting him drag himself against it. He curses and picks up speed.

I jerk in surprise when Kalliope's fingers find their way between my thighs again. Her eyes meet mine, looking like an angelic devil. Both fingers circle my clit at the same pace he pumps into our mouths.

I moan, vibrating my mouth for him. His hips are hitting the sides of our faces now, and to my absolute shock, I'm loving every second of this. The feral way he fucks our faces is empowering on a level I didn't know sex could give.

Something in my mind cracks open, shifting my entire perspective on sex. There's power here, even when on my knees. Taking a fierce male such as Legend and reducing him to ashes through my raw sexuality is empowering.

Kalliope lowers her torso a bit more so she can push her fingers inside me. My thighs part instinctively, allowing her to go deep. She pumps her fingers up and down, matching Legend stroke for stroke.

His movements shift into a staccato pace, and I look up, grinning at his pinched expression. As if he's in pain, but I know better. Especially as his head snaps back, and he roars toward the ceiling. Wetness smears across my cheeks and mouth, his cum making an absolute mess of our faces.

He jerks a few more times before letting go of our heads. We separate our faces, but Kalliope continues to work me with her hand. She pulls out and jerks her head toward the bed.

"Legend is going to finish you with his fingers."

"Don't have to tell me twice." I jump onto the bed and face him. Adoration softens the lines of his face as he kneels in front of me. Bringing his hands up to my legs, he spreads them apart, fingers digging into the thickness of my thighs.

"Keep them there," he commands with a grin. I nod, watching Kalliope come sit beside me. One, then two of his fingers prod my entrance. They're bigger than hers and immediately stretch me.

I grit my teeth, trying not to panic and clench my muscles.

"Easy," Kalliope says. She brings fingers to my swollen and sensitive clit and begins tantalizingly slow circles. The pleasure immediately relaxes my muscles, my core eager to be filled.

He moves his fingers slowly, letting my body adjust to the new size. The girth brings a new flavor of pleasure I haven't had yet, and I lose myself in it. He curves those deliciously thick fingers, hitting my G-spot perfectly.

"Faster," I demand.

He obeys, picking up speed. Kalliope keeps her circles slow and methodical. The difference in speed and sensation is too much. The

301

orgasm grips me, squeezing my muscles impossibly tight. As if on cue, they slow to a stop.

I look down at them, panting as I complain, "What the *hell?* Why did you stop?"

Legend smirks and winks at me. "We can make that even better."

"How?" It's difficult to not show outrage at the interruption.

He holds up three fingers, and I moan at the sheer thought of it. I nod, spreading my legs, eager to know what else he can do. He inserts half of one, then the other. He twists just a little and prods with the third. The stretching is delicious and painful all at once.

Kalliope continues with her methodical circles. I look at her. "Faster."

She grins and obeys, picking up speed. Then Legend's third finger is in me, and there's a sharp pain. I gasp, my body shocked at the sensations.

"Shhh," he assures me. "It's okay. Relax."

He moves again, and my eyes slam shut as I bring my legs up higher and wider. He accepts the invitation and pumps even faster. The pleasure is too much. I'm so full of sensations and emotions. It feels so fucking good; I cry. Nothing should feel this good, not even—

The orgasm slams into my senses, ripping me from reality. Pleasure like nothing I've ever felt cascades along my body, electrifying my skin and making it more sensitive. They both continue at the same pace, but Legend pants out, "That's so good. You're doing so good."

Those words ring me dry, and every muscle in my body tightens further. The orgasm rises and crests again, chasing the first. My core pounds, demanding everything.

My scream rips from my throat, feral and fierce in its intensity. The kind where I swear I've just time traveled all over again.

It's a slow return to reality. The stars in my vision fade, revealing Kalliope's Cheshire grin — it's full of pure alpha satisfaction.

Slowly, my legs lower, and Legend carefully removes his fingers. I'm like an overcooked noodle, lying there, waiting for a wheelchair because I don't think my legs will work. My eyelids grow heavy. I just woke up and already need a nap.

"Fuck, that was hot," Legend says, blowing out a heavy breath.

Kalliope stands and says smugly, "Told you."

Confused, I frown. "Told him *what?*"

She licks her plump lips. "That you would be incredible to spend time with."

Legend nods and pads over to the bathing area. As the sound of water splashing echoes in the room, he says, "Fine. You're right. Again."

Kalliope hops up with a spring in her step, heading to the drinks station. "I should've bet coin."

I prop myself up on my elbows. "You guys are so weird."

She sashays away, ass jiggling deliciously. "Yes, well, you need someone to be weird with, right?"

I think of Piper and grin. "Yeah, that's true."

Piper is going to be so proud of me. She probably didn't think I'd ever have sex on this trip. She's going to die when I tell her what's happening. Last month, I worked fourteen hours a day at the lab, munching on chips for breakfast, and eyes blurring over the endless screen time.

Look at me now — fresh from my first kidnapping, giving blow jobs, and pretty sure Legend just made me shake hands with the goddess with that orgasm.

Life is unreal. Gone is the virgin nerd.

Wait. I canted my head to the side. "Am I still a virgin?"

They stop what they're doing and look at me.

Kalliope raises an eyebrow. "Does it matter? What qualifies as losing your virginity anyway, where you're from?"

I chew the inside of my cheek. "When there's a dick inside someone."

Legend barks out a laugh. "Then there are a lot of virgins around here. Not all females choose to have male consorts."

Kalliope reaches for a robe and wraps it around her body. "Yes, virginity is just a construct, Saira. We enjoyed each other's bodies and experienced pleasure. Isn't that all that matters?"

I make a little *moue*. "Well, that's true, I guess."

Piper is going to be stoked. I'm not a virgin anymore.

There's a knock at the door, and the three of us go silent. We've successfully staved off reality for a moment, but everything we've been trying to forget hasn't forgotten about us.

Kalliope's entire demeanor changes. Legend watches her walk to the door and open it. Zenab is on the other side, looking exhausted.

"We found Daeva."

Chapter Thirty-Four

A Color Named "Dastardly Bitch"

Telling Zenab to meet at her office in an hour, Kalliope summons breakfast. Apparently, she ordered a whole feast and also had them bring me a change of clothes. Both show up quickly, and we all wash up, getting ready in record time.

None of us talks about what will happen next. With no additional information, what is there to bring up? Instead, to distract us from the impending conflict, I pull out my different electronics. I try to explain to Kalliope what a movie is, and she playfully demands to watch one. When I explain they're hours long, she cheers up at my promise to show her one soon.

Finally, we're heading to Kalliope's office. If you can call it an office. It's more of a mix between an atrium and a study, with a huge domed window and shelves upon shelves of books.

In the middle is a table that can seat up to sixteen. They're all empty except for Zenab, whose expression is grim.

Zenab doesn't even wait to give a debrief. We're still trying to sit down as she barrels forward. "They found her at the edge of the forest near Averdeen. The sentries claim she was confused and furious." She pauses, giving me a nervous look.

Kalliope pauses in getting comfortable. "What is it?"

"She's claiming Saira is dead, and that she escaped the Vulturians."

A laugh bursts out of me before I can stop it. "I'm in excellent shape for being dead."

Zenab nods, hate written all over her face. Clearly, her devastation from the initial news has faded. In front of us is the former general, furious at the betrayal. "I don't know exactly what she'll say happened, but I'm sure it will be interesting."

"Does she think I'm dead?" Kalliope asks, reaching for the gold-trimmed velvet jacket Zenab chose.

Zenab shakes her head. "No, she knows you're alive."

"Pity. That could have been even more entertaining."

Zenab bites her lip, finally hesitating in her anger. Instead, she looks worried. "That isn't all, Kal."

Kalliope sighs. "I cannot *wait* for this female to be dead and stop being a claw in my side. What is it?"

"She told me privately that she'll demand a Scrap to challenge you for leadership. Claims you ignored her warnings about the Vulturians and caused dozens of Amicums to be killed in the attack."

My jaw almost dislocates as it drops open. "You have *got* to be kidding me. No one will believe that for one second."

Kalliope freezes, her gaze turning icy. "She's gone insane."

Legend, sitting next to me, swears and drums the table impatiently with his fingers. "When does she want to have the Scrap?"

"Tomorrow."

Dread scrapes along my bones. Tomorrow? "What exactly *is* a Scrap?"

All four of them look at each other with grim expressions. Kalliope clears her throat, eyes still simmering with wrath. "Amicums can challenge a lordess to a Scrap in an effort to change a power structure. It's a two-part battle. If one warrior wins both parts, they're the clear winner. A tie ends with the crowd deciding on the winner. However, sometimes, a competitor can win both parts of the Scrap and still lose if they aren't popular."

"So it's essentially always up to the crowd," Legend adds.

306

"Daeva has done equal amounts of support for this land," Zenab says grimly. "She has followers, who most likely helped her plan this coup. We don't know who they are, but some are most likely influential."

"She's taking advantage of that fact," Legend growls.

Kalliope takes a deep, calming breath. "When is she assembling the Great Hall?"

Zenab grimaces. "Now, Your Grace."

Kalliope stands. "Well, let's do this." To Zenab, she says, "Make sure the younglings remain protected. No matter what happens in the next twenty-four hours, they need to remain protected. Abstain from involving the Guardians for now. We'll need to take time to interrogate every single one of them before they can be trusted again."

"Of course, Your Grace. I'll see to it immediately."

To me and Legend, she says, "Follow me."

The five of us file out of the office. Zenab bows to Kalliope and rushes off. Kalliope leads us in the opposite direction, down a narrow hallway. I struggle to keep up, my body still aching from the abuse it's experienced in the last couple of days. Legend stays next to me, attention scanning the hallway for any potential threat.

Finally, Kalliope slows and stops in front of a wall, right next to a simple wooden door. Beyond it, I can make out the faint sound of chatter.

I assume we're about to walk through the door, but then Kalliope pushes a carved flower, and a short, hidden door opens, tall enough for me to walk straight through. The only way I would have noticed it is if she had pointed it out. Otherwise, it blends in with the molding. This manor not only has a maze-like layout, there are secret compartments *in the walls?*

She turns to face me with a grim expression. "They think you are dead. You need to stay here until Legend brings you in, understand?"

My heart aches at the idea of her being away from me for even one second. I know she's more than capable of defending herself, but these last couple of days have taught me anything is possible. "Will they hurt you?"

Joy soars inside my body as she brushes a soft kiss against my lips. "No, I'll be alright. She's shackled and unable to shift. I need Daeva to set herself in a trap of lies. If she still believes you are dead, then this is a perfect opportunity to prove to the entire court who she is."

She cuts Legend a look, who nods in whatever silent exchange they're having. Kalliope disappears beyond the door, leaving us alone in the hallway.

"Let's go, Gem," Legend says, pushing me toward the dark space.

With a sigh, I do as he says and step into the darkness. It's surprisingly tall inside, which is good, or else Legend would be in a lot of pain. Moving aside to make room for him, Legend motions for me to be quiet. He presses a button on the wall and it swings shut silently. Darkness envelopes us.

I'm about to ask how I'm going to see when Legend grabs my hand and pulls me down the narrow walkway. We turn a corner, and I'm relieved to see pinpoints of golden light streaming through the walls, revealing dancing dust. On the other side of the wall, the voices are more clear. Legend leads me further down the passageway until he stops and points to one hole.

Bending over, I press my forehead to the light, shocked to see a massive atrium with wooden panelled walls. Immense windows bring in bright light on one side, and a raised dais at the front of the room. A single chair, made of white wood, sits at the center. On its purple cushion sits Kalliope, surveying the room with a detached expression. Almost bored.

Throughout the room, a large gathering of Amicums loiter in gossipy groups, not shy about pointing at Daeva. Most of them are in true-form as well, wearing colorful garments. My stomach sinks; it's like this is a show for them.

Below the dais, in the center of it all, stands Daeva. Faintly glowing shackles bind her ankles and wrists. Seeing her face again kicks my heart into a sprint; my still-healing bruises throb as a reminder of what she did. When my breath hitches with anxiety, Legend's hand comes to my back. It's a welcome comfort.

Daeva's staring up at the platform with a serene expression, her sharp, pale features like icicles. I follow her line of sight, and my heart thumps harder when Kalliope calmly walks to the edge of the platform, looking down at Daeva, the would-be usurper.

Kalliope's voice rings clear and powerful as she says, "General Stryder, you stand accused of treason, murder, and kidnapping. What say you to the charges?"

Daeva snarls, her sharp fangs flashing in the sunshine. "I am innocent of these charges and demand to face my accuser." Her expression turns smug when she looks around and sees no one coming forward. "See? No one can offer any form of evidence because I'm a victim, too." She shoves her hands up. "I was kidnapped, and yet, you've thrown me into these barbaric chains."

It's a convincing show. My eyes flick to Kalliope's, wondering if she'll admit I'm alive. Instead, she says, "Please explain what happened to your fellow Amicum, Legend. He was left for dead before you kidnapped my guest, Saira. He almost died."

Gasps and murmurs of shock fill the room. Kalliope's eyes skate over the crowd with a blank face. Daeva does the same, the recalculation clear in her expression. She takes a step forward and holds her hands out.

"Your Grace, my lordess, my friend, please let me explain."

Kalliope's face flickers with disdain at the various nomenclatures. "Proceed."

Daeva paces, even with her ankles hobbled. Instead of looking at Kalliope, she addresses the crowd. "I am being accused of treachery, which does not exist. I have served the people of Ilorna for most of my life. I've fought alongside and for each one of you."

My jaw clenches when people nod in agreement. Noticing this, Daeva raises her shackled wrists again.

"This is what Lordess Kalliope thinks is a respectable treatment for loyal followers — shackling her most loyal soldier because of rumors and speculation. We were both kidnapped, but I'm being punished for escaping? How is that fair?"

Everything inside me screams to run in there and slap her. She's not even trying to deny what happened to Legend. It's a distraction from the truth. How is Kalliope staying quiet?

Daeva paces the edge of the crowd, looking them in the eye. She knows every single one of them — nothing about this is impersonal.

She continues, shoving a finger in Kalliope's direction. "Your Grace, you accuse me of something you have no proof of. I am innocent of these charges. I'm a victim, and this treatment is abhorrent and a blight upon the customs we revere."

Kalliope looks down her nose at the female. "Explain what happened to Legend and Saira. You have yet to do so."

Daeva bows her head, shoulders sagging. "I never attacked Legend. It was the Vulturians, Your Grace. I hear it was a mix of wolfsbane and nightshade, which can cause hallucinations when combined. Both Saira and I were kidnapped, presumably to hold for ransom." Her voice catches, and she looks up with an anguished expression. "I tried to follow, tried to bring Saira back, but it was all so chaotic."

Daeva raises her chin in defiance, with tears falling down each cheek. "I tried to save her, Your Grace. There was nothing to be done."

Does anyone notice that this makes little sense? Whispers slither through the room. Some look like they believe the words. It makes me nauseous. How has she gone this long, fooling everyone?

Kalliope's features soften. Sorrowful, even. Even though I know it's for show, it also must be eating her up inside, seeing someone she's known her whole life lie so easily. "That sounds horrific, my friend."

Bolstered by the title of friend, Daeva paces again. This time, she brings every raw emotion possible to contort her face into torment. "Your Grace, I barely made it out." Her expression twists with regret as she takes a deep breath. "It pains me to say, I might have found her if you hadn't made my own sentries hunt me down, Your Grace."

Kalliope's expression is downright sinister as she turns away from Daeva and walks to an empty chair in the middle of the seated Amicums. Dropping heavily onto the cushions, she pinches the bridge of her nose between two fingers.

"It is my regret that we have reached this point." Her voice is soft, but my blood quickens with the edge of something building inside the tone. She straightens, placing one hand on each chair arm, digging nails into the wood.

Daeva nods slowly in agreement. "I understand, Your Grace. I know the one-form has grown important to you."

Kalliope scoots to the edge of her chair. Everyone's focus snaps to her, the tension growing. There's a sense of imminent danger, although Daeva seems oblivious as she continues.

"I know the one-form was important, and please know I tried everything. I'll leave with my Guardians at once to find her body."

Kalliope shifted, leaning on one arm, bringing a growing claw to tap at her mouth in thought. "I do not think that will be necessary, but thank you."

Daeva frowns, looking around the room. "Your Grace? Do you not care about the one-form?"

"Of course I care, but you do not need to find her. Because she is already here, General."

"That's our cue," Legend whispers, ushering me out of the walkway and up to the small door. It opens with an ungodly squeal, catching the attention of everyone watching as he leads me inside. My skin heats from the unwanted attention.

However, it's a delight to see the crowd process who just walked through the door, and that I am, in fact, not actually dead. Eyes widen, and all decorum's forgotten as some shout and point excitedly. It turns into pandemonium.

Kalliope tracks me as I stride to the center of the room, stopping a few feet from Daeva. If looks could kill ... her eyes are glaciers, but her normally pale cheeks are flushing to a violent pink. She's caught and knows it.

Everything she's ever done to me assaults my mind; her punching me repeatedly. Offering me to the Vulturians as an appetizer. All the times she ever made fun of me. Made me feel less than.

This female has gone out of her way to try and destroy me, all because she's a close-minded bigot with a grudge and a god complex. Well, I'm not the same person she met weeks ago. Straightening, I lift my chin and give her my best smirk.

I can't help it — I wriggle my fingers in a condescending wave. "Sorry to spoil the party."

"You," she hisses, taking a step forward. All pretense of sorrow evaporates. In its place is bigotry and hate.

A deep growl echoes against the walls, catching everyone's attention. Kalliope catapults onto her feet, fists barely concealing fully formed claws.

"Take another step, and we'll skip this farce and right into sentencing."

The words trigger Daeva, who whirls to face her. "You tricked me," she seethes. "You knew the one-form was still alive."

"Which is it, Dae-Dae?" I grin when she snarls at the nickname. I motion to my body. My outfit hides most of the bruises, but the ones on my face and neck are visible. "I thought you saw me torn to shreds? Or maybe you should take a little responsibility for what you did."

"I didn't say that — I said they took you, then attacked me."

The anger of her betrayal comes to a boil. I stride toward her, unafraid. *I'm not a fucking wallflower anymore.* She can't shift, and Legend keeps pace with me, ready to spring into action. Stopping a few feet in front of her, I put my hands on my hips.

"That's a fucking *lie.*"

The whole room gasps.

Pointing at her hateful expression, I declare in a booming voice, "You almost killed Legend. You attacked me and forced me onto a Morgoth. You gave me to the Vulturians and were so full of yourself, you couldn't help but reveal your plans." I motion to the crowd. "You said everyone here would just go along with it."

A cacophony of whispers fills the room, and some Amicums shout with shock. Kalliope holds up a hand, and everyone quiets. Daeva's face is now a shade of red so crimson, if it were a shade of blush, its name would be *Dastardly Bitch.* It's glorious. She gnashes her teeth, the best she can do without being able to shift.

Unwilling to admit what she's done, Daeva throws her head back and laughs. "You stupid one-form. There are many things you don't know or understand. This is one of them."

"Then explain it." The command booms from overhead, and we look up to Kalliope. The whole room falls silent. "Tell everyone what exactly happened. Now we've proven Saira is not indeed dead, so your story requires recalculation."

Looking around, it's clear the friendly faces from earlier have dried up. Smirking, I watch the realization hit her like a thrown brick. It's so satisfying to witness real justice in action. Daeva draws herself up with as much confidence as possible. "I will not defend myself further. I assumed Saira was dead. Her being alive proves nothing, except the fates graced her with an escape."

"You told the Vulturians about a deal you made," I spit out with venomous rage. "They set a trap to kill Her Grace, so you could come here and appear to rescue everyone from the chaos you created."

Daeva whirls toward me, straining against her manacles, trying to shift and failing. Her eyes turn pure black, and her ears round at the edges. A smattering of leopard spots shows how hard she's trying to shift and kill me. Legend steps forward, partially shielding me from view. It thaws my heart even further. I know that if it came down to it, he'd die trying to protect me. I wrap a hand around his elbow, and he looks down, expression stony. At my grateful smile, his mouth flickers upward for a split second before flattening again.

Daeva's chains glow brighter, and her shifting stops. I've never been more grateful for restraints in my life. Instead of continuing to spew threats or trying to attack, she pauses. Straightens. Turns back to Kalliope.

"Lordess."

The respectful title makes the hair on my neck raise. Kalliope arches an eyebrow, and the audience is rapt. Daeva takes the scene in and relaxes. They're all putty. She preens at the attention, giving a feline grin.

"Lordess Kalliope, I challenge you to a Scrap."

Kalliope's smile is slow and feral. The crowd murmurs excitedly, but all I can do is watch Kalliope and the way she homes in on Daeva. It's raptorial and unrelenting. She licks her lips, and I can't help but wonder if she's imagining Daeva's blood on her tongue.

Next to me, Legend lets out a deep chuckle. To me, he mutters, "Kalliope is going to wipe her existence out of these lands."

His confidence boosts mine. Intertwining our fingers, I grin. "I like the sound of that."

On the dais, Kalliope struts to the edge. Peering down at Daeva with a smirk, she raises her hand. The room instantly quiets. Her power is intoxicating.

With a voice made of sharp steel, she declares, "Challenge accepted."

Chapter Thirty-Five

Another Day In The Amicum Neighborhood

The rest of the day moves in a blur. Daeva's brought down to the lone holding cell in the manor's basement. Because of the Scrap, Kalliope's required to draft and send correspondence to all lordesses, warning them of potential leadership changes.

While she does that, Legend escorts me to breakfast. He hasn't left my side since my rescue. Maybe it's my imagination, but sometimes, it looks like guilt weighs down his expression. How can I convince him the kidnapping wasn't a failure on his part?

Even now, as I take a bite of crispy meat, his gaze is like a magnet, forcing me to return his staring. Dabbing my mouth with a napkin, I place it on the table and say, "I can't claim to know you as well as everyone else, but something tells me you're beating yourself up."

Despite casually draping himself in his normal chair, Legend stiffens. "What makes you say that?"

Lifting a cup of coffee, I gesture to him. "There hasn't been a single innuendo, and you won't stop staring. It isn't your normal M.O."

"M.O.?"

"*Modus operandi.* It's Latin for normally acting like an insatiable flirt."

His expression, so stoic until now, softens. "Would you prefer my flirting right now?"

"No, not if you aren't feeling flirty," I admit. "But you're watching me like I'm going to float away like a balloon if you blink too hard."

The tension in his shoulders melts a fraction. Leaning forward, he grabs a fluffy roll and takes a bite. After a moment of consideration, he says, "Saira, my life's dedicated to protection. Not only Kalliope, but everyone else as well."

A muscle feathers in his jaw as he contemplates his words. "Under said protection, you were taken." Those jewel-toned eyes flick away from my face in shame. "I was too confident. If I'd shown more caution, Daeva would never have gotten away with you."

I place a hand on his arm, squeezing it. "Legend, I don't blame you. No one anticipated Daeva's betrayal."

Dropping the half-eaten roll on the table in disgust, he says, "No, we didn't. Perhaps that was our mistake. The signs were there if we'd looked closely enough. Our mistake almost cost you your life."

His confession squeezes my heart painfully. Like Kalliope had after the village attack, he's beating himself up. There's most likely nothing I can say to make this better, but it's worth a try.

"You came for me. All of you did. That means everything to me, Legend." When he continues to look away, I roughly grab his chin, forcing him to look at me. His eyes flare with surprise. "It's worth something to *me*, Legend. This journey is unbelievably lonely — and it's just beginning. But finding people out there ready to fight for me? Die for me? Makes it all the more worth it. Being here, experiencing everything so far, continues to strengthen me. That's impossible to truly regret."

Emotions swim in his eyes as glittering unshed tears. Cupping his jaw, I murmur, "No matter what my future holds, I'm glad to have met you. I want my incorrigible flirt back." When he doesn't respond, I plead, *"Please."*

The word cracks his demeanor. Voice hoarse, he says, "Gem, I can't live with myself if something happens to you."

My mouth draws down in a frown. "I have to leave soon, Legend. As much as I'd love for you to tag along and intimidate everything that will try to eat me, you can't. The best you can do is help me prepare with training. How does that sound?"

Eyes lighting up at the suggestion, that familiar panty-dropping grin flashes. "I'd love nothing more than to help you train."

"That settles it, then," I say, returning the smile. "After the Scrap, you can teach me how to take on an oversized brute."

Face heating with unmistakable lust, he purrs, "I'd love to teach you how to take on something oversized."

Laughing, I slap his arm. "There's my shameless flirt." Satisfied, I take a sip of my coffee. Legend's spirits appear lifted, if the endless dad jokes and flirtations are any indication.

Yet, my own words rattle around in my brain. *I have to leave soon.* The statement is more like a threat than a promise. Part of the reason I stayed in Ilorna was to train and prepare for any future dangers. That decision was made weeks ago. When will it be long enough?

Something deep down inside my gut tells me the answer, but I shove it away.

Dreams of Piper and the anxiety of the Scrap led to an awful night's sleep. I spent half the night staring at the ceiling. As a result, morning arrives too quickly. My mind and body crave real rest, and the exhaustion leaves me emotionally raw. Despite my best attempts to meditate and calm my racing thoughts, everything I've been trying to ignore refuses to disappear.

Guilt presses down on me like a wet, weighted blanket. I can't help but feel like I'm failing my family. This mission's about saving them, not dilly-dallying. I've spent weeks here, beyond what Dad would probably consider acceptable.

Now I'm in love with two people, one of whom might die in front of me today. These emotional entanglements are confusing, and wonderful, and terrible, and consuming. A part of me yearns for the simplicity of a lab. Where things have order, even when the outcome is unknown. There's nothing about this reality that is orderly or contained.

Kalliope's thigh shifts over mine as she turns in her sleep. On my other side is Legend, one of his arms slung over my hip, completing this Saira Sandwich. If I could do it over, would I have stayed here?

I'm still not sure. I can already tell love is excruciating, and we haven't even gotten to the goodbyes yet. So yeah, I'm not sure if it's been worth it yet.

A snarl interrupts my thoughts as Legend stuffs a pillow over his head, blocking sunlight peeking from between the curtains. Kalliope stirs, then sighs, rolling away from me. I watch her stare off into nothing, face flat with resignation.

Today, she has to kill someone she considered a best friend. I can't even imagine what that would be like, and I technically did it with Piper. Not quite the same, but enough to have empathy. Snuggling into her back, I bring an arm around her ribs and hug her tight. One of her slender hands covers mine, intertwining our fingers.

She curls into my hold. For a moment, time suspends as I try to offer the silent support she needs. It aches when she lets go, but I don't force her to stay with me.

With a heavy, frustrated exhale, Kalliope swings out of bed and drags her palms across her face. Accepting defeat against the inevitable morning light, Legend stalks to the door, pulling the rope to signal for breakfast. He looks to Kalliope, and for a split second, worry etches his features. Before she notices, his expression smooths, and when he catches me watching, he winks. It's an appreciated brave front.

Meadow arrives with trays full of protein and pastries. I make a beeline for my favorites, although I can't turn down the pile of pan-fried meats.

As Kalliope picks at her food, Meadow sections off her hair into tight braids. She clicks her tongue in disapproval when Kalliope doesn't eat as much as she needs, especially after the last few days.

When I ask about it, she says, "There's no need to puke in the arena."

Fair enough.

After weaving Kalliope's braids into an intricate crown, Meadow leaves and returns with a pile of armor and leathers. Kalliope follows her to the dressing area, allowing Meadow and Legend to fret over every tie and buckle. There are flashes of red metal, but I'm too distracted by getting myself dressed. I don't take in what she's wearing until Legend cinches in the last buckle.

The effect is breathtaking and intimidating all at once.

Kalliope looks like Aries in female form, with stunning red leathers wrapped around her body, with knee-high laced black leather boots. On her shoulders are thick, pad-like pieces of ichor–colored leather with small, red spikes reaching outward. The crown of braids atop her head emphasizes her regalness. The tension in her expression yanks at her features, sharpening her cheekbones.

A hush blankets the room as everyone takes in their lordess, ready for a fight to the death. She looks at each of us with a grim smile. A knock at the door breaks the trance. The anxiety I've been trying to shove down rolls over me in crushing waves.

It's Zenab, who also looks sick to her stomach. She's wearing simple fighting leathers the color of rich soil, and her curls are pulled tightly into a bun atop her head. It's a severe effect.

She swallows hard, then says, "It's time, Kal."

The silence cutting between us is heavy and full of dread. Legend's expression is unreadable, but something tells me it's going to be like that for a while. He can't support her if he's falling apart.

I, however, can't make the same promise.

The journey to the arena feels like a dead man's walk. Legend stands between Kalliope and me, with Zenab leading the way. Dread creeps through my veins, creating the urge to scream about the unfairness of it all. I know it's the "Amicum way," and it's not my place to judge, but

I'm nauseous all the same. It's easier to pretend this is just another day in the Amicum neighborhood.

The arena is a couple of miles away from the manor, which isn't far when Legend allows me to ride him in manticore form. Apparently, he's also allowed to shift when on official Cohort business.

When we reach the arena, I'm struck with how similar the outside resembles the Colosseum in Rome. Crowds of Amicums loiter on the outside, while others climb stairs to the different levels of seats.

They all look excited, and I hate them for it. Kalliope could die, and the crowd's acting like this is a circus. So many things about Amicum culture are interesting, but this one only breeds resentment.

We walk into a hallway in the back of the arena where almost no other Amicums are. For the few lingering, Kalliope doesn't spare them a second glance. She's introspective, barely interacting with any of us. It's a new side of her that's both alarming and fascinating. It's easy to forget that under her commanding and austere lordess facade, she's just a person, trying her hardest for everyone.

Since Daeva's demand for the Scrap, she's kept herself busy with her duties. Not an inch of nerves has shown, minus her slowly turning inward. Legend doesn't appear worried, but I also think he's putting up a good front for everyone's sake.

We stop in front of a wrought-iron gate, the only thing standing between us and the crowd. Beyond the gate is a stretch of soft beige sand that glows in the searing sun. There are no weapons or places to hide. Last night, I tried to imagine what the arena would look like. Surprisingly, just like the outside, the inside also resembles a coliseum. Staggered up to the top are rows of stone benches, with a good five feet in front of each bench, presumably to allow variously sized shifts.

It's packed to the brim, and the noise is a cacophony, making me wish for headphones. The screams are pinpricks across my brain, spiking the adrenaline already pumping in my veins. The onlookers are a mix of true-forms and shifts. No matter the form, their excitement is palpable. According to Legend, there hasn't been a lordess vs. Cohort duel, ever.

In full regalia, Kalliope looks ready to take on every rebel and Vulturian all at once. Even if I could have a chance, I'd never want to go up against her.

Somewhere on the other side of the arena is Daeva, the slimy liar looking to dethrone Kalliope out of a misplaced sense of ownership.

I hope Kalliope whoops her ass.

Zenab steps forward and rests her hands on Kalliope's armored shoulders. She touches different pieces of the armor, adjusting and straightening them like a mother hen. Tears glisten in her eyes. "You wear your mother's armor."

Kalliope grimaces in resignation. "It feels only fitting due to the accusations."

Zenab nods in understanding. Biting her lip, she looks down at the stone floor. Her voice carries devastation as she says, "I'm loath to say it, but after what Daeva has done, her death is the only solution. She'll keep trying if you let her live."

Inhaling a deep breath, she brings a hand to Kalliope's dipped chin and lifts it. Kalliope's face contorts with different emotions, the main one clearly heartache. "Do not feel shame for doing what needs to be done. Your mother would be proud."

Zenab straightens and snaps back her shoulders, every inch of the interim general. Temporarily out of retirement, she's taken charge of Daeva's role while a replacement's promoted. She gives a quick bow in deference, which Kalliope returns.

Kalliope focuses on me, and I feel so inept to offer any kind of encouragement. What do I know about going to kill your friends? I've only left mine to die.

She reaches for my hands, and I'm surprised to find her palms are dry and warm. Mine are disgustingly damp. Sweat beads at the curve of my back, and my heart thrums in my ears.

"What if you die? There's still so much I want to share with you." The words are acid on my tongue.

Kalliope's mouth curls at the edges, and she brings her forehead to mine. "Death can't and won't change how I feel about you. I love you,

JENNA AVERY

Saira Andromeda." My heart stutters at the words. When I open my mouth, she cuts me off. "Don't. I know it's too hard for you to say it, and I understand why. But I'm not about to walk into that arena with it unsaid."

She looks to where my invisible Scout rests on my wrist. Last night, the three of us agreed it's smart for me to prepare for the worst — that means wearing my travel outfit, and my backpack's hitched over Legend's shoulder. Kalliope gives me a wry smile. "I don't plan on dying, but if I do, just know I'm grateful for the day a bear tried to kill you in the forest."

I hiccup a laugh, tears freely streaming down my face. I'm such a coward to not say the words, but I shove the shame into a deep hole in my mind. Maybe someday; not today.

Instead, I say, "I'll never live that down, will I?"

Kalliope kisses the tip of my nose. "Most likely not."

"Definitely not," a small voice adds. We look over to find Ginger, red faced with swollen eyes. To my shock, she's wearing simple, white armor. Her hair's pulled back into a chunky braid. Attached to her hip is a slender sword with a silver hilt. If Kalliope is Aries going to war, Ginger is Aphrodite ready for battle.

She flings her body at Kalliope, who catches her easily.

Their embrace is heart-wrenching as Ginger quietly sobs into Kalliope's shoulder. They exchange whispers, nothing my lame human ears can pick up. When they break apart, Ginger furiously wipes at her tears and whirls around, rushing away.

Kalliope turns to Legend. He brings a hand to her jaw, stroking his thumb along her cheek. Their foreheads nuzzle, like two lions showing affection.

"I'm not worried," he says, voice firm.

They share a feather-light kiss, then she says, "Me neither."

A horn blares, startling me. Kalliope doesn't even flinch. They share one last kiss, and she steps back.

Taking a deep breath, she turns towards the gate, and it slowly opens.

322

Chapter Thirty-Six

A Bird Named Fruit Boop

As Kalliope strides into the arena, Legend and Zenab lead me up a staircase. It winds up six floors before spitting us out onto a covered veranda. A thick white cloth tarp blocks the intense sun, flapping in the breeze. The balcony is free of a railing, offering a quick death to the ground if one gets too close to the edge.

Six chairs made of dark wood rest in the center of the platform, with one bigger than the rest. Ginger stands at the edge of the platform, attention riveted on the sandy arena.

She spares us a glance. Her swollen eyes are alight with crackling anger, like a lightning storm over an emerald field. "I'm ready for this bitch to go down."

"You're clothed," I half-heartedly jest. It's like joking at a funeral — and I immediately regret it.

Her expression remains solemn as she purses her lips, turning her attention back to the arena. "If Kalliope somehow fails — but she won't — I plan on entering that arena immediately. No matter what, she's carrion today." She glances at me again. "Did you know the stables burned down? They're gone. The Vulturian rebels set it on fire, with some Amicums still inside." She looks back at the arena, cheeks flushing red. "She could never die enough times to make up for the friends I lost yesterday."

On a whim, I walk over and throw my arms around her. Her body tenses, then relaxes as she returns the hug. I hold on until she's the first to let go.

"I'm so sorry, Ginger," I whisper, the words catching on the emotion lodged in my throat.

Her eyes water as she dips her chin. "Thank you. I'm sorry for you, too. Today's justice is deserved."

The moment's shattered when the crowd roars in exaltation. We look into the arena and find Daeva and Kalliope stalking to the center of the arena. All of us rush to take a seat.

My fingernails dig into the smooth wood of the armrest, adrenaline pumping in my arteries and grasping me in a chokehold. It's like a movie come to life, but it's too real. There's too much dust and screaming. The blood pumping furiously in my ears is like drums, a morbid soundtrack to the scene.

"She'll be alright, Gem," Legend whispers, putting a hand on one of mine and squeezing. "Only the strongest and fastest can become a lordess and retain the title. This isn't her first Scrap, either."

Unfortunately, his words aren't having the impact he hopes. Daeva was the general for years for very good reasons. Kalliope is *down there*, possibly about to die. Tearing my eyes off Kalliope, I evaluate Daeva.

The chains are gone. She's wearing gray leathers but they cover portions of her body. It's a vest-like top with shoulders that flare out, but allow freedom of movement. In place of pants, she's wearing the equivalent of a leather kilt. It swishes with each step, stopping right above her knee. To my shock, she's barefoot. In the sunlight, her milky white skin glows like moonstone. The visual is too ethereal for comfort.

The crowd's volume increases, rattling the stone structure. Neither challenger glances away, locked onto one another like the predators they are. The excitement in the air is catching, and a flutter of anticipation courses through me. I'm terrified for Kalliope, so much so that it's hard to think. Hard to breathe. But my gut tells me she's stronger and faster. Otherwise, Daeva would already be lordess.

Zenab's mouth's set in a grin line as her eyes track their every movement. It must be so incredibly difficult, watching two people you helped raise battle to the death.

"So what happens now?" I ask.

Her eyes flick to mine, their intensity pinning me in place. "This first portion is a duel in true-form with a weapon of their choice."

Two other doors open, revealing attendants holding different weapons. One holds a short sword. The other holds a thick metal spear, the metal gleaming. Not glancing at the attendants, they hold out their hands for the weapons.

Daeva smirks and speaks to Kalliope, but it's impossible to hear it over the roar of the onlookers. Whatever it is, has Kalliope tensing even further. Daeva's eyes flick to me, and the smirk grows feral. I gnaw the inside of my cheek, shoving away the leftover fear from the kidnapping. *She can't hurt me anymore.* This is her recompense, not her absolution.

"Now medics check them over for any issues," Legend narrates as two different Amicums walk up to them, visibly inspecting their bodies. Kalliope's fully healed from the battle with the Vulturians.

The anticipation crawls up my skin, breaking out in goose bumps. Screams from the crowd offer encouragement to Kalliope. No one screams Daeva's name.

Anxiety causes me to shiver, catching Zenab's attention. She places a hand on my shoulder, giving it a firm squeeze.

"Don't fret, Saira," she assures. "Kalliope has not only practiced dueling countless times, but as Legend said before, this isn't her first Scrap. This arena is familiar territory. She knows what she's doing."

The words don't calm me, though. "But has she gone up against someone as talented as *her*?"

Zenab considers the question, then says, "Aside from training with me? Not that I recall — but they have practiced together for years. It's tradition for an entire Cohort to practice together."

"Won't that make it worse?"

"Probably," she admits, consternation flitting across her face before it's smothered. "But also, it makes sure the crowd knows whoever wins is truly the strongest and the best. That's why everyone is so thrilled — it's only natural to seek the best leader possible."

"It's barbaric," I mutter.

She shrugs. "It is the Amicum way."

"It's a godsdamn show."

"It's evidence," Legend corrects. "There are no mistakes or mis-interpretations. Only the strongest prevail, and that's how nature works."

It's not your culture. This isn't the time or place to demand an explanation. Understanding it won't smooth over the deep fear curdling in my stomach. Shifting uncomfortably in the chair, biting back more questions, I jiggle my leg to disperse some of the agitation crackling in my veins.

Legend gently places a hand over mine, offering a comforting smile. It doesn't stave off the worry, but I squeeze his hand back.

Time slips by like grains of sand in a windstorm as Daeva handles her sword with expert grace, twisting her wrists to warm them up. Kalliope twirls the spear in deft, rapid circles. They begin to pace around each other, waiting for a signal. My free hand finds its way to my vibrating rib cage, pressing against my rattling heart. I'm desperate to freeze this moment, keeping Kalliope safe.

The horn blares, and they lunge with unbelievable speed. The crowd roars when the two collide, their weapons a blur as they move in a familiar dance. For every parry, the other blocks it with familiar ease. It takes everything in me not to cover my ears from the overwhelming sounds.

Kalliope moves like water, ducking and twirling, lashing out with the spear. Daeva bends backward so far her knees bend at almost ninety-degrees, expertly avoiding what would have killed any other normal being.

The dance continues for a few minutes before first blood's drawn. *Kalliope's blood.*

My warrior lordess barely falters as the slice on her forearm bleeds freely. Crimson droplets stain the pale sand, a stark contrast. Tears blur my vision, and I furiously wipe them away, desperate to not miss a single second. Kalliope needs my strengths, not weaknesses.

Daeva grins, her fangs flashing as she increases her speed, sensing weakness. As she spins to the left, Kalliope anticipates and parries the other way, bringing the tip of the spear against Daeva's calf. To my extreme joy, Daeva stumbles before rolling away from the follow-up stab. I stand and whoop. Daeva catches my reaction, and her expression darkens. I hope it distracts her.

They pause, chests heaving. Perspiration glistens on their skin. The breeze picks up, fraying Kalliope's braids further. They made a mess around her face, sticking to the sweat.

Kalliope says something, and Daeva shakes her head. Whether denying or disagreeing, it's impossible to know. Kalliope bares her teeth and snaps them like a dog. Daeva returns the sentiment, and they lunge again.

Their quiet exchange bothers Daeva enough to slow her down. The sword swings turn sloppy. Her icy skin flushes a vibrant red. She screams a desperate threat, working the crowd into a froth. The floor vibrates from the stomping and screams. Adrenaline throbs in my temples, indistinguishable from the pounding.

Slash. Stab. Dodge. Duck. Jab. The weapons slam together so hard, I can finally hear the ringing of the sword. The sand kicks up into dust, swirling around them.

They begin trading blows. Daeva receives a slash across her cheek and thigh. My body breaks out in a cold sweat as Daeva slashes the sword across Kalliope's left shoulder, forcing the spear to clatter to the ground. Kalliope somersaults, barely escaping Daeva's sword.

The urge to scream Kalliope's name is strong, but it'll only distract her. I'm helpless as Kalliope sprints to Daeva, dodging left and right, intent on attacking Daeva with her bare hands. She lands a couple of punches, and blood pours from Daeva's nose. Legend joins me in my whoop of joy. A sliver of hope shines in my heart as Kalliope headbutts Daeva, breaking her nose.

In spite of it all, Daeva doesn't falter — she delivers precise slashes of the sword, forcing Kalliope backward. She glances over her shoulder, looking for the spear. Whirling around, she sprints for the weapon, sliding on her knees in the sand when she gets close enough.

She whirls around, aiming to thrust the spear forward, but Daeva's too fast.

The leopard shifter's sword sinks into Kalliope's right pectoral, stopping her short.

I scream, reaching toward Kalliope as if I can somehow halt the blade. This can't be happening. It isn't real. Legend lurches forward, a panicked cry ripping from his throat.

Ginger surges from her chair, striding to the edge of the platform, toes ready to tip forward. Zenab hisses, a hand flying to her bandolier of daggers. She pulls one out and stabs it into the arm of her chair, viciously twisting it into the wood.

My heart stutters even as adrenaline courses through my veins. The crowd's energy sinks rapidly, and suddenly, it's deathly quiet. All except for the crow of victory from Daeva's nasty mouth. She let go of the weapon, throwing her arms up as if urging the crowd to join in her joy.

None of them do, but it doesn't appear to bother her. Ginger lets out a slew of inventive epithets, her freckled face red and blotchy with rage.

It's quiet enough to hear Kalliope's grunt of pain as she painstakingly removed the sword still stuck in her armor. Her chest heaves as her hands come up flush against the blade and slowly push it out. Blood gushes, slipping through her fingers as it falls to the sand. She grimaces, falling forward. Even prostrated before her enemy, Kalliope glares up at Daeva with unimaginable hatred.

Kalliope holds up three fingers, and Daeva spits blood at her feet, grinning.

Zenab shoves off the chair, a vein pulsing in her forehead. "It can't be!" she booms. "How did that even happen?"

Tendons strain in Legend's neck as he stares at Kalliope, his fists clenched so tight his knuckles turn white. In a low growl, he says, "This is centaur shit."

"What does this mean?" I ask, my voice shrill.

Zenab cracks her knuckles. "Kalliope forfeited the first round. Forfeiting provides the loser one more chance to try. Now they duel in the second part."

"When they shift and fight as Amicums?"

Ginger's face goes white as a sheet when Zenab says. "Yes. Until someone gives up or dies."

The four of us hurry back down the hallway by the gate, rushing to Kalliope as she limps past the gate. They're given an hour break to take healing balms and rest. Amicums are incredibly fast healers, and their healing salves and draughts work with the magic in their bodies. They're less effective on me, but work wonders for them.

I'm frozen in shock at the pain written all over her face. She'd put up a strong front, but there was clearly more hurt than she let on in front of the audience.

"Kalliope," I gasp, rushing over to help. Legend steps around me and scoops her up, carrying her down the hallway. Zenab leads the way, with Ginger taking up the rear.

Kalliope's head lolls over to look at me. "It looks worse than it is."

The blood has seeped down her crimson armor, leaving dark streaks. "It looks like you're close to bleeding to death."

Legend grunts, giving me an irritated look. To Kalliope, he says, "Let's get you to the healers."

"Can they fix it?" I follow them, desperate to help, to do *something*. I'm a scientist, for fuck's sake. Back at home, they call me Dr. Andromeda. Here? I'm useless. More than useless.

Ginger snatches my arm, preventing me from following too closely. "Give them space, Saira. The healers will help her."

All I can hear is Kalliope's gasps for air. That sound will echo in my dreams for the rest of my life.

They stumble into a room, and Legend places Kalliope onto a surgical cot where an Amicum in true-form waits, wearing lavender breeches and button-up shirt. I rush to stand beside him, watching the scene, feeling utterly helpless. Ginger and Zenab stand by the doorway, leaning against each other for comfort.

As Kalliope leans back against a pillow, the healer cuts away the leathers. The blood flows more freely now. She's deathly pale, panting from the effort of existence. The healer barks orders at her assistant.

"You need to fix it," Kalliope gasps at the healer. "I have less than an hour to go back out there."

If Kalliope doesn't go out there, it's an automatic forfeit. Then we're all dead. To her credit, the healer doesn't respond, focused entirely on cleaning the wounds.

The leathers fall to the floor with a wet *thunk*, and the healer grabs clean clothes and a tub of balm. Cautiously, making sure not to interfere, I walk to Kalliope's other side and grab her hand. It's cold and sweaty, her grip far less strong than fifteen minutes ago.

Her eyes meet mine, unfocused. "Saira."

My name is a question and a statement. I squeeze her fingers gently. "I'm right here."

Legend whispers to the healer in an urgent tone, catching Kalliope's attention, but I lightly yank on her hand. "Hey. Look at me."

Her head wobbles back and forth. Terror grips me, and I lean over to wipe away stray strands of hair from her brow. Her skin is clammy. She winces and sucks air through her teeth as the healer applies the balm. It's time to distract her.

"Do you want me to tell you about the time I saved a baby bird?"

She grimaces as Legend lifts her torso to pour a concoction down her throat. She drinks it, making a face at the taste. "Of course."

The room fades away as I dig into my memory. "When I was six years old, I was playing outside in my backyard when I came across a nest that had fallen onto the ground. Crushed eggs surrounded a lone baby bird with barely any feathers. The mama was nowhere to be found, so I figured I could be its new mama."

She gives a small *mmm*. "How kind of you."

It had been such an impulse, scooping the baby bird into my tiny palms and carrying it inside.

"I tried to find information on how to keep it alive, and didn't have any bird food. So I fed it cereal."

Her brow furrows. "What's cereal?"

How the hell do you explain cereal? "Um, it's like grains and sugar mixed to form shapes and tastes?"

She blinks rapidly. "Shapes?"

I laugh. "Yeah, well, I thought cereal shaped like fruit would be a good meal for a baby bird."

"Was it?"

I shake my head. "I never got the chance to find out, because my mother discovered my contraband pet and drove me to a nearby rescue where people could take care of it."

Her eyes flutter shut, but she says, "Did it live?"

I grin. "They named him Fruit Boop, and when he was old enough, they released him back into the wild."

The healer wipes away where the sword wounds used to be. They're entirely healed now. Between Amicum healing speeds and their weird magic elixirs, her healing time's significantly reduced. Relief loosens the tension in my shoulders. She's going to be fine.

Kalliope's eyes are brighter and more aware than five minutes ago. The healer pats her on the shoulder. "You're good enough to shift now."

The healer steps back and Legend immediately takes her place, holding onto Kalliope's arm as she sits up. Every muscle in his body is taut, straining with fear and concern. "Kal, you need to rest and drink some liquids."

Kalliope pats his hand. "I look worse than I feel." She shares a small smile with him. "That whelp of a dirty bitch won't survive the day, I promise."

Their foreheads rest together, and he inhales her scent. Legend's lower lip quivers slightly before clamping down on it with his teeth. When he straightens, we make eye contact. For a fleeting second, he lets me see the devastation he's desperate to hide from her. He's a protector — and it's the one thing he can't do right now.

My heart breaks for him. For both of them. This universe is new to me, but for them, their entire world's fallen apart in a matter of days. I ache to wrap my arms around them both.

The healer reappears, handing over a silver goblet. Kalliope, already moving with more confidence, grabs it and guzzles. I let go of her hand so she can swing over the edge and stand. Her legs aren't strong enough, and she stumbles. Legend leans forward to support, but Kalliope waves him off.

"I'll be fine. I require a few extra minutes to recuperate."

She drinks another goblet as Ginger hands her a loose tunic. The leather top is ruined, but she won't need it for the next trial.

When the second goblet is done, she looks at me. "Have you saved any other animals since?"

I grin, grateful for the levity. "No, but it seems like animals keep saving me."

She laughs. "And we're happy to do so."

The lightness evaporates as the ten-minute warning horn rings. Kalliope straightens and takes a deep breath. With a shockingly assertive stride, she walks out of the room, pausing to give Zenab and Ginger quick forehead bumps. Legend and I exchange a glance and follow as Kalliope marches to the iron gate. Time for take two.

Chapter Thirty-Seven

Death: The Crowd's Decision

The crowd's excitement reaches its crest as Kalliope steps back into the arena. More of them are in full and partial shifts. Perhaps in solidarity for what's to come.

My nerves are as tattered and worn as a ribbon left in a storm. Anxiety is a living thing inside my body; writhing in my veins; vibrating my bones.

The tension drives me to pick at a thumb, drawing blood. All of us return to our spots except Ginger. She skips sitting altogether and begins pacing at the edge of the platform.

Daeva and Kalliope meet in the middle again. Both look strong and healed — but that blonde bitch wears a self-satisfied smirk. A newly found feral part of me wants to claw it off her face.

Bending at the waist, I place my chin in my palms, ready for it to be over. No one will say it, but Kalliope wasn't in great shape after the first battle. The idea of Daeva winning this round? I can barely contemplate the possibility. Stamping down my fear, I concentrate on the arena.

Legend estimates this battle will be less than five minutes based on past Scraps. All our futures rely on the next five or so minutes. It does nothing for the knots in my stomach.

The females circle one another. A loud whistle sounds, and with a shimmer in the air, a black wolf and snow leopard are pacing in a circle.

I lean over to Zenab, who's rubbing the back of her neck anxiously. "What are the limits?"

She doesn't even glance at me. "Any form, at any time. First to yield is the loser and can be executed."

I stifle a whimper. This whole thing is barbaric, at odds with what I thought a matriarchy would be. Back at home, women had all kinds of ideals about what a matriarchy could look like — but it wasn't a world full of shifters.

The horn blares. The predators are a blur, tussling and wrestling around each other. Teeth snap. Blood's drawn immediately, trickling down from Daeva's hind end. They spring apart, a plume of dust whirling around their forms.

Kalliope snarls, spittle flying from her jaws.

Bolting upright, I rush to the edge of the platform. Zenab does the same and screams in encouragement. Legend stalks to stand beside us, quivering with intensity.

Daeva roars, baring her fangs. She flicks her three-foot-long tail, her enormous paws silent as they circle each other again.

An unseen signal has them rushing to one another again. They fly upward on their hind legs, paws and legs gripping while their teeth gnash against each other. Kalliope finally finds the edge she needs — a mouthful of Daeva's throat. With impossible strength, she jerks one way, then the other, slamming the snow leopard to the ground. I jump up and down, screaming with elation.

She shakes her head like a dog, violently shaking Daeva like an unruly stuffed animal. It doesn't last; huge gray-brown paws flash six-inch-long claws. They dig into Kalliope's shoulders.

Kalliope releases her hold, but it's too late. Daeva snaps her mouth forward. Snatches a paw. I hear the bone snap all the way from here. I let out a keening sound, a hand coming to my mouth. Even at this distance, I see mangled toes. How could she keep going now? The fear I've been trying to ignore bursts forth, walloping my heart into a vicious staccato.

Kalliope's form shifts. A massive grizzly shakes its thick trunk of a throat, roaring with rage. On its chest is a star-shaped patch of white fur. Legend sucks in a sharp breath, his body turning rigid next to me.

The snow leopard hisses and takes a step back. The crowd goes wild. Some even shift into different versions of bears of different colors. White. Brown. Black. Gray. Despite my dread, a part of me can appreciate the incredible sight. The deafening roar of bears echoes against the arena's walls.

The broken paw doesn't even seem to faze Kalliope as the grizzly gallops forward, enormous jaws bared. Even with the thousand-pound frame, the bear's speed is phenomenal. She's as fast as a galloping horse. A thick layer of fat protects all the vital organs. It's genius.

Daeva dodges, but her long tail doesn't get out of the way fast enough. Kalliope takes a mouthful and clamps down, biting it in half.

The sound that comes out of Daeva's mouth is music to my ears. It's a keening, moaning roar, and she whips to the side, leaping onto the bear's shoulders. Digging all four paws into Kalliope's back, she sinks her jaws into the bear's spine.

Tears burn my eyes. Breathing becomes impossible. Legend's hand reaches for mine, clutching it for dear life. We share a glance, mirroring terrified expressions.

With one great shake, Kalliope shrugs Daeva off like a fly. The snow leopard lands on its side like a discarded stone. She's on all four legs immediately, then it's gone. A shimmer of air and a thick emerald green snake twenty feet long slithers through the sand like water, missing a portion of its tail.

"*What the fuck?*" I whisper.

Legend's voice is thick with fear when he says, "A basilisk. She can't manifest their powers, but they're deadly even without the breath."

Daeva doesn't wait — she strikes as she rushes Kalliope, raising half of her body upward. Kalliope stands up on two legs, which might be a mistake. Daeva strikes.

For a second, I think she's going to bite the bear, but instead, she strikes like lightning as she wraps round and round the bear.

335

"*Kalliope!*" I scream, aching to jump in to help.

The mythical snake begins to squeeze.

Kalliope roars, but the sound's cut short as her lungs are slowly crushed.

There's a shimmer, and the basilisk falls into a heap on the ground as a chestnut horse leaps out onto the sand, kicking the snake straight in the face.

Daeva wavers, dazed from the hit. Kalliope hobbles away with the injured leg. She's wheezing and moving slower, but she's able to gain distance from the snake.

After only a moment of hesitation, the twenty-foot snake shimmers, and Daeva becomes a golden lion with a flowing mane. The horse shimmers, and a black lion turns ice-blue eyes to the golden lion.

My lungs burn, and I suck in air, realizing I've been holding my breath this whole time. Legend hears my panting and rubs between my shoulders. Our attention's snapped back to the arena when two equal roars turn into cries of pain. The lions are slapping each other with outstretched claws, digging fangs into each other's faces.

Kalliope gains momentum and slams Daeva to the ground, sinking teeth into Daeva's shoulder. A slab of skin and meat peels away, exposing bone.

"Get her, Kal." Legend's words are a breathy prayer. This is the most helpless I've ever felt before. They're equals in almost every way, with years of training together prohibiting any significant advantage.

Not giving Daeva an inch, Kalliope strikes for Daeva's belly, raking claws through the soft skin. Ribbons of blood pour out. Daeva's keening cry feeds the crowd's frenetic energy. It's a balm to my need for revenge — after everything she's done, it's the least she deserves.

Daeva falters, flipping herself upright and galloping away from Kalliope's form. To my surprise, Kalliope doesn't follow. The battle has worsened the injury on her leg. It's unable to hold weight, hanging loosely off the joint. Across the arena, Daeva shifts into a snow leopard. It looks worse for wear now. This time, when Kalliope shimmers, it's terrifying to watch her form grow and grow and grow.

A wyvern the size of a two-story building appears. In the sunlight, its shimmering blood-red scales glisten, reflecting dots of light all over the arena. Kalliope whips the wyvern's club tail across the bloody sand. Dozens of tiny, needle-sharp horns jut from the crown of her head to her throat.

"I can't believe she pulled it off," Zenab says, incredulous. Legend hums in agreement.

I'm about to ask what she means when Kalliope carries her bulk on her wing talons and one leg, carefully dragging the other one. A forked tongue slips from between the wyvern's scaled, dark black lips, tasting the frenzied excitement of the crowd. Hopefully, she tastes Daeva's fear, too.

Daeva paces and hisses while searching for weaknesses.

Kalliope lowers her long, snake-like neck and opens her maw. Orange boils brightly in her throat before she roars and a steady stream of fire rushes toward the snow leopard.

Daeva bolts, but not in time. A streak of blisters appears along her flank, forcing the snow leopard to tuck and collect her hindquarters, forcing a quick retreat.

Kalliope doesn't move as her reptilian pupils track Daeva, scurrying along the edge of the arena. Half the crowd begins to boo and share their disappointment as Daeva tucks tail.

It's so incredibly satisfying.

Kalliope charges, the platform vibrating with each pounding step. She doesn't go far, already taking up half the arena. Daeva whips to the left as Kalliope's talon swipes the air. The two-pronged hooked talon catches Daeva mid-jump, slicing from sternum to groin. Blood pours freely onto the dirt. She crumples into a ball of blood and guts.

Daeva shimmers and the bitch appears in true-form, clutching her guts with one hand, holding up the other with three fingers. Legend leans down and gathers me in his brawny arms, hooting with joy and relief. I giggle, feeling lighter than a balloon. It's over.

"She's yielded," Zenab gasps.

My brows crease with confusion. "Why didn't she become a wyvern?"

"Daeva is powerful, but an Amicum's shifting size depends on its current state of health and power. Kalliope has always been the strongest — her shifting skills are unmatched." She grinds her teeth before saying, "Something Daeva should have considered before starting her ill-advised coup."

The wyvern disappears, and Kalliope stands in the arena, lungs heaving for air. It's impossible to tell at this distance, but I'm sure she's exhausted. Everything took less than an hour and a half, but relativity made it pass like years.

Daeva falls to her knees, using her hands to hold everything in. Kalliope ignores her. Instead, she slowly spins to eye everyone in the stands. The stone under my feet vibrates from the tremendous power of the stomps. The celebration of true power from their lordess.

I want to prostrate myself in awe. Her expression's carved with ferocity and determination. All her braids are in shambles, and her long hair waves in the stiff breeze, dust swirling around her.

Ginger cups her mouth and crows out into the crowd with joy. Legend whoops, grabbing the mare shifter and spinning her. She snarls like a crabby cat, but her grin belies the threat.

Looking at Zenab with a wide grin, I ask, "What's next?"

An emotion I can't place passes over her face as she says quietly, "The crowd decides whether to kill the loser."

I hope they vote to kill Daeva. I search for some form of shame or guilt at the thought, but there's nothing but righteous satisfaction. Dozens of Amicums died because of her. She plotted my kidnapping and eventual spit-roasted death. Failed in executing a coup. There's no way the raucous crowd chanting Kalliope's name will let Daeva live.

Chapter Thirty-Eight

Nothing But Ashes Upon Stone

Kalliope

The instincts of different animals are at war inside me, desperate to either flee or attack. As much as I want to look up to the viewing platform, my wolf demands my prey never leave my line of sight.

The healers look over the betrayer, reinserting her innards and sealing the wound with the healing salve. It's better than she deserves, and I'm confident the crowd will agree.

Chunks of caked dirt mixed with sweat and blood glob onto my skin. Her blood crusts around my mouth; its tangy, its coppery taste barely satisfying the edges of my hate. We were practically littermates. We spent our entire lives training together and lending support when our parents died. In my eyes, her choice is utterly unforgivable.

Her eyes lock onto mine, even as she grimaces with pain. To my left, a healer touches my shoulder.

"Lordess, I need to heal your wound."

Lifting the limb away from my body, I allow her to tend to the injury as I consider what form of death will be delivered.

The bitch, who was formerly a dear friend, bares her teeth at me. I return the sentiment. Gone is the youngling who laughed with me

339

in the training camps. We comforted one another when our mothers died. I trusted her with my family, friends, and the protection of this land. Every Vulturian attack in the last few months was her fault. Every murdered Amicum and one-form is on her head.

From the start, Daeva never gave me a moment to consider her capable of a coup. Or held so much hate in her heart. It wasn't always like this. Before the war, she was a carefree youngling, full of mischief and laughter. The war and the years hardened her. Beyond repair, so it seems.

Her mother would be ashamed. Even if it hurt, I know her mother would be on the dais, accepting the inevitability of this sentencing.

So even if it pains me to kill Daeva, one of my dearest friends, it is what needs to be done. She cast the first stone, and it must be returned in kind.

There is no way the crowd will let her cowardice stand. It would have been easier if I had won both rounds, but now it is time for the people to decide. It is the better outcome, though. Now they are a part of the decision, and their established confidence in me will only bolster my claim.

And it is what I have always had — a claim. Anyone who wanted to challenge me as lordess has always had a fair opportunity to do so. This is not my first time in the arena, but it never led to an execution. Daeva is special. You do not get to enact a coup, fail, and then go live in exile. Shifting into the largest form possible, a wyvern, only proves my capability and strength.

Memories of the recent attack are a barrage in my thoughts. Dead friends littering the ground, slain by Vulturian rebels. The stable turned to ashes and rubble. The scent of burned flesh inside the charred building. Finding Legend near death. It was almost too late to find Saira.

Unforgiving rage explodes in my chest, boiling my blood. No, Daeva does not deserve mercy. Even if it were an option, I refuse. The time for mercy, for peace, is past. I know my Cohort and partners approve; that's enough for me.

340

The healer finishes with my arm, and I twist it around, testing for any missed injury. Satisfied the healer did her job, I watch as Daeva stands, assisted by the other healer. Weak whelp.

We know what to do next. Turning my back on Daeva, almost willing her to try something. I would have every right to kill her if she did so, without the crowd's approval.

I stop in the center of the arena. She stands a few feet away from me, spitting out blood from a couple of missing teeth.

"When they choose me, I'm fucking your one-form half to death before I flay her alive. Then I'm going to make Legend my slave and make him piss on your corpse every day before I make him serve me all night."

The words further fuel the boiling rage inside me, and I lose control for a second. The thought of her hands on either washes my vision with red. Claws burst from my fingers, and fangs flash as I snarl. "You don't deserve them. Don't even fucking look at them. You're carrion, you inbred bitch."

Fear flickers across her face before the smirk returns. "I bet she tastes good."

"Better than your foul innards will."

This weakens her attitude as her eyes land on the dried blood smeared on my face. She opens her mouth to say something, but the horn blares. Good. I want no more of her words.

On cue, the crowd goes quiet. The shaded tarps snap violently in the wind. It's an ominous sound when paired with the silence.

As the current reigning leader, it's my duty to speak first. My voice cracks with the need for water, and I lick my dried lips. Never show weakness. "To my people." I spear Daeva with a pointed glare. "And I mean *my* people. I've been blessed with the honor of serving you for ten years. In that time, I have gotten to know every single one of you. Have I been a perfect leader? It is unlikely I will reach perfection, the same as you. However, I am confident that together, we have worked to not only rebuild our world with our mothers at our side."

I look at all the familiar faces. At the Amicums that have given me nothing but respect because it's what they receive every single day. My mother taught me to make everyone feel seen, even when it scrapes the dregs of my energy. Her sage advice will make today's outcome what it deserves to be.

"We have exceeded our mothers' dreams. Together we have built something worthy of pride, and is not a credit for me to claim. You are who I serve. And if you feel as if someone else could help you continue to build a world worth striving for, I will die for your right to decide."

I take a step back, giving space to whatever lies Daeva spins. Looking at her with a farce of respect, I patiently wait. She hesitates, her skin paler than usual. The healers can fix a wound during a duel but not replenish lost blood. She should be in bed instead of standing.

But Daeva is where she belongs.

She clears her throat. Her voice starts out hoarse, growing stronger with each word. "To *my* people." She throws me a childish scowl. "My mother served this country before me, and it has been a lifelong dream to live beside you and serve in the role of lordess. Most of you have known me since I was a youngling, and that should mean something."

Low murmurs filter through the crowd. The tone isn't optimistic. Animal instinct increases her desperation. "Kalliope wishes to repress others while exalting only some. How is this fair? I want this land to flourish, and you can only do that with someone willing to step up and make things right."

The Amicums shift impatiently. There are mutterings of disgust and disdain. The words don't equally resonate. Daeva either does not notice or does not care because she continues.

"If you allow me to execute Kalliope, we can move forward with the general plan of expansion, provisional licensing of growing—"

Her words stop short when a piece of dung's thrown at her feet. My gaze jerks to the crowd, scanning for the offender. No one appeared to move, but someone had to have thrown it. A flick of movement to the left and another piece of dung lands behind Daeva.

Their verdict is clear. The grin splitting my split lip is painful, but assuaged by her dismay.

A rain of excrement falls from every direction. It hits the sand with wet plops. A particularly large piece lands on top of Daeva's pale hair. She hisses and tries to dig it out, only to have one land on her arm.

The surrounding ground becomes shades of green and brown. She screams at the crowd.

"How *dare* you! I've defended you with my life. I'm dedicated to *you*." Her claims only further enrage the crowd. She's forced to stop when some flies into her mouth. I laugh.

Spitting out the shit, Daeva is furious, shaking a pointed finger at the stands. "You are all so *ungrateful*. How could you deny me—"

I tune her out. Looking up at the platform, I'm pleased to see Saira looking like a youngling given a sweet cake as a reward. Zenab's face shines with elation, and Legend stands proudly, offering an encouraging nod. Ginger stares at me, embers of unforgiving hate in her face.

Make it hurt, she hisses in my mind.

Gladly.

Realizing the inevitable, Daeva crumples. Now literally knee-deep in shit. Thin, graceful fingers clasp together as she begs, "Kalliope. Please. I am nothing but sorry. I did what I thought was right. You understand, right? It was for the *people*."

"You put Ilorna at risk for ambition. You murdered and harmed others for misguided beliefs and falsehoods." I sniff the air dramatically and sneer. "You stink of putrid lies." Finally, I let the wolf slowly take over, controlling the slow progression of fur and claws. Only the most powerful Amicums can do it, and I am feeling dramatic.

Before I give way to it entirely, I say, "When this is done, all records of you will be destroyed. Your name will be forbidden and eventually forgotten. Your legacy, from this moment forward, will be nothing but ashes upon stone."

She stares at my wolf in fear as I snap in her direction. The throbbing of my broken paw can't place a dent in my rage. The crowd roars and shifts into wolves and hounds, howling for blood. All around us, energy crackles with retribution.

And it's my job to deliver.

The coward scurries away, tears smearing the filth on her cheeks. She's on borrowed time and knows it. "Please, Kal, please. You don't have to do this. You have the power to spare me. Exile me. Let me go somewhere else and never return."

The wolf in me, my mother's wolf, has no pity for this prey. My paws burn in the hot sand, the heat battering my black fur. She holds her hands up placatingly as I stalk toward her slowly, savoring the sour taste of her fear. She flinches as my snarl flings spittle onto her face.

Daeva whips around and tries to bolt, spots rippling across her skin I'm faster. Leaping in the air, my wolf lands on Daeva's back with all four paws. Her face crunches into the sand. Ribs crack under my paws.

"Kal, *please*—"

My fangs sink into her skull, buckling under the pressure of my jaws. Like a cracked eggshell. A single moan of agony before permanent silence.

With one powerful jerk, her head severs from the spine. Keeping the momentum, I allow it to fly through the air. Blood drizzling from my maw, I watch it roll comically across the sand. Her face's forever frozen in an expression of horror. I feel *nothing*.

Then the entire arena howls as one. Recognizing me as their true lordess, the one worthy of the title.

I tilt my head back and join their cries of victory.

Chapter Thirty-Nine

Is That A Banana In His Lap?

Saira

It's impossible to explain the extreme relief coursing through my body as Kalliope's wolf exits the arena, meeting us in the hallway. The moment the gate closes, my arms are around her bloody neck. The smell of iron is repulsive, but the desperation to have her in my arms is stronger.

"Oh, goddess," I sob into her wet fur. Some of the wetness smears along my face. *She's alive.* "I thought you were going to die."

I squeeze even tighter, and the wolf whines.

"Gem," Legend says quietly. "She'd like to shift now."

"Oh." Letting go, I sit back as she shifts. Her arm's still broken, and she cradles it with the opposite arm. Yet, despite her injuries, her eyes shine with victory. The frenetic energy of battle comes off her in waves, making her more like a goddess of war than ever before.

"You were stunning," I breathe, coming to stand in front of her. "I've never seen anything like it."

Her grin is bloody, an untamed beast in human skin. "I'm ready for a drink, a fuck, and something filled with cheese."

Zenab comes up and lays a hand on her shoulder. "That was incredible, Kal. You showed Ilorna exactly who's most qualified to lead them."

Kalliope gives her a dry look. "That's one way to put it."

Legend chuckles and brings a hand to the small of her back, coaxing her forward. "Come, my love. Let's get you a healing tonic and a bath."

She grabs one of his hands, and he leads the group down the hallways. Ginger falls in step with me, bouncing on the balls of her feet.

"What did she say to you down there, Kal?" she asks, cheeks flushed with excitement.

Kalliope glances over her shoulder, her own cheeks flushed. "The usual words of bravado, but in the end, she begged."

"Damn," Ginger whines. "I wish we could've been closer."

"Any closer and we would have been in the battle," Zenab reminds her.

Ginger juts out her lower lip. "What would be wrong with that?"

"Bloodthirsty mare," Legend mutters, earning an insulting gesture from Ginger. He chuckles and lifts Kalliope's uninjured hand, brushing a kiss against her knuckles.

The same healer as before rushes up, offering another tonic. As Kalliope takes a swig, the healer wraps her injured arm in gauze. From what I've seen, the break will heal within an hour or so. It's a relief to know that seeing her in pain is temporary.

A servant comes up with a platter of drinks, her face flushed with excitement. "Your Grace, the celebratory drinks as requested."

Legend raises an eyebrow at Kalliope. She shrugs a shoulder, smirking. "I knew I'd need a drink after."

All of us grab a drink, the goblets full to the brim with clear liquid.

Zenab raises her cup, eyes shining with pride. "To Lordess Arnoux. May she continue to lead with kindness, ruthlessness, and fairness."

"To Lordess Arnoux," everyone intones, grinning ear to ear. Taking a sip, I gasp and sputter at the strength of the alcohol.

"Wha-what *is* this?" I ask, gagging from the unforgivable burn.

Ginger giggles, then takes a big swig of the devil water. All of them do. I'm the lightweight, apparently.

"It's persnickle, a rare celebratory drink," Kalliope explains, taking a sip of the drink as if it's only water.

Okay, then. It's a bit ironic that the first edible thing I truly dislike in Ilorna is a celebratory drink. Legend bumps my shoulder and jerks his chin at my still-full goblet.

"I'll drink it if you won't."

Curling a lip, I hand over my cup. "Be my guest."

We take a few more minutes to chat, allowing Kalliope to regale us with her perspective. My heart rate has barely begun to drop from witnessing it all, so the details make me a bit squeamish. I'm grateful when Kalliope finally announces she needs to go greet the waiting crowd.

I don't really understand what crowd she's referring to until we reach the main entrance to the coliseum. Amicums are already waiting outside, yelling out Kalliope's name like she's a celebrity. All that's missing is cameras flashing.

Legend sighs, unsurprised when she lets go of his hand and steps into the fray without a glance back. The Kalliope we know and love has returned. We exchange a look, and he gives a good-natured grin.

"She's going to be a moment; want a ride back?"

"Sure." I glance at Ginger and Zenab. "See you back at the manor?"

Ginger wastes no time in shifting. There's a shimmer and a white Pegasus with a chestnut mane stomps her hoof, nodding her head furiously. Zenab chuckles and nods, then sinks into the crowd of Kalliope's fans.

Legend leads me to an open space at the perimeter of the crowd. No one pays us any attention, which is perfectly fine. Today wasn't about me.

When we have enough space, he shifts into the manticore, his wings shifting to give me space to mount his sleek back. Adjusting my backpack, I slide on without an ounce of effort. When I'm comfortable, I tap his furry shoulder. He chuffs and bounds forward in wide, powerful strides. His beautiful wings flare out and pump furiously, boosting us impossibly high into the sky.

I close my eyes and experience it all. The wind in my hair. Sunshine heating my skin. His warm body under my splayed fingers.

I open my eyes and let the wind make my soul sing. Because right now, life is incredible. How many times will I be able to say I rode a manticore?

The trip is short, and Legend lands on silent paws with cat-like grace in front of the manor. I slide off and pat his shoulder. He purrs and butts his head into my cheek.

Scratching behind one of his ears, each bigger than my fist, I say, "You really are just a big kitty cat."

His purr turns into a rough chuffing. I step back as the air shimmers, and then the breathtaking male is in front of me, snorting with amusement. He leans down and pinches one of my ass cheeks, and I squeal, batting him away.

"Bad kitty."

Still laughing, we walk into the manor, and I assume we're going back to his room, but he leads me back to mine.

"Why are we here?" I ask as he opens the door and lets me go in first.

He closes the door behind us and looks at my backpack. "Because you need to put your things away."

True. Slinging the heavy thing off my shoulders, I carry it back to the armoire. Unbuckling my utility belt, I shove it next to a pair of boots.

Standing, I turn to him, feeling awkward. The room is quiet, minus the crackling fire that Meadow keeps burning day and night. He watches me, scanning my face for a clue to how I feel. After the anxiety, fear, and adrenaline, all I want to do is touch someone. Touch him.

Not at the expense of Kalliope being hurt or angry, though. Legend would undoubtedly do nothing to hurt her, so it's easy to trust he won't invite or start anything that might break what we've developed.

Sensing my apprehension — because of course he does — Legend smells his armpits and scrunches his nose. "I'm ready for a bath. Watching Kalliope fight for her life was one of the most stressful moments of my life. I've sweated through my clothes."

"Same," I admit. "Daeva put up a good fight."

348

He nods, heading toward my tub. It isn't as big as the one in his room, but it should be able to fit his broad shoulders. As he turns the faucet, he reaches for one of the many bottles and pours copious amounts of it into the water. Exhaustion isn't a strong enough word for how I feel, but it's soul-level tired. How's Kalliope? If anyone deserves a bath and a nap, it's her.

"Do you think she'll be back soon?"

Legend slips his shirt off, tossing it to the floor. "Probably." He pauses and then grins. "Maybe. She takes her duty seriously. Always has, even when we were younglings."

Taking off my clothes, I ask, "Was it weird growing up with someone you eventually became romantically involved with?"

He frowns, slipping off his pants. My attention immediately zeroes in on his length. Even when not aroused, the size intimidates. Catching my glance, his tongue flicks out, swiping against his bottom lip. As if he's already imagining the taste of me. "No. It felt natural, actually. Even in our youth, I felt protective of her. Watching her step into her power and surpass everyone was like watching a butterfly unfurl its wings for the first time."

He steps into the tub, taking up most of the space on one side. Holding a hand out for me, I'm able to ease in on the other side, nestling between his long legs.

I scoop bubbles onto my body, enjoying the way they pop and tickle my skin. "But when did you decide to take it beyond being protective?"

His mouth twists in thought, his focus far away in a memory. "When I passed my youngling training, I already knew being her Guardian was all I wanted to be. So I went off to Guardian training. We were separated for three years."

"Who protected her during that time?"

Legend's eyebrows sink together in irritation, like he can't stand the thought of anyone else protecting her. "Random Guardians."

"Did she sleep with them?"

"I don't know, and I don't care."

My brow shoots up. "Truly?"

349

"Truly. I might be her consort, but she's free to be intimate with whoever she wants, and I am, too."

"She doesn't get jealous?"

He shrugs, splashing water. "Of course not. She knows I'm dedicated to her. Enjoying the flesh of others is about experiencing the full breadth of life. It doesn't reflect loyalty if we are open and honest about it."

The freedom in their dynamic relationship is beautiful. They make it look natural, like it's how relationships should be. Being raised in a society that perceives jealousy as a positive trait in relationships, it's almost unbelievable they don't experience jealousy, too.

Legend dunks his head under the water. When he pops back up, his long strands are slicked back. Bubbles speckle his face, neck, and chest.

I lean forward and pop an enormous bubble under one of his eyes. He flashes me a grin. Pointing to the bottles of shampoo, he says, "Want a head massage?"

"Do Amicums shift for fun?"

He guffaws, the expanse of chest muscles heaving. "You're a quick learner, Gem. Already sharing common Amicum idioms." He grabs a bottle of shampoo and twirls his finger. I turn and squeak when one of his big arms wraps around my waist and tugs me closer.

Oh, my. Is that a banana in his lap, or is he just happy to see me?

Choosing to ignore his growing thickness, I ask, "So do you sleep with others often?"

He fills a cup of water and runs it over my sweaty strands of hair. I duck my head back to make it easier for him. "Not really. Rarely without her. I'm extremely picky and only attracted to certain kinds of sexual partners."

My eyes close as he pours shampoo on my hair and works it into my scalp. His talented fingers are a blessing from the heavens.

His words sink in. "You're picky? How?"

"Well." His voice grows husky, and his fingers slow, pressing and circling through my hair. "I'm attracted to strong females."

"Mmhmm." My mind goes blank as chills run down my spine. I've always been a sucker for head massages.

"And ..." He leans forward, shifting my hips into his even more. Warm breath tickles my ears as he continues. "I'm attracted to females who are comfortable with their own bodies. Willing to explore all the pleasure their bodies can offer. Not everyone can truly step into their power in such a way."

My lungs freeze, his words sending a zing of need straight to my core. I want to identify with his words. The desire to be more than I am right now is overwhelming.

He leans back and washes the shampoo out. When I can finally breathe deep enough, I ask, "Do you think that could be me one day?"

The only sign he's not pleased with the question is the pause of his fingers rubbing soap into my shoulders. "Saira, what makes you think that isn't you already?"

Insecurity unfurls, turning into sticky feelings of inadequacy. "Because I'm so inexperienced. I don't like my body. People have judged it my entire life. I'm not built like ..." I think about how most of the Amicums I've seen are graceful and slender. "I'm not beautiful like those here."

Water sluices down my shoulders, down my back, and he says nothing. Fear and doubt press down on me, and suddenly, I don't want to be here anymore. I'm embarrassing myself. It's why he won't say anything. Doing this without Kalliope was a mistake. We should wait for her.

I lean forward, about to move away, but one of his hands spreads against my soft belly, keeping me in place.

The emotions have taken over, though. Memories of slicing comments from peers and family carving into me, the invisible scars now splitting open. A tear slides down my cheek. I feel absolutely bonkers with these emotions suddenly appearing. He's going to think I'm one card short of a deck, bursting into tears randomly.

"Let me go, please," I plead, biting my quivering lip.

The hand disappears instantly, and I move to the other side of the tub, curling my knees to my chest. I can't even look him in the eye.

JENNA AVERY

Shame courses through me, digging its claws deep into my heart. This is humiliating, randomly losing my shit like this. There's so much else going on. So much death. Betrayals on levels I'll never understand.

And here I am, crying about how pudgy I feel.

"Saira." Legend sounds so patient, and I can't stand it. Now I'm the antithesis of what he wants. He'll never want me ever again.

Tears mix with the bathwater as they drop onto the surface.

"I'm sorry," I whisper. "This is absolutely stupid of me."

Chin in my hands, I look up at him finally. His expression is full of nothing but compassion.

"Saira, it's okay to cry. Someone, or someones, has hurt the absolute Afterworld out of you. It sounds like where you come from, females are treated like objects, viewed as broken if they don't fit some idealistic construct. Crying sounds like a reasonable response."

Taking a shuddering breath, I nod. "That's exactly what it's like."

He shakes his head. "Such things would never be acceptable here. You're judging Amicums based on the warriors you're around. Most of the ones you spend time with are naturally built for guardianship and battles. But Amicums come in so many body types. And not a single one of them is judged for being on either side of the spectrum."

My tears dry up, and I unfold my body. "Really?"

With a solemn nod, he motions for me to come back to him. "Yes, really. Now come here. I have something to show you."

Scooting forward, I go to turn again, but he stops me. "No, face me."

Oh. He grabs my hips and lifts me up slightly, adjusting me to sit on his lap. He's still hard, pressing into the soft folds of my belly. My breasts brush against the hard muscles of his chest, the smattering of hair scintillating. He shifts me closer by bringing my hands to my back and tucking me forward.

It's an intimate position, flushing our bodies together, aligning us perfectly. His fingers graze my back, up and down. Soothing my emotions until they're barely a rumble in my mind.

Black eyelashes frame shamrock-green eyes, searching my face for any other flicker of pain.

"Saira," he whispers. "I'm in love with you. I think you're beautiful, just as you are. Whether you gain muscles as big as a Clydesdale or become willowy as a doe, I'm going to want you."

He's in love with me. Both of them are, and yet ... it's impossible to say it back. It's a line I can't seem to cross yet. Soon enough, I'm leaving them and this is a piece of me I'm struggling with leaving behind. But my heart and soul is right there with them. Completely.

Legend doesn't pause or wait, expecting me to say it back. His hands come to my rear, pushing my hips forward to grind against him. I gasp at the sensation of him sliding between my thighs.

Instead, I focus on the mind-blowing sensations of Legend gripping my hips and rocking me back and forth. "I love how brave you are." Feeling him slide back and forth between my slickness brings forth another gasp. "I love how smart you are." His fingers tighten, digging into my ample flesh. "I love how funny you can be."

One of his hands comes to the back of my head and tilts my face until I'm looking at him. Eyes glazed with lust, he feathers a kiss against my lips.

My sanity is reaching its limits as he shoves me so far forward, the tip of his cock prods at my entrance. His kiss smothers my moan, chuckling in his throat as I jerk my hips, trying to sink onto him. His words have triggered something deep inside of me, and my instincts demand him inside me immediately. To claim. To enjoy.

"Please," I beg. "*Please.*"

He smirks and teases my entrance again. "Are you sure? It might hurt at first."

My nod is so desperate, it might break my neck. "I need you."

Without another word, he lines us up perfectly and guides my body down his length. My body stretches easily at first, ready and eager, but the further I sink onto him, the more resistance there is.

"Breathe," he murmurs. "Look at me."

My world narrows down to eyes the color of spring as he works himself into me. I whimper, and he kisses me slowly, diving into my mouth like my oxygen will be his own.

Finally, each intense inch is in me, and he's fully seated inside. Spreading and filling me. I never knew it could be this way, offering a sensation of completion.

"Take what you want from me, Saira," he whispers against my mouth. So I do. Slow at first, I gyrate against him. The first couple of times feel strange, the way he pushes against my inner walls. My body liquifies at the stimuli. Eager for more.

My speed picks up, and he grabs my hips, helping me. Guiding me. He peers down through the water to watch our joining. I do the same, enthralled with the way my body rides his.

He tilts my hips, allowing my swollen clit to rub against his pelvis. It electrifies everything, blinding me with euphoria.

"Legend," I pant. "I'm so fucking close."

"Give it to me, Gem. Give me all of you."

Our speed is so uncontrollable, water splashes everywhere. Bubbles cover the floor and walls. Half the tub is emptied by the time my orgasm rips reality from me, arching my back, thrusting my breasts in his face. He takes the opportunity to grab one in his mouth, and he bites down on my nipple, roaring with his own release.

I'm buried in pleasure, filled with impossible gratitude to the universe for allowing me to know what it means to be cherished. Every morsel of insecurity and doubt ignites and turns into ashes.

By the time I come down from the sense of bliss, I find him watching me with wonder.

"You're so fucking stunning." He crushes my mouth to his, possessive and dominating. For the love of gods, I already want more.

"She's definitely stunning, and that was also one of the fucking hottest things I've ever seen."

I gasp and twist to find Kalliope leaning against the wall, biting her bottom lip. She looks bloodied, exhausted, and ... *very* interested in what she's looking at.

Chapter Forty

Piper Is Going To Be Ecstatic

Unfortunately, there's zero room for her in the tub and almost no water left. I laugh as Legend helps me shift off him and wince at the loss of him inside me. I'm going to need him again. Soon.

He gets out of the tub first, grabbing our towels. "How was your victory lap?"

Kalliope looks less wired than she was an hour ago. Now, exhaustion etches deep into the lines on her face. She pushes off the wall and shrugs. "Not much different from the other times I've had to put an overreaching whelp in their place."

Legend wraps his towel around his waist, not even bothering to wipe water off his limbs. Instead, he towels me off, trailing kisses down my belly as he squats to dry off my thighs.

Between kisses, he says, "Would you like a bath, Your Grace?"

Kalliope chuckles darkly. "I need a bath, a meal, and a three-day nap."

Tucking the towel around my breasts, Legend kisses the top of my forehead and turns to Kalliope. "I think we can make all three happen. Let's get you cleaned up."

Bolstered with renewed energy, she's naked in five seconds flat. Bruises and half-healed cuts speckle her body, but she doesn't even seem to notice.

Legend does, though, running his fingers over the ones on her neck and sternum. "Want me to get a healing pack?"

She shakes her head, and he turns to restart the bath. The floor squishes with his footsteps, the large puddles of water still needing to be mopped up.

Kalliope steps into one puddle and looks down. "Honestly, that's impressive."

"What can I say? Things get wet around me."

Kalliope and I glare at Legend, who gives us a shit-eating grin and shrugs.

After cleaning up the sopping mess, I get dressed while Kalliope sinks into the tub with a loud hiss. Legend stays with her, murmuring words as he pampers her. And to my surprise, jealousy doesn't appear. She deserves someone to love her the way he does.

And for the first time in my life, it's something I truly want for myself.

Piper is going to be *ecstatic*.

Smiling, I pull on a shirt and pants. As I'm buckling my belt, there's a knock on the door. Opening it, I can't help but show Meadow the happiest of smiles.

"Oh, Meadow!" I swing the door open wide enough to give her a hug. The last time I saw her, all of us were in shock at what had just happened.

She returns the hug. "I'm so glad you're alright, Miss. Do you need anything? Healing balms or tonics?"

"No, I'm okay for now. I look worse than I feel right now." Not entirely true, but I've already taken multiple tonics. It doesn't work as well on human bodies, so I'm afraid of overdosing.

There's a splash behind me, and Kalliope giggles. Meadow glances over my shoulder with a knowing look. Suddenly remembering why she's here, she straightens. "I've come to see if there's anything Her Grace needs; I heard the battle was riveting."

I grin. "'Riveting' is certainly one word for it. Kalliope said she's hungry. Can you bring some food and wine?"

She gives the smallest of curtsies. "Of course, miss. I shall return momentarily."

I close the door and turn around, catching Legend toweling off Kalliope, then wrapping it around her torso. When he's satisfied it's snugly tucked into itself, he wraps one around his waist. She peers up at him adoringly, and he presses a hand against her cheek, rubbing a thumb over one of the fading bruises under her eye. They're looking at each other like not even all the stars in the universe could distract them.

Walking over to my bag as quietly as possible, I pull out my camera. Quickly adjusting my settings, I bring it to my eye.

It clicks, capturing the look between them forever. The reverie's broken when they hear the sound. Both sets of eyes turn to look at me, curious.

Holding up the camera, I cringe. "Sorry, I was taking a photo."

Kalliope reaches for one of my brushes and runs it through her wet hair. "What is a fo-toe?"

Standing, I hand it to Legend when he draws closer. "It freezes moments in time."

His brows shoot up. "What does that mean?"

I tilt the camera to press a button to show him the photo. His jaw drops with shock. "Magnificent. You've had this the whole time?"

I grin. "Yeah, but I never wanted to take it out. Didn't want people to think I was stealing their souls or anything."

Kalliope reaches for a robe hanging on the wall. Padding over to us, she peers over his arm. Before I can stop him, his thumb moves the dial, and photos of my family come up.

"Wow." Kalliope's eyes shoot to mine. "Who are they?"

I stumble back, not wanting to look. "My family."

Kalliope frowns, but Legend, so enthralled, misses my reaction. "They seem so happy." His thumb pauses, and he tilts the camera. "Who's this? She looks like you."

It's Piper, sticking out her tongue with a kooky grin, holding up a peace sign. It was taken six months before we separated, lying in her bed. I'm next to her, holding up the camera, kissing her cheek.

It's like a punch in the gut, air whooshing out of me. She's so achingly beautiful and happy at that moment. The day before, Dad confirmed he had enough supplies to create two Scouts — but no more.

Later in the evening, I had to break the news to her.

Exhaustion sits on my soul, dragging down any sense of happiness I'd gathered. There isn't even enough in me to cry. Staggering to my chaise, I drop onto the cushion like a stone.

Legend places the camera near my bag and rushes over. "What's wrong?"

Kalliope beats him to me, squatting next to the chaise. "Saira, what happened?"

Numb all over, I point to the camera resting on the bag. "I haven't had the guts to even look at those. Because I knew it was going to hurt too much."

And my fear's confirmed.

Legend looks pained. "I was unaware. I'm so sorry."

Exhaling a deep breath, I try to pretend it's no big deal by waving him off. "It's not your fault. I wasn't thinking."

Kalliope puts a hand on my shoulder. "Why don't you want to look at the photos? Isn't your family the whole reason you're here?"

My emotions are too raw right now with everything that has been happening in the last three days. The Vulturians. Finally having sex. Kalliope almost dying. And now this. It's too much.

A lone tear breaks free, and I wipe it away. "Yeah, but it's agonizing. I miss them so much, you know? Piper's my best friend. We're only a year apart in age, and we grew up together."

Kalliope wipes another tear rushing down my cheek. "I understand completely. Piper is important to you, and even if you'll be able to get back to her one day, you still had to leave a version of her to die, which is awful, no matter how you look at it."

There's a knock, and Legend moves to answer it. Meadow has arrived with food and wine.

Kalliope rubs a hand against my cheek. "Saira, maybe it's time you looked at them. It's a blessing to have photos of the ones you love. Plus,

I'm positive Legend and I would love to learn about the people you're jumping worlds to save."

I laugh out a sob. "Okay, sounds good."

So that's how we spent the rest of the day: eating, drinking, and going through the happy moments of my family. When I'm all cried out and the food is all gone, I offer to show Kalliope what a movie is.

Turns out, action films are her favorite. Shocker, I know.

Chapter Forty-One

Doing It For The Plot

"Eyes up here," Zenab orders, pointing two fingers to my face, then hers. She flips the sword in her hand like it's an extension of herself. The sword in my hand is *not* an extension of myself, that's for damn sure.

It's heavy, and my palms are so sweaty, I keep dropping it. My shoulders shake with every attempt at lifting it. With only three weeks of training under my belt, I'm still a newbie, but over a month ago, I wouldn't have even been able to pick up this sword.

Getting into literal fighting shape is nothing like the movies.

It's impossible to show on the screen how the lungs burn after running for thirty minutes. No matter how good they are, actors can't show the pounding headaches and dry mouths caused by learning footwork for another hour.

Licking my dry lips, I wince as my left bicep cramps.

"I'm trying," I seethe, gritting my teeth with the effort. "I'm pretty sure my arms are about to fall off!"

"I could go grab a mace?"

"I don't even know what that is, but no, thank you."

Zenab's gray curls sway in the wind as she cocks her head and raises her sword. "Then continue."

She's merciless. I asked for this, after all. I ignore the burning in my shoulders and raise the sword.

It's been two weeks since all the chaos went down, and now I'm back to my normal training routine. Ginger's focused on rebuilding the stables, so she hasn't been around as much. Every day, it's Zenab training me in the art of stabby-stabs in the morning, and Kalliope teaching me how to ride and fight various shifts in the afternoon. Legend appears randomly, mostly to look handsome and give words of encouragement.

In my heart, I know it's time to leave. Ilorna has been home for almost two months, and this kind of training helps strengthen me for the upcoming unknowns, but the time to leave is approaching.

As my body shakes, Zenab raises an unimpressed eyebrow. Her springy gray curls are tied back into a bushy bun, and the loose shirt she's wearing already has sweat stains. Yet, when she notices me slowing down, she sucks on her teeth derisively and points her sword.

"You can handle doing this for fifteen more minutes."

"Fine," I bite out. "But my reward better be something sweet."

She smirks. "I'm sure Her Grace will be happy to oblige."

"I said sweet, not spicy." I stick out my tongue.

Her laugh is loud and full. "Fair enough." She points her sword at me. "Arms up!"

By the time she grants mercy, I'm barely able to reach up and wipe sweat off my forehead. Flopping down into the dirt, I take deep gulps of air to steady my thundering heart. Zenab takes a seat beside me, folding a leg underneath her butt while leaning an arm against a propped up knee. She takes a sip out of a waterskin before passing it to me.

"It takes time, Saira. You're doing well, considering."

I sit up and take deep gulps of the water, then pass it back. "Considering what? I sat in a lab chair for years?"

She laughs. "Well, yes. You've only been here for a few weeks. There hasn't been a ton of time for you to focus on training."

I suck in a deep breath, willing my heart to slow down. "I have to leave soon."

Zenab sips from the waterskin and puts the cap back on. "Where will you go?"

"I'm not sure," I admit. "Wherever I end up, I guess."

Last week, at an intimate dinner, I told Ginger and Zenab who I am and what my mission entails. Neither was surprised that I didn't belong here; Ginger was smug, mentioning something about winning a bet. It's been a relief, being myself and not worrying about being considered an alien or witch.

Zenab kicks her legs out and leans back on her hands. "Are you scared?"

Massaging my sore forearm, I nod. "Absolutely. This is my fifth stop and the most pleasant. Which isn't saying much, since I almost died multiple times and got kidnapped." After a pause, I add in a whiney tone, "And eaten. Things keep trying to eat me."

Zenab chuckles. "Life would bore without some thrills."

"I could live without those kinds of thrills," I mutter, inspecting a blister on my palm. "Why can't I get dropped off at an ocean where whales talk and I can turn into a mermaid or something?"

"Who says you won't?" she asks, giving me a half smile.

"Fair enough." I look at the sun; it's almost peaked in the sky. "Please tell me the torture's done for the day."

She stands and holds out a hand, grasping my arm to lift me up. "Yes, for today. Kal will kill me if you aren't ready in time for the trip this afternoon. You better hurry and find her."

Nerves flutter at the mention of the trip. Kalliope mentioned wanting to take me somewhere this afternoon, but maintained her refusal to say where.

After giving her a quick hug of thanks, I leave the training area and head back to my room. Finally, after weeks, I'm able to get through this brick maze without getting lost.

As I walk through the hallways, I wave at familiar faces. After the Scrap, the resident Amicums started going out of their way to get to know me. Slowly, this place has felt like home. Which is comforting and alarming. Ilorna, despite the drama I've experienced, offers a lot of charm. Even though I can't shift — and trust me, I wish I could — the culture is still warm and open enough; I think the family would thrive here.

The anxiety of leaving is consuming at this point. Every day, I go through my pack and make sure everything is in place. My travel outfit's been cleaned thoroughly and is ready for me to slip on again. It's more loose than it was a few weeks ago, but I'm not surprised. Daily workouts and no junk food work wonders.

After a quick bath and bites of the food left in my room, I hurry to the courtyard to meet Kalliope.

The afternoon has turned overcast, and the ground is still a little muddy from the rain earlier this morning, encasing me with the scent of petrichor. It's a scent that will always calm my racing mind and make my heart happy.

The sound of boots on gravel interrupts my thoughts. I turn to watch Kalliope striding over, a wide grin splitting her beautiful face. She's been so down these last couple of weeks, seeing the familiar swagger makes me return the grin with one of my own.

She gives me a brief kiss on the cheek, making my heart skip. "You ready?"

"Are you going to tell me where we're going?"

"Nope." She pops the P with a sly smile. I'm surprised she's picking up my mannerisms. "Better to be a surprise. Now hop on."

The air shimmers and expands, revealing a black wyvern shaking its massive body like a dog, groaning. Kalliope snakes her horned head in my direction, chuffing in demand as she slips a massive shoulder to the ground.

My arms cry a little as I scurry up the scaled arm, but I push through the burning sensation. Grabbing a spike for leverage, I swing a leg over the meaty shoulder blades. It still feels precarious, simply because, well, there's a ten-ton lizard between my legs.

Suddenly, at eye level with the roof of the manor, I look around us. Even with the sun hiding, the gardens explode with rich greens and flowers of all colors. Amicums focusing on gardening lift their gaze and waves at us. I returned the greeting.

A rumble vibrates underneath me, bringing shivers down my spine. I playfully slap her shoulder. "Knock it off and let's get out of here."

She chuffs again, taking crashing steps toward the field next to the courtyard. When there's enough space, she rears up and spreads her midnight wings, slamming against the air until gravity has no choice but to release us. I lower my torso close to her neck, letting my center of gravity keep me in place as we take to the skies.

Once we ease from vertical to horizontal, I'm able to sit up and look around. Now the land seems as familiar as the back of my hand. The forest stretches for miles. The homes dot along the estate where the staff live.

The overcast clouds are lower than I realized, and we're gradually sifting through them. When I was a child, I daydreamed about touching clouds. I imagined they were as fluffy and tangible as cotton candy. I hold out a hand, letting my fingers pierce the misty rain droplets.

There's nothing up here to pierce the peaceful silence. A part of me wishes I'd never discovered what the joy of flying can bring. For the umpteenth time, I wish there were a way to shift. I've stuffed samples into my pack for Dad with the silliest hope that he could create a technology to turn me into a shifter.

A ridiculous thought.

For a while, Kalliope and I cruise, reaching the sunny skies above the layer of clouds. Then she tips a little, banking toward something I can't see. We're sliding back into the clouds, and I tremble against the chill. Thank the gods for these leathers.

Once we're back through the seamless blanket of gray, I spot a small town in the distance. Some buildings look charred, but people move around with purpose. I recognize the town center with its tiny merchant stalls and statue of a bear in the center.

The town we helped save all those weeks ago.

Knots twist themselves in my gut. I never expected to return here, but Kalliope seems to think it's a good idea. Why?

Before I'm ready, we're landing in the same field on the outskirts of town. She dips her shoulder, and I slide off, landing with new-found grace.

A moment later, Kalliope stands in front of me, cheeks ruddy with windburn. She's smiling, but it falls when she sees my frustration.

"Why are we here?" I demand.

Her brow furrows as she tilts her head. "I thought you might want to see the progress of a town you helped save."

All this town reminds me of is how weak I was. It was a catalyst for growth, but I don't remember the moment fondly. "Why would you want to bring me where I almost died?"

Understanding softens her expression. "Ah, well then, why don't I show you?"

Before I can insist on a better answer, she's walking past me toward the town. People noticed us landing, so a group is already gathering to greet us. Many are eager to offer goods and food, praising Kalliope for her protection and support. She declines them but welcomes hugs and handshakes.

I trail behind her, begrudgingly accepting the same greetings. Touching so many strangers isn't on my list of favorite things to do. As we walk between the buildings, I observe repairs in full force. While some homes are still ashes, a few are freshly built. These people have chosen to move forward from their pain and embrace change. There's something admirable about this choice.

We reach the town center, where a larger group has gathered. The people cheer, rushing forward. My pulse races wildly, and I step closer to Kalliope. Sensing my hesitation, she grabs one of my hands, weaving our fingers together.

"Don't fret, they're just grateful. No one will harm us," she promises.

And she's right. We're handed food. I accept a buttery roll and almost swallow it whole. It's so good. Some even try to shove jewelry into our palms and pockets. It feels impossible to say no, especially as they do it without asking.

Finally, we come to a stop at the bear statue. A plaque attached to the stone base reads, *Dedicated to Noraya Earthbane, for keeping the town of Jarice safe from harm.*

Kalliope notices me reading the plaque and says, "That's Legend's mother."

I stare up at the roaring bear in awe. I didn't even know Legend's last name was Earthbane. Noraya seemed fearsome, all nine feet of her. "She saved these people?"

"Noraya was their head Guardian during the war, defending it from multiple Vulturian attacks. She perished in a battle, in bear form, but not before killing the entire patrol who stopped for what they thought would be some fun."

The bear looks familiar. I notice the patch of star-shaped fur chiseled into the metal. "You shifted into her during the Scrap."

She nods. "It felt right. Without her sacrifice, so many more would have died."

I want to ask more questions about the female who gave Legend life, but we're interrupted by a woman stepping forward from the crowd, holding a basket of wildflowers.

Her braided hair's loosely held by a red ribbon. Next to her is a little girl clinging to the apron tied around the woman's waist. It takes a moment to recognize them without dirt, soot, and blood coating their bodies. But then it hits me.

Meegan and her mom.

Now I understand why we're here. I squeeze Kalliope's hand in silent gratitude. She returns the silent sentiment, then releases her hold to accept the basket.

Kalliope's fingers graze the petals. "Thank you for your generosity."

The woman nods her acceptance of the gratitude, but her focus is entirely on me. The urge to look away is strong, but I find it in myself to lift my chin and meet her gaze.

The crowd goes silent, watching in anticipation. As if this moment was planned.

Meegan peers up at me with those big eyes, sucking her thumb anxiously. Resting my hands on my thighs, I lean forward until we're eye level. She's tinier than memory serves.

"It's good to see you, Meegan."

She removes her thumb from her mouth with a wet pop. "You're the one who saved me."

I nod. "Yep, that's me. I'm glad you're okay."

She nods eagerly. "Yes, Mama says you're an angel." Her eyes scan behind me. "I don't see any wings. Are you really an angel?"

The question shocks me. My mouth opens and closes. How the hell do you answer this kind of question? Finally, I say, "No, I'm just a person. Like you. I did what I knew was right."

Meegan gives a toothy grin, revealing two missing front teeth. "I want to be an angel like you one day."

I boop her nose. She giggles. "Then make sure to do what's right at all times."

Turning solemn, she nods. "I promise."

I straighten. "Good. When I come back, I'm eager to hear about all the things you've done."

"Thank you so much," her mother says, tears shimmering in her eyes. "She's my only daughter, and her father died before she was even born — she's my everything." The woman swallows thickly. "I am in your debt, always."

Unable to figure out what to say next, I nod my head, neither agreeing nor disagreeing. I can't make saving her daughter a situation worth a favor, but it seems to give her relief that I appear to be agreeing. Without another word, she and Meegan blend back into the crowd.

The rest of our visit is spent with Kalliope asking what they need and how the Amicums can help. By the time we're heading back to the field, I'm emotionally exhausted.

Right before she shifts, Kalliope turns to face me. "Are you okay with us visiting the town? I needed to check in with them and figured you might enjoy coming to see how they're doing."

I glance over my shoulder back at the town. "I'm ashamed to say I haven't thought about them. So much has happened since the attack."

Kalliope steps away from me to shift, but not before she says, "I thought it would be good for you to understand the difference you can make, even with a single choice."

The wyvern shimmers into existence, and I'm climbing onto her back, trying to digest the afternoon. When this trip first started, I didn't know how it would turn out. Sure, there were concerns about being eaten or sucked into a black hole. Maybe being blown into a million atoms and failing entirely. Those seem like feasible outcomes, albeit not ideal.

Saving people? Falling in love? Neither existed in mine nor Dad's imaginations. Having this wonderful female not only saving my life, but showing how I can affect others positively? It's mind-blowing.

I want to save my family, but maybe it's time to view this trip differently. Now that I've seen enough to know that whatever comes next, it's easy to accept things will be nothing like I expected. Collecting data is still vital, but maybe I can view this as a personal adventure. Seek out the adventure as I complete the mission.

Do it for the plot, right?

Chapter Forty-Two

The Kitchen Never Leaves The Heart

Today, I'm telling Legend and Kalliope it's time for me to go ... in three days.

It's been almost two months since I landed in Ilorna, and I can't lie to myself anymore: I've overstayed my time here. This experience has been wonderful, training during the day and spending time with them at night.

Sometimes, it's easy to forget my purpose. To sink into the day-to-day challenges, working toward something tangible. Saving my family is more of an abstract idea and far less tangible than the sensation of a sword in my hand or spending endless hours in bed with my partners. It's the first time in my life I've allowed myself to focus on my wants and needs.

That's become the issue, though. As the days pass, so does my motivation to leave. The further The Mission slips from my mind. It was something I thought about all day, every day, and now ... now I think about it maybe once a day.

Yesterday during dinner, Kalliope mentioned my leaving eventually, and for a split second, my brain couldn't comprehend what she meant.

When it dawned on me, shame ate me alive. It's not that I forgot The Mission, but rather, I've been enjoying living my life. After years in school and labs, it's been wonderful spending every day outside, getting to know my body, experiencing lust and love, and enjoying existence.

The truth was undeniable, though, when I realized how far I'd strayed from The Mission. My instincts tell me I have enough samples and documentation. There are other places in Ilorna I could see, but it's unnecessary to present a well-rounded argument for bringing the family here. Which means it's time to go.

The decision to leave fills me with dread and excitement. I'm not sure how Kalliope and Legend will respond, although it'll undoubtedly be supportive. I pondered all night how to tell them. Finally, in the early hours of the morning, while wrapped up in their limbs, I realized I wanted to share something of my life with them, as they have with me.

I look over to memorize Legend's angelic features relaxed in sleep. His mouth is parted as he breathes in deeply, the exhalation tickling the hair above my ear. On my other side is Kalliope, her muscular arm laying over my chest. Her soft, naked body curls around mine, keeping me toasty warm. The three of us sleep in the nude, and let me say, waking up to him without clothing on is transcendent.

The love I have for both has deepened these past few weeks, but the words stay tucked in a corner of my heart. I won't dare say the words. I can't. It'll hurt too much, especially if I'm never going to be with them again. Neither seems bothered that I haven't said it back. They never pause and wait for me to say it. It makes me feel like I'm a coward; I'm not sure I deserve them. The very least I can do is break it to them gently.

Getting antsy, ready to get this conversation over with, I squirm between them. Instantly, Legend's eyes flutter open, flicking over my face, making sure everything is okay. Then a smile curls his kissable lips, and one of his hands settles on my belly.

"Good morning, Gem."

At the rumble of his voice, Kalliope stirs. Long nails press into my torso as she stretches like a cat and pulls me further into her. Her forehead nuzzles my mass of curls, and a deep purr rumbles in her chest.

This is my favorite way to wake up.

I trail a hand along Legend's arm, loving the valleys and curves of muscles. I spent my life not touching men, and now I can't seem to stop reveling in the silky steel of his body. "Mornin'. I have a surprise for you both today."

He perks up a bit at that. A curl falls across his forehead, enhancing his boyish grin. "Oh?" Deft fingers walk down to the apex of my thighs. My back arches when two of his fingers split to trail along the seam of my core. "Does it have anything to do with you using me as a chair today?"

As his finger finds the perfect spot, I gasp at the shooting pleasure lighting up my nerves. "No? Yes? M-m-maybe?"

One of his long fingers sinks into my body, and stars glitter in my vision. He shifts more onto his side, resting on his palm as he watches my expression. Kalliope's eyes are still closed, but her hand roves up to one of my breasts, gathering it in her hand and massaging it. Legend's thickening cock presses into my hip, and my hand can't resist wrapping around the hot flesh, smiling as he jerks in my grasp.

"Gem ..." His tone is a warning. He adds a second finger, pumping into me with steady, forceful thrusts. My thighs part all on their own, allowing him to deepen.

Kalliope's hand comes up to my face and tilts my head toward her, bringing me into a slow, sensual kiss. My whole body softens as they take over. Legend's mouth descends on one of my breasts as his thumb presses into my clit, moving it in sync with his fingers pumping. His hips thrust sensually, and I tighten my hold around his cock. Legend groans against my breast, biting my nipple.

I moan and shove my hips up, already desperate for him to fill me even more. He shifts to hover over me, and Kalliope shifts over to make space for his thick thigh. He swiftly replaces his fingers with that glorious, thick cock with one hard thrust. I groan into Kalliope's mouth. Legend pushes up my knees, watching himself slide in and out of me.

Kalliope breaks the kiss and brings two of her fingers to my lips. Obediently, I let her shove them into my mouth, sucking and licking them until they're covered in spit. Her expression is devilish as she brings them to my clit. The sensation shoots bolts of electricity skittering across my body. Legend thrusts faster, his fingers digging into my thighs, undoubtedly leaving marks.

"Cum for me, Gem," he commands. Kalliope draws one of my earlobes into her mouth and gently suckles it. I gasp for oxygen as the sensations overtake my body. Lifting my hips to allow Legend to get deeper, he brings a hand to each ass cheek, holding my hips up so he can slam into me harder than ever. Sweat coats his chest, beads dripping down his abs. He's transfixed on where we're joined, face full of concentration.

His enthrallment is my undoing. My orgasm tears into me like a tornado, decimating my awareness as pleasure explodes through my limbs, lighting up every nerve ending.

"That's it, baby," Kalliope murmurs in my ear, her fingers never slowing down. "Give him your pleasure."

Through the pulsing waves of orgasm, I hear Legend growl and slam into me so hard, the ferocity rocks my entire body upward. A scream rips from me, and the orgasm intensifies on the final pulse.

Then my body's a limp noodle, the orgasm having jellied every muscle possible. Legend's breathing hard, gently lowering my hips to the mattress. It feels like a loss as he slips out, sitting back on his heels. Kalliope's fingers slow down, then trail away from my core. She brings them up to her mouth and licks them clean. My cheeks burn with the salaciousness of it, but it's also the sexiest thing ever.

"Well," I say breathlessly. "Good morning to you both."

Kalliope rolls to her belly, then arches her hips up, stretching her arms forward like a cat. Legend's gaze homes in on her bare ass, the endless hunger for her reappearing. His hand lashes out, smacking one of her ass cheeks. She grins over her shoulder and spreads her legs. An invitation he's too weak to resist. We love a good simp, and Legend is one of the best.

With a mischievous bite of his lip, Legend says, "Almost, but not quite yet."

After the pre-breakfast festivities, the three of us get dressed for the day, but when Kalliope asks if I'd like an escort to training, I shake my head.

Opening the bedroom door, I step into the hallway. "I'm skipping training today. I want to surprise you both for lunch. Can you meet me in the kitchen at noon?"

Legend and Kalliope exchange a look. Kalliope tilts her head, furrowing her brow.

"The kitchen? Whatever for?"

I give them a mischievous smile. If I'm able to make the dish I want to, it'll be a delectable surprise. "You'll just have to wait and see. I promise you'll love it. Just point the way to the kitchen." Despite my weeks here, I've never been to the kitchen. With a sheepish chuckle, I ask, "Um, where's the kitchen?"

Legend closes the door behind him and points down the hallway. "The kitchens are that way. Ask a servant if you get lost."

Kalliope gives me a doubtful look, combing her fingers through her tousled hair. "Ellie might not take kindly to your meddling in her space."

"She'll be fine. Ellie will be delighted." Legend doesn't exactly sound positive as he picks a stray hair from the sleeve of her shirt between two fingers, then allows it to flutter to the ground. Catching my uncomfortable expression, he flashes me a grin with sharp canines. "Personally, I want whatever Saira is concocting."

I grin and begin walking in the direction he pointed. "Thanks. See you soon."

It's still early, so the manor is quiet save for the random sound of disembodied coughs and the clatter of items echoing down the hallways. I take my time, pausing to admire paintings I haven't spent time examining before. Amicum culture celebrates art, if the vast amount decorating the manor is any indication. The statues and busts punctuating the floorboards are carefully chiseled with precision, bringing each marbled Amicum to life.

If I'm able to return, maybe I can ask for lessons. Learning how to paint with oils sounds like a lovely alternative to cleaning beakers and typing into a computer for days on end.

When I finally find myself at the entrance to the kitchen, I inhale the scent of bread. Standing at the top of the three steps leading into the space, I study the space.

I'm instantly in love. This kitchen is nothing short of heaven.

It's large enough to hold three stoves and multiple ovens. Counters line the walls, with one gigantic island made of a solid piece of wood in the middle.

The walls are smooth terra cotta, and the windows are circular, like polka dots. My eyes rise to the high ceilings, appreciating the exposed wood beams and industrial-looking lights spotlighting different sections of the room.

It smells of bread and something spicy. Somewhere, a chicken clucks. Pots and pans clang against stoves and spoons. The energy is busy, but not hectic.

As one, the room turns its attention to me. One portly female pauses as she kneads a ball of dough the size of my head. Frizzy strawberry-blonde curls flare out from under a light green skullcap, framing her heart-shaped face. Another female, holding a metal bowl full of something she was stirring, stares at me, mouth agape.

The other dozen females have also frozen in their tasks. Is it weird to have me down here? My ears burn from the attention.

I give a sheepish wave. "Uh, hi. I was kind of hoping I could make something?"

The female kneading the dough slaps her hands together, and flour flies into the air in puffs of dust. "Is there something we can do for you?"

I'm not sure why I thought the reception would be more welcoming, but it feels like I'm overstepping. Kalliope's warning comes to mind as I say, "Um, I'm actually craving something specific."

The heart-faced female snaps her fingers, glaring at the others. The sounds of cooking fill the room again as everyone jumps back into their tasks. I'm impressed with the commanding presence of this female. I step down the steps, waiting for her as she scoots through the aisle full of cooks, making her way to me.

Stopping in front of me, she looks up at me and crosses her plump arms, glaring. Her dress is simple, wrapping her curvaceous form with dark green cotton. Her bib apron is an even darker shade of green, stained with flour and other substances. She scents the air, but it doesn't offend me anymore. She now knows I'm a one-form, but there's no look of disdain or suspicion. Well, she *does* look suspicious, but I think it has more to do with my unannounced appearance.

Cheeks ruddy from the warmth, she looks me up and down. "We do all the cooking here. Are we not up to snuff for your liking?"

Her question drops into my belly like a boulder. Flustered, I shake my head violently. "No! The food is incredible here. The best of my entire life, if I'm being honest."

The genuine compliment lands. Her features soften, and her tense shoulders relax. "What can we make for you? We enjoy serving the manor, and I'd like to create whatever you'd like."

I sense eyes on us, but I'm dedicated to my mission now. Lowering my voice, I'm surprised my voice wavers as I say, "Look. I haven't been home in weeks, and I won't be back for a long time. I never thought I'd say this, but I miss cooking, and I thought maybe today I could do something that reminds me of home." After a second thought, I add, "Kalliope said Ellie might let me?"

My words must trigger something because understanding lights up her face. "Take the heart out of the kitchen, but the kitchen never leaves the heart."

Relieved she gets it, I nod. "Exactly. I just want some taste of home." *And a memory.* But I don't say that. With her, I don't think it even needs to be said. Food is emotion.

Uncrossing her arms, she motions around the room. "What are you craving, dear? We have multiple stoves and ovens. We're still prepping for breakfast, but I'm sure we can find room for you."

"Do you have pasta?"

She raises a silver eyebrow. "Pasta?"

Yikes. I'd been hoping for a more positive answer — making pasta from scratch will take longer. "Yeah, like noodles?"

Cocking her head, she squints and looks to the ceiling, probably trying to recall if she's ever heard of it. Finally, she shakes her head. "I can't say I recall ever hearing of 'noodles.'"

They have queso here, but not noodles? I'm about to rock her world. There's obviously flour here, so I barrel on. "Oh boy, I'm about to introduce you to something transcendent. What about milk and cheese?"

She bustles over to a shelf, pulling off baskets and bottles. "Of course."

Perfect. "I'd like to make something called macaroni and cheese."

She shrugs, still too ignorant to know how her life is about to change. "Color me intrigued. What do you need?"

A thrill kick starts my heart. I can pass on a little bit of Mom into the heart of Ilorna. There's zero doubt Ellie won't love the invention of noodles. I list the ingredients, and she nods. Motioning for me to follow, she leads me to an empty spot on the island. "You can start here and let me know of anything else you need. This kitchen is my kingdom." She sticks out a flour-caked hand. "You can call me Eleanor. Ellie for short."

Ah, the cheeky female, not introducing herself when I first mentioned her name. I shake her hand, smiling as a chunk of dough falls to the tiled floor. "Thank you, Ellie."

And so begins the journey of making noodles from scratch.

Chapter Forty-Three

The Recipe For Dairy Ambrosia

In the rare instances I found the time to cook, between writing my dissertation and helping Dad in the lab with research, I always focused on comfort meals. Usually, it was some of Mom's favorites. One of the first things I kept was her recipe book. In it was a homemade macaroni and cheese recipe. She'd claimed it was from her grandmother.

She spent multiple afternoons teaching me how to make it. We'd lick the saucepans clean, and celebrate the gooey cheese pulls. It's one of my favorite memories of her.

Mixing the dough ingredients, I revel in the feel of it. Since they don't have a pasta maker, I make do with flattening it out with a rolling pin until it is as thin as possible.

I'm so focused on the task, I don't notice the kitchen going silent. The only sound is the rolling pin smooshing the dough. Wiping my brow with a floured hand, I pause in confusion.

Then a familiar voice says, "My curiosity got the better of me."

Kalliope watches me as Legend peers down at the pasta. My heart leaps with joy, and it's impossible to hide the impulse to grin like a maniac.

"You're here early."

Kalliope peers around the room, her gaze settling on my busy hands. "We couldn't wait."

Legend leans over and places a chaste kiss on my cheek. "Hello again, Gem."

Before I can say anything else, Ellie walks up, wiping her hands clean with a towel.

"Apologies, Your Grace, this one was quite insistent that I let her invade the kitchen and take over."

I laugh. "I was polite about it."

Kalliope chuckles. "It's fine, Ellie. Please bring over something for Legend and me to sit on, if you'd be so kind."

The kitchen relaxes and gets back to work. Ellie calls out to a servant and commands two stools to be brought over. The servant, whose name is Valeraya, rushes them over. They sit, leaning their elbows against the counter, examining the mess I've made so far.

Kalliope leans over the pasta, looking intrigued as she asks, "What in the world is that?"

Pride swells in my chest. "I'm making macaroni and cheese. My mother taught me the recipe, and I thought maybe you would want to try it."

Legend swallows a bite of an apple. "I don't know what makinroni is, but I love the sound of cheese."

"Me, as well," Kalliope agrees, plucking the apple from his hand and taking a bite before handing it back.

Valeraya wavers, looking desperate to please Kalliope. With a sweet, quiet voice, she pleads, "Can I bring either of you something, Your Grace?"

This is turning into a party, so I might as well give them a crash course in the concept of brunch. "Do you have champagne?"

Valeraya looks to Ellie, who nods with permission. "Yes, Miss."

"Orange juice?"

Valeraya's eyebrows furrow. "Yes, freshly squeezed this morning, Miss."

I clap my hands excitedly, forgetting they're covered in flour. A white puff floats in the air, and a chunk falls on Legend's thigh, and he picks it up, tossing it into his mouth. He smacks his lips, like it's the most delicious thing he's ever eaten. What a ham.

Raising my eyebrows, I ask, "Have either of you had mimosas?"

Kalliope and Legend exchange a glance before looking back at me. Kalliope grimaces. I'm tempted to chuck a dish towel at her doubtful expression.

"No?" she hedges.

I pluck up a nearby dish towel and throw it at her face. It smacks her face, eliciting a chuckle as she catches it before neatly folding it. "I don't like that look of doubt, *Your Grace.* You'll be regretting it soon enough."

Her eyes flicker at the sultry way I say the title. I can't wait for the payback later.

The kitchen is cozy; the warmth seeps into my bones, relaxing my tired muscles. Or maybe it's the champagne. Hard to say.

The five of us — Kalliope invited Valeraya and Ellie to enjoy some mimosas — are all grinning like idiots. I've learned Valeraya is brand new to the kitchen, fresh from her final training as a baker. It explains her eagerness. As I'm finishing up the last of the bow tie pasta, Ellie tends to the strawberry tarts for tonight's dessert, while Valeraya stirs something in a pot.

Ellie chuckles as she tells a story about Kalliope as a youngling. "And then she gets caught by her mother, who gives her a sound thrashing for trying to bite the dignitaries in the buttocks."

Kalliope laughs, her cheeks flushed. "I was five and learning how to shift. I wasn't aware of how sharp tiger teeth were yet."

Legend chuckles. "But you sure found out quickly."

Ellie snorts, popping the tarts into the oven. "I'll say. Lordess Kailen commanded Ginger to shift and bite Kalliope in the buttock multiple times, to help with bite inhibition."

"And did it work?"

"It backfired." She laughs. "My daughter, being the Amicum she is, made it into a competition. Ginger challenged Kalliope every single day to see who could shift and bite each other. For weeks, you could hear their squeals and Lordess Kailen's hollering through the halls at their misdeeds."

This is the third story shared about Kalliope as a youngling, and it makes me love her even more. She was full of pranks and tricks, according to Legend and Ellie. Normally, she's more reserved around others, so it's a delight to know there's yet another layer for me to discover.

"Mother was so exasperated, she eventually banned shifting for an entire month." Kalliope takes a sip of her mimosa, smiling at the memory. "That was enough to get us to quit."

I'm still stuck on what Ellie said. "Ginger is your daughter?"

The chef extraordinaire laughs loudly. "Yes. She gets her attitude from her father. You can blame him for it all, if you'd like."

I snort with amusement. "I'm not sure anyone can be blamed for Ginger, except for Ginger."

Ellie's eyes twinkle. "I couldn't agree more."

Looking at the completed rows of pasta with deep satisfaction, I ask, "Is there a saucepan?"

Ellie glances at Valeraya, who springs into action. When that appears, I tap a finger against my chin. "I also need cream, cheese, salt, butter, flour, and bread crumbs."

"What kind of cheese?" Ellie asks, already headed to a corner of the kitchen.

"What kind do you have?"

Ellie lists off the options. Some I don't recognize; some of them are familiar.

"Parmesan, Gruyère, and cheddar."

Valeraya is off in a flash, retrieving all the ingredients. While she does that, I place a pot on the stove, humming with happiness. As the pot of water heats, it's easy to pretend I'm not about to have one of the most difficult conversations of my life. Bad news is best delivered over good food. It's what Nana believed, so I might as well try it out.

Valeraya arrives with arms full of ingredients and tumbles them onto the counter. She's so full of infectious youngling excitement.

Kalliope leans over and touches Valeraya's arm. "Thank you so much for helping."

She beams and stands taller. "It's a pleasure, Your Grace."

Assessing the ingredients, I nod to myself, then look at Ellie. "Do you have a high-edged pan that can go into the oven?"

She nods and leans down, brandishing a copper pan and places it on the counter.

Alright, time to make some magic. The process of making the sauce is a familiar ritual, soothing any leftover edges of stress the champagne didn't remove. The smell of butter and cream makes my mouth water. Here comes the best part: melting the cheese.

As I mix them together, Legend says, "That smells incredible, Gem."

"Wait until you actually taste it."

Dumping the fresh pasta into the empty pan, I turn to grab the bubbling concoction. The sauce spreads along the pasta beautifully, reminding me of the queso we had the first day I met Kalliope.

With the finishing touches of breadcrumbs, I slide the pan into the oven.

Turning back to my friends, I put dusty hands on my hips. "And now we wait."

Twenty minutes later, Legend sighs and pats his flat stomach. "Gem, I'm starving over here."

I point to his almost-finished mimosa, ignoring the growl of my stomach. The champagne already makes me feel like my head is a shining bubble. "Keep drinking and be patient, you big complainer."

His eyes dance with unbridled amusement as he obeys, finishing what's left and motioning toward Kalliope to the next unopened bottle.

The waiting is excruciating. Even though Ellie shares another story of youngling adventures, the minutes pass slowly. My mouth is already watering, imagining the gooey marriage of cheese and pasta.

Finally, the timer Ellie set finished. With satisfaction, I pull out the slightly burned and bubbling concoction. My stomach growls in demand. Perfect.

"Bountiful goddess, Saira, what is that?" Legend's voice fills with awe. Kalliope moans, and the sound makes me almost drop the pan. The most appropriate reaction to macaroni and cheese.

With a racing heart, I place it down on the counter. When I ask for bowls and forks, Valerya rushes off. While we wait, I help Ellie clean up the mess I made. She's insisting on helping, but I can't just sit here while she does it.

Face flush from the champagne, Kalliope refills our mimosas and toasts. "To trying new things and devouring cheese until our bellies hurt."

"Sounds gouda to me." Legend's smug grin makes me laugh. I throw a kitchen towel at him, which he catches with wicked reflexes. "You cheddar not try that again, Gem."

It hurts to admit, but I'm going to miss the hell out of his cheesy jokes. For a second, my iron grasp on my emotions slips, forcing me to bite down on my quivering lip. *Focus on the cheese.* There will be plenty of time for emotions ... *later.*

Oblivious to the turmoil in my mind, Kalliope groans, folding onto the counter, dumping her head onto her arms. "Why did Inanna decide to give me this male?"

"Inanna didn't need your parmesan to bless you with my good looks and excellent jokes."

Ellie points a spatula at him. He flinches, as if she's slapped him with it more than a few times. The reaction wipes away my sorrows, and I smile as she commands, "Knock it off, *Paul*, or I'll tell them some embarrassing stories I'm positive you want to keep secret."

Before Legend can retort with another cheesy joke — pun intended — Valeraya appears with the forks and bowls. Grabbing a ladle, I dip it into the glorious meal and spoon out a little into everyone's bowls.

Legend hovers the steaming mass of cheesy noodles an inch from his nose. The salacious sound he lets out spreads warmth through my core. I need to hear that sound again, preferably in my ear while he's inside me.

Sitting down, I examine my portion. Golden brown splotches crisp the cheese, still bubbling. Mom would be so proud. My fork poises above my serving when I realize everyone is staring at me, then to my fork.

Laughing, I dip the fork into the noodles and show them a glorious cheese pull. Blowing on it, I know it's still too hot, but my patience is thin. It burns the roof of my mouth. The pain is worth it. The flavor is an explosion. Salt. Cheese. Cream. And the pasta is incredible.

The four of them dig in and, for a few seconds, they chew slowly. Kalliope closes her eyes and slumps against the table dramatically. Legend pounds the table with a fist, moaning salaciously. Valeraya hums with appreciation, and Ellie stares at the bowl so hard, it's like she's demanding it unlock hidden secrets.

Her eyes flutter up to me and in the most serious tone, she says, "You're not allowed in this kitchen ever again ..." Before I can protest, she winks. "Unless you give me the recipe for this dairy ambrosia."

The threat makes me bark out a laugh. "Deal."

Legend brings his bowl up to his mouth and shortens the distance for his fork to travel. "I am nothing but a servant in any way that encourages you to make this every day."

His use of *every day* pierces me deeply, but I shove it away and grin. Beaming with pride, my heart reaches a fullness I've never felt before.

Kalliope's eyes are closed, and she's chewing slowly. We all pause, waiting for her reaction. Her eyelids flutter as she opens them, her expression full of too many emotions to name. "I didn't think I could love you more, but I was dead wrong."

Her words flip flop in my belly. I ache to say the words back, but instead, I shovel another bite into my mouth.

In less than ten minutes, the five of us gobble the entire dish down. Legend pats his belly, this time in satisfaction. "I'm going to have to go to the practice mats to work that off."

Valeraya declares her thanks and hurries off to take care of the growing pile of dishes.

Ellie comes up to me, giving my arm an affectionate squeeze. Before she walks away, she says, "Any time you want to come down here, dear, just say the word."

Legend and Kalliope stare at the empty dish, as if willing more to appear.

"I'll leave the recipe with Ellie," I promise. This is a good segue to why I've brought them here, but my thoughts race faster than I can grab them. Do I really need to leave in three days? *Yes. You do. Quit being a coward.*

Kalliope wags her finger at me with fake admonishment. "You better. And I'm not sharing next time."

"What about me?" Legend protests.

She sighs. "Fine. I'll share with you. And that's *it*. You must guard it from any thieves"

Legend nods sharply. "I'll protect the martoni and cheese paste with my life."

It's tempting to correct him, but hearing it pronounced that way is too cute. Everything about this moment is too cute; I hate to break the levity. The upsetting words sit poised on the tip of my tongue. Their possible devastation holds me back. There's also the possibility that they won't care, and that will ruin me instead.

No matter what, this is crushing. Nothing about this situation is pleasant or ideal. There's no good time to break up with someone, let alone two people.

No more waiting, Saira. Time to get it over with.

I clear my throat, and they look at me. It's breaking my heart, knowing their joyous expressions are about to evaporate. Legend must notice something in my expression because his happiness melts into concern.

"Gem? Are you alright?"

His perceptiveness is a battering ram against my tightly bound emotions. I take a deep breath and blow it out hard. Heart hammering, I say, "It's time for me to leave."

Their faces fall, as expected. My heart plummets with them, the painful emotions I've been trying to hide under a truckload of macaroni and cheese rushing to the surface.

Kalliope's eyes shine with unshed tears. "When?"

"In three days."

Legend swears, rubbing a hand down his face. Kalliope's eyes never leave my face as she stands. When her arms open, I fall into their strong embrace. The kitchen grows quiet as everyone seems to notice the energy shifting in our little corner. Legend's hand comes to the back of my head, stroking my curls.

"Three days?" he asks.

I nod against Kalliope's chest. Her arms squeeze me in tighter, as if I'm about to slip through her grasp like a ghost.

Legend hums like he's pondering something. Finally, he says, "How much sex do you think we could have in three days?"

Chapter Forty-Four

Having Morals Is Painful

With less than forty-eight hours left in Ilorna, Kalliope surprises me with a visit to a place she calls Burnel. It's apparently a sacred gathering spot for both Amicum females and one-form women. Established three years after the war, it offers an opportunity to continue nourishing the connection between the two species. No men or males allowed.

So, it's basically heaven.

When Kalliope's eagle lands on a grassy knoll, I hop off and look down the hill toward Burnel. It comprises a large pond with a tall, pillared rotunda in the center. The pillars are pure white with terracotta tiles on the roof. Long strands of sheer curtains hang between the Grecian-style pillars, flowing gently in the wind. Dark green vines wrap around each pillar.

Overflowing pots of bright flowers flank the pale stone path leading to the rotunda. My eyes widen at the lily pads in the turquoise water — they're the size of small cars. Femmes laze around on them with pillows and blankets, munching on snacks. Some of them are naked, and others wear various styles of flowy outfits. In the water, dark shapes swim around. Some are even mermaids.

Small buildings buffer the edges of the pond, their open doors revealing tables, lounge areas, and groups of femmes chatting.

Kalliope comes to stand next to me, bringing an arm around my waist. "What do you think?"

My stomach flutters with excitement. "It looks magical."

She chuckles, leading me toward the first building. "I enjoy spending time here. It's quiet, relaxing and, most importantly, I can leave my responsibilities behind for an afternoon."

We stop in front of a desk on the outside of the first building. A female with long blond hair greets us with an inviting smile, revealing sharp canines. With a feline snout and golden spots smattering her face, she looks exotic in her toga-style clothing, every inch of visible skin also covered in golden leopard spots. Her eyes light up when she realizes it's Kalliope.

"Lordess Kalliope, we were not expecting you." She stands and gives a small bow, then looks at me. "You must be Saira. We've heard so much about you. We've been hoping for a chance to meet you." She looks back at Kalliope. "Would you prefer the rotunda today, or shall we find you a private space?"

"Hello, Janessa. Private, please," Kalliope says, giving me a sly grin. The flutters in my belly intensify. While I miss Legend's irreverence, it's exciting to have an afternoon with Kalliope and no one else. It's a rare occasion, one worthy of cherishing.

"Of course," Janessa says, checking a slip of paper. "It looks like your usual suite is available. If you'll follow me." She pauses and tilts her head. "Would you like a tour? Since this is Saira's first time? We recently added a few features you may not be aware of."

"Yes, please." Kalliope ushers me forward to fall in step beside Janessa, trailing behind us.

Janessa tucks a strand of hair behind her round ear. "Follow me, please."

Her legs are long, so it's a hustle to keep up with her. We walk through the building, passing by groups of femmes chatting on soft-looking lounge chairs. Between each chair are tables with snacks and glasses filled with various liquids. Melodic laughter echoes in the rooms.

We pass through a hallway with many doors, some either opened or closed. She pauses in front of each one.

"This is the mud bath room. It's by appointment only, so please inform me or one of the attendants if you'd like to reserve a spot. This is the steam room. No appointment is required; you're welcome to walk in at any time."

We walk past an open door where naked femmes are being beaten with branches. "Here, you may enjoy a unique experience with the falenjoli leaves. It may look abrasive, but I assure you, your skin will never feel softer."

I've never been to a spa, so all of it sounds intriguing. Except for being beaten by branches. Maybe that's something to work up to.

We turn a corner and enter a wide, open space devoid of walls. Matching pillars support the relaxing space, with sheer white curtains pulled open to block some of the sunshine. Soft music plays from somewhere. Circular garden tables dot the room, with groups of femmes sitting in the comfortable chairs.

Janessa pauses. "This is the only restaurant in Burnel. The menu's set, but with enough notice, we can custom make any meal you wish. Please give at least two hours' notice and we can accommodate any craving you may have."

I look over my shoulder at Kalliope. She's walking with her hands clasped behind her back, quietly observing everything. Catching my eye, she smiles softly. An eternity of those smiles will never be enough.

Janessa moves on, leading us down another hallway. "Our private suites are stocked with various drinks, robes, and snacks. Each room has its own attendant." We stop at a room, and she opens the door, stepping aside so we can walk in.

It's quaint yet luxurious in the design. Its layout is like an over-the-water bungalow. Candles light the space, even though there's still plenty of light. One side of the room holds a massive bed with pure white cotton sheets and blankets. Fluffy pillows dot the bed, and colorful abstract art hangs on the walls.

On the other side of the room is a white marble bar with dozens of bottles. Next to it is a closed door, which I assume leads to a bathroom. Toward the edge of the room, there's a wooden patio with lounge chairs and fabric privacy shades on either side.

"It's beautiful," I murmur, walking to the edge of the room. Thanks to the privacy shades, there's no one to watch us if we choose to get naked. Or more. It's the latter that has my stomach fluttering in anticipation.

I turn to Kalliope. "This is all ours for today?"

"Yes, do you like it?" Her voice has an edge of anxiety, like there was a chance I didn't like this place.

I giggle. "Do I *like* it? I'd live here in a heartbeat."

"This rope right here will summon your attendant. They're always close by." Janessa motions to a teal rope hanging from the ceiling by the front door. "Is there anything else I can help you with?"

"No, that will be all. Thank you, Janessa." Kalliope flashes her a polite smile. I offer a little wave to Janessa, who gives a small bow and steps out of the room, closing the door behind her.

I look at Kalliope expectantly. "What now?"

She flashes a wicked grin. "Now we make love until they kick us out."

A couple of hours later, I'm famished and well fucked. Looking around at the rumpled bed, I smile. A mess worth the effort. Minus the enormous one I'm leaning against, the rest of the pillows lie on the floor. My body's satiated and ravenous at the same time.

Kalliope pads over to the rope completely naked and gives it a gentle tug. Her skin glistens with sweat. The urge to lick it off is strong.

I adore spending time with Kalliope and Legend, just enjoying existence. Our chemistry together is something I could never have expected. Even in the last few weeks, I finally feel like an adult. Not simply because of the sex, but because of the true autonomy I'm able to embrace.

After spending most of my life solely focused on studying and researching, it's been incredible actually *living*. Before, I moved through my days in a fugue with tunnel vision. Now, life is more colorful and intense than I ever thought possible.

"What would you like to eat?" Kalliope purrs, walking toward me slowly. Her hips sway back and forth, flexing her muscular abdomen. She's athletic yet soft in all the right places. I eye her pink nipples and lick my lips.

"How long do you think it'll take for them to —"

The answer to the unfinished question comes as a knock at the door. Kalliope winks and walks to the door. No robe. Just naked.

When the door opens, I hear a soft voice. Kalliope looks over her shoulder.

"What would you like to eat?"

"Is there a menu?"

Kalliope asks, then, "Tell me what you would like and they'll make it."

I bite my lip, thinking. Finally, I shrug. "Platter of sandwiches and pastries?"

Kalliope relays the request and closes the door. She walks over to the bar and peruses the drink options. "Would you like some wine?"

"Something fruity?" I offer. She grabs a bottle of purple liquid and two glasses.

Pouring them carefully, she says, "How are you feeling about leaving?"

The topic sours my mood slightly. Choosing to leave tomorrow was my decision, but that doesn't mean I'm leaving without regrets.

"I'm sad," I admit. "Ilorna has been the best experience of my life. I'm afraid to leave, knowing I most likely won't return."

She tilts her head, carrying two glasses to the bed. "Even after being kidnapped?"

I laugh, grabbing one of the glasses. "Yes, even after that. You and Legend accepted me wholeheartedly. I don't understand why, honestly. Some random woman showed up in the woods, and you naturally said,

'Sure, come live with me and mine for however long you want.' Why? What about me made you do that?"

She sits next to me, taking a sip of her drink. I do the same and hum with appreciation for the flavor. Something tells me the next place won't have the same level of amazing food. My life doesn't have that kind of luck. I've probably stretched the limits of my luck just by finding this place and falling in love.

Not that I can admit the latter part out loud. The sip of wine sours in my stomach. I need to stop thinking about these kinds of things — I *need* to live in the present.

"Well," Kalliope says, looking out past the bungalow's edge for a moment. "I don't know, really. Maybe it was your sarcastic wit." She looks at me, grinning. After taking another sip of the drink, she places it on the nearby table and turns to face me fully. "Perhaps it's unexplainable."

The conversation she had with Zenab in the greenhouse springs to mind. I swallow hard. "I heard you that day in the greenhouse with Zenab."

"Oh?" She lays down on her side, making lazy circles on my thigh. Her finger encircles a small fading bite mark. "And what exactly did you hear?"

I shiver as her hand goes a little higher. "That you were falling in love with me."

"Mmm," she hums, bringing her fingers up to the vee of my thighs, pressing a finger against my clit. She holds it there. The lack of motion does more for me than if she were rubbing it. "I was falling in love with you."

She rolls closer to me, removing her finger in favor of licking a slow path up my thigh. I suck in a sharp breath, my heart picking up speed with her words. "I fell in love with your bravery." She nips one thigh, making me groan. "I fell in love with your wit." The opposite thigh gets the same treatment. My legs widen of their own accord, eager for more.

Her words plant an ache in my heart as a ball of emotion lodges in my throat. She keeps saying that word — *love*. She loves me. Both of them do. And I'm too much of a coward to say it, but admitting it out loud would require doing something about it. Maybe new expectations would appear. After all, who the hell leaves behind people they love?

You already did.

My conscience is unkind today, but not wrong. I left my whole family. Sure, there was a purpose to it, just like leaving behind my partners has a purpose ... but this feels different. I don't know how to explain it or put it into words, so it's easier to bottle it up. Pretend that everything is normal. It's totally normal for your partners to admit their love, and you don't say it back, even if you feel it.

Totally normal.

These thoughts are making everything worse. Even as her tongue flicks against my clit, the urge to cry intensifies. What if I never get this ever again? I'm not foolish enough to believe that all relationships are like this. I might've been a virgin, but I'm not dumb. Kalliope is special. What we have is special..

She's completely oblivious to the turmoil wrecking my mind right now. After a long, talented stroke, she murmurs, "I fell in love with the way you embrace growth."

I wish she would stop saying that damn word. Tears prick my eyes as my skin heats with pleasure. The dichotomy is intense. It's as if my body threw out the manual about how to process both things at once. From between my legs, she looks up, glowing with desire.

Nope. I can't.

Noticing my tears, she abruptly stops and sits up. When she realizes how upset I am, she grabs a blanket and wraps it around me. "What's wrong?"

The question breaks the emotional dam, and tears fall freely. "I'm going to miss you so much, Kal. You and Legend, Zenab, Ginger. Tomorrow, I'm going into the unknown, and so much has already tried to eat me." The moment I mention being eaten, my chest heaves with a jagged sob. She scoots up closer.

"Hey," she says quietly. "Hey, it's okay. It'll be okay."

"It won't," I lament, now completely unable to stop. It's an emotional release, completely proportionate to the fear trying to overwhelm me.

If I were a shittier person, I'd stay here and be safe until I died of old age.

Having morals is painful, which is why so many people don't have them. Right now, I wish I were a selfish person. Deep, deep down ... I wish I'd never created time travel.

I mentally dig a grave in my mind and shove that thought into it, covering it right up. It's never worth considering ever again. I'm leaving, and that's all that matters. There's no time or space for regrets right now. I've made my choice, and I'm sticking with it.

"You're capable," Kalliope says firmly. Her hands bracket my cheeks, turning my face to look at her. Sadness pulls at the edges of her eyes as she says, "Listen to me, Saira. You are so much more than the version of you I met in the woods all those weeks ago. I've seen you train with Zenab. You're fast and capable. You've survived multiple attempts on your life. It might happen again; it might not. The most important thing for you to remember is to never hesitate to stab whatever it is trying to kill you."

The joke hiccups a laugh between the sobs. "I don't even have a knife."

She sighs, offering a small smile. "That's easily remedied, my love." Her thumbs wipe away the trailing tears on my cheeks. "You'll save your family, Saira. One day, you'll be home with Piper, laughing about all the adventures you had. You can tell her how you were loved by a lordess. Tell her how fiercely you were cherished."

At the last word, her voice catches, tears finally shimmering in her golden eyes. She hasn't cracked since I announced my departure, but I think it's a brave front; just like Legend does sometimes. They'll never ever say it, but I know they want me to stay. I'm glad they don't ask — I'm not sure I'd be able to say no if they did.

Taking a sharp breath, she briefly shakes her head, as if clearing away the heavy emotions. With a wide smile, she rubs her thumb against my cheek. "I'll never forget you, Saira. It's been such an honor."

While the water works have slowed, the agonizing regret grows. The urge to admit the depth of my feelings is overwhelming, like the love inside me is a beast, rattling against my bones. It's a silent war, one I'm not willing to reveal. Instead, I croak out, "I don't know how to move on."

"You have to," she says firmly. Dropping her hands, she grabs one of mine. "Now that you've discovered a new part of yourself, it's time to go discover more. And if you somehow find your way back here, we'll happily keep you."

I don't want to tell her how impossible it is. Instead, I allow myself to cling to the delusion of maybes. "If there's a chance, I'm taking it."

Kalliope's kiss is chaste and comforting. I'm going to miss her unwavering support. Against my lips, she whispers, "Good. I'm going to believe Inanna will bring you back to me."

I never really asked about their goddess Inanna, but if it takes praying to a goddess for a miracle ... What could it hurt? I send up a silent prayer to Inanna, hoping she'll hear a one-form. "I hope she's a good listener."

"Very." Kalliope brushes off the last of my tears and hands me my glass of wine. "Here. Drink. Let's pause these worries in favor of enjoying these last moments fully."

I take the drink gratefully. It tastes better this time, as the weight in my belly lightens. My feelings aren't gone, but they can wait on the back burner. "Pausing the tears sounds like a great idea."

So we drink and we make love. The afternoon is full of laughter and quiet confessions. For a moment, time waits to exist. It denies its purpose to spare me a few merciful seconds here.

It's easier to pretend tomorrow will never arrive.

Chapter Forty-Five

The Last Saira Sandwich

Today is my final day in Ilorna. Last night, the Cohort and I had dinner together. It was cozy and full of laughter. Every second with them matters, and I'm determined to remember it all. It's a struggle, but Legend and Kalliope have been more than willing to distract me from my worries.

That's why, two hours before I'm slated to leave, Legend's talented tongue circles my dusky nipple, and I'm unable to stifle the moan that escapes me. Kalliope's mouth covers mine, greedily swallowing the sound of pleasure. Her slick heat covers my hand as I plunge two fingers in and out of her.

This is it — our last time together.

The thought struggles through my focus, but the way Legend grips my hips, directing the way I ride him, nothing else matters.

He's so deep inside me; it's almost too much as I tilt my hips, grinding my clit against his pelvis. He growls, his thick fingers digging into the curves of my ass, guiding my hips. Desperate.

Expression twisted in concentration, Legend's eyes lock onto where we connect, mesmerized by the lewd sounds our joining makes.

Kalliope pushes him down, forcing his head onto the pillow. A brief sound of protest is smothered by her swinging a thigh over his head, lowering onto his waiting tongue as she faces me. They moan together in unison.

My pleasure reaches new heights as he holds onto one of my hips, sliding the opposite hand between my legs, finding my clit. A sinful moan escapes from between my lips, and I toss my head back, eyes closed. It's easy to imagine myself as a goddess, blessing him with my curves. Every thrust is an offering, pushing me to new heights.

As Legend works an orgasm out of each of us, Kalliope leans forward and kisses me, the intensity an asteroid to my senses, leaving a crater of need. One of her hands cups the back of my head as the other tweaks one of my nipples.

The sensations and sounds of the moment are too much. My hips buck and pick up speed. I'm chasing this orgasm like it's the last thing I'll ever do. Kalliope cries out, grinding against Legend's mouth as two of his fingers tease her.

The explosion of pleasure arches my back, slamming my breasts into Kalliope. Her strong arms wrap around my sweat-sheened torso, supporting me as the pulses in my core rip free into a roaring orgasm.

Then it's Kalliope falling apart in my arms. I continue riding Legend like the universes depend on it while he releases my hip and brings the hand to Kalliope's body, sliding it up her torso, pausing at her neck. The thick fingers wrap around her delicate neck, squeezing hard.

She gasps and arches her back. Red streaks trail as he drags fingers along her pale skin, stopping at one of her breasts. He grabs it with possessive roughness, eliciting a whimper of approval from both of us.

Our desperation reaches a fevered pitch as we each edge toward our own pinnacle. Who knows where I'll be in three hours? If it's my time to die, I'll be damned if I don't die with the memory of Legend's thick cock inside my body and the taste of Kalliope on my lips.

As Kalliope's orgasm crests into jerking movements, Legend moans his pleasure into her pussy. The vibrations push Kalliope over the cliff of pleasure, and she screams his name.

I feel him swell and twitch inside me. His body tenses, and he thrusts deeper, filling me with cum.

Then it's over, the sexual fervor petering out into sweaty gasps for air. After a moment of recovery, Kalliope swings off Legend, leaving a wet mess along his mouth and jaw. He licks her cum off his mouth, looking quite pleased with himself.

"That was amazing, Gem," he purrs, grabbing my hips again before I can lift myself off. Biting my lip, I grind one more time on him. With a regretful grimace, I swing off his glorious body.

Instead of acknowledging the finality of it all, they insist on taking one more bath with me. It's platonic but filled with gentle caresses and words. They take their time washing and scrubbing my sated body. It's odd, having two people bathe you at the same time, but their ministrations soothe the raging anguish swirling in my gut.

When the water grows cold, they help me dry off and get dressed. It's unnecessary, but I can't begrudge them this act of service.

Once I'm dressed, I triple check my belongings, making sure everything is in its assigned place. Tucking Piper's locket under my shirt, I strap the Scout around my wrist, then turn it into the hologram of a leather wristband.

As Kalliope and Legend dress, I squat down in front of my pack and compulsively check the pockets. Earlier today, Meadow brought some pastries to bring along. It was a teary farewell, and I hugged her small body tightly. I could never express enough thanks for everything she's done, but I repeated my gratitude until she playfully demanded I stop.

We decided our farewells should be in the area where Kalliope and Ginger originally found me. All of us, including Zenab and Ginger, are going to travel there for the final goodbyes.

Meeting in the courtyard in front of the manor, all of us take to the skies, with me riding Kalliope's golden eagle form. Zenab's black lion has beautiful iridescent wings, right beside Legend's manticore shift. Ginger takes up the rear as a snowy white Pegasus with a red mane. As we fly through the clouds, I close my eyes and hold out my arms. It's easy to pretend I'm an eagle, too, joining my friends on a trip to the ocean.

I might not be able to shift, but I can pretend.

The ache in my heart thumps, like a throbbing sickness inside my chest cavity. Deep down, I know my respite in Ilorna is coming to an end. It's like my body has a sixth sense that I'm about to be on the dinner menu again. It's at this moment I realize Kalliope never gave me a dagger. Disappointment stamps down the fragments of happiness left inside of me.

I'm so doomed.

Einstein would have a heyday with how time is treating me right now. It's like quicksand, sucking away my remaining moments; the more I attempt to live in the present, the faster the seconds fly by. As much as I try to calm the festering anxiety, it's impossible when Kalliope begins a slow descent back to the ground.

Ginger stops by the pile of boulders, the ones I'd originally encountered when the bear appeared. I hop off Kalliope, landing gracefully, even with the backpack on. I run my hands over her soft feathers. When I step back, she shifts into her true-form.

The rest do the same, and for a moment, we stand there, silent. Of course, they have no clue what comes next. I look around and find an area devoid of objects.

Pointing at the spot, I say, "I'll travel from there. Make sure no one is too close. I could end up taking you with me."

"So you're saying there's a chance we could join you?" Legend says, hopeful. Kalliope playfully slaps him on the chest with the back of her hand. He cringes, then grins. "What?"

A stab of emotion cuts a serrated line in my heart, but I shove it down. Instead, I chuckle like I'm not about to beg for that very thing and walk over to the spot. "We never tried it, but do you want to chance being spliced into a million pieces?"

"Maybe," he says with a jutted lower lip, but we all know he doesn't mean it. I'm not resentful that they're not actually trying or willing to travel with me. Where I'm going, they don't belong. I mean, I don't either, but this is their home.

"BB, do you think you'll land on a bear again?" Ginger quips.

"I told you I'd already been in the woods for a week," I snipe. My attitude makes her grin.

Kalliope snorts with amusement, coming to my side and wrapping me up in a hug so tight, thoughts temporarily stutter into silence inside my mind. I return the embrace with equal intensity, hating every second of this goodbye. She was both my redemption and release. I owe her so much, more than I can verbalize.

If she hadn't saved me in the forest from the bear, I wouldn't be here.

If she hadn't killed the Vulturian in the village, I wouldn't be here.

If she hadn't saved me from being a juicy steak, I wouldn't be here.

If she hadn't loved me, I wouldn't know what it feels like to be ripped apart and stitched back together by selfless devotion.

My grip tightens as she moves away, pouring every molecule of emotion into it, hoping she can sense how I feel.

I love you; I love you; I love you.

The words blaze through me, incinerating any stability left. My whole being cracks in half, letting out jagged sobs. For the first time, love feels like a curse; an unshakeable burden shackled to my soul. I hate it.

I can't live without it.

As I release the tumultuous show of emotion, she comforts me with a hand stroking my back, murmuring words of adoration.

"You're so incredibly brave, my love. You have the soul of an Amicum, and the heart of a Guardian. You're leaving, but you're also going somewhere." Her voice breaks into emotional shards, and she swallows hard before she says, "We'll think of you every day, even if years pass. I'm going to pray to Inanna each evening for your return, even if it's in my dreams."

I'd like to say the words make me feel better, but they don't. But I can't sit here, letting this anguish continue. I have to leave.

Inhaling a shuddering breath, I release my desperate hold on her body. Roughly wiping away the wetness on my cheeks, a sheepish smile tugs at the corners of my mouth. Her own eyes are red, glittering with unshed tears. Her eyebrows shoot up as she remembers something. From her belt, she removes a small but bulging leather pouch.

"Take this."

It's heavy, and my hand dips when she places it in my palm.

"What is it?" I loosen the ties and peer inside; it's gold coins. With a gasp of shock, I try to hand it back. "I can't take this."

Legend walks to her side and crosses his arms. "You can, and you will. Maybe you won't need it. In case you do, there's enough there to buy a castle."

My throat tightens as I hide it in my utility belt's largest pocket. They always think of everything because they only want the best for me. "Thank you."

Zenab steps forward, also looking like she's about to cry. "I had something made for you."

We all watch her unstrap the blade attached to her belt and around her thigh. In her palm, she offers me the thigh holster and dagger. I take it from her, inspecting the smooth hilt. It's made of cold, black metal, tipped with a wolf's head at the end. A black wolf. Oxygen lodges in my lungs as I tentatively wrap my fingers around the hilt and reveal the blade.

When I separate it from the sheath, the obsidian metal glints in the light. A tear broke free from the corner of my eye and plops onto the grass. This isn't just a gift — it's a token of belonging.

She says softly, "In case you run into something that needs a good stabby-stab."

The generosity is too much, and the tears return. I close my eyes, willing them away. It's a losing battle, but I'm able to stave them off a little longer. I throw my arms around her chest, almost dropping the dagger.

"It's beautiful," I choke out. "I'll *definitely* stab something with it."

She returns the tight embrace, her bandolier pressing uncomfortably into my chest. I don't care — she's been just as formative in my growth as my partners. "I hope you think of me when you do."

"Absolutely." I release my hold and raise it again and examine the holster; its beautiful craftsmanship. I might need to find an excuse to stab something, even if it's just an apple. Although something on this level probably deserves a baptism by blood. Looking down at my thigh, I ask, "How do I attach this?"

Zenab points at the one attached to her opposite thigh. "Just wrap it around your thigh and attach it, similar to a belt."

Opening the metal clasp, I wrap the holster around my thick thigh. It's a perfect fit and makes me feel like a badass. Definitely stabbing something more than food with this bad boy. And with the training she and Legend have given me, I have a fighting chance — at least a fighting chance to stab someone without hesitation. No guarantees on the outcome..

Lower lip quavering, I rasp out, "Thank you so much, Zen."

Zenab gives me one last hug, then claps me on the shoulder. "Remember your training, Saira. Never stop moving."

"I'll make you proud," I promise. She grins, clearly confident I'll keep my word. To my surprise, she shifts into the obsidian lion, the shining feathers like slick oil as she takes to the skies.

Looking toward Ginger, I wait to see what she'll do. She looks so small right now, especially as sadness weighs down her features. Her hands clasp in front of her as the crown of curls falls in luxurious waves around her naked body.

"You know," I say slyly. "I thought you were such a bitch when we met."

Her sad eyes spark with familiar mischief. "How ironic, considering I thought you were useless."

"Have I proved you wrong?" I ask, raising an eyebrow.

She lifts her chin. "Have I?"

We hold our staring contest until she breaks and rushes forward. "Oh, BB, I'm going to miss you."

And now, I'm hugging a naked Ginger, something I would've never done when we first met. Maybe I'm indoctrinated, but it's not so bad. More squishy than expected, and I'm afraid of putting a hand in the wrong place, but I also doubt she'd care.

"I'm going to miss you, BB," she says into my jacket, voice cracking with emotion. "It's been an honor to know you."

"Oh, Ginger." I wrap my arms around her shoulders, hugging her tighter. "I'm going to miss your sassy ass."

We hold the embrace for a moment longer, then she steps away, wiping her cheeks. "Don't let any bears eat you, okay? And come back if you can."

Before I can say anything else, she shifts back into her Pegasus form and flaps her wings furiously until she's up in the clouds, red mane like fire in the sunshine.

Abrupt exit, but not unexpected.

Finally, it's Legend's turn. The man who showed me that the things I assumed were flaws, weren't. There are so many things about him to love — his irreverence; devotion; masculinity. Never once has he given a reason to doubt his sincerity. He's chosen love and loyalty as a profession; I admire the fuck out of that.

He wraps those big arms around me, enveloping me in his safe embrace. I rub my face into his chest, inhaling his citrus scent. Legend taught me there's power in sex, and not the corrupt kind. Since we met, he's encouraged me to embrace my body and sexuality. Due in part to him, I'm no longer the nervous wallflower from weeks ago. The version of me today owes him so much, including the newfound confidence thrumming in my veins.

"I'm going to miss you so much," I mumble into his shirt. The tears won't stop now. Neither will the agonizing ache throbbing through every molecule in my body. How can I possibly ever move on from these people?

His fingers graze up and down my back, soothing my shaking body. In a voice as quiet as silk, he says, "I'm going to miss you too, Gem. But I want you to go out there and enjoy every second possible."

Enjoying anything past this moment sounds ridiculous. How am I supposed to *breathe* without them, let alone move on? "I'll never stop wanting to be with you, though."

He pushes me back and ducks his head to make eye contact. Unshed tears wobble at the edges of his dark lashes. "We don't know if you'll return. So you can't move through the rest of your life like you'll be able to return. I know it hurts right now, but you need to continue looking forward."

"That seems impossible." My voice quavers with the words. How could I ever move on from them? I'm in the middle of my first breakup — technically — and I had no idea heartbreak could feel like rolling in glass while drinking acid. Moving on feels like a betrayal.

"He's right," Kalliope says. She wraps her arms around me from the back, turning me into a Saira Sandwich. I close my eyes, trying to memorize every sensation of their touch. Their scents. Their warmth. One last time, I try to release as much of my love into them, hoping it'll transfer like osmosis. The words are *right there*, souring my taste buds, but they're gagged behind a wall of fear. I'm such a coward.

Into my ear, Kalliope murmurs, "You know we won't care if you return and have been with six dozen partners, Saira. We know how you feel about us." I open my mouth, ready to say something, *anything*, but she shakes her head. "We understand why you can't say it, but actions will always be louder than words. Nothing will change these truths, even if you never return. Don't you *dare* let the memory of us hold you back."

"I won't," I say with determination, but inside, I'm fucking dying. Shriveling up into a human-sized wasteland.

They release me, and Legend cups my face, kissing me. I desperately savor every flutter of his lips. The reverent way he holds me. It would be a feat for anyone to top this.

When he finally releases me, Kalliope kisses my forehead, then each cheek. Her embrace ends with the best kiss of my life. It's sweet and claiming. The smell of a campfire will always remind me of her.

Inside me is a feral beast of heartbreak, whipping through every quark available like it's a race against time to rock bottom. On the outside, I'm giving them both a brave, wobbling smile. Underneath this suit of skin, I'm hurtling toward emotional devastation.

I step back, and they release me. It's time. Anything beyond this point is procrastination and draws out the pain. There's enough pain to feast on in the coming months.

"I'm going to try to come back," I say through gritted teeth, desperate to bite back the wretched sobs begging for release. The words have been said more than enough times, even if they can never be guaranteed.

Legend offers me his signature smirk even though his face twists with regret and grief. With a voice rough with unshed emotion, he says, "I'd very much like to cum on your back."

The spicy dad joke surprises me so much, I snort out a laugh that chokes out into a half-sob. "Smart-ass."

"Better than a dumb-ass." Kalliope chuckles sadly, knowing about the inside joke with Piper. My heart squeezes painfully. Ilorna has severed a piece of me as a price for this joy. It can keep it. They can keep it.

I look at the two people I love more than the air in my lungs. "All of you have a place in my heart. Thank you for taking me in and helping me discover myself."

"I love you," Legend and Kalliope say simultaneously. They reach for each other's hands, an anchor for one another. I'm glad they can live their lives together.

I love you; I love you; I love you.

My mouth opens, ready to release the declaration. Then I snap it shut. Now is *not* the time.

I slide the mask down over my face, and the screen whirs to life. Oxygen flows into the small space.

"Goodbye," I choke out, although they probably can't hear it. One more minute; I just need one more fucking minute. They stand there, in the exact spot I first laid eyes on Kalliope. My vision waters as I remember how she leaned down to offer a hand and ask me if I was alright. All of the moments with them flash before my eyes. The laughter and joy. The pain and agony. The all-encompassing love that nudged me into discovering myself.

I'm stepping into the unknown, but because of them, I'm prepared for whatever comes my way.

Kalliope leans against Legend, tears falling freely down her pale cheeks. His eyes glow as his tears wet his face. Together, they're beautiful. Together, they'll be okay.

My fingers press down on the button, squeezing my eyes shut in denial, refusing to look at the countdown.

The world rips in half, right along with my soul.

Epilogue

I land on my hands and knees, soggy vegetation breaking my fall. There has got to be a way to land more gracefully post-travel. Luckily, the nausea isn't as strong this time, and while I heave a few times, nothing comes up.

Instinctively, I look for Legend and Kalliope. *They were just here.* But they aren't here. They'll never be here. Being hit with a sledgehammer in the chest might hurt less than the bone-rattling anguish ripping through me right now. They're gone. I left them.

I *left* them.

A sob hiccups from between my lips, but I bite down, refusing the escape of another. *This is not the fucking time to fall apart, Saira. You have no idea where you are.*

Inside my mind, I create a little box — Pandora's Box, if you will — and shove every morsel of pain into it. Closing the lid, I shackle it with determination. Around it curls the beast of heartbreak, slumbering as it guards what's left of my heart. Ready to lash out at a moment's notice.

Time to focus. A sense of numbness sluices through my body, wiping away every source of grief threatening to buckle me. It's a blessing to feel nothing. Absolutely nothing.

Sitting up, I take stock of my surroundings. The air is sticky; the humidity is thick enough to dampen my hair. Moisture beads on my exposed skin. It seems to be nighttime, or, at least, I assume that until I look around and spot a large grouping of ginormous monstera leaves blotting the sun. They're easily twice my height, swaying slightly in the dense forest beyond the leaves.

Sitting back on my heels, I take stock of the situation. It's a relief there are no nearby explosions or the smell of death in the air. No sharks. No fire tornados. Maybe this will be like Ilorna with an advanced matriarchy ready to save me.

Unlikely, but a girl can hope.

Well, there's no time like the present. I go through the motions of taking samples and logging information. The air is breathable, so it's safe to put the mask away. In about thirty minutes, I've collected samples from everything nearby.

When I'm done with the science portion, I try to peer between the thick stems of the plants. All there seems to be is even more greenery. A few birds call out above, and there's a cacophony of bugs. That seems to be about it, though.

This situation's familiar, but hopefully, there are no bears nearby.

One foot after the other, I work my way through the overgrown foliage. Vines act determined to yank me backward.

"Should've packed a machete," I mutter, ready to punch some of the tall grass.

The trees reach upward to impossible heights. If I squint hard enough, blue skies are visible between the thick branches. Down here, though, it's more like dusk.

After what seems like hours, it's time to lie down. My eyes can barely make out the shape of anything. It's officially nighttime. Not a second too soon; another step forward might be impossible. With a gusty sigh, I don't even look for a prime location. Everything looks to be the same. So far, there have been no signs of locals, people or otherwise.

Unpacking my tent, I pop it open and go through the motions. Without a nearby water source, I'm forced to sip from my rations. Ideally, they're only there in dire need. Tomorrow, I'll need to find a river or something similar.

I'm frustrated to discover that all the surrounding wood is too wet to catch fire. It's balmy, but a fire would be a comfort. Exhausted and defeated, I crawl into the tent and zip it closed. Shoving the pack into the tent, I tuck my utility belt into the top zipper. Then I loosen my boots and set them aside. It's stifling in the tent, but instinct tells me it's not safe to sleep out in the open.

After a lot of readjusting, I'm finally able to doze. Tomorrow, I'll wake up and find a town or city. I'll be fine. *I can do this.*

I'm not sure what makes my eyes pop open, but my instincts scream to keep still. Straining, I try to hear what woke me up. The forest is quiet. All the bugs and birds are silent. Water drips into a puddle somewhere.

Something outside my tent sniffs at the zipped-up entrance.

The hairs on my skin raise. Heavy breaths push the soft tent sides in and out. Whatever it is takes a step, and the ground vibrates. Another step kicks my heart into a gallop. It's *massive.*

A clicking chortle *right behind me* almost makes me scream. I slap my hand over my mouth. It sounds reptilian, like a ... like a ...

Dinosaur.

No, that's not possible. Even if it isn't a dinosaur, *something* is out there. Afraid of being eaten alive in the tent, I scoot forward and slowly unzip the tent. Even when done carefully, it's impossible to fully muffle the sound. There's a snort and loud hissing. Not too far away, there's a response. So there's more than two. Great.

Carefully peeling apart the flaps, I look beyond the clearing in front of me. A nearby puddle ripples as the ground shakes once, twice, three more times. It's on my left now. The sun must be rising because the outlines of trees are vaguely more visible.

Then, an enormous toothy jaw creeps into view, looking around the edges of my tent. Frozen in place, all I can do is make eye contact with the glowing eyeball of a T-Rex-looking motherfucker. It's the color of worn bark, with streaks of red and blue flaring from its nostrils to its glowing gold eyes.

The stench of rotting meat almost makes me gag. At home, the schools teach students about dinosaurs, and there are so many movies about them. There's nothing to prepare you for the predatory assessment of one. Or the decayed bits of meat lodged in their fist-sized teeth.

In a rotten bit of luck, a part of the tent flap adjusts. It triggers something in the T-Rex. I screech as it rears up and bellows to the skies. There's another response from the forest, but closer.

Oh, fuck, oh fuck, oh fuck.

Shrieking, I dive out of the tent right before it's slammed away. My foot snags on the entrance, tripping me, but my newfound reflexes, thanks to training, means I'm already up and bolting into the woods. Mud soaks into my socks as my legs pump, fueled by terror.

Behind me are shrieks and more clicks. Whipping behind a tree thicker than a car, I press myself against the moist bark.

My exhales come out ragged, and I hold a hand up to hide them. My balance's thrown with each of the enraged steps. They're close. So close. It's hard to think, to remember what I've learned about dinosaurs.

What the hell am I supposed to do? A small voice in my head reminds me of the dagger on my thigh. Yanking it from its sheath, my knuckles crack from my death grip on the hilt. I skid to a stop, pressing against a tree. I can't tell the difference between blood pounding in my head and the sound of their footsteps.

After a couple of minutes without a confrontation, it's clear they lost interest. All I hear is tearing, more chortling clicks, and finally, the steps fade.

When ten minutes of silence have passed, I lower my hand, re-sheath the dagger, and take a deep breath. It's shaky, and my lungs still constrict from fear. As much as I'd like to keep hiding, there's no way I can live in soggy socks. If I'm lucky, the dinosaurs left my boots alone.

The first thing to catch my eye in the clearing is shredded silver fabric. Well, goodbye, tent.

Pieces of it flap in the breeze. Ten feet away is one of my boots. I scan the ground for the other one as I put the boot on. Nothing.

What am I going to do if I can't find it? I don't see my pack either. What if I have to walk around a world with dinosaurs with only one shoe and that's it?

The panic threatens to take over. Worst-case scenarios roll through my mind over and over as I stomp through the dense brush. Just as I'm about to lie down and cry, I trip over the second boot.

"Ah-ha!" My cry of victory is too loud, but I don't care. Now I have both boots on ... even if my socks are soaking wet, and I may very well develop some weird fungus soon. A little further off, I find my sleeping bag. Rolling it up, I tuck it under my arm.

Now to find my pack.

And ... it's nowhere. With each piece of tent I pick up, my hope rises, then plummets. By the fifth piece, I dread the worst. What if they ate it? All the research is on there. Food. Supplies. Ellie's pastries. My heart pounds in my ears, and my skin prickles with fear. It would be devastating if that happened.

What would I do?

How would I continue?

I'd fail my family!

Dropping the items, I shake my hands and take gulps of air, pacing as I hum in an attempt to stave off the threatening tears. I don't want to be here. I want to be in Ilorna. I want to go back.

The last thought hiccups out a sob, and I slap a hand over my mouth.

Breathe.

I'm going to go into a full-blown panic attack if I don't chill out. I can't survive if I can't think clearly. Putting my hands on my knees, I bend over, steadying my breath. My body is shaking violently from the shock and the adrenaline drop. It's been thirty minutes, and the backpack is nowhere to be seen. They must've taken it with them, for whatever reason.

My shoulders slump with defeat. Things went from bad to worse. No pack, no research, no pastries, no water. And damn, I'm thirstier than a middle-aged mom at an all-male strip club.

Might as well keep trudging along. Without a single idea of where I'm going, I focus on putting one foot in front of the other.

Because I'm brazen, I follow the huge tracks left by the predators. Not like I'm looking for more trouble, but a teeny tiny part of me hopes they've dropped my pack somewhere.

In a tiny corner of my mind, I send a silent prayer to the goddess Inanna. Kalliope says she's a good listener; I desperately want someone to be paying attention to me. To prove I'm not alone in this jungle full of predators.

My hope's rewarded. I spot the pack a few inches deep in the muck. A hole punctures one strap, and the other seems a little frayed, but otherwise, it's in good shape.

Thank the goddess.

Kneeling, I go through and check that it's all there. The pastries are a little squished, but waste not, want not. Needing a quick win, I pull one out and take a bite. The creamy texture offers a brief respite from the racing fear still coursing through my veins, but it also makes my heart ache.

I wish I'd stayed in Ilorna.

No. I can't keep thinking that — I'll go mad. The beast of heartbreak snorts in agreement inside my mind. The rest of this journey *needs* to be objective. *I* need to be objective. I failed once; I won't do it again.

Mentally cleansed of emotion, I lick the leftover cream cheese off my fingers. As I grab my pack and begin trekking through the forest, there's an extra spring in my step. Sure, I no longer have a tent, but the pastries are intact. Yes, I'm entirely alone in the world, but I survived another attempt on my life.

Gotta focus on the good things.

Right?

Acknowledgments

T his book was a labor of love — ever since I first watched *A Kid in King Arthur's Court*. Since the first bit of encouragement arrived back in 2020, this book and Saira's story have nipped at my heels. I didn't know exactly what this story would be, and this poor thing has really been through it, y'all.

From originally being a six-book novella series to a thicc duology, it's been my growth book. My writing style and process evolved right along with it, so Saira will always hold such a special place in my heart.

I'm so incredibly grateful to my husband, Josh, who always made sure I had the time and sanity to work on this story. Thank you for finding my editing meltdowns humorous enough that you never got mad. When I started screaming at my manuscript during the final draft, wondering, "Who the fuck wrote this slop???" you just freshened up my water bottle and kept me fed.

This book has been through so much evolution and has had so many eyes on it, I can't remember everyone that's helped me. However, if you had a part in this book through beta reading, thank you so much for all of your support.

To everyone who listened to me rave about this book in-person, your patience and enthusiasm kept me fed.

Of course, I need to give a big shout out to my Happily Ever Authors crowd! I met y'all at the very end of my drafting/proofing, but the late night writing sprints, critiques, and lamentations literally gave me life. I would have never known interiority was a weakness if y'all hadn't kept saying, "Yes, but how does she *feel?*" This book is 100% better because of your support, and I'm so godsdamned grateful!

To my newfound writing cohort, I actually named the Cohort in Ilorna years before I knew you all, but I feel like we could also sit in a pub, drinking a beverage, and maybe enjoy a cheesy snack or two. Thank you for your kind critiques and uplifting words!

And to my dear readers — thank you for reading! I wanted to create an FMC who wasn't just some whiney, skinny white bitch who's just sO tInY. Representation matters in literature, and it's my hope Saira's story has and continues to be a source of inspiration for those inevitable challenges life throws at us that sometimes feel like personal asteroids.

You don't have to be the Chosen One to make a story that matters to others.

About Jenna Avery

The origin story of Jenna Avery is complex, weird, and requires numerous alcoholic beverages to regale. The current story? She's an elder millennial with a penchant for evolving and growing. This is a polite way of saying her ADHD makes her choose a new hobby every three months. By the time you read this, who knows what she'll be into. Just ask. Otherwise, she lives with her horde of kids and pets, a golden retriever husband, and a rotating residency of soon-to-be-dead plants.